I had sneaked onto the freight without being seen. We gained more speed, working our way up to maybe thirty-five miles per hour. Then the cars began that gentle side-to-side rocking that makes you sleepy. I was suddenly very tired. I was about to crash, and if I weren't careful I would doze off, lose my grip on the ladder, and fall under the wheels to a frightful death. What was I going to do next?

"All right, Adams. Don't move a muscle."

I turned and saw the muzzle end of an automatic aimed at my head.

Also by Rick Boyer
Published by Ivy Books:

BILLINGSGATE SHOAL

THE PENNY FERRY

THE DAISY DUCKS

GONE TO EARTH

THE WHALE'S FOOTPRINTS

MOSCOW METAL

A Doc Adams Suspense Novel

Rick Boyer

IVY BOOKS • NEW YORK

Ivy Books
Published by Ballantine Books

Library of Congress Catalog Card Number: 87-4025

ISBN 0-8041-0292-9

First published by Houghton Mifflin Company. Reprinted by permission of Houghton Mifflin Company.

Printed in Canada

First Ballantine Books Edition: February 1989
Second Printing: December 1990

for

Paul Bennett

professor, author, poet,

teacher, wise counselor, and my friend

Rubik's Cube

IT STARTED WITH A DEAD CAT. BUT IT SURE AS HELL WASN'T Tom Sawyer. So you ask yourself: what do three crows, a spilled box of kitty litter, two paint cans in the basement, a yardstick, the Rubik's Cube puzzle, and a broken-down steam shovel have in common?

Plenty. And exactly none of it was nice or fun.

1

IT WAS THE NOISE THAT FIRST DREW OUR ATTENTION. A horrid sound. A monstrous, gurgling cry of agony that we could hear fifty yards away as the animal ran to us, tripped and staggered by his own convulsions.

And all from a seven-pound cat.

Moe turned from the chessboard and looked across the lawn in horror. Through the low birch boughs and golden leaves, I could see the cat jumping in the air, performing twisting aerial stunts as it bawled in strangulated voice.

"Is it something hi's killing?" I asked.

"No Doc. It's the cat. Something's terribly wrong wid it—"

I stood up and hopped away from the low wooden table where we were playing chess. I called the cat. My cat.

"Claude! Claude!"

For a second the animal managed to look at me. In that instant, I saw in the stricken yellow eyes all the fear and agony of wounded living tissue, all the suffering of the animal kingdom condensed in time and distilled in space. A heavy stream of reddish vomit erupted from its mouth. And then a frenzied, strangled yowl. The cat rolled on its back, its four feet working in a blur, clutching and clawing at cruel demons that weren't there.

I couldn't stand another second if it, and ran inside the house. When I came back out, Mary was shouting after me and running over the fallen red leaves in the bright autumn day.

"Charlie! Charlie, no! Don't you dare!" she screamed.

Claude was on his stomach when I got to him, bubbling his breath in a puddle of vomit and mucus. There was also a foul smell of excrement. I aimed right behind the head and squeezed, and the horror stopped.

When I looked up, Mary was screaming at me with anguished eyes. Moe stood with us, looking like an Old Testament prophet, gazing down at the dead cat. He shook his head slowly in sadness.

The muzzle of my .22 target pistol wept faint smoke.

2

AN HOUR LATER, I PLACED THE SHOPPING BAG FLAT ON THE table. The table was waist-high stainless steel and had a shallow gutter molded around its perimeter to catch fluids. Two hairy brown hands, standing out against the pressed white linen of the lab coat, reached for the bag. Dr. Raymond Perrucci slid the newspaper out. On it rested Claude's remains.

"The blood is from the gunshot wound?" he asked, pointing to the brown stain on the newsprint.

"Mostly. And also from the projective vomiting. I deliberately shot in the neck because I wanted you to examine the brain tissue."

Ray leveled his keen, mustached face with mine for a moment. He knew my reasoning. Without comment, he turned and opened the first file drawer in a big gray cabinet. Under *A*, for Adams, Dr. Charles. Not *C* for Claude. He took a number of cards in his hairy paw. Five of them: three dogs, two cats. Make that one cat.

"If you're suspecting rabies," he said, "it can't be. We vaccinated Claude last March."

"I never suspected that. I'm thinking of a very strong and fast-acting poison, like strychnine. What else could produce those horrible symptoms?"

He shrugged his shoulders and looked over at Mary, who stood frozen, with wet eyes, looking at our dead friend. I suppose I just don't cry for cats. Still, I was attached to this one, who would rear up in the morning and brush each side of your face with his mouth in greeting, just like a French premier to a war hero.

"Well, an examination of the brain tissue should yield something. From the convulsions you describe, it sounds as though the central nervous system was definitely affected. Was the animal sick previously? Listless, without appetite?"

"No," said Mary. "He was fine. Whatever it was, it was sudden."

Then I also suspect a poison," said Perrucci. "One that's very fast and deadly and causes convulsions. Strychnine is a very good guess, Doc. Trouble is, it's rare nowadays. It used to be found in most rat poisons. But now they use warfarin. As you probably know, warfarin is an anticoagulant and kills by causing internal bleeding. It's pretty slow acting compared to what you've described."

"Are you suggesting rat poisons because you think Claude may have eaten a mouse that had eaten poison?"

"Well, let's put it this way: with a cat, the possibilities of ingestion are fewer than with dogs. Cats are fussier eaters. Dogs will try to eat just about anything, including deadly plants. The most common poison fatality now, especially this time of year, is ethylene glycol, or antifreeze. People change their radiator coolant and spill the antifreeze on the ground. It's got a smell that dogs like. They lap it up and die. Cats don't do this. They like meat, preferably live meat."

"So you think it was probably a strong rat poison that did it?"

Perrucci shook his head slowly.

"I don't know what I think right now, except that it was some kind of virulent toxin. We'll have to see. Doc, you want a complete workup on this?"

"Absolutely. Hundred percent. Tissue samples. Microscope work. Examination of organs. The works. Even an X-ray, if it'll help. This cat was our favorite of all time, and only three years old. As Mary says, he was in the pink just this morning. We want to know exactly what happened to him. If nothing else, we can make sure it doesn't happen to our other animals. They roam around the house and grounds pretty freely, you know."

"Ray, you think it could be deliberate poisoning?" asked Mary.

The vet nodded. "Oh yeah. There are cat-and dog-haters out there. People don't like dogs for messing up their lawns, or digging. Or barking. People don't like cats because they kill songbirds, yowl at night, and because they're cats. You name it."

"How do these people poison pets?" she asked.

"Usually not in very sophisticated ways. Standard approach is to take a piece of raw meat—say a beef kidney, which has a taste strong enough to cover the poison—and lace it with poison you can buy over the counter, like rodent poison or weed killer. These poisons are the organo phosphates and act on the nervous system. But they don't act that quickly, and the animal only dies after its liver is destroyed, which may take a day or even a week. Horrible."

"But this was so sudden," I said.

"So it seems, Doc. Arsenic we can rule out. It's deadly, but not rapid. Cyanide is the quickest of all, and the deadliest. But with the cyanide compounds there aren't the violent symptoms; the animal usually simply drops dead. I just don't know yet; there are hundreds of poisons. I'm sorry, too."

We trudged out to the car, took the winding road down the pine-covered hill where the animal hospital sits, and went back home. I sat on the back terrace with the four remaining animals: Danny, the yellow Lab; Troubles, the drahthaar bitch; and Flack, the wire-haired dachshund. There was also Phoebe, the gray tabby, who already seemed to miss her playmate. They all looked healthy and happy. So far.

"Mary, I know they're not popular in New England, but I'm thinking of putting a fence around the back yard."

"Jeez, Charlie, the neighbors will hate us for it. Couldn't you just fix the gates on the stone fence?"

"Well, it won't keep the dogs in, other than Flack, who can't even jump over a shoebox."

"I know. And no fence can keep in a cat. Look, honey, the dog runs we've got are fine. When the dogs are in the yard, we'll watch them."

"Ohhhhh. I don't know. . . ." I sighed. I had a helpless feeling that things were out of control and there was nothing I could do.

I went over to the tiny birch grove with its wooden table and rustic chairs. The plastic thermos jug, milk, sugar, and cups were still on the table. The tea inside was still warm. Moe hadn't had time to bring over his antique Russian samovar, so we'd used the jug. Less aesthetic, more efficient. Isn't that the way nowadays? The chessboard was still there, with the Staunton pieces on it. The clock was still, with both its buttons in neutral. Chess clocks count down, not up. But I could determine the elapsed time: six minutes plus on my clock, a little over four on Moe's. Ten minutes. Then I thought of something. I called Mary over from the garden, where she was collecting a batch of fall snow peas.

"Mary, it seems to me that just after Moe and I sat down to play, you came out with the milk and sugar for the tea, right?"

"Uh-huh. Your were just setting up the pieces, I think."

"That's the way I remember it, too. And guess who followed you out the kitchen door?"

"Claude?"

"Yes. I remember him parading across the lawn in your wake. Then he went away somewhere. When we next saw him, he was leaping and staggering across the yard, dying. Look here: ten minutes on the clock. Actually, closer to eleven minutes. That's all. So Claude had to leave the premises, get into trouble with whatever or whoever killed him, and come back, all within that time."

"That's not very long."

"No. It sure isn't. It'll be interesting to see what Ray turns up from the autopsy."

"I'm going in to cook something," said Mary, "and maybe drink a split of wine while I work. Want to help?"

"No. I want to take a little walk around the neighborhood.

Claude couldn't have gone far at all in that amount of time. I'll bet that where he ran into trouble isn't a hundred yards from where we're standing."

By the time I got my coat from inside, Mary had put the big French enameled kettle on the range and poured a jar of her home-canned tomatoes into it. She was cutting up Spanish onions as I went out the kitchen door.

"Creole gumbo," she said. I heard the pop of a cork as I crossed the terrace and headed down the sloping lawn toward my neighbors' houses along Old Stone Mill Road.

They were all nice people. At least, we had always thought so.

3

Our neighbors in Concord, Massachusetts, are few and far between. On the other side of Old Stone Mill Road from the Adams house lies the wide, up-sloping expanse of McCloed's Orchards. Dean McCloed's house is large but not visible from the road. The field is planted in apple trees, which give way to a dense woods fifty yards distant. It was from this field that my mercenary-soldier friend, Laitis Roantis (pronounced LIGHT-us Ro-WANT-us), was shot by a sniper the previous winter as he left my house. He survived, though. He always does.

Since I had seldom seen Claude, or any of my pets, over in that field, I began my stroll in the opposite direction, to the rear of the house. Beyond our terrace is the Japanese teahouse and bonsai garden, the tiny birch grove where Moe and I play chess, and then the small, garage-sized guest house, which is really a log cabin. Here our property ends. There is a narrow gully that runs along the property line. At one time it was an unpaved alleyway, used for work vehicles. But no more. Now it's grown over with grass. In the spring, the water table is high there, and your feet squish as you walk along it. I walked up and down this gully for twenty minutes, looking at my neighbor's houses. There are three of them.

The neighbors to the west are Jim and Maureen Burke,

longtime friends who graciously look after our dogs when we're away. They have pets of their own, and it was inconceivable to me that they'd have set out poison. To the east live John and Florence Rutner, an older couple in their early seventies. Though not close friends of ours, they are decent, peaceful folks who travel abroad often. They have a Rottweiler to keep watch over their place while they're away. A hired man arrives in a truck daily to feed and clean up after it. Now and then I can hear Samson—that's the Rottweiler's name—moaning and growling like the Hound of the Baskervilles. Dog-lover though I am, I won't get near their place with Samson around. John and Florence were away somewhere—Singapore or the Middle East—for six weeks. That ruled them out.

That left the third neighbor, a fairly recent addition to the neighborhood, a widower named Emil Haszmanay. I had only met him twice, and he had seemed pleasant enough. Haszmanay was a Hungarian refugee, a scientist who worked at the Lincoln Laboratory, located on the Lexington-Bedford line. He was retiring—almost reclusive—and seemed to spend most of his time in his fine brick house with its ivy-covered walls. I strolled up from the gully and headed for his house, which was dark in the falling light. My eyes swept the lawn as I walked, looking for a telltale container, can lid, or ripped package that could have held the fatal dose of whatever it was. I saw nothing, not even a partially eaten carcass of a field rodent. The windows of the Haszmanay residence were all dark. I rang the bell, waited. No answer. Rang again, waited. Not home. But his Buick Skylark was in the driveway.

I walked around the house, which was sizable. I looked particularly closely around the foundation, behind and through the shrubbery—anyplace where a dog- or cat-hater would set out poison. It was clean as a whistle. Out in back was a delightful patio terrace with a small fountain and birdbath in the center. Oh-oh. Prominent birdbath. Cat-hater. Wait a minute. *I* had three Plexiglas tube feeders outside my study window, and I also owned cats. I couldn't, shouldn't, assume anything regarding Emil Haszmanay until I talked with him.

I walked around the grounds twice more. Nothing drew my attention. I stood on the edge of the lawn and gave the house a final once-over. You could tell that Haszmanay was an electronics expert. There was a satellite dish placed unobtrusively on a rear corner of the roof and above it a metal mast with aerials on it. Other than that the house was unremarkable, and very well maintained. I noticed a telephone lineman's tent high on a pole beyond the trees. But I wasn't sure whether it was even on the Haszmanay property.

Then from behind me came a commotion that resembled the distant barking of dogs. A whole pack of them. But it wasn't. I knew well what it was, and seconds later a big V of Canada geese shot into view from behind the pines. They were flying low, heading for the Great Meadows Wildlife Refuge. They passed thirty feet over my head, making a big racket. *Branta canadensis*. My favorite bird. Jet pilots have seen them flying at incredible heights. They fly at night and don't get lost. They can live to be sixty, and they mate for life. When a bird dies, its mate grieves. I watched the wide skein sail on over the hill and heard their raucous talk grow faint.

Well, I'd struck out. I decided to stroll over to the Rutners', and was far onto their property before the big dark lump on the lawn leaped up and barked a deep, booming warning. Old Samson had been asleep, and it was my feet rustling the dead leaves that had roused him. I was thankful for the stout welded-wire fencing between us. Samson settled down when I spoke to him, but still didn't seem too jovial. I walked around the Rutner place. Nothing unusual here either. I walked south, crossed Old Stone Mill Road, and stepped over the low stone wall and into Dean McCloed's orchard. I paced up and down it systematically, working my way farther and farther into the field. I saw nothing, and then it was too dark to continue. I headed back to my house.

Mary was leaning over the kitchen sink, cussing. I saw blood seeping from her right thumb.

"Dammit, Charlie! Why do you keep the knives so sharp?"

"Oh. Sorry. Guess it's my background in surgery. And you know what they say. A sharp knife is a safe knife."

"Hell it is. I barely touched my thumb—and look!" She dried it on a paper towel and held it there until the bleeding stopped.

"Want a Band-Aid?"

"No. It'll just get wet and soggy. Jeez, maybe I shouldn't have had that split of bubbly; I got a little careless. Would you get the door?"

I opened it to let in Ray Perrucci, who said he'd just stopped by on his way home. He followed me into the kitchen, where I made him a cup of cappuccino.

"We're still not sure what the substance was," he said, blowing into the cup between sips, "but it was definitely a toxin. The lab ruled out strychnine. My current guess is zinc phosphide, or a similar compound. Zinc phosphide is a rodenticide that will produce symptoms like the ones you described, Doc. My guess is that an animal ingested the poison, then Claude ate the animal shortly afterward. I have to ask you, do you want the remains for burial?"

"Not after an autopsy," said Mary. "But what about the ashes?"

So we arranged for that, and then Ray dug into his coat pocket and retrieved a small envelope, the kind vets put capsules in.

"But I did find something else interesting," he said. "It seems that even before he got hold of the poison, Claude was in danger. Somebody was out to get him. Look here."

He took a pea-sized object from the envelope and held it between his thumb and forefinger. I took it from him. It was a lead pellet, the kind used in air guns. It was roughly hourglass-shaped, with a conical point on the front end and a hollow base on the back. I handed it to Mary, who examined the tiny object with hatred in her eyes, twirling it between her fingers.

"The bastards! Charlie, let's find out who did this!"

"It's not as easy as it sounds, Mary. There are precious

few kids around here, and nobody else I know owns an air rifle."

"I found it in the lower rib cage, back toward the animal's flank. The wound was recent, too. So be careful with your pets. A pellet like that wouldn't hurt a dog unless it struck it in the eyes. But a cat's different. Some of these air guns are powerful, too. I've heard of some made in England and Germany that pack damn near as much punch as a twenty-two."

"But this didn't kill Claude?" asked Mary."

"No. The cat died from a strong toxin. All this did was cause some internal bleeding. But it's a good bet that whoever shot your cat also poisoned him. A cat-hater is a cat-hater is a cat-hater. Seems like he's using everything he can to rid the area of them. I'd keep Phoebe indoors for a while and notify the police. They can keep a watch out for anyone using an air rifle."

Ray finished the coffee and was on his way. He said he'd let us know the specific poison used as soon as the lab reported it to him. Then, as a precaution, we would keep the proper antidote on hand and be better prepared if the cat-killer struck again. He said he would bring Claude's ashes over the next afternoon. I let him out the front door and returned to the kitchen, which smelled of the rich gumbo. Mary had just added the roux, and the okra was making it thick and sticky with its juice. She picked up the pellet again and look at it closely, then dropped it into one of my pipe ashtrays and put the ashtray on the shelf.

"Let's save that pellet, Charlie, and give it to Brian," she said, referring to our friend Brian Hannon, chief of police in Concord. "Then if we find somebody with an air gun, we can match the pellets. Right?"

"Hmmmm. I don't know if air guns leave ballistics marks on pellets, but there's no reason to assume they don't. Brian would know. Good idea. And let's follow Ray's advice and keep Phoebe close to the house. When's dinner ready?"

"In twenty minutes," she said, adding the file powder. "I'll add the shrimp in the last five minutes—and, I know, leave the shells on."

"Right," I said.

* * *

It was a gumbo and a half, and I dove into it, chewing the shrimp, crabmeat, and chunks of smoked sausage, then biting off big hunks of sourdough bread and washing it all down with beer. Afterward Mary settled herself on the sofa.

"Thought you were going to throw a few pots tonight," I said.

"No. I don't feel so hot, Charlie. I think maybe I got a bad shrimp in that gumbo. I'm going up to bed and watch TV, okay?"

So she toddled up to the sack, and I lighted a fire in the fireplace, because it was cold out now, and settled down to read magazines.

Ten minutes later I heard a thump on the ceiling, so I went to the stairway and called up to Mary. But all I got for an answer was the water running in the john. I went back to the magazines.

A few minutes later I heard her scream. I ran up the stairs three at a time. Mary was stretched out in the bathroom, retching her guts out. I felt her head. It was boiling hot. Way, way too hot. I carried her back to bed but she wouldn't stay put. She kept moving and thrashing, unable to lie still.

Then I got on the phone to Emerson Hospital, where, as it happens, we both work. I ordered an ambulance and flew back downstairs, as if in a bad dream, to look for something to counteract the food poisoning. But as I looked frantically through the cupboards and shelves, I suddenly realized it was not food poisoning. Not at all. Because I was staring at the ashtray, and at the tiny pellet inside it.

And then I knew.

I grabbed the phone tight and tried to call Ray Perrucci. But my hands were shaking so much I couldn't dial.

4

MARY'S CONDITION, SO FRIGHTENING AT FIRST, HAD BEGUN to stabilize within a few hours of the initial attack.

"But why not *us*, then?" asked Ray as I led him down the hospital corridor. "I mean, we both picked it up, too."

"No. Mary cut her thumb just before you showed up. She picked up the pellet, just like we did. In fact, I think she picked it up twice, holing it between her finger and thumb. Maybe she squeezed it, too. But the difference was that whatever was on it entered her bloodstream through the cut. Now I want that lab to—"

"They're on it right now, Doc. Good thing they're open twenty-four hours a day. But listen, I bet your brother-in-law's going to have the answer quicker. It's much easier to determine the toxin from the actual agent than from tissue samples."

Now Ray followed me down the corridor to the lounge area, smacking his fist into his palm and cussing that he'd been so stupid.

"Hell, Ray, there's no way you could suspect the pellet itself as the poisoning agent. I mean, how many times has that happened? A dart, maybe, but not a pellet—"

"Doc," he said suddenly, "I think I know what the poison is! I'll be right back."

Before I could question him, he hustled back down the hall to a pay phone. I bought a Coke and headed back to Mary's room. She was now out of intensive care, but we needed to identify the toxin so further treatment could proceed. As I walked along, I felt a hand on my shoulder and turned to see Moe Abramson, who no doubt had just gotten through seeing his psychiatric patients on Wheeler Four.

"She's gonna be just fine, Doc. Don't worry. Mind if I come along wid you?" I shook my head. "Good. Hey, you shouldn't drink Coke, Doc. Stuff's poison. Coke's got—"

"I know what it's got. After what got into Mary, though, a Coke's nothing. I'm only drinking it because there's no whiskey here."

"Tch! tch! tch!" he clucked, and we went in to see Mary.

If it's possible for a Calabrian to look pale, Mary Brindelli Adams was doing her damnedest at it. Her black hair looked even darker against her face now, and against the white pillow behind it. She smiled at us, and I kissed her.

"How do you feel?"

"I ache everywhere, Charlie, like a fever. And I'm still spitting up a little blood."

"Well, you do have a fever, a fever of unknown origin. But as soon as we identify the poison, it won't be mysterious anymore. The blood is probably just ruptured capillaries from the vomiting. You know that happens in extreme cases."

She sighed deeply and closed her eyes. Moe and I stared at her a while, then I sat down next to the bed.

"Are you going back to the office?" I asked Moe. When he nodded, I asked him to leave a note for my assistant, Susan Petri, to reschedule Monday's appointments.

"How about Tuesday's?" he asked.

"Keep 'em. Maybe I'm an optimist, but that's day after tomorrow. I think by then she's going to be well enough for me to go in to work. Hi Brian."

Moe turned to see the sandy-haired chief of police poking his head into the room. It was followed by another head, the big, swarthy, pudgy face of Detective Lieutenant Joseph Brindelli. Mary's kid brother.

"How is she?" asked Joe.

Mary opened her eyes at his voice and weakly held out her arms. They embraced as Joe leaned over his sister's bed, talking softly to her.

"See you a minute, Doc?" asked Brian. I walked out into the hall.

The short, stocky man stared up at me intently, his blue eyes gazing into mine as if trying to read an unfathomable secret.

"Well?" I asked.

"This thing is more serious than we first suspected," he said. "Joe took the pellet to the state lab at Ten Ten Commonwealth Avenue. I think I told you that."

I nodded and heard running feet behind me, drawing closer.

"Well, they ran it through. Turns out it's not a standard pellet that's been coated with poison. No. The whole damn *thing* is poisonous. What it is—"

"Thallium!" shouted Ray Perrucci, out of breath from hoofing it up the corridor from the phone. "The lab just confirmed it, Doc. What it is is thallium."

Brian nodded in agreement.

"Yeah," he said. "And not only that, it's *irradiated* thallium. Radioactive thallium. They say it's the nastiest poison ever devised."

The three of us stood and stared at each other.

"So what does this mean?" I asked. "Does she have radiation poisoning too?"

Brian gave a short nod and said, "Yes, but she'll recover. Ought to be no problem. But you should know that the guys at the lab said there would be liver damage. She could lose some of her hair. We've got to keep a close watch on her kidney function. She'll be longer recovering than we first thought."

I stared at the wall. I could hear Joe and Mary talking softly in the room. Who would do this? Who would concoct such a monstrous thing?

"This is no cat-killer," I said. "This is something bigger and meaner."

"Exactly. That's why Joe and I want you to come down to Ten Ten Comm. Ave. with us. Okay?"

We waited until Dr. Rachel Danzeck arrived from the state poison center in Cambridge. She was an expert at treating poisoning. Blood and urine samples taken from Mary confirmed the thallium poisoning and also, thank God, the relatively minor dose she'd gotten. Minor dose! Good Christ, I'd hate to see a regular dose. But then, I had: Moe and I had seen what a full-blown dose had done to my cat. Dr. Danzeck treated Mary with small doses of Prussian blue. She told me that Prussian blue—potassium ferric hexacyanoferrate—is used as a binding agent, combining with the thallium in the gut and keeping it from being reabsorbed.

"Looks real good," she said just before we left. "But she'll be laid up for a week."

"What about the radiation poisoning?"

"Don't worry about the radioactivity. They irradiate the thallium for fast absorption. It should have no lasting effects. But the poison itself takes a long time to excrete. We'll watch her closely for the next seven to ten days."

"You're the expert, Dr. Danzeck. Tell me, who would make a poison like this?"

She looked up, surprised.

"C'mon, Dr. Adams. You mean nobody's told you?"

"Told me what?"

"It's made by the Russians. The KGB. It's one of their favorite revenge and assassination weapons. It even has a nickname."

"Which is?"

"Moscow Metal."

5

WE PARKED IN FRONT OF THE GREEK RESTAURANT ACROSS the street from Ten Ten Comm. Ave., and went inside the big brick building that had twenty or so radio masts on the roof. Ten Ten is the main headquarters of the state police. Joe and Brian and I rode the elevator up to the top floor, where the lab was.

"They put it up on top of the building so they could vent it easily," said Joe. "You know, acid fumes, explosive fumes . . . stuff like that. You ever meet Karl Pirsch? Ha! A crazy Kraut. But loves his work. And, Mother Mary, is he good at it."

We went through industrial-type double doors and into a huge room filled with glassware, gas burners, sinks, and tubs. There was also an array of more specialized equipment Joe had explained to me once: polarizing microscopes, comparison microscopes, spectroscopes, gas chromatographs, and specialized photography equipment. Eight people were in the room, but one stood out above the rest: a tall egret of a man, thin as a rail, with a great beaky nose, a shiny bald head, a bush of curly white hair on each side of his long face, and a pair of wire-rimmed glasses. I thought he was going to sell me a Vlasic pickle. The man wasn't smiling; he wore an expression of barely controlled rage.

"*Yesss?*" he asked in a demonic hiss. The white lab coat was wrapped tightly around his frail form, so that it overlapped like a double-breasted coat. The man recognized Joe and peered hawk-like at us over his spectacles.

"Ah! Lieutenant Brindelli," he snapped, motioning us forward with a wave of his arm.

"That's Pirsch, I take it?" I said to Joe.

"Gee, how'd you guess?"

The thin man advanced and shook my hand with remarkable ferocity, pumping it fast, like a two-stroke engine.

"Dr. Adams. Ah, yesss! And how is your wife?"

He said it like this: *Und how iss your vife?*

"She's going to be fine. But it'll take time."

"Hummmph! Of course. Thallium is most deadly. Now watch."

Pirsch directed us to a marble countertop, pulled a Bunsen burner to the center of it, and turned a red knob at the end of the burner's hose. He squeezed a flint lighter above the tube of the burner, and a blue flame appeared with a pop. Then he took a small envelope from a drawer—the same envelope, I think, that Ray had given us—and let the pellet slide out onto the marble slab. He picked it up with a big pair of forceps and held it just over the flame. It glowed red, then yellow. But above it rose a bright green flame. As green as a parrot's tummy.

"Ha! You see, gentlemen? The green flame, a dead giveaway for the metallic element thallium. A heavy metal, similar in some ways to lead. Isolated in eighteen sixty-one by the British chemist William Crookes. The name thallium comes from a Greek word meaning 'green twig.' They got the name from the flame it produces when heated."

"And it's deadly poisonous," I said.

"Oh, yes. Your wife is fortunate, although I am sure she has suffered as well. Thallium salts act on tissue much as the lead salts do. The swine!"

"Who?" asked Joe.

"Whoever did this! And the FBI wants to know who it was, Lieutenant. That is why Chester Harwood is waiting downstairs in your office right now," said Pirsch, turning off the burner. He dropped the pellet back on the countertop to cool and fetched an electronic device from a shelf on the wall. It was the size of a lunch pail. When he switched it on and removed a chrome wand from the handle, I recognized it as a Geiger counter.

"Now listen," ordered Pirsch, and he passed the wand over the pellet, back and forth. Each time the wand passed over the pellet there was a loud static clicking, and the needle on the instrument's case buried itself. I watched the needle oscillate back and forth, in and out of the danger zone, in horror.

"You see? Irradiated thallium. They get the thallium from flue residues of industrial furnaces. When thalliferous pyrites are roasted, they leave salts behind. That's what they start with. Then they cook up the thallium in a nuclear reactor. What's left is this." He pointed at the tiny pellet accusingly. "Thallium is bluish-white metal, rather soft. See? It makes a perfect substitute for the lead pellet. And it doesn't take much . . . or very long, either."

"Thanks, Karl," said Joe, shoving his hands down deep into his coat pockets and rocking back and forth on his heels. "Have you shown this to ballistics yet?"

"Of course I have! What do you think—"

"Easy Karl. I just asked, is all."

Pirsch spun around and retrieved a clipboard. Stuck on it were close-up photos of the pellet and a written report on a preprinted form. Pirsch cleared his throat.

"The projectile was fired from an air gun—there are no powder residues whatsoever—having a barrel at least nine inches long and a left-hand rifling twist, with twelve lands."

He paused and looked up. "That means the barrel of the weapon is German-made, by the firm of Weihrauch. It is a spring-piston type, in twenty-two caliber. This type of air gun, modified in England to produce even higher velocities than the standard German issue, and known as the Weihrauch-Viper, will send a twenty-two caliber pellet from the muzzle at a velocity of just under a thousand feet per second. I daresay that had the pellet not hit bone it would have passed clear through your cat."

"Would it have survived then?" I asked.

Pirsch quickly shook his head. "Oh, no. The result would have been the same."

"Doc, Brian, let's go on down to my office now," said Joe.

We left Karl Pirsch and his industrious staff and got off the elevator at the fifth floor. Joe's office, which he shared with his partner, Kevin O'Hearn, and two other detectives, had the typically depressing look of a public, state-operated building. Drab green high-gloss walls around the room's lower half. Above the chair rail, dirty beige with hair stains and finger marks. Old acoustical tile on the ceiling—the kind with holes in it. Fluorescent ceiling lights with shades that looked like the insides of old ice-cube trays. Old linoleum floor in green and white checker-board, curled up and shipped around the edges. Desks made of gray metal with bent drawers that didn't close all the way. Used styrofoam coffee cups with dried brown stains in the bottom and old stinky cigarette butts mashed into them. Then add a few gobs of chewing gum and pieces of stale submarine sandwich. Smelled great. Windows with metal frames, chipped putty, and metal Venetian blinds that hung all lopsided and bent.

"Who designed this?" I asked my brother-in-law as I sat down in an old oak armchair. Kevin O'Hearn moved his beefy, puffy form around in his chair and glanced back at me with his pink face, winking.

"I believe, Doc, it was I. M. Pei. Or perhaps Mies van der Rohe?"

"Thought so, Kevin," I said. "Jeez, no wonder you guys work in your car all the time." I jumped up.

"Where are you going?" asked Joe.

"To throw away these goddamn coffee cups and old sub wrappers," I said. When I got back, after washing my hands twice, I saw a man in a shiny gray suit hanging his hat on the rack. He came forward and gripped my hand.

"Dr. Adams. Yes. Chet Harwood. From the Bureau. Pleased to meet you. And this—where the hell is he?—Joe, where's Sid?"

Harwood looked around angrily just as a short, thick,

graying man with a big long nose and steel-rimmed glasses strode into the office. He wore a floppy trench coat.

"Oh, there you are. Dr. Adams, this is Sid Wanzer, my partner."

"How ya doin'?" Wanzer said, as he gave my hand a quick jerk and sat down in a far corner in one of the swivel chairs. He slumped there in it, with a bored and vacant expression on his long face.

I turned and looked again at Chet Harwood. He seemed to be about fifty years old, trim, businesslike, with thin tortoiseshell glasses. Black hair and light skin. Irish? No: brown eyes. Black wing-tip shoes. White shirt with two pens in the breast pocket. No telltale bulge under the armpits. But when he removed his suit coat I saw what looked like a Walther .380 auto stuck in a tiny belt holster near his right kidney. He sat down and looked at all of us. I studied him some more. Looked like a lawyer or an accountant. If he ever had to carry a sawed-off, he'd probably take it to the scene in a Hartmann belting-leather attaché case. Thoroughly professional. A typical Fed. But I was glad to see him. After what had happened, very glad.

Harwood took out a notebook, paused, and asked whether anyone would object if he taped the interview. We didn't, and he nodded quickly to Wanzer, who opened his briefcase, set a little pocket cassette recorder on the table, and switched it on. Wanzer had hazel eyes. I noticed that his sloppy, bored appearance was a bit deceptive, for he set up the electronic device with speed and precision, then returned to the chair and slumped in it. I looked at his eyes again, behind the bureaucratic steel-rims. They had a slightly slanted, Mongol cast to them, much like Laitis Roantis's peepers. Was Wanzer a Lithuanian? A Czech?

"First, Dr. Adams, I have heard that you know why the Bureau is so interested in this incident."

"I was told the pellet is a KBG assassination weapon."

"Right. Now, other parties may now have and use these pellets. But as far as we know, they're limited to Russian spies and enforcers. What we're curious about is, why in *your* neighborhood?"

"Why indeed?" I said, shrugging my shoulders. "I take it no state agency was interested in killing my cat."

"Right. We think that's a safe sassumption. But even if the shooting was accidental, that still means that somebody discharged the weapon in your neighborhood, Doctor. Either a neighbor or a stranger, but somebody did it. And somebody had the poisoned pellet. A pellet that, as far as we know, could only have been manufactured in the Soviet Union by Department Five of the KGB,"

"What's Department Five?"

"Let's just say it's the one responsible for keeping agents in line."

"Rather like internal security?"

He nodded, adjusting the volume knob on the recorder.

"So which of my neighbors is it?"

"That's why we're here, Doctor. We're hoping you can point us in the right direction."

I described the Burkes and the Rutners briefly, mentioning occupations, time lived in the area, hobbies and mutual friends, and so forth. Harwood wrote furiously in his little notebook. Then I mentioned the retiring neighbor directly behind me. After quickly running the facts and recollections through my mind, I said that the likeliest candidate for any kind of international hanky-panky would be Emil Haszmanay.

"Tell us about him, please," said Harwood, leaning forward, pencil in hand.

"Well, I'm not accusing him," I answered. "It's just that I've known the other neighbors for years, and I think they're impossible candidates. By elimination, then, Haszmanay is the most likely. He moved in two years ago. I don't know much about him except that he's a refugee from Hungary and works at the Lincoln Laboratory. He lived somewhere in California before coming to New England. I haven't talked with him recently. I suppose Mary and I should have invited him to dinner, but we never got around to it. Maybe it's because he's such a loner, and he isn't married. Now, as a matter of fact, I went by his house yesterday, just after taking the cat to the vet's—"

Harwood brightened at this and asked me for all the details. I filled him in as best I could, which wasn't much.

"And you say Haszmanay wasn't home, but his car was there?" asked Harwood.

"Right. He stays indoors a lot of the time. Maybe he didn't hear the bell. I see him outside now and then, working in his garden."

"Are there any other regular visitors?"

"Not that we've noticed. But his house is scarcely visible from ours. And he's a widower, too, and that probably curtails his social life. I don't think he has a ladyfriend, either."

I noticed that Harwood wasn't writing anything in his notebook.

"Did you try calling him?" asked Harwood.

"No. The vet came over just after I got home, and I forgot."

"Is there anything else you can tell me about Mr. Haszmanay? Which of your friends or neighbors knows him best?"

"There's just not very much. I think I know him better than the others, because he seemed drawn slightly more to me than them. Maybe it's because of my medical training. As a scientist, maybe he felt he had more in common with me. But, believe me, he's a loner."

"Did he ever mention his job or his past to you?"

"Only briefly, in passing, once when we talked over the fence, so to speak. If I remember right, he came to the U.S. in fifty-six, just after the Hungarian revolution. He's an expert in radar and electronics. I think when he was in California he worked in Livermore. A good place to start might be the Lincoln Labs. Have you tried them yet?"

"No. But we will."

I sat back, grinning. Then Harwood caught on, and he stared up at me.

"You already know all about Haszmanay, don't you?" I said. "You jotted down everything I said about the other neighbors, but when I mentioned Emil, you wrote nothing. I'll bet you've already got a file on him, right?"

Harwood cleared his throat and put the notebook down. I noticed Wanzer break into a broad grin and scratch his ear.

"Uh, as a matter of fact, yes. But we still cross-interview as often as possible, trying to get different viewpoints. You can be assured that your interview with us helps."

"Well I hope so. I'm not saying I'm the most important physician in the world, or the only one with a family. But I have a sick wife I'd like to be with. Did you get any new insights?"

"Yes," replied the special agent, "as a matter of fact, I did. You said Haszmanay was attracted to you more than the others in the neighborhood. This could be important to all of us. You see, Dr. Adams, you are drawn into this affair by circumstance. You're a part of it, without choice."

"What affair?"

He squirmed in his chair a millimeter or two before answering. Then he glanced around at all of us.

"I'm going out on a limb here. Perhaps I shouldn't do it, but in this instance I feel I have little alternative. What I'm going to tell you should be kept secret. Agreed?"

"Absolutely."

"Good. This is especially important because your safety may be involved. Considering what's happened already, I'm sure you realize that this isn't kid stuff."

I nodded.

"Emil Haszmanay is what he told you: a first-rate scientist, now engaged in what we'll call 'vital projects relating to state security.' Follow?"

"A weapons expert," said Joe.

"Call him, what you like," snapped Harwood, half turning in his chair. "Just remember, you never heard it from the Bureau. Anyway, let's just say that for some time now, we've been very interested in the activities of Mr. Haszmanay."

"He's giving secrets to the other side?"

"I did not say that. I never *will* say that, and I won't say more. Just remember, the kind of work he does is sensitive. Everyone involved is subject to the most rigorous surveillance. You were right, Doctor. We *do* have a full file on

Haszmanay. You don't miss a trick. But we didn't compile it just to keep ourselves busy. All I can tell you is that the Bureau has good reason for watching him. Now, I'll also admit that it may turn out to be unwarranted."

"Hell it will . . . ," murmured Wanzer, shoving a stick of gum into his mouth.

Harwood jerked his head around and shot a glance at him. "C'mon, Wanzer," he snapped, "let's keep our personal hunches out of it, okay?"

Everybody was quiet for a second. I looked down at the curled and cracked linoleum. I hadn't asked for any of this. There I was, sitting out in my back yard playing chess. Next thing I know, my wife is almost dead, and I'm dodging poison pellets and the KGB. What gives? Why me?

Sid Wanzer, the same sleepy-eyed, bored look still on his face, began tapping his leather-soled shoe on the linoleum in a fast tattoo. The man appeared to be a strange combination of sloth and energy. He sniffed loudly twice, cleared his throat quickly, and folded his arms, looking at the floor.

"Why don't you just pick Haszmanay up and grill him? Find out one way or another?" asked Brian. Good old Brian—always the direct approach.

Harwood rose and went over to the smudged window. He looked out at the cars creeping along Commonwealth. He rocked up and down on his toes.

"Believe me, it's always tempting," he said finally. "But that's not the way it's done. The trick is to undertake surveillance without the subject being aware of it. That way, if our suspicions prove correct, we find out enough to bust the whole operation, discover who his superiors are, who runs the network. We can also arrange it so he feeds them false information. It's a tricky game. Cat and mouse."

"And you want me to participate," I said.

"No. But we would like you to cooperate. Keep your eyes and ears open. I've seen already that you have very good powers of observation, Doctor."

"It's my profession. Physicians are trained above all else to observe. To look for what's wrong . . . out of place. Okay, I'll use my eyes and ears on Emil. But I'm telling you, I hardly see him. And if I snoop around, he's liable to get suspicious."

"I don't want you to snoop. All I want you to do is tell me, either directly or through Joe or Brian here, if he contacts you, or if you see anything interesting. I'll give you phone numbers where I can be reached quickly. I've worked with Joe before on a couple of cases, and Brian and I have had previous contact. I see no reason why we can't all keep in touch about this matter."

Then he turned from the window and placed his hands on a chair back, leaning slightly forward and looking down at us. It sure looked impressive. Did they teach the special agents that at the Bureau?

"And finally," he said, "don't make any more out of this than it is. This is merely one of a dozen or so similar cases I'm handling right now. In fact the only reason I'm here is because of the pellet. Now that it seems to be over, with no deaths—uh, no human deaths—perhaps things will slide back into normal again."

"Normal?" whispered Brian. It was a whisper that hissed. It was a menacing whisper. I know that whisper; he's used it on me a lot. "With some nut out there in my town shooting things with a silent gun? A gun the inflicts hideous death? With a pellet made in Moscow? *Normal?*" Brian was on his feet now. "C'mon, Chet!"

"Okay, okay," said Harwood, holding up his palms. "I know it's weird, and scary. But we've come here to assure all of you that Concord won't become a killing ground. What we'd like to see is a thorough investigation by your own department, Brian. Something strictly local and low-key regarding the shooting incident. Your men can look around, call on Haszmanay, maybe get inside his residence. You can say that not only was a pet killed, but Mrs. Adams came close to death. We're dealing with a serious menace here, right? *But*, don't mention thallium, the KGB, or anything else. As far as you and the town of Concord are concerned, it's just some local nut poisoning pets. That way his suspicions won't be aroused. But be thorough, and a little stubborn. Maybe you can shake something loose that will help us."

"Now you're talking," said Brian.

"Maybe I've said more in this meeting than I really should have. If so, I'd appreciate your confidence—and silence. Two of you are police officers, and silence is part of your job. That leaves you, Dr. Adams. I guess I have to take your word that you won't say anything about what I've told you to anyone, with the possible exception of your wife. However, it's been our experience that telling even one person seriously jeopardizes confidentiality."

"What you've said about Emil—and it isn't much—won't go further than my house. You can count on it. And I'll keep you discreetly informed of anything going on over there."

And with that, the interview was over. I sketched out a rough map of the neighborhood for Harwood, with landmarks thrown in, and explained where the various people lived and what they were like. Sid Wanzer stood behind us, snapping his chewing gum. It was Juicyfruit; I could smell it. Then the two of them took off for their office in the J.F.K. Federal Building, and the three of us went back to Emerson Hospital to see Mary.

"Quite a neighbor you got," said Brian on the way back. "We'll pay him a visit first thing tomorrow."

6

Later on that Sunday afternoon, I brought Mary back home in the car, then set her up in a rented hospital bed in my study. The study, which is just behind the living room, looks out into the back yard. Next door to it is Mary's beloved atelier, her pottery studio. Adjoining both rooms in back is a small greenhouse, light and airy. I knew that Mary would much prefer to be downstairs in the middle of things than up in our bedroom. She was semiambulatory, but still weak. The fever had left soon after its origin was discovered and the Prussian blue began to have its effect. She worked the bed's controls so that she was sitting up and requested her favorite medicine.

"Make it French roast, Charlie. In a big mug. And can you put on some music?"

I did what she'd asked, then opened the big sliding doors between the study and the living room, which were usually shut. This gave her a nice view and a lot of space. And since the bed had wheels, I could move her into the kitchen, too. Once she was settled, I realized I wanted some fresh air. And my curiosity was working overtime. I decided to go for a walk. I dropped my pocket thirty-five-millimeter camera into my sport coat, took a walking stick from the umbrella barrel in the hallway, and called the dogs. All three of them.

It was cloudy outside and looked like rain, so I put on an Irish tweed hat.

I assured Mary I'd be back in forty minutes and went out the back door and across the lawn toward Emil's house. The dogs fanned out ahead of me. Danny and Troubles ranged back and forth, testing the ground and the wind for scent. Occasionally they looked up. Flack kept his nose to the ground and shuffled his low-slung body through the fallen leaves, never glancing up. That's the difference between retrievers and hounds. Dachshunds are hounds; they have great noses for following scent on the ground, but they can't see worth a damn. We were looking for nothing in particular, but I figured three keen noses would be a help if there were anything to find.

My feet squished softly in the low gully at the property line, and I walked through a hedge and up Emil Haszmanay's lawn. I noticed again how well maintained his house was. The brickwork was in excellent repair; the wooden window trim and the pillars of the front entranceway were freshly painted cream yellow, semigloss. Even the ivy on the walls was neat. Clean windows, immaculate lawn. He had to have help to keep the place this well. Rang bell. No answer. Car still in driveway. Had he gone away? Often people leave their cars in the driveway when they go on a trip to give the appearance that they're home. But Haszmanay's garage door was open, and I saw his riding lawn mower and a lot of other equipment just inside. He would have locked up if he were really away. So what did it mean? Would Brian and his men find him inside his house tomorrow, dead?

Who knew? I moved away from the front door and walked down the drive. The dogs had crisscrossed his property without showing anything but passing interest. There was the birdbath and bronze fountain, and something I hadn't noticed earlier: a half-completed flower bed. Freshly dug earth. Emil, or his hired help, had been putting in bulbs for springtime. The bulb planter, with its funny-shaped, tubular blade, was leaning against the brick wall of the house. The dogs came up, sniffed at the garden, and walked on. It was darker now, and the sky was low and leaden, with rolling layers of stratus clouds that had the metallic look of crumpled lead foil. I felt a few drops of cold rain. It had rained the previous night, too. That's why my feet had squished in the gully. But last night I hadn't really noticed the rain, or much else, because I had thought Mary was at death's door. There was the telephone lineman's tent up on the far pole, but no one was working there because it was Sunday. Three crows sat on top of it, bobbing their heads. I walked on to the end of Emil's yard. There was a thick patch of brush there separating his property from the Rutners'. The dogs showed keen interest in this. But was it something sinister or just a burrowed woodchuck or passing coon?

I peered under the thick bushes, now spiky gray with their leaves gone, and saw Danny sniffing and growling at a spot on the earth. What was it? Probably just a urine scent left behind by a passing male dog. But, looking through the bushes, I realized that this spot would be an ideal hiding place, even in wintertime. And it was right where my property joined Haszmanay's and the Rutners'.

It seemed to grow colder even as I walked across my yard. By the time I crossed the terrace to the back door, the cold rain had changed to sleet. I went inside and built a fire in the kitchen wood stove. The stove has fireglass in the front doors, so you can see the flames dance inside. When it was going full tilt, I wheeled Mary in and poured her a mineral water.

"No wine, hon. Not for a couple weeks, at least."

"Well, I don't want it anyway. And besides, I'm not worried about my liver; I'm worried about my hair, Charlie. It's falling out in clumps!"

She was starting to cry. I tried to cheer her up by describing the ski lodge I was taking the family to over Christmas, but she wasn't listening. I poured a drink and sipped it, rocking up and down on my toes and looking out the window. The sleet had now changed to real snow.

"Honey, it's snowing out. Snow in October, can you believe it?"

She grunted, and I watched the white specks fall earthward in the dying light. The back yard was soft gray now.

Soon it would be white. But who knew how long it would stay? Mary stopped crying and looked at me.

"What are you thinking about?" she finally asked.

"I'm thinking about crows," I said.

7

MORE OF THE SAME WEATHER THE NEXT MORNING. I LOOKED out the bedroom window and saw low sheets of gray clouds. Drifting flakes blew around the windowsills, and tiny steams and rivulets of snow blew along the terrace tiles below and formed into little mounds of white in the corners. I reached over and gently rocked Mary back and forth. She rolled over and opened her eyes. She didn't look well, and had been up half the night with cramps and diarrhea. The Prussian blue was helping her, but it had its side effects, too. I ran my fingers through her hair, and she closed her eyes. She put her hand on mine. It felt cold and damp, as did her forehead.

"Can't you sleep?"

"Uh-huh. So I don't want to go downstairs yet. Let me have another hour up here."

I went downstairs and made coffee. After drinking two mugs, and going over the *Boston Globe*, I returned upstairs and snuggled with Mary in bed, thankful she was going to be okay. I was exhausted from being up all night at the hospital Saturday. I lay next to her and tried to decide if I should go into the office after lunch and see the patients Susan had not rescheduled. I supposed it would depend on how Mary was doing. . . .

I know I was asleep, because it was the dogs barking

downstairs that woke me up. Sitting up in bed, I heard the faint chime of the doorbell above the racket. I went down and opened the front door amid a cluster of whirling, barking dogs. Brian Hannon was standing on my stoop, blowing big clouds of vapor from his mouth.

"How's Mary?" he asked, following me into the kitchen and pouring himself a mug.

"Not too good. She was running to the john all night, and she's in pain. I think she's got a couple more days of misery ahead of her, too."

He shook his head slowly and swore, lighting a Lucky.

"You believe this weather, Doc? You believe it? Friggin' snow, for Chrissakes. Remember eight years ago, we had snow in May? Jeez, covered my lilacs. . . ."

"What brings you here? Want to talk to Mary?"

"No. I want to go inside Haszmanay's house."

"Really?"

"Yeah. Nor for an official search; we'll need a warrant for that. For suspicion of felony. See, I figure we can talk to Haszmanay legit, just the way Chet Harwood suggested. We're investigating the incident. But we called his residence early this morning. Nobody home. We then called Lincoln Labs. Hell, it was twenty minutes before they'd even speak to us. Weren't convinced we were the law. Talk about buttoned up. Anyway, Emil Haszmanay always comes in to work between seven-thirty and eight. As of eight-thirty this morning he wasn't in. He's got no time off scheduled, and he has always called in sick promptly in the past."

"So he's missing," I said.

"Yeah. Missing, or dead maybe. I say there's a good chance we'll find the late Mr. Haszmanay next door. I suspect foul play. Ergo: suspicion of felony. Ergo: no search warrant, just go in for a look, not a search. I brought some help with me. Are you working today? I'd like you to come, too."

"Not working till P.M., if then. Why do you want me?"

" 'Cause I've never laid eyes on Haszmanay. You can identify him."

"And you think he's dead in his house?"

"A good chance, Doc. Put it together: poisoned pellet from air gun. Pellet made in Moscow. Haszmanay, Hungarian refugee involved in defense secrets, doesn't answer phone and hasn't gone in to work. Car still in drive. *Hmmm?*"

We went up to say goodbye to Mary, but she was asleep, so we went over to Haszmanay's. We stood at the front door, with two officers behind us, and rang the bell. No answer. We walked around the house, looking in the windows. Appeared vacant. We returned to Haszmanay's front door. Before long a detective in a trench coat pulled up in an unmarked cruiser and walked over to us, carrying an oversized attaché case. Brian introduced him as James Billings. Billings placed the case on the stoop and opened it, revealing rows and rows of neatly packaged tools, mirrors, and small drills. He selected two tools. I knew what the tools were; on a previous case, Joe had personally demonstrated the use of the pick and torsion bar. The pick pushes up the tumblers in a lock, and the torsion bar keeps tension on the cylinder and the tumbler bars so they don't slide back down again after they're pushed up by the pick.

I hang around with classy people. Only the best.

Billings inserted the torsion bar into the bottom part of the keyhole and twisted it slightly, then proceeded to "rake" the lock in the front door. When he had the tumbler pins pushed up in their proper position, he was able, using the bar, to turn the tumbler set and cylinder within the lock, and there was an audible *clack* as the door unlocked. But still it wouldn't open; Haszmanay had fastened a chain lock as well.

"Well, he didn't leave by the front door," said Brian. "Whadduyuh think, Jim? Should we try the kitchen door?"

"Nah," said Billings, and took two more tools from the case. One was a mirror the size of a lady's compact, mounted on a thin jointed metal rod a foot and half long. It was made so that you could bend and adjust it any way you wanted. At the rod's end was a clamp. The second tool was another jointed rod, but instead of a mirror it had a spring-mounted, three-pronged gripper that could be worked from a plunger on its opposite end. Billings inserted the mirror through the crack in the doorway, clamped the rod to the door, then adjusted the mirror so that he could see the reflection of the slot for the chain lock. Then, with both hands now free, he took the other rod in one hand and drew the door back so that it was almost closed. I looked over his shoulder and saw him adjust the rod, then manipulate the gripper so that it grabbed the end of the chain in the slot. In less than a second he had pulled the chain out, and the door swung open.

"Hey, where can I get those tools?" I asked.

"Bet on it," said Billings, and packed up his case.

"Might as well stick with us a while, Jim," said Brian. "We might need you again." The five of us went inside.

The house was spotless and tastefully furnished. The living room had gray-painted wooden molding, even around the fireplace, with a Federal bull's-eye mirror over the mantel. There were hunting prints and Audubon prints in gilt frames. Bird lover. Ergo: cat-hater. I knew it. Ming rugs, parquet oak floors. Traditional furniture with some Chinese influence. Leather-topped desk in study alcove. Bright porcelain vases, cobalt blue and scarlet on white. Trim kitchen. Not well furnished, but nice. Haszmanay clearly did not cook. Family room that was turned into a big study, with computer, printer, and very impressive-looking radio with microphone.

"Ha!" said Brian in a coarse whisper. I turned to see him holing his finger to his lips. Mum's the word, he way saying, we're in the residence of a master spy. Okay, but if he is a spy—was a spy, I thought to myself—why is the radio out in public view?

We went through the dinning room, which had a nice mahogany highboy, a nice brass chandelier, nice buffet and table, and nice everything else.

"For a man not born here, he certainly seems fond of American furnishings," I said, looking at the prints from the Hudson River School that were hung over the Regency wallpaper.

Brian leaned close and whispered softly, "Don't you see? Perfect cover."

We came back to the kitchen again. Well, Emil Haszmanay wasn't on the first floor. I saw Brian's jaw drop.

"Look," he said, pointing at the back door. The back door had a chain lock, too. And it was fastened. Brian had the two officers check the downstairs windows. They returned in a flash to say they were all snibbed. Brian let out a slow breath of air and rolled his eyes upward.

"Then he's up there," he said. "Morrissey, you and Fields watch the downstairs while we go up. Billings, give the basement a once-over and then follow us up, okay? Oh, and you might as well call the meat wagon. No sense waiting for it later."

We went back to the small marble hallway and started up the staircase, which curved up around a big brass hanging lamp. The house sure was exquisite. It was too bad our errand wasn't more pleasant. Where would we find him? In bed, having passed peacefully in his sleep? In the tub, drowned? Slumped unceremoniously in some corner, dead from a sudden stroke or a massive heart attack? I wasn't looking forward to it.

"Good thing you're a doctor, Doc. You can give a preliminary opinion on cause of death. By the way, you still are a regular doctor, aren't you?"

"Well, I went through med school and practiced internal medicine for four years, if that's what you mean. I wouldn't—couldn't—take on a practice now. But I know all the basics."

"How come you switched over to oral surgery?"

"Because of stuff like what we're doing now," I said. "Also, I really do like surgery, except the tooth-pulling. I'm good with my hands. Here's the bathroom. You go first."

He advanced to the half-opened door of the john, then paused, waving an arm in front of himself and half bowing.

"Naw. After you, Alphonse."

"*Mais non!* After you, Gaston."

"Nah. I think—"

"Move it, Hannon!" I barked, giving him a gentle knee in the behind. He growled and opened the door, pushing it with his thumbnail so as not to leave prints. Vacant bathroom. Except for drawn shower curtain. Oh-oh. Brian peeped around the edge, then flung it back. Empty stall. I breathed a sigh of relief.

We went back out into the hall and opened the first door we came to. Brian gingerly turned the knob with two fingers wrapped in a hankie, opened it a crack, peeked in, and then went through. Spare bedroom. Checked it out. Vacant. On to next door.

"Okay, hotshot. Your turn," he said.

"Why me? You're the police chief."

"Open it, Doc." I did. A linen closet. Sheets, pillowcases, towels, blankets, some mineral oil, toothpaste. No body.

"Ha!" I said, pleased with myself.

"Goddammit, linen closets don't count. Now, do the next one."

I tried the next door. Master bedroom. Appeared vacant. Bed made. Bedroom had its own bathroom. Door open only a crack. Oh-oh.

We fought a minute or two over who the lucky guy was going to be. Finally I pushed the door open with a pencil, half shielding my eyes. Empty bathroom. Toothbrushes, razor, everything where it should be. Even hairbush and comb. Shower curtain already pulled back, revealing tub. Everything orderly.

But we weren't out of the woods yet. There were more doors to try. Bedroom closet. Vacant. Back into the hall, following it to the end. Brian turned the knob carefully, with the hankie, as he had before. He opened the door a crack and kept pushing it open, peering in and around. It was a third bedroom, turned into yet another study. Big desk with many papers on it. Chair and sofa, vacant. That left only the upstairs porch, the door of which was open. We could see it was empty. On our way out, Brian tried the only door we had forgotten. He tugged absently at the spare-bedroom closet door, and it came open.

Nothing. Empty coat hangers.

"Hey chief, need any help?" asked Billings, coming up the stairs. He worked his way down the hall, looking in the rooms, frowning.

"So where is he, Chief? Where's the stiff?" he asked.

We both shrugged at him.

"Well, the cellah's clean. And the windows are locked from the inside. So where is he?"

Brian looked heavenward for an answer. He saw the trap door to the attic. There was a rope hanging from it. He reached up and pulled it down. Fastened to the trap door was a wooden ladder that unfolded and reached the floor.

Again, Brian swept his arm and bowed. This time, to Billings.

"Okay, Jim, do your stuff," he said. So Billings reluctantly oozed his way up the wooden stairway, flashlight poised, mouth set tight. Just before he disappeared up through the trap, he shot a dirty look at his chief.

But darned if the attic weren't vacant as well. Funny, but I sort of thought it would be. I sat down on Haszmanay's bed and looked out the bedroom window. Over the trees, I could just see glimpses of a wide, gambrel slate roof. My house. I looked all around the neighborhood and then turned to Brian.

"Well? Haszmanay is nowhere to be found."

"I know, I know. Jeez, Doc, whadduyuh think I am, dumb?"

"No comment."

"Okay," he said, after a long, weary sigh, "let's do it again."

So we went through the house once more, from the basement on up. When we were finished, I again sat on the bed in the master bedroom.

"So what'd he do?" asked Brian. "Fly up the chimney?" I gathered it was a rhetorical question.

"I don't know. But Emil Haszmanay sure kept his house locked up tight. Maybe he was cautious, or just plain scared. Maybe he feared for his life."

Brian was fed up and disgusted. He stomped downstairs and out through the front hallway with all of us trailing behind. We were met out front by the boys from the ambulance, who were wheeling a litter up the driveway.

"Tell 'em to forget it," said Brian. "False alarm."

After the ambulance, the two officers, and Detective Billings left, Brian and I sat in Haszmanay's living room. Brian fidgeted, patting all his pockets.

"Shit! I left my weeds at your place, Doc. In the kitchen, I think."

"Well, it won't do you any harm to do without for a few minutes. It'll amaze your lungs, for one thing. And also, how do you know Haszmanay would want you to smoke in his house?"

He was frowning at his feet, which were propped up on a hassock in front of him. His feet wiggled back and forth in nervousness, and he frowned at them, then squinted at me.

"Emil's dead. Besides, he smoked too. Look at the ashtrays."

I noticed them, as I had when I first arrived. I took a walk into the kitchen and opened the refrigerator. Imported beer: Grolsch. Veggies, cream, lots of cheeses. White wine. And Camels. A half-empty carton of Camels.

"I guess it's okay. You were right. Haszmanay was a Camel man."

"Mmmmmm . . . ," he said, joining me in front of the refrigerator. He took out the carton and shook out a pack. I watched him, saying nothing.

"And don't give me that holier-than-thou look, Doc," he growled. "It irritates me." He lit up.

I still said nothing. Still frowning, Brian shook out his match, held it under the faucet, and dropped it in the wastebasket. He was looking at me as if his theft were my fault.

"Okay . . . so where is he?" he said, drawing in the smoke and letting it out in a loud hiss.

"I guess he's either dead or—"

"Or what?"

"Or flown the coop. To God knows where. You know, Brian, I get a funny feeling being here right now. I get the feeling that this could be my house."

He swiveled his balding head to stare at me, dribbling smoke out of his nose.

"Whadduyuh mean by that?"

"As I walked around in here—and around the outside, too—I kept getting the feeling that if I *did* own this place, I'd furnish it just the way he did. And I somehow knew that if

Emil smoked, he'd keep his cigarettes in the refrigerator, just the way I used to when I smoked."

"You smoked cigarettes? What kind?"

"Camels. See? See what I mean? Haszmanay and I are soul mates. Or *were* soul mates."

"Oh, yeah? Well, your so-called soul mate killed your kitty and almost did your wife in. How do you fit those minor details in, eh Doc?"

I sat in the easy chair and thought a while before answering.

"I'm not convinced he did. I think there's a lot we don't know abut Mr. Haszmanay."

"Well, I wish Chet had told us more. I guess I better get back to the office and call him. Meanwhile, we better leave. We still don't have an official warrant, you know."

So we went back out. Brian came inside and had another cup of java. I helped Mary downstairs. She and Brian hugged, and she sat down for her breakfast: a big bowl of cottage cheese. Mary said she was feeling much better, almost chipper. So I decided to go in to the office. Brian noticed his Luckies on the table, so he switched packs, leaving the Camels in their place, then left.

Something was gnawing at me, but I hadn't mentioned it to Brian. Just before I left for the office, after having propped Mary up in the living room, I made a phone call to the Town of Concord's Municipal Services Building. Then I kissed Mary goodbye and said I'd be back at four.

All right, I wasn't snooping. I was just looking around a bit. I rang twice but knew there'd be no answer. I looked around behind me, and up and down Orchard Lane, the street that Haszmanay's house faced. Nobody in sight. I tried to do this scouting casually. Did it work? Who knew? I walked up the driveway and into the garage. It was quarter to five and the daylight was beginning to fade. What was in the garage, anyway? Snow blower, lawn mover, power weed whacker, electric hedge trimmer . . . all those suburban survival tools.

Long aluminum ladder hanging on the rear wall. Perfect. I lifted it off and carried it out. Boy, the metal was cold. I stopped, leaned the ladder against the brick wall of the house, and put on a stocking cap that I pulled down low. Then I buttoned my parka up tight and carried the ladder over Emil's lawn, through some brush, and over a meadow. I don't think anybody saw me, but I mean, hell—a big ladder like that, it could glint in the sunlight.

Fighting my way through a small copse of young pines was tough, but I finally made it. I propped the ladder up against the pole and began climbing. Twelve feet up, the steel climbing bars commenced, and I took them the rest of the way up. I grabbed the hanging flap of the tent and shook it. A big, glossy black bird sailed out past my face, not saying anything.

Then I took a deep breath, steadied myself, and yanked back the canvas tent wall.

A foot and a half from me, a face stared back.

That is, I assumed it had once been a face.

Two bloody sockets, pecked into red-brown ooze. They were set on a field of ripped, dangling, and clotted tissue that had been skin and muscle once upon a time. The big grin was intact, of course. I mean, you can't eat teeth. It was trying its damnedest to be a face. It just wasn't making it.

8

WHAT DO YOU MEAN, 'BETTER CALL THE MEAT WAGON back'?" said Brian. "Where are you, anyway?"

"Home," I answered, opening the wood-stove doors and poking the hot embers inside. "When I got back from work I sort of continued our investigation of this morning. I had a suspicion, and a call to the Municipal Works Department confirmed it."

"You found Haszmanay? Dead?"

"No. I found some other guy dead, but not Emil. This guy's beefy, not thin, and had black hair. I found the body up in the lineman's tent."

"Where? Lineman's tent? What lineman's tent? What the hell *is* a lineman's tent, for Chrissakes?"

"Look, just get the ambulance. And then call the municipal building and have them bring one of those cherry-picker utility trucks over here."

He told me to quit playing games and come clean. So I told him exactly what had happened.

"And you mean the stiff is still up on that pole?"

"Uh-huh."

"And the ladder's still there and everything?"

"Uh-huh."

"So some little kid could climb up there now and get a free peek at the Faceless Wonder?"

"Uh-huh."

"Do you realize you're a total nincompoop?"

"Uh-huh."

"Okay, look: go out to the goddamn pole and stay put. I'll get on the wire and be over there as soon as I can. And Doc?"

"Hmmmm?"

"Don't do anything else. Just don't do anything at all, okay? Just *freeze*."

So I went back outside with a flashlight and trudged back across the various community lawns and through shrubbery until I was again at the utility pole. Sometimes I just can't help but get the feeling that Brian doesn't think I'm all there upstairs.

Well, let me tell you: getting the guy down out of that tent was a bitch. First, getting the cherry-picker rig, and the men to work it, was a challenge in itself. It was after hours, and most municipal employees don't like to work at seven in the evening. Maneuvering the truck through thick brush in the dark to get to the pole was also a chore. Finally the truck was positioned, and the driver got out and climbed into the little basket at the end of the hydraulic arm, worked the levers at his side, and brought the contraption to rest at our feet. I swept my hand in front of Brian and bowed.

"Okay, Monsieur Gaston, climb aboard. Do your stuff."

"Up yours, pal," he growled under his breath as he climbed in with the driver.

They were up there only long enough for Brian to take a peek inside. "Down," I heard him say to the driver. "*Down*, goddammit!"

He stepped out of the little basket and paced to and fro, breathing deeply and spitting constantly. Finally, as if on sudden impulse, he disappeared into the bushes and puked. He reappeared shortly afterward, with red face and watering eyes.

"Jeez, Doc, that's awful, huh? Just ate the face away. Keee-*riste*!"

"Yeah, I guess I should've warned you. We'll go back to the house afterward and unwind."

"Let's go now. This thing's, uh, bigger than I first thought. We're gonna need a full lab team out here to do it right."

Brian requested that the cherry picker remain on site but that the men stay in the cab so as not to disturb the scene. Likewise he told the ambulance attendants to wait in their vehicle on the street until the team arrived.

"And turn off your beacon, for God's sake," he said, pulling up his coat collar against the wind. "I don't want half the town here looking on."

Back at our house, Brian washed out his mouth and drank an ice-cold Coke. He belched slowly, tentatively, and said he felt much better. We went back across the fields to the pole, and the lab team arrived within an hour, without flashing lights. But it was fully dark now, and cold. We watched men scurry back and forth from the street to the utility pole, bundled up and carrying flashlights. The utility truck had trained its spotlights on the eerie-looking canvas tent. They didn't even bring the body down until after nine. They didn't use the cherry picker for that. They lowered it, wrapped in a plastic body bag, in a rescue litter with a block and tackle. We watched as they carried it away.

"Where will they take it?" I asked.

"Straight to the state lab in town. I've notified Ten Ten Comm. Ave. We ought to be seeing Joe pretty soon, too. Any homicide, the state must come in, right from the start. Frankly, I'll be glad when they get here; this is bizarre enough I don't wanta take any chances."

The lab team approached with a wrapped bundle.

"What's that?" Brian asked.

They placed it on the ground, near a hissing gas lantern, and pulled back the wrapping. Lying there in the bright white light was a scoped rifle.

"Where'd this come from?" he asked.

"It was undah the guy, Chief. You know, undah-neath.

He died of a gunshot wound inna chest. Maybe he shawt himself, but I don't think so."

"Why not?"

"Cause there's no powdah residue on the coat. An' also, the gun's only a twenny-two."

"Looks awful fancy for a twenty-two. Doc, look at that hand-checkered stock."

But I was already reading the manufacturer's name on the barrel: Weihrauch.

"Looks like our friend Karl Pirsch was right on the money, Brian. This is the souped-up air gun he described, remember?"

Just then another man brought over the contents of the corpse's pockets. There were three items: a single-bladed folding knife, a hand-warmer in a red felt bag, and a green tin can, the size and shape of a shoe-polish can. It had a screw-on lid, and some words in German written on it. Below that was a picture of a pellet. Brian lifted the can with gloved fingers and shook it tentatively. It rattled.

"Be especially careful with this," he told the technician. "Don't even open it. Dust it all for prints."

The man nodded and began to turn away. Brian grabbed his sleeve and turned him around.

"That's it? No wallet? No IDs? No car keys? Spare change?"

The man shook his head and departed. Brian blew a breath of air out, his cheeks puffed out in a balloon like Dizzy Gillespie. I knew what that meant: he was frustrated. I felt a clap on the shoulder and turned to see the dark, stubbly face of my brother-in-law. Brian turned and nodded, then gazed at the pole with a thousand-yard stare.

"Hey Joe," he said, "You wanna look at the site a little bit?"

"Nah. I'd probably just screw it up. I'm better at reading the lab report when the pros are finished."

"Did you bring your men?"

"Just two for now, to help out. I know your guys are great at packaging evidence. I called Chet Harwood as soon as

Doc called me. He's going to notify all kinds of specialists to look at the corpse. You're sure it's not Haszmanay, Doc?''

''Positive. I've only talked with him at length two or three times, but I know face structures, even with most of the flesh gone. This guy, whoever he was, isn't Emil. He's bigger and taller, for one thing. And he had hair. Dark hair. Emil's balding, with wispy white hair. Harwood will back me up on it. By the way, what was Chet's reaction to these developments?''

''Hard to read,'' said Joe, ''but he was very interested and wants to talk with you.''

''Well, let's go back to the house and warm up. I'll heat up the rest of that gumbo Mary made, and we'll wait for preliminary findings on the stiff.''

Joe, never famous for his delicate appetite, inhaled three big bowls of gumbo with noises akin to those made by a feeding walrus. He chewed the big hunks of smoked andouille sausage. He crunched up the big Gulf shrimp, shells and all, which is how they're tastiest anyway. In between gulps, he tore off big sections of a French baguette and slathered them with unsalted butter. When he was finished, his eyes still wearing that glazed, ecstatic look, he poured himself a generous tumbler of red, lighted a Benson & Hedges, and sat smoking.

''Let's see. We've got a missing Haszmanay. From a house that's well kept and, to all appearances, undisturbed. Also locked from the inside. Swell. Then we've got this would-be assassin perched in a lineman's tent, no doubt for a good vantage point. The preliminary examination suggests that he died from a gunshot wound to the chest, fired from a distance. He's go no ID, no nothin', except more nasty pellets, a knife, a hand-warmer, and the German air rifle.''

''And the small folding canvas camp stool he was sitting on,'' added Brian.

''Okay. So I say we look for a vehicle that's strange to the neighborhood and that hasn't moved. That'll be the car he came in. He stowed the keys and his wallet somewhere nearby. I'd say we've got a good chance of recovering them once we find the car. First, of course, we'll check to see if the prints on the vehicle match those of the marksman. Once we've made the vehicle, we check the registration with the state and, at the same time, search for the keys. Where we find them, we'll also find the cash and the IDs."

Brian nodded. "But then who shot him? Haszmanay?"

"Maybe," I said. "Or maybe whoever shot him also took Haszmanay away."

"But how?" asked Brian. "How'd they get him out of that locked house?"

"The ladder," I said. "Oh, I forgot. The ladder I used was Emil's. And before I carted it over to the pole, I checked the lawn around the house. There were two depressions—rectangular—in the grass just below the master-bathroom window. I put the ladder next to them, and the feet matched the depressions."

"So what you're saying is, somebody used Emil's ladder to climb up into the john window and get him—probably in the dead of night."

"Uh-huh. Looks like."

"Why the hell didn't you tell me, Doc? Jeez! And disturbing the evidence and everything. Keee-riste! Remember, Chet himself said no snooping. You're snooping your ass off. I want it *stopped*!"

"Okay."

"So. So tell me more. Tell me all you know," he continued.

I shrugged my shoulders and said there was nothing more, which made him mad. He did the Dizzy Gillespie breath-blow again, and Joe shot me a wink.

"But maybe something will occur to me if we go back to Emil's house again. I like that place; it fascinates me. Joe, you'd really like it, too."

"What about me? Or don't I count?" asked Mary, who walked in from the dining room. She walked slowly, unsteady on her feet. She was grabbing her white terry-cloth robe around her neck to keep warm. She scuffled over to the wood stove, and I jumped up and got a chair for her. I settled her in front of the hot, tinking metal and watched the color come back into her face.

"You want to come?" I asked her.

She waved her hand absently in our direction.

"Oh, Charlie, I'm just too tired. And hungry. Am I going to have to have more cottage cheese?"

"What do you want?"

"There's half a frozen lasagna in the freezer."

Joe was up on his feet in a second and making a beeline for the freezer around the corner. I noticed Brian was smacking his lips and looking appreciatively around him.

"Whadduyuh say, Charlie? Should we put out some plates for these bachelor types?"

"Why not? But Joe, you already ate, didn't you?"

"Huh? The gumbo? An appetizer, Doc. C'mon!"

So we ate the lasagna, hot Italian garlic bread, and a big Greek salad while we talked about the strange neighborhood events of the past several days.

"I'd like to go back to Emil's tomorrow morning as soon as it's light," I said.

"Sounds good to me," said Joe. "You seem to be doing pretty well so far, Doc. Mary, I take it the guest room is ready?"

9

NEXT MORNING, A POLICE COURIER FROM BOSTON DELIVered a search warrant to my house. The warrant was for the Haszmanay residence. Joe thought it would be a good idea to have official clearance, so the previous evening, after his light meal of gumbo and lasagna, he'd called headquarters and made the arrangements. I trotted back into the kitchen, amidst a swirl of barking dogs, and told Joe he had to sign for the envelope. Then I went upstairs and checked on Mary, who'd suffered a slight relapse and hadn't slept well. I brought up a tumbler of iced Poland Springs water for her, and her medicine. When I returned to the kitchen I saw Brian dragging on a freshly lit Lucky while he fiddled with the coffee machine.

"Jeez, Doc, this wop coffee alla time. Can't you just make the regulah stuff?"

"Hmmmmph! Why'n't you just go to Ho-Jo's, then?" said Joe, sitting down at the table and opening the envelope. I made a cup of American coffee (whatever that is) for Brian, and ten minutes later we were out in the cold, walking to Emil's house.

"I'm not sure you should come with us, Doc," said Joe. "This is official police business."

"Well, he went with me yesterday," said Brian. "I mean, Doc's the only one who can identify Haszmanay."

"You know I won't disturb anything," I said.

"Yeah. Okay, just keep it quiet. I have to admit I like the way you notice things, Doc. Keep an eye peeled, eh?"

When we got inside, Joe gave a soft whistle.

"Hey, this is okay," he said, taking in the furnishings and the decor. "This is as nice as your place, Doc. Reminds me of it, too."

"Hmmmm. That's interesting. Because I told Brian the same thing."

"The lab teams are going to show up after lunch," said Joe. "Chet and the rest of the Feds will be here, too. This is our last shot at going over this place solo. Even so, don't touch anything."

I nodded and went straight for the upstairs porch. That room, with windows on three sides, had intrigued me from the first. I looked at the big desk with all the papers on it. Messy. Why messy, when Haszmanay was obviously neat, even compulsively so? I looked at the papers. Old bills. Statements from the oil company, gasoline charge receipts. Bills from Filene's department store. Junk mail. Nothing important. Why, then, were they littering the desk? Open the desk? No, I couldn't, at least without asking Joe to help. I looked out the windows, especially the two that overlooked the back. The windows all had pull-down shades and curtains, too, which could be closed by cords. What were the curtains made of? Heavy material. As heavy as corduroy. If the windows were shut and you drew all the shades down and then closed all the curtains, what would happen?

I would be pitch-dark in the room. Yes. And also quiet. Very quiet.

"Well?" came a voice from the doorway. It was Brian, with Joe standing right behind him.

"I thought you said they put the ladder up to the bathroom window? This isn't the bathroom."

"I know. Can I clear this desk off?"

"You may not, even for a good reason. What's the reason?"

"I want to get up and sit on it."

"That's not a good reason," said Joe. "As they used to say in the South End, that's a jive-ass reason."

"But these papers aren't important. Why did he leave them here? The rest of the house is so neat. . . ."

"Well, why do you want to climb up on the desk and sit on it? Mind telling us?" asked Brian.

"Because there's a great view of the lineman's tent from the top of the desk. Take a look out the center window and see."

"I'd rather not," said Joe. "Let's not touch anything until after the lab teams come and go." Then he and Brian left, and I was alone.

If you shut all the windows and pulled down the shades and drew the curtains, I thought to myself, and left that middle window open . . . maybe pull the shade down halfway and draw the curtains almost shut, leaving a crack about eight or nine inches wide . . .

"Hey, Doc, quit daydreaming, will ya? Joe and I got the ladder in place. You were right; fits perfect. Wanta take a look?"

"Nah. I'm going home for a second and check on Mary. When you're finished you can find me in my study. I'll fix us all some lunch."

He raised his eyebrows, shrugged, and went back to the master bathroom. I went downstairs and into the little first-floor study. I leaned over the desk and peered again at the framed certificate that hung on the wall. I lifted it off the hook and took it with me.

"Karl? Karl Pirsch?"

"Yes. What may I do for you, please?"

"Karl, this is Dr. Charles Adams. I understand from Joe Brindelli that a team from your lab is coming out to Concord early this afternoon."

"Yes. We leave in three hours." He said it like this: *Ve leaf in ssreee owasss.* I asked him if he was coming out too. He answered that he wasn't planning on it.

"Well, the only reason I'm calling you directly is that

sometimes the chief of police here, Brian Hannon, doesn't think I know what I'm doing, since I'm not a professional. But I—"

"Wait, Dr. Adams. I believe Joe said it was you who found the body of the assassin?"

"Uh-huh. I had a hunch."

"Okay. Then I will listen. What is it?"

"First, what does the word *Schutzenfest* mean?"

"*Schutzenfest* is a sport shooting match among friends."

"That's what I figured. I've heard the term used at the gun club I belong to. I think the Adolph Coors Company sponsors one every ear, if I'm not mistaken."

"Yes. That would be correct, since Coors is a German brewing family."

"Okay," I said, reading the words off the framed certificate, which I held in my hand. "Now I see a pair of crossed rifles and a stag's head, and a lot of Gothic script here. But it says Budapest. Do they speak German in Hungary? I thought they spoke Magyar, or Romany, or something like that."

"German is still occasionally used in Hungary, Doctor."

That answered that. I asked Karl a few more questions, and the upshot was that he decided to accompany the lab team out to Concord. I told him I'd meet him at the Haszmanay residence around one-thirty. Then we rang off, and I went up to see Mary, who was still in bed. I crawled in and cuddled with her a while. She was still weak and woozy, but she liked the contact.

"How's the hair? It looks like it's going to stay after all."

"Oh, Charlie, I look so awful. I feel so bad. I'm never going to get well. . . ."

"Yes, you are. You'll be right as rain in a week, and your old self in ten days. I'm going to fix some lunch for Joe and Brian. You want anything?"

She said she just wanted to sleep. "Gee, Charlie, this'll do wonders for my body. I've lost almost six pounds already."

"Oh yeah? Well there was nothing wrong with it in the first place."

"Oh yes there was. Too fat."

"Well then, I like women who are a little too fat. I can't stand skinny broads."

I defrosted some of Mary's potato and leek soup for lunch. I would have maybe a Dixie Cup's worth, no more. Joe and Brian came in and slurped up several bowls apiece. I finished my mug of coffee and rinsed the dishes.

"All right. I'm going for a run now, then a sauna. I'll see you guys over at Emil's when the lab team gets there," I told them.

"Why don't you just leave it alone, Doc?" suggested Brian. "I mean, shouldn't you be pulling teeth or something?"

After loping five miles in the cold fall air, I had a long think in the sauna bath. With the temperature at a little over a hundred and sixty, and my pulse working itself practically to death, a lot of blood was going to my head. The sweat ran off me in sheets and soaked the redwood decking I sat on. I went over various scenarios in my mind. Over and over and over them. A key element would be the time of death of the marksman in the lineman's tent. Joe said they'd have that little tidbit when the team arrived. I went out, showered, sat in my terry-cloth robe for fifteen minutes, then went back into the inferno again. After the second dose I dressed and returned to my study with a mug of cold mineral water.

My thoughts kept returning to Mr. Emil Haszmanay. What sort of fellow was he? It seemed that Chester Harwood of the FBI was doing his damnedest to insinuate that he was a traitor/spy, or close to it. Possibly. But my personal impressions of him, and those I had after visiting his house, hardly reinforced this image. I saw in my mind's eye, based on the composite sketch of these impressions, a man who had fled tyranny, loved America, was delighted with his newfound status, and was circumspect. So he couldn't be a traitor/spy.

On the other hand, these qualities were exactly those needed to make him a superspy.

* * *

I brought Mary down, wheeled her hospital bed into the kitchen, and made her some coffee.

"I'm getting hungry," she said. "Finally."

"Well, have your cottage cheese now. If you're still hungry tonight we'll have steak or lamb."

"Charlie, you seem so worried lately. Is it me? Is there something nobody's telling me?"

"No. You're going to be fine. It's just that I can't make sense out of what's been happening around here lately."

"Well, the police and the FBI don't seem confused. They seem to know where they're going."

"I know. That's why I'm worried."

I watched Karl Pirsch direct his assistant. The middle pair of curtains in Emil Haszmanay's upstairs porch study was carefully removed from the slide rod and placed inside a clear plastic bag.

"Great, Karl. Remember: the central inside edge of each."

"Don't worry, we'll have the results before the end of the day."

"And what about the body on the pole? What does the lab have for time of death?"

"Approximately seven A.M., day before yesterday. Sunday morning. It's a good fix, because the corpse, being outside in the cool air, showed hardly any decomposition. We are performing a very thorough workup on this."

"Seven Sunday morning? I was at the hospital then, hoping Mary would live."

Pirsch said goodbye and hopped into a black sedan with the Commonwealth of Massachusetts seal on the door. I left to go to the office; I had an extraction at three and then a preliminary workup on a patient slated for a mandible resection the following week. Susan Petri, bless her heart, was full of sympathy and optimism. Believe me, I needed it. I was sick of death, near-death, corpses, poison, and hide-and-seek. After the second patient departed, I collapsed into my office chair and stared across the desk at the Winslow Homer and Andrew Wyeth prints on the far wall. I was drained. I looked at Homer's *Coot Hunter in the Adiron-*

dacks. I wished I were there, coot or no coot. I could picture in my mind a mist-covered lake at dawn . . . with Brady Coyne and me gliding silently across it in a canoe with fly rods . . .

Susan came in and left some material on the desk.

"You look tired," she said. "Why don't you go home? I'll be here to get the phone and make appointments."

Well, I didn't need persuading. I stopped at Moe's office, two doors down the hall. Nobody home. The beach rock near the chessboard was pointing away from his chair. After making my move, I turned the rock so the painted arrow on it was facing Moe's chair. At no time did I look inside the fish tank to glimpse Moe's repulsive sea-creatures—my day had been trying enough.

I left the building and drove toward home, but before heading up my driveway I swung past Emil's house and watched the men from the lab coming and going, toting carefully wrapped parcels, sealed vials, and envelopes, all containing evidence. Joe had left temporarily to investigate a call. Brian wandered in and out, taking mental notes. Then fatigue hit me again, and I went home.

"Charlie, you don't look so good," Mary said from her hospital bed. "Are you coming down with something?"

"Maybe. Aren't we a fine pair? Scoot over."

I climbed into the hospital bed. Mary had made a cozy fire in the wood stove, and we lay there snuggling, watching the flames dance on the other side of the fireglass. The stove tinked and purred. I closed my eyes and fell asleep.

When I woke up, it was midnight. I sat up and felt the room rock and sway. Fever. I fell back on the pillow and slept again.

When I woke again, it was early morning, and Mary was leaning over my bed and kissing my forehead.

"You're the sick one now," she said. "Your forehead's like an iron. Want some ice water?"

"Yes. What time is it?"

"Quartei after eight. Karl Pirsch, the lab man, called last night after you crashed. He said to tell you that he found ample powder residues on the curtains he took with him. He says a firearm, probably a rifle, was fired from the upstairs porch, at a distance of less than eight feet from the curtain."

"Ha! Knew it!"

"So why didn't anyone hear the shot?"

"Because the room absorbed at least eighty percent of the blast, that's why. To anyone outside, the shot would sound like a car backfiring. A small car, maybe a Volswagen. And how many people are even up and around at seven o'clock Sunday morning? So it was Emil Haszmanay who shot the man in the tent, probably in self-defense."

She placed her hand on her hip and stared, her head cocked to one side.

"Joe and Brian know this?"

"I don't know. Even if they've been told, they probably don't believe it," I said, stretching and yawning. Stretching feels so good when you have a fever. "What do I have? The flu?"

"Wouldn't surprise me. You've been going full blast for the past four days. Remember, you didn't get any sleep at all Saturday night. And you've been out tramping in the wet and cold, climbing up telephone poles—"

"Utility poles. Well, looks like I won't be much good at work today."

"I've already called Susan at her apartment and told her you wouldn't be in."

So I spent the day mostly sleeping and listening to the radio. I hardly ate anything, but drank three quarts of ice-cold mineral water.

I felt a tad better by six, but not much. Mary was pacing the kitchen restlessly.

"Jeez, Charlie, this *would* happen now. Guess what? I felt so much better this afternoon I told Janice I'd go shopping with her for about an hour tonight. I better call and—"

"Why? I'll be okay, Mare—I'm a big kid now. I can even go toidy by myself. You still hungry? Why don't you ask Janice if she'd like to go out for dinner? If I get hungry I can always scrounge something here."

She thought it was a great idea, and soon she was bundled

up and ready to go. I warned her that she would probably tire easily and asked if they were going to the mall.

"No, just over to Lexington Center. We should be back before ten. Oh, there's Janice honking now. Bye!"

After she left I grabbed a stack of magazines and slid back into the hospital bed, watching the flames in the stove and reading. Danny, the Lab, came in, did two tight turns on the kitchen floor, and sank to his belly on the linoleum. He sighed once and fell asleep. I read until the lapping and purring of the flames made me feel like dozing, and then I got out of bed, locked the back door, turned off the kitchen light, and threw another hunk of wood into the stove. I sank back into the covers, stretched and groaned, and drifted off.

Danny woke me up fast. I was sitting up in bed, startled. He barked again, a rolling, thunderous chorus of deep barking, and in the dim light I could see the dark patch of raised fur along his back. He was at the basement door, head low, lips raised in a snarl. Troubles rushed into the room and joined the ruckus. I shushed the dogs, who kept whining and growling. But then I heard it too: a faint scuffing and bumping below me.

Somebody was in the basement, fumbling around in the dark.

I was out of bed before I realized it. My breathing was hard and fast, not only from my illness but from the adrenalin rush. I moved quickly to the basement door and slid the bolt shut. I went upstairs and came right back down carrying my auto pistol. I grabbed the battery lantern from its perch on the shelf, crept back to the door, and listened. Someone was coming up the cellar stairs, tripping in the dark. I heard the sound of falling on the stairs, and that was all the cue I needed. I unlocked the door and yanked it open, shining the light down into the darkness. My pistol was up and ready. The dogs lunged forward, stopping halfway down the stairs, raising the roof with their racket. They were all mouth and fangs, both of them.

A crumpled person lay at the bottom of the stairway. He was trying to move his arm.

"Who is it?" I demanded. But I couldn't even hear myself over the dogs.

I went down the stairs, the dogs slightly ahead of me and ready to pounce. I'd never seen them in such a nasty mood. I saw an old gray head, moving slightly back and forth in fear. I reached down and grabbed him under the arm. His clothes were wet and very cold. He raised his head; I heard the chattering of teeth. And then he looked up, into the beam of light. I hardly recognized the man.

"Emil! Where have you been? What's happened to you?" I asked.

"Help. Help me—"

I carried him up into the kitchen and sat him in front of the stove. He was shivering violently now but had the strength to grab my arm.

"Help me, Doc, please," he said, gulping. "They're going to kill me."

10

I SAT STARING AT THE FLAMES IN THE WOOD STOVE AND wondered what to do. I should call Brian, and tell him to send some men over immediately to interview Haszmanay, and perhaps take him into custody. I should call Joe and tell him to alert Chet Harwood. Or maybe I should call Chet myself. Right now.

You hear that, Adams? *Right now.*

But I sat and did not do any of the above. Some inner voice, or hunch, or set of ethics, or *something*, made me wait. Wait at least until the shivering, exhausted wreck of a man beside me could pull himself together enough to tell me what had happened, and why.

"Emil, you want coffee or whiskey?"

"Whiskey. Please," he said. "With some hot water." He was scarcely able to talk because his jaw was clenched shut with the shivering. I mixed some blended whiskey in a glass with warm water and gave it to him. I moved him closer to the stove and unbuttoned his tattered and dirty trench coat to let the warmth seep into his chest. A trench coat? Hell, no wonder he was freezing. He tossed off the whiskey and had another, then seemed to settle deeper into the chair. His jaw stopped shaking, and his limbs were still. He breathed deep, ragged sighs. I put on some coffee. By the time I went and sat down again, he was asleep. His clothes were damp, almost wet. He needed a hot bath and dry clothes, and then a warm bed. My watch said 8:15. Mary could walk in any second, but I probably had an hour at least before she would return. Though still weak and feverish, I moved pretty fast. I began by running a hot tub upstairs in the boys' bathroom—now the guest bathroom—and putting out some warm clothes for Emil. They'd be too big, but they were dry at least. Rousing him was difficult, but once awake, Emil let me half carry him upstairs and dump him into the tub.

"You sure I can leave you for a second? You're not going to pass out and drown?"

"No. This is great, Doc. But I can't stay long. They're going to—"

"I heard. We'll talk more about that later." I took his wet clothes in my arms. I went down to the cellar and dumped them in the washer. Then I paused and turned around, looking at the window. The question had suddenly occurred to me: how had he gotten inside my house?

I found the answer in the old coal bin. The coal bin is an ancient wooden cage at the far corner of the furnace room. The wooden bulwarks are five feet high, enclosing a space seven feet by ten. From the foundation wall above, a metal coal chute projects down over the bin. The door to the chute was ajar. Emil Haszmanay, in a fit of strength born of desperation, had managed to kick it open, snapping the metal latch that had held it in place. Then he'd slid down the chute, landing in the bin like a sack of coal. A rather unceremonious entry for a research scientist.

Why hadn't he simply rung my doorbell?

Easy: for the same reason he'd covered his desk with junk mail, escaped from his own house via a ladder from the second floor, and disappeared for two days. People were after him. Chet Harwood, the marksman in the tent, the KGB, and Lord knew who else. And he'd come to me, just as Harwood had predicted he might. Old Chet Harwood was pretty slick on predictions. He was a pro, a government lifer. No doubt fugitives like Haszmanay exhibited regular, predictable patterns of behavior that made them easy to track and intercept. It certainly seemed as if mild-mannered Emil Haszmanay was cornered on all sides. Poor guy.

Wait a minute; don't get carried away, Adams. From all that's been revealed to you, this mild-mannered guy has been busy undermining U.S. security and selling our defense secrets to the Soviet Union.

I returned upstairs to see Emil emerging from the boy's bathroom in my khaki pants and flannel shirt. I gave him wool socks, a pair of fleece-lined slippers, and a thick Norwegian fisherman's sweater to wear over the shirt. We returned to the kitchen, where I heated up a can of soup and threw a frozen rib-eye steak into the microwave to defrost. Haszmanay seemed almost chipper. But something was making him fidget.

"Would you by chance have a cigarette? I'm dying for a cigarette."

"Sorry, but we don't smoke them anymore," I said, and watched his face fall in disappointment. "I guess you'll just have to—hey, wait a minute—"

I felt around the windowsill in back of the kitchen table. Sure enough, there was the almost-full pack of Camels Brian had swiped from Emil's refrigerator. I flipped them over to Haszmanay.

"*Hmmmmm!*" He said, stuffing a white cylinder into his mouth and setting fire to it, "My brand, too!"

"Uh-huh—must be a miracle," I said, watching him sit there and inhale huge lungfuls of smoke. I had him stand under the range hood in the kitchen and turned the exhaust fan up all the way. To further mask any cigarette smell, I lighted a pipe. I'm so glad I quit cigarettes. But I still have occasional dreams about Camels. Emil sat happily sucking in the poison, letting the smoke dribble out his nostrils for the full taste, the way Laitis Roantis does. Then I served him his dinner, which he inhaled also.

"Tell me," I asked him as he sat huddled over the stove, the light of the flames playing on his face, "where did you hide the rifle?"

He stared at me, transfixed with fear. "You mean they found out? How?"

"*I* found out. I was with the police when they went through you house. You must've left the neighborhood, or you would have seen us tramping in and out. Nice house, by the way. But where did you hide the rifle, Emil? Or did you take it down the ladder with you when you left?"

He sighed in resignation. He had a bald head with a ruff of snow-white hair around the sides and a Santa Claus nose on which perched wire-rimmed glasses. He looked elfin, like a kindly old grandfather. I saw that he'd borrowed Jack's razor while upstairs, too, and had shaved off his three-day stubble.

"So I'm wanted for murder too, eh? Well, I have some important things to do before they catch up with me. Where did I hide the rifle? Down inside the walls. It's hanging by a cord in the attic, down between the studding. The only thing visible is the top of the cord, tied to a nail. When they kill me, you can keep the rifle."

He said *when*, not *if*. Emil was certain he was going to die. That made me uneasy. I looked at my watch again; time was getting short. All things being equal, I didn't want Mary to know he was hiding out in our house. She tends to get upset about little things like that. For starters, I was breaking the law by not turning him in. I'd rather she stayed out of it.

"Follow me," I said, and led him back down the cellar stairs and into the furnace room, which held the cagelike coal bin. The furnace room was also where we stored the camping equipment, because it was the warmest, driest room in the cellar and kept the sleeping bags and tents free of mildew. From a set of pine shelves, I took down a mattress pad, a jumbo sleeping bag, and two thick woolen blankets. I spread out the pad and the blankets in the coal bin—which had not held coal in forty years—then rigged up a mechanic's "trouble light" with a forty-watt bulb next to the bag. This, Emil could switch off and on as he pleased, and the light wouldn't shine much beyond the walls of the bin. With the furnace-room door closed, it couldn't be seen at all. Meanwhile, the dogs had all grown used to the new occupant, so no alarms would sound from that quarter. But just to be on the safe side I put them out in their runs for the night.

I went upstairs and cleaned up the telltale dinner dishes, then rejoined Haszmanay in the cellar. I sat with my back against the wooden bulwark and listened to the oil furnace purr. The cellar was warm, dark, cozy. I saw that Emil was reclining on the pallet, almost asleep, with a lighted cigarette in his hand and an ashtray perched on his chest.

"Thank you, Doc. Ohhhh . . . This feels so good and warm. I slept in a lumberyard last night. . . ."

"Before you nod off, can you tell me about it? I should tell you I'm under strict instructions to turn you in. I still may have to."

He nodded slowly, sadness written on his face.

"The horrible part is, I cannot tell you much," he said, looking down at his chapped hands and the cigarette smoldering in between his fingers. "I wish I could be open with you. And I know I can trust you. But you see, my situation is such . . . the whole situation is such . . . that it is impossible. I thank you so much for helping me. I'm sorry."

Then he drew on his cigarette again. That was it? *"I'm sorry"?* Well, it wouldn't do. Should I get rough with him? Threaten him? No. He'd already been through hell, that was plain enough. Threats and rough stuff wouldn't faze him.

"Well, Emil, I'm sorry for what's happened to you, too. I think. But believe me, unless I know more about these, uh, impossible circumstances, my inclination is to call the cops in about ten minutes. I mean, hey, there was a man killed here this weekend, and my wife almost died."

He looked up at me with wide eyes. "Your wife, Mary? Almost died? Oh, my God—"

"Now, you say they're going to kill you. Who's going to kill you—and why?"

"The KGB is going to kill me. They're going to kill me for betraying them. They tried to do it on Saturday but failed. Instead, Doc, they hit your cat. . . ."

"Uh-huh. And the cat was dead within two minutes. Mary picked up that same pellet and got some of the thallium into her blood through a cut on her hand. She damn near died of it, too."

"Thallium!"

"Irradiated, radioactive thallium. A revenge weapon of the KGB."

"You see? It was meant for me."

"Well, then, let's get help. What the hell are you skulking around in the cold for? I know some FBI people who can help us get the KGB before—"

"No. No Doc," he said, holding up his hand. "I can't go to them now. They think I've betrayed them."

I thought about this for a second or two.

"Wait a minute. You say the FBI thinks you've betrayed *them*?" I asked. "Why do you say that?"

"Why do I say it? Well, because it's now obvious. My contact in the Company—that is what we call the Central Intelligence Agency—has avoided our most recent appointment. He has grown colder and more distant toward me in recent months. There are a hundred signs that point to his suspicions. So why I say it is obvious. The question is, Doc . . . the real question is: why does he feel this way? As far as I know, my behavior and actions have been exemplary. So I seem to have enemies on both sides . . . and nowhere to go."

"You've been in contact with the CIA? Are you saying you're a double agent?"

"Yes. I have been for some time now. And of course I now wish I had never become an agent at all, to say nothing of a double agent. I haven't the courage or the nervous system for it."

"I still don't see why you can't go to the right people on our side and tell them everything. You have your rights. You're protected by them."

"Ah! But the intelligence agencies are not like other institutions, you see. Here, even in America, the CIA often operates outside the framework of our Constitution—"

"Ahhh, c'mon, Emil, get off it—'

"No. No Doc, I'm serious. But wait—"

He took another drag, stubbed out his cigarette, and cleared his throat.

"Listen. I am not trying to change the subject, Doc, but I really cannot say much more about why it's impossible to go now to my Company contact, or even the FBI. Let me instead give you a brief history of my life here. Maybe then the situation will begin to make more sense. Okay?"

"Fine," I said, glancing at my watch. "But be brief; Mary's due back any minute now, and I want to be upstairs in bed when she returns."

"Yes. Okay. I first arrived here in late nineteen fifty-six, after the Hungarian revolt. I came here as a refugee scientist. But really this was just a cover story, for I was actually sent here as a spy, a Soviet illegal."

He paused to shake another Camel out of the rapidly shrinking pack and light it. I looked at him, amazed at this confession. But Emil Haszmanay proceeded as if he'd told me nothing more than where he'd gone to college. I also noticed that the more he talked and relaxed, the more pronounced was his accent, which resembled a German one. Actually, he sounded most like Bela Lugosi as Count Dracula, or perhaps Peter Lorre, punctuating his speech with thick rolling *R*'s and guttural *G*'s. It made him seem almost sinister.

"As you might imagine, with my cover story I was welcomed here practically with open arms. I gained cover as a research fellow in such scientific and university communities as Ann Arbor, Madison, Chicago, and finally Berkeley. My instructions were to do nothing until I was 'activated' by a command from Moscow. This is the pattern for most Soviet illegals. They lie low, leading quiet lives totally within the law. They make occasional contact with their superiors to touch base and receive financial help if needed. But, during this inactive period, the planted spy does nothing at all except his 'cover' occupation. This lulls the agency of the host country into thinking the planted agent is merely a grateful immigrant. You see?"

He paused to rearrange the sleeping bag, then lay down on it. I could see his eyelids begin to droop.

"Now, in my case, financial help was not needed because I found myself very well paid. I liked America from the start, and felt ill at ease about my future assignment—whatever it might be. I knew that sooner or later the directorship would feel the time was right and would have me start feeding information to my superiors in the U.S. Believe me, I wasn't looking forward to it."

"You call yourself a Soviet illegal. What's a legal? Is there such a thing?"

"Oh, yes. In the foreign service—the diplomatic corps. Most of the embassy staff of any nation has diplomatic immunity, which means they cannot be prosecuted or tried for espionage. It's no secret that large portions of most embassy staffs are associated with the intelligence services of their native countries. In the case of the Russians, the percentage is almost total. But they still rely on illegals—there are thousands and thousands of them in America—some in very sensitive positions of government and industry."

"So you're a Russian spy."

"Yes and no. No, I am not, in that I am now working much more for the United States than for the Soviet Union. But one cannot quit the KGB, Doc. It is rather like the Mafia. Once you are in it, you stay in. For life. To try to leave, or switch sides, is death. You have seen for yourself that I am now to pay the ultimate price for betraying them."

His hands shaking, Emil snuffed out the Camel. I rose and pried open the coal-chute gate to let the smoke out and to hear Mary's car door slam when she returned.

"I was activated in the mid-sixties and began to pass information on. Most of it concerned the guidance systems for medium-range missiles. I did a good job, but my heart wasn't in it. I had grown to like this country . . . then to love it. And also I remembered what had happened in my own country in nineteen forty-eight. It did not take me long to realize that I was not a very good Communist. I wanted out. But again, once in, you stay in. The only way to leave is—as we say here—feet first."

"So what did you do then?" I asked.

"The only answer was to make contact with the other side and become a double agent, with the hope that eventually America would shield me from KGB revenge. So that is what I did, in Berkeley, in early nineteen seventy. I contacted the

CIA there and began life as a double agent—giving secrets to both sides but always giving the edge to the Americans."

"That seems, uh, rather dangerous."

"My God, Doc, if you only knew. It is certainly not a life I would have chosen for myself. I am basically an intellectual . . . and a coward, sad to say. But, as it happened, things went well for me for the next ten years. I was in Livermore then, and gave my fellow illegals enough good information that they didn't suspect. In fact, they considered me one of their premier agents. And my double role enabled American intelligence to make big inroads into the Soviet spy apparatus on the West Coast. When the FBI rounded up several key illegals I was one of them—to divert suspicion, of course. After a lengthy 'investigation,' the Bureau finally let me go, and I requested permission from my superiors in the KGB to move East. Regretting what I had been put through, they agreed. I came here at the end of eighty-three to work at MITRE and then Lincoln Laboratories. I continued to report to both sides. But seven months ago, things got out of control—"

"The KGB found out you were doubling on them?"

"Well, I knew they were beginning to suspect it. I could tell by lots of little things. They were watching me much more carefully. They could not apply the usual pressure of a captive loved one in Russia because I am a childless widower; my wife Sonia died in fifty-nine, when I was still inactive. So the only thing they can threaten me with is my own death."

"What happened last Saturday? How did my cat die?"

"Oh, I am so sorry about that. But you should know this: the cat saved my life. Let me start at the beginning. Since I was aware that the KGB was watching me more and more closely, I was busy being a model illegal. My contacts with the Company—the CIA—were alerted too, and they were keeping away. I was passing on good stuff from Lincoln Laboratories on the development of the SDI system, which is now call Star Wars. My superiors were very pleased, since the Star Wars defense system is of utmost importance to the Soviets now. It transcends all other matters. I thought I was therefore in the clear. But it was not true. I am marked for death as a traitor. They almost got me; it was your poor cat that saved me."

"What happened?"

"I was in my side yard about one o'clock, planting bulbs—"

"Right. I remember seeing the bulb planter leaning against the side of your house, and the newly dug bed."

"Yes. Well, your cat came up to me. Both of them do, and I pet them. Sometimes I feed them sardines and tuna fish. Anyway, I picked up your cat and was holding him in my arms—across my chest—petting him. Even in the outside air, I could hear him purring like a little motor. I walked around the side of my house toward the back door, because I wanted to take him into the kitchen and feed him."

Haszmanay lighted another Camel and continued.

"As I rounded the corner of my house into the back yard, I heard a distinct *thump* right in front of my chest. Your cat squalled and jumped up about three feet in the air, scratching my arms. Then it hit the ground and took off running across the yard toward your house. I watched it run, and then heard it making the ugliest noises in the world—"

"Uh-huh. That's when he came running into our yard."

"I'm sorry, Doc. If it weren't for me, it wouldn't have happened."

"So what happened after Claude got hit and jumped out of your arms?"

"At first I couldn't put the pieces together. The thump and then the leaping cat. It was maybe three or four seconds before I put the events together and figured it out. And then, out of the corner of my eye, I saw that canvas thing hanging up on the telephone pole. I wasn't looking directly at it; it was the flapping of the canvas door that made me notice. The flaps drew back for an instant, then closed again. It was very quick, but long enough for me to realize what had happened. The man in the tent had not noticed the cat in my arms until after he'd pulled the trigger. He was aiming right for my chest, you see, and had probably been waiting for the opportunity to shoot me for several hours. His aim was excellent, but he hit your cat, not me.

"When I noticed the canvas tent up there behind me and saw the door flap open and shut, I managed to keep my head and pretended not to see it. I walked back around the house, back to my garden, as if nothing out of the ordinary had happened. I did not want the killer to know I'd seen him.

"I went in the front door, locking it behind me. Then I crept to the back door and locked it, too. I went upstairs to my study with a pair of binoculars. Maybe you are wondering why I didn't just call the police. Well, I had a good idea who the man in the tent was. Not who he was specifically, you understand, but I knew he was KGB. Therefore, a call to the police would not do much good. So I watched him first, to see what he would do next. He assumed I was still around the side of the house, you see. I watched the tent on the pole. It was absolutely still for the next several hours. Then, just before dark, in the dim light of dusk, a man emerged quickly from the back side of the tent and climbed down the pole, then went into the trees and brush, taking a small stepladder with him. Obviously it had been leaning against the pole in the thick brush and had not been visible to me. The pole seemed to be in between property lines, in a wooded place nobody paid much attention to. If I had not been watching carefully, I never would have seen him in that light. After the marksman left, carrying no gun, I waited nervously up in my study. About twenty minutes after I saw him leave the tent, I heard my doorbell ring again and again—"

"That was me, Emil."

"Ah. I thought it might be the killer. So, needless to say, I did not answer it. After a long wait, I left the house, took my ladder from the garage, and had a look at the tent. There was no weapon up there, which meant he had taken it apart and carried it out underneath his coat. All I saw inside was a small folding stool on the plywood floor. At first it was my plan to set a trap in the tent. When I examined the pole, I realized it was not for telephone lines, but for power lines. I thought of using my knowledge of electronics to tap into these lines and rig some kind of device that would electrocute him, perhaps even making it appear accidental. But I discarded this idea as too complicated and risky. No, I decided to repay him in kind. I decided to shoot him before he shot me. And since he did not know I had even seen him, I knew the odds of my pulling it off were good."

"So you got up very early the next day, Sunday morning, and you waited for him him to return to his perch. . . ."

"Yes. I assumed he would return for the remainder of the weekend, expecting me to be out in my yard again, offering him an easy shot. He arrived early, at six-thirty, just before daybreak. By then I had my study windows shut and the shades and curtains drawn. All that was open was one window, just above my desk—"

"And you set up a bench-rest there, just like in a *Schutzenfest*, and you sat up on your desk, your rifle braced right on the target—"

"Correct. I watched him climb up the pole in the predawn light, through my riflescope. Then he left the front flap open while he sat down on the small canvas seat. I saw him cock the air rifle with a spring lever—"

"Then you shot him, right in the chest, from inside the curtained room."

"Exactly. And the rifle was a good eight feet from the opening in the window. Not much of the noise escaped outside, and it was early anyway. I expected him to fall out of the tent and into the thicket. I had thought I might even have to drag him to my car and somehow haul the body away. This frightened me. But I was lucky; he stayed up there on the platform. Only an arm flopped out below the canvas. I was confident I had killed him, but I waited thirty minutes to see what was going to happen. When it was clear that nobody had noticed the noise and there was not the slightest movement in the tent, I went outside and climbed the pole. I pushed his arm back inside the tent and let the flap fall back into place. In all my years as an illegal, it was the first time I had ever hurt anyone, ever."

"And then?"

"Well, I did not recognize the man, whoever he was. I felt for his wallet. He had no identification on him, which did not surprise me. I climbed back down and took the short stepladder three houses down the road and leaned it against a garage. For all I know, Doc, it's still there. It was very cool outside, so I knew there would be no immediate decomposition and odor. I calculated that I had a day's head start before Department Five would wonder what had happened to their assassin. So I went back home, hid my rifle where I mentioned, and dressed warmly in sweaters and a trench coat, then returned outside to lean my tall ladder up against my bathroom window on the second floor. The previous night, I had gone through all my papers, burned any that were important and possibly incriminating in the fireplace, and scattered the ashes in my front shrubbery. I had also packed basic possessions I would need in an old suitcase, which I had ready. After setting up the ladder, I went back inside, locked all the doors and windows from the inside in the hope of confusing pursuers, and then climbed down the ladder and replaced it in the garage. It was still very early in the morning.''

''So you took off at a moment's notice.''

''Well, yes. I had no choice, did I? And it may prove to be ultimately stupid. But is was the best I could think of at the time. I knew Department Five would discover the dead marksman before long and would send more men. I needed to get away, and fast. I walked to town and took a cab to a motel in Acton, where I spent Sunday night. I paid in advance and left the suitcase there. I do not think I'll go back.''

''And where have you been since then?''

''Around. I'm afraid to stay in one place too long. Maybe I shouldn't have returned. But I had to find out what was happening around here, for reasons I cannot yet tell you or anyone. And I was so cold. I did not know it would be so cold this early. . . . I had to come inside. I tried the other neighbors' house because I knew they were away. But they have that big dog—''

''You were smart not to try there. So you walked around my house, desperate, and finally pushed the old coal chute open. Gee, if you were any bigger, you wouldn't have fit. So what are your plans now?''

''I need time to sleep, then think. Do not worry, Doc, I won't be here more than a day—I can't be.''

''Well, it hardly takes a genius to realize you're in a lot of trouble. And danger, too. I still think you ought to go get some help. I know the chief of police here in town. Maybe he—''

''The problem is still more difficult than you realize,'' he said urgently, a lost expression on his face. ''What I must do in the next few days, I must do alone. If I tell people about what is happening, they will detain me, perhaps lock me up. And I cannot have that. I must be free to roam about now. After it's over, I don't care what happens—''

''What, Emil, After *what's* over?''

''I can't tell you. Yet, anyway. And also, think of this: the Company is no doubt convinced that I have been forced back to the other side—that I'm again working primarily for the KGB. It is not true, but that is what they think.''

''So what you're saying is, you're caught in the middle, with nowhere to get help.''

He nodded, looking at the floor.

''I shouldn't tell you any more. Not because I don't trust you; I am trusting you right now with my life. But if I tell you certain things it might jeopardize your safety. I will say this much: there is a major security leak at Lincoln Labs right now. An extremely serious leak, and it is in my own department. I'm certain that as things now stand, considering my past history, the American intelligence community is convinced that I'm behind it. I'm not.''

''Can you prove that?''

''No. Not now. But I will be able to very shortly. How I am going to do it, that is what will occupy my time for the next week or so. That is, if Department Five doesn't find me first.''

''And they're probably out combing the woods for you right now,'' I said. ''Emil, why don't you take the train in to Boston early tomorrow, hop a bus to some small town, rent a car there, and drive somewhere safe?''

Hmmph! I wish there were such a place. No. And I have things to do here. I know where the leak is coming from in the lab. I'll tell you one thing, to allay your suspicions if nothing else. Ten days ago I happened to intercept a routine memo in my department. That is, it appeared routine to the casual eye. Hidden in the memo was a microdot. Do you know what a microdot is?"

"I think so."

"A microdot is no bigger than a period at the end of a sentence on a typed page. In fact, that is what they are often disguised as. They are actually supercompressed text that can be read by a special microscope device known as a microdot reader. Until recently I had such a device hidden in my house. I glanced casually at the memo at first because it appeared to be strictly routine, but then I thought I recognized the microdot in the message. After all, as an illegal, I was trained to look for such things. I took the memo home with me—thus violating every procedural and security regulation of the lab. I managed to return the memo the next day, unobtrusively. But the person who composed the memo now knows it was missing. Furthermore, the person who was supposed to intercept the memo—who is not the person to whom it was addressed—also knows that someone else has seen it. Do you begin to see the difficulties involved?"

"Yes. Well, what did the microdot say?"

"I'm not sure I should tell you. But I am tempted to, because if I don't—and I am killed—then the discovery of the leak will die with me. On the other hand, if you know about it, then you will be in danger too. I don't want that. I'm sure Mary wouldn't want it either. I'm placing you in enough danger just by being here."

"Do you think you were followed here?"

"No. I took great pains not to be."

"Do you want to come back if you need a place?" I asked.

"Yes, but I don't—"

Through the old coal chute we heard the slamming of a car door. Mary was back. I told Emil to lay low, with his light off and no smoking, for another hour at least, until we went to bed. I told him there was a toilet in the back room that worked.

"But don't flush it except when you hear water running upstairs," I cautioned, and I went up, not locking the basement door behind me as I usually did.

"Well, you recovered, hon?" asked Mary as she entered the kitchen. I, of course, was sprawled in the hospital bed, thermometer in mouth. She removed it and had a look.

"Jeez, Charlie, hundred and one. Who'd have ever guessed that by this time I'd feel better than you? I think I'll sleep in our bed upstairs tonight. It's so cool up there. You want to stay down here?"

"A good idea. Even this room feels cold because of my fever. And it would be bad if you came down with the flu on top of the poisoning. Now, don't forget, we've got to go in for your tests tomorrow. With Dr. What's-her-name."

"Dr. Danzeck. Rachel Danzeck."

"Right. Well, when she gives the thumbs-up, you can stop taking that Prussian blue, which should make you feel even more chipper."

She bent over and gave me a kiss on the cheek, put a big tumbler of ice water near the bed, and went upstairs. I had forgotten to ask her if she'd bought anything. Silly question.

I suddenly decided I'd feel a bit safer, sandwiched between Mary and Emil, if I had my pistol. I was thinking this after I had popped two aspirin and drained the glass of ice water. Before I had a chance to act on the thought, I fell asleep.

I awoke with somebody standing over me. I was frightened at first, then realized it was Emil, leaning over my bed in the dark. He was once again dressed in his own clothes—now dry. I felt his cool palm on my forehead.

"Tch! Tch! Tch! You're sick, Doc. You had better stay in bed today and rest, yes?"

"What are you doing here?" I asked in a harsh whisper. My throat was hot and dry; I got up and chugged fresh ice water and looked at my watch. Five fifteen, and still dark out.

"I am taking off now, while it's still dark and nobody will see. I would like to return tonight, if it's okay with you."

I found myself nodding. "Where are you going now?"

"Into Boston. I'm going to buy a hair piece and get some new clothes. Maybe another pair of glasses. I'll come back late tonight, God willing."

"Okay. Good luck, and be careful."

He stopped, then came back and leaned over me again, whispering urgently.

"If I don't return, you will know what has happened. Department Five has caught up with me. Now listen to me, Doc. I have been thinking it over; I am going to tell you something important. Is your mind clear?"

"Clear enough."

"Good. Here is the most important thing the microdot said. There was a lot of extraneous information on it, but this is all you need to know. Something is going to happen Thursday, the twenty-eighth of October. I assume it has something to do with the lab, but perhaps not. The message did not say what would happen, just gave the date: Thursday, the twenty-eighth."

He patted my cheek in kindly fashion.

"Goodbye, Doc. Please keep this secret until I return. I'll come in the same way. But now I'll leave by your back door—is this all right?"

"Fine. Need any cash?"

"No. I still have plenty. If it goes well, you won't recognize me when I return. And, who can say? If I get lucky, I may have more to tell you."

Then I heard the back door open slowly and shut quietly. He was gone. I silently wished him Godspeed, and fell back to sleep.

11

YOU FEELING ANY BETTER, CHARLIE?" ASKED MARY AS SHE poured me a big mug of dark roast coffee.

"Not much. The sleep did me some good, but I've still got a little fever. How're you?"

"Better and better. In fact, my hair's stopped falling out. I feel positively chipper."

"Good. Why don't you go in and pull teeth for me?"

"No thanks. But I'll call Susan when she gets in and tell her you're still down for the count. And I can go to the hospital by myself for my checkup with Rachel Danzeck."

I eased back onto the cool pillow and realized that I would be home all day, and probably alone for most of it. Were my sudden illness and Mary's lightning recovery merely a coincidence, or had fate interceded so that I could help Emil when he came in out of the cold? Who knew. I sat up, drained the coffee cup, and took some aspirin with four large swallows of ice water.

I thought again of Chet Harwood's little lecture in Joe's office, of his uncanny prediction that perhaps Emil would seek me out. I was disobeying the instructions I had been given. Joe and Brian wouldn't be pleased with me. And Chet would be angry. I was going against FBI orders. I was possibly endangering national security and aiding and abetting the enemy. Aiding and abetting . . .

"You okay, hon? You're frowning and grimacing. Are you in pain?"

"Oh, no. I just don't like missing this much work. But I think I should stay home another day or so and rest and get over this."

"Absolutely," she said, and picked up the wall phone to call my office.

Dr. Charles Adams, of Concord, Massachusetts, we find you guilty of aiding and abetting an enemy agent. You are therefore guilty of treason, of betraying your country. You are guilty of contributing to the overthrow of the United States of America. . . .

Oh shit.

12

After Mary left, I got out of bed, put on my robe and slippers, and went down to the furnace room. The old coal bin was empty and neat as a pin. The pad, sleeping bag, and blankets had all been rolled up and returned to their proper places on the shelves. In my workshop I found the trouble light, with cord coiled neatly, hanging on its customary peg. Emil's ashtray I discovered under the workbench, cleaned and free of butts, which he had no doubt flushed down the toilet in the dead of night. The clothes I had loaned him were there too—neatly folded. There was absolutely no trace of his overnight visit. I marveled at the way he'd covered his tracks.

But then apprehension rose in me. If he was so skilled at deception, was he deceiving me as well?

I paced around in the tiny coal bin, smacking my fist into my open palm in frustration. What if Mary were now endangered? Or the boys, when they came back from college for Thanksgiving break? I was tense now, and the doubts I had had earlier were renewed and stronger than ever. Best to call Chet Harwood and Joe right away. Perhaps they could pick up Haszmanay when he returned—*if* he returned—and then I'd be out of it. Or else I could keep mum until he came back, then tell him that I could not harbor him any longer. He would have to leave.

That's it, Adams, ditch the issue. Let the others worry about it.

I went back upstairs and got dressed. I was angry with myself. I sat on the edge of our bed putting on my socks and shoes, then stopped.

But maybe the reason you're waffling is because you suspect he's telling the truth, I thought to myself. Maybe you sense he's a decent guy who loves this country as much as you do—probably appreciates it more—and who's in a desperate fix. He needs help, and you're offering it. And maybe what you're doing takes more guts than simply turning him in.

Well, I thought, it all depends on whether or not he's telling the truth. If he's sincere, you're doing a heroic thing. If he's lying, you're a traitor.

I sighed, forearms across my knees, and lowered my head. I still had a fever, and it seemed to brighten and intensify my thoughts.

I believe him, I said to myself finally. He's telling the truth, and he needs my help. And, God help me, he's going to get it.

With that minor question resolved, the rest would be easy. It's never the action that's hard; it's the hemming and hawing beforehand that gets you down.

"Why, Dr. Adams, what are you doing here?" asked a surprised Susan Petri, who was standing in front of the full-length mirror in my office, brushing her lovely chestnut tresses. Isn't that what they're called? Tresses? Anyway, she had a dynamite head of hair, and everything else to match. Men aren't supposed to notice those things about women nowadays, or mention them at least. But I'm mentioning it anyway. Pretending not to notice Susan Petri's, uh, feminine appeal is like riding in a caravan across Egypt and pretending the pyramids aren't there.

I collapsed into my office chair and sighed. I felt as if I'd just run the marathon. But all I'd done was drive across town and walk through the parking lot. I was sick.

Susan put a palm on my forehead and pronounced me unfit. I was used to hearing that line. I told her I had only come in for a consultation with Moe.

"Why?" she asked innocently. "Are you feeling mental?"

"Just about," I admitted, and went down the hall to Moe's office. He was hovering over his new fish tank, a tall, octagonal model with salt water in it. And, bless his heart, he'd stocked it with gorgeous fish. Moe said they were tangs and clownfish. They were brilliant blue, yellow, orange and white. And they had normal mouths, too, not horrible sucking nozzles covered with whiskers. These bright and cheery creatures were a far cry from the blotched and freckled, pinkish, purplish, brownish monsters that inhabit his other tank. I made sure not to turn my head in that direction as I peered at the new creatures, or I'd see some horrid, muzzle-mouthed bottom-feeder, and get the dry heaves.

"So how's Mary, Doc? And what's new wid you?"

"Mary's just about recovered. And now I've got the flu. After we talk, I'm going home to bed."

He pushed me down into his snazzy leather swivel chair, eyed me sympathetically, and frowned.

"Tell me what it is," he said. "I can tell it's bad."

So I did, without getting specific or naming names. He sat behind his desk, running his hands through his trimmed beard and saying, 'Hmmmmmm . . . hmmmmmmm."

"Well?" I asked.

"Sounds like a classic conflict between the individual's obligation to the state versus his obligation to his fellow man. Hmmmm . . ."

Then he quoted Malraux, Marcus Aurelius, Machiavelli, Tolstoy, Stonewall Jackson, Plato, Thomas Paine, Reinhold Neibuhr, and the *Bhagavad Gita*.

None of them helped. I asked him, since he was so damn smart, what *he* thought I should do.

"I can't really say at this point," he said. "But it's tricky.

I mean, if he is a spy, you're in what's colloquially known as deep shit."

"Do tell. Listen: mum's the word—to everyone. Especially Brian."

I left and went back to the car. Well, so much for the theoretical, philosophical approach. Now I needed the pragmatic viewpoint, the "kick-'em-in-the-ass" school of thought. And fortunately I knew just the guy who could give it to me.

Luckily, I found a parking place that was near the BYMCU club in downtown Boston and where my car wouldn't be stripped in ten minutes. I walked in, crossed the gym floor, and went into Laitis Roantis's little office. The stock Lithuanian, who killed his first man—a Nazi soldier—when he was twelve years old, was sitting back in his chair, feet on desk, blowing smoke rings at the ceiling. He was wearing a suit. Kind of. It was old and frumpy, baggy and tight at the same time. Roantis wasn't made to wear suits. Military fatigues, tiger-striped stalker outfits, and white karate robes were more his style. On the old gray desk rested a Japanese sword in a black scabbard that was wound with a red silken braid. The hilt was gold. High on the office walls on all sides were portraits of Asian men. Most of them were old-timers with white, stringy beards, sitting cross-legged on reed mats with placid expressions on their faces. There was Japanese writing on these pictures. I knew that the writing represented messages of blessing and best wishes for the career of Laitis Roantis, most honored and skillful student of these famous fighting men from Okinawa and Kyoto. There also were banners and sashes on the walls that had been presented to Roantis at various tournaments in Asia.

And there were other goodies up there, too. There were throwing knives, Ninja *shuriken*, or throwing stars, Gurkha *Kukri* knives, Balinese *Kris* daggers, blowguns, Ninja *shuko* (metal hand-claws that enabled the wearer to scale a stucco wall or take off a face), *Num Chucks*, garrotes, and a host of other treats. Laitis is good with all of them.

"Hiya Doc," he said, flipping up his shirt cuff to look at his watch. "In about an hour, let's walk down to the Dunfey's and get up some draft Bass. You can buy. Better yet, let's go now."

"No. I've got a fever and I want to take steam first. But mainly I drove all the way in here to talk to you about some important things."

"Like what?"

"Like spying. The CIA, KGB, and all that. You know anything about this stuff?"

He took his feet off the desk, stretched and groaned, and admitted he had been in the temporary employ of the "Company" more than once. And of course I knew that he hated the KGB, and the Soviets in general, with that special sizzling vehemence one sees in refugees from Eastern Europe, who saw their native lands enslaved at the close of World War II.

"Now Laitis, we trust each other. Those high jinks in North Carolina proved that. I want to walk through the Common with you after my steam bath and tell you a few things that you must keep secret."

"Okay. And then you want advice?"

"Yes."

"Good. Cost you some draft beer."

"Done."

I entered the wet steam chamber and sat for a quarter of an hour, came out, showered, rested and cooled, and went into the sauna for its dry heat. Came out soaked in my own sweat, showered, rested and cooled, back into the steam, et cetera, drinking lots of water between visits and alternating between wet and dry heat. As I dressed I felt weak as a kitten, but I knew I had helped my body get rid of bad stuff.

"You seen Tommy Desmond around anywhere?" I asked Esteban Fernandez, the huge, rotund Filipino who was, as usual, jazzing up the air of the locker room with his elegant Burmese corona. He slipped me a fresh one, which I pocketed with thanks.

"I think I heard he went over to Ireland for a couple of weeks, Doc. Where's he from?"

"Galway."

"Yeah. I think there. Hey, Doc, you got a gawdamn *tattoo*

on your arm! Hey, wait, it's just like Tommy's! It's a picture of *Daisy Duck*—"

"Uh-huh. Well, it's a long story, Esteban. Roantis was in on the caper too. He can fill you in. Listen, I hope Tommy isn't into anything, uh, shall we say, *political*, during his visit to the old country."

"Oh, I think he's done with that stuff."

"Well, let's hope so. Thanks for the cigar."

Roantis and I left the gym and cut diagonally across the intersection of Tremont and Boylston streets, which put us on the Boston Common, America's oldest public park. There were two mounted patrolmen on the corner, sitting astride those handsome, blocky Morgan horses. Roantis glanced this way and that, his keen gray eyes always in motion. If Boston had gotten any snow the day before, there was no evidence of it now. We walked up the middle pathway of the Common. Before I spoke I looked all around. Nobody nearby. I told Roantis the details and then asked for his frank advice. He told me to walk slower; he was having trouble keeping in step with me. A young man who had been behind up passed and soon was thirty yards ahead. Roantis walked at my side, staring ahead at the young man, who was dressed in a parka and wearing earphones. On his back was big pack on an aluminum frame.

"Think it's really safe to talk out here, Doc?" he said in a clear voice.

"Sure. Don't you?"

"See dat guy up ahead of us? I bet he's hearing every word. I'm going to run up there and—"

Before Laitis had even finished his sentence, the man ahead, who was definitely out of earshot, turned quickly around and faced us for an instant, then broke into a high-speed run up the path. Roantis and I followed, and I was gaining on the kid until the flu and fever made all my energy give out. I slowed to a trot, panting harder than I had in months. The young guy in the parka was way up past the Frog Pond now and dashing up the stairs at the far end of the park. He disappeared on Beacon Street. He had run away from us very fast, which meant that whatever was in that big backpack wasn't really heavy. Roantis and I sat on a bench and huffed and puffed. When our breathing returned to normal, I asked Roantis how he had known the man was listening to us.

"I can spot a tail easy, Doc. Part of my training. Dat guy was good, trailing us front and back. People don't expect tails to be in front of them. He was waiting for us when we left the Y. Bet he had a strong directional mike on him somewhere, with a li'l parabolic disk. The disk, like a miniature TV dish, is hidden in the rucksack, you see. It picks up voices through the canvas and goes onto a tape that's running. He monitored us with those earphones. Hell, they look just like those Walkman phones. I think he picked up everything you told me."

I was so shocked I couldn't say anything for a few seconds.

"That means I was tailed all the way into town. But I didn't see—'

" 'Course not. You weren't supposed to."

I sat down on a bench and wiped my forehead, then leaned forward, put my elbows on my knees, and sighed. Roantis wiped his mouth and reminded me of the draft beer I'd promised him.

"It'll probably be safer talking in Dunfey's," he said, "because of all the people and noise."

Well, after that little episode in the Common, I was ready for a beer too. We went down into the The Last Hurrah, a basement emporium underneath Dunfey's Parker House, found a small table in back where we could watch the room, and ordered two big Bass ales and a plate of oysters on the half-shell. Roantis gulped down the beer and three oysters before lighting a cigarette and leaning over close to me.

"Here's what I think, Doc. For what the hell it's worth. I'd like to meet this Emil guy. I think I'd like him, and we've got more in common than you might think. But whether I do meet him or not, I'd say the chances are he's telling the truth. And also, as I've said before, I trust your instincts. So should you. So, *one*: I think you're doing the right thing. But, *two*: you got to get out of it. The risk is unacceptable. You say he feels that the KGB, the Company, *and* the Feds are all after him. Has he given you a detailed reason for this, or is it just a hunch? If he doesn't have any real evidence that the CIA is after him too, he should stick his neck out and contact them. Otherwise, I'd be suspicious of him."

"So, either way, I should call it off?"

"Yep. The risk level is unacceptable for a man with a family, understand? You're placing Mary—and maybe Jack and Tony—in too much danger."

I took two big swallows and wiped my mouth. I couldn't believe the advice that Roantis, former commando and mercenary soldier, had just given me.

"Jeez, Laitis, you certainly *have* changed, haven't you?"

"Ha!" he chuckled softly, "that's what Suzanne's been saying. I think that last episode of the Daisy Ducks really set me thinking, Doc. I realized how lucky I was to be alive after the life I've led. Now I'm getting older and more cautious. You can't have dis guy under your roof any longer. That's just the way it is. Yeah, he's in trouble, and we're sorry. But in a sense he asked for it. Do what you can to get him away safe, then stay out of it."

"Looks like they're onto me already."

"Who? The kid with the backpack? How d'you know it wasn't one of our guys, huh?"

I looked around absently at the fine old wood and Tiffany lamps. I nodded slowly. Roantis was right. And he's personally seen enough of the rough stuff to be a voice of authority. We left the bar and walked back to the BYMCU. My legs felt tired and achy. I drove home, eyes continually scanning the rear-view mirror. Hell, if there was a tail following me, I sure couldn't see it.

I stopped at the store and bought some beef short ribs, then drove home, parked in the driveway, and walked around the house toward the front door. I stopped dead still, staring at the ground. Footprints in the melting snow, near the bushes in front of my house. Emil's tracks—going up to the coal chute. The freakish, early snow had all but melted in Concord. I hadn't noticed the prints that morning; and since he'd left before dawn via the back door, Emil hadn't considered them either. But there they were: melted-down footprints in the faint snow, brownish-green against gray-white. As plain as day.

I thought about cutting a spruce bough from one of my trees and swishing it over the tracks to spread some snow and cover them. That's what they do in the movies, which probably means it's dumb. And the snow was really and truly almost melted; in a few more hours the footprints would be invisible. But perhaps the biggest reason I finally walked right past the tracks and into the house was this: it was too late. If anyone had done even rudimentary snooping around the house, they would have seen Emil's trail leading right to the coal chute.

This latest discovery, plus the wired kid in the Common and Roantis's stern warning about "unacceptable risk," brought all my doubts and fears back full force, and they gnawed at me like a plague of locusts.

I sighed as I placed the shopping bag on the kitchen counter. Well, at least I had decided one thing: this was to be Emil's last night under my roof. That thought allowed me a measure of relief. I removed the packet of meat. I was going to make a big pot of braised ribs. If nothing else, it would make the house smell nice and cheer me up.

I took a heavy Dutch oven and put it over low heat, dumping in two cans of beef broth. Then I cut up two big onions in half-inch slices, taking the rings apart so they formed layers of white circles on the broth. I dredged the ribs in a mixture of flour and hot paprika, then browned them in oil in a hot skillet. When they were done I put them in the broth on top of the onion slices and poured the drippings over them. Then I added sliced potatoes and celery, seasoning, and a jar of home-canned tomatoes. The flour on the meat and the skillet drippings would thicken the broth, and we would have the stewlike mixture over egg noodles. Then it occurred to me that I had, with the addition of all that paprika, really make a goulash. Was it for my Hungarian friend? Yes, there would be plenty of food. So much, in fact, that Mary would never miss a couple of large portions. When the mixture in the pot began to bubble and send out good smells, I went in to the sun porch and took a thin volume from the bookshelves. If I remembered correctly, my situation had literary parallel.

So I climbed back into the hospital bed with my little book—a novella, really—and sipped ice water and read and smelled the aroma from the dutch oven. At three o'clock I fell into a doze and didn't wake up until Mary came home from shopping at six.

"Well, Dr. Danzeck pronounced me fully recovered," Mary said, adding a cup of dry red wine to the pot. "Gee, this smells good!"

"So you're fine now? And you don't have to take that Prussian blue anymore?"

"Nope. And best of all, I won't lose any more hair. You've obviously gone shopping. Did you go anywhere else?"

"To the office, briefly, but it was a waste."

"Well, thanks for cooking this surprise, Charlie. Gee, it's got a lot of that hot paprika in it. . . ."

I got out of bed, tasted the stew, grabbed a beer, and returned to the sheets, where I stretched and groaned. Mary gave me a queer sideways look.

"Charlie? Is there something you're not telling me?"

"Hmmm? No, why?"

"I don't know. You're just a little . . . distant the past day or so. Is it the flu?"

"Must be. But it hasn't affected my appetite," I said, patting the bed next to me. "C'mon, Mare, grab an ice water and join me. We'll watch the news together."

So she did. And after the news we ate the ribs and a big salad. After that, Mary went through the doorway into her atelier to throw some pots. I returned to my little book, which I finished and put in the pocket of my robe. Then I watched the fire in the wood stove, smoked a pipe, and sipped beer until I fell asleep.

13

I WAS AWAKE AGAIN AT ELEVEN. MARY HAD GONE UPSTAIRS. Though she'd been given a clean bill of health, I knew she tired easily. I went up there and looked in. She was sound asleep. Odds were she'd sleep through the night. I went back downstairs, put the two big dogs out in their runs, and made some coffee. If I drink coffee after noon, or tea after two, I'm awake till three or four in the morning. Every time. The java would insure that I'd be alert when—and if—Emil returned. I smoked and read, tried an old movie on television. I fussed and fidgeted, waiting.

At quarter to one, there was a faint sound from the basement stairs. Flack, the wire-haired dachshund, barked shrilly twice, and I hushed him, opening the basement door all the way. I heard more clumping and muted scraping and went downstairs. Peeking around the corner of the coal bin, I saw a strange man turn and face me.

"Hello, Doc. It's me," said a familiar voice. It was Emil, all right, but in strange garb, and with a different face. He now had a full head of long dark hair that covered his bald head and his white fringe of natural hair. A long, dark, wool coat covered him, and he'd pasted on a bushy mustache—which appeared obviously fake—and substituted dark horn-rims for his granny glasses. If the desired effect was to change his appearance, then it certainly worked. But the rig wasn't professional-looking. It looked like a disguise.

I fetched the trouble light, and he got the blanket, foam pad, and sleeping bag. When we had gotten his little campsite ready, I asked him to tell me everything that had happened.

"Wait till I get my ashtray," he said. "You know I can't talk without smoking."

I followed him into my workroom. He looked around at the power tools, the organized racks of hand tools, and my half-completed projects and remarked that his own workshop was very similar. But was it any surprise to me that Emil had a workshop in his basement, or that it closely resembled mine?

Emil took the ashtray from its hiding place. We doused the light and walked back to the furnace room through the dark hallway.

"What's that?" he said in a hoarse whisper. "I almost tripped over something here. . . ."

I turned on the hall light and saw the cat-litter box sitting there. Emil's foot had kicked it. I picked it up and put it back against the wall. I could see, and smell, that it was still unused. I told Emil we kept it there is case the cats—make that cat—got caught in the house. But in three years they'd never once used it.

"Then why do you keep it around?" he asked.

"Well, there may be a first time," I said. We went back into the furnace room and into the little coal bin. The furnace hummed and purred behind us. Emil donned his big dark coat, sat down, and lit up.

"Gee, Emil, you really ought to quit, or try to cut down."

"I thought of it. But I like it too much. And, frankly, there's very little left that I enjoy. Besides, how long have I got, anyway, eh? No, I'm a smoker, Doc, and never far from my Camels."

"So how was you day?" I asked.

"Busy. I'm tired tonight. After I left here I walked into Concord Center in the dark, where I phoned a cab. I rode the cab to Lincoln, then took the train into town, where I bought this stuff at a magic shop in the Combat Zone. The coat, I got at Goodwill. How does it look on me?"

"Ridiculous."

"I thought as much. But it's necessary. I hope it will fool anyone who's looking for me."

I hadn't the heart to tell Emil how crude and pathetic his attempt at security was. As a sometime spy, he should have known better. But then, Roantis once told me that most "spies" aren't the James Bond type, men who span the globe seeking one deadly assignment after another. No, they're professional drudges, bureaucrats or scientists who ride the trolley to work and whose dreary lives are not glorified or enhanced by their sneaking out an occasional document or going through reams and reams of technical data. Such people had little instinct, Laitis said, for the way the other half of the intelligence networks operated. Those were the enforcers, the assassins and thugs who kept the drudges in line and who punished even minor infractions with keen and practiced brutality. The booky types, the information-gatherers like Emil, had no real appreciation of how sophisticated and dangerous those other people could be. But now Emil knew; the man in the lineman's tent had shown him.

"I spent the rest of the day around town here looking for a place to go to ground for the next several days," Emil continued. "So far, I haven't found a place that's well hidden and in the right part of town."

"And where's the right part of town?" I asked.

He shook his head slowly, dragging on the cigarette.

"Not sure yet, Doc. But maybe out west, toward the railroad tracks. I just don't know."

"Any more developments at Lincoln Labs?"

He hesitated a second before replying.

"Yes, I think so," he said in a low voice. "But Doc, it's clear that I can't return there, under any circumstances. And yet I know something's up. There is more information to be gained. Listen, I'm going to give you two names. One is a man I trust completely. The other one is the person I suspect of passing information to the KGB."

"Wait, Emil. I'm not sure I want to get any deeper into this thing."

"I know. But just listen to these two names. Don't write them down. Then, if I don't come back, at least you'll know where to begin. The first name is Howard March. He lives in Lexington, and he's a trusted friend. On him, you and the government can depend completely. The other name is Roland Williamson, who lives in Belmont. I'm almost positive he is the source of the leak I uncovered recently. Remember the microdot I mentioned? It came off a memo from his office. Now remember: the message was not complete; it only mentioned that the event is to take place on the twenty-eighth—that's exactly two weeks from today."

"Howard March. Roland Williamson. Howard March—good. Roland Williamson—bad. Thursday after next. October twenty-eight. Fourteen days from now, something happens. We don't know what or where. Emil, won't there be another message, under another microdot?"

He thought for a second, then shook his head. "No, the dot I chanced to intercept was probably the *second* of a two-part message, not the first. They've probably known for some time what the event will be and where it's to take place. This message only provided the exact date. But who knows? I could be wrong. One thing's for sure: I can't go back inside the lab to find out."

He stretched, yawned, and settled back on the thick wool blankets with a groan. Behind us, on the other side of the wooden partition in the big basement room, the furnace snapped on and hummed. The sound made me think of sleep. I knew Emil wouldn't be awake long, so I hustled upstairs and put the water on to boil and the rib stew on low heat. Dammit, I wanted a cigarette. The tension level had to be high—higher than my conscious mind was admitting to.

Twenty minutes later I re-entered the basement with a big bowl of hot buttered egg noodles with ladles of ribs and stew on top. Emil was ecstatic and dove into it.

"Ooooh! Paprika! You've made goulash, Doc. The only thing that would make it a hundred percent Hungarian would be a bottle of Bull's Blood."

"Coming up," I said. I went down the hall and into the old laundry room, which we've converted into a small wine cellar. I took out the appropriate bottle, went up to the kitchen, drew the cork, and brought the wine down with two glasses. Emil was delighted.

"I take it you've heard of Joseph Conrad," he said. "Well, this book he wrote reminds me of—"

"Is it this one?" I said, pulling out *The Secret Sharer* from the pocket of my robe.

"Ha!—I can hardly believe it, the way we think alike," he chuckled, leaning back with the glass of red in his hand. The empty bowl lay on the blanket in front of him. He seemed, momentarily at least, wonderfully content for someone whose life was threatened. "As we say in America, we're on the same wavelength."

We both stared for minute at the thin novella, the story of a young sea captain who rescues and hides a fugitive from the law—doing so on the spur of the moment, and on his basic intuition.

"It's really—" He stopped suddenly, and I looked up at his face. There was fear on it. He put a finger to his lips. "*Shhhhhh!*" he whispered.

I waited a minute. "What?" I finally asked, in a whisper.

"Thought I heard," he said so softly I had to lean close to hear him, "a faint tapping or scraping on your wall."

I sat still and listened again. "Nah, don't think so," I whispered back.

But then I heard the shrill barking of Flack upstairs, directly over our heads, in the living room. Something outside the front of the house had alarmed him. I went upstairs; if nothing else, he might wake Mary. I hushed the dog, put him in Mary's atelier, and returned to the furnace room, which was now dark. Emil had doused the room light and the trouble light in the coal bin and was lifting up the metal door of the coal chute. He opened it about four inches, listening intently to the night sounds outside. I joined him, letting the cold air sweep over my cheek. Nothing. Emil sat down on the blanket, and I was just starting to lower the door back into position when I heard a car door shut, far away down the road. I looked at my watch: 1:38. Too late on a Thursday night—Friday morning, actually—for house guests on Old Stone Mill Road. I closed the chute, joined Emil on the blanket, and turned on the light.

"I've got to tell you a few things, Emil, to explain why I'm afraid you can't stay here anymore."

I told him about the episode in the Common and the kid wired to the gills with listening apparatus. Emil cringed. Then I mentioned the footprints leading to the coal chute. He cringed again.

"So what it boils down to is this: the KGB is two steps ahead of us. It's only a matter of time before they nab you."

"And I know who it will be, Doc. The worst, the most feared of them all . . ." He stared at the wooden wall of the coal bin, six feet from his face. His eyes were unfocused, dreamy with dread.

"What? What are you saying?"

"Listen to me," he said quietly, still staring at the wall, but with a far-off look in his eyes. Was he dreaming of eternity? "Listen to me—"

"I'm listening, Emil. I'm all ears, for Chrissake. What?"

"About the message I intercepted at work. I never mentioned the person who was to read the hidden message, the man for whom it was written. . . ."

"No, you didn't. Do I know his name?"

"No. You should be thankful you've never heard the name. But you will now. Because I must tell you. In fact, he's one of the reasons I'm so afraid—for both of us, now. The other reason is that I don't entirely trust the American side. Something's out of place in the Company. But the other man, the man who was to receive the message on the microdot . . ."

"Well?"

"He is called TALIN. T–A–L–I–N. It's a code name. A code name for the old pro of Department Five here in America. The most ruthless and most feared KGB enforcer of them all, or so it's said. If I could help our side capture or kill TALIN I would be a hero. But it is not likely to happen."

"Why not?"

"Because the odds say that TALIN will get me first. He has not failed in ten years. Maybe fifteen, or however long he's been operating here. He's deadly as a cobra."

"What's he look like?"

"Nobody knows. He has deep, deep cover. But there is one identifying mark, so the legend goes. It was revealed by a KGB agent in East Berlin who came over to our side. He was a big help to the Company for a while, but then Department Five caught up with him and killed him shortly afterward. They used a Kremlin water pistol on him—a squirt gun filled with prussic acid. Are you familiar with prussic acid?"

"Yes, sad to say. A friend of mine was killed with it up in Lowell. Death is instantaneous, and the effects are like those of a massive coronary. Usually an autopsy doesn't even reveal the true cause of death."

"Yes, Doc. Exactly. Well, the Company was sure that Hans Schuyler had died of a heart attack, too, until they caught on to the Kremlin water pistol. Anyway, Hans claimed to have known TALIN in his younger days, when the two of them were in *Spetsnaz* training together in the Ukraine—"

"*Spetsnaz?* What the hell's that?"

"*Spetsnaz* is the Soviet elite armed forces, similar to the old Nazi Waffen S.S. Anyway, during training, according to Schuyler, TALIN caught some fragments of a defective grenade. It was a white phosphorus grenade, and pieces of it landed on his upper back on the left side. It left a horrible scar there. 'You see that,' Hans said, 'watch out!' "

"Are you saying this just to cheer me up?" I asked.

He tried to smile. "Well, it was long ago. And who knows if it's even true, eh?"

Then he nodded slowly, sadly, and put the wineglass down. I looked at it. It was as if the wine had suddenly turned to vinegar. The festivity was over. They were closing in. And, like the young captain in Conrad's novel, I now had to draw my ship up under the black mountain on the coast and say farewell to my stowaway. I only hoped he could make it to shore. I gathered the bottle, dish, and glasses and trudged upstairs as he rolled into the sleeping bag. When I went back down to turn off all the lights, I saw a brief flare and flicker as he lighted a cigarette behind the partition.

Six A.M. I was fully awake, having slept most of the previous two days. I felt better; if I had a fever, it was only a degree or so. Where was Emil? Still asleep, I figured, since it was only four hours since he'd gone to bed. I hopped up, put on my robe, and tiptoed downstairs. Soon Mary would be stirring—if Emil was going to take off, he had better be quick. I rounded the corner to the coal bin, expecting to find him bundled up like a kid in a crib. I was shocked.

The bin was clean and neat, as it had been the previous morning. Everything, including telltale butts and ashes, had been taken away. But there sat Emil, on the concrete floor, still as Buddha. I didn't like the look on his face.

He threw a forefinger up to his mouth, silently saying *shhhhhh!*

"What's the—"

"Shhhh!" he said aloud. Barely. He pointed to the foundation walls, sweeping his finger around, a worried and intense look on his face. He made a writing motion with his hands. I silently crept upstairs and returned with a pad and pencil. Emil wrote on the pad and handed it to me. On it were two words:

SPIKE MIKES

I mouthed the word *what?* He pointed at the pad and then around the foundation walls again. I wrote on the pad:

STAY HERE QUIETLY. NO SMOKING. I'LL GET YOU AFTER MARY LEAVES.

At eight-fifteen, I was in the hospital bed feigning a light doze when Mary popped downstairs and felt my head.

"Better, Charlie. I'd stay home one more day, though, if I were you."

"I'll play it by ear. You look like you're going out."

"I'm going to do a few errands after coffee and a croissant. You want one?"

I said yes, and we ate, drank coffee, watched the *Today* show, and talked. Then I went upstairs and dressed. Just before Mary left for the mall, an hour later, she stood in the front doorway, keys in hand, and said, "Well, we're both almost well again. After those three days of hell, it seems that we're finally back to normal around here."

I nodded faintly. Sure, toots. Sure.

I went back to Emil, who was still sitting there like a scared Buddha. He motioned for me to follow him. He led me to the boys' bathroom on the second floor, where he turned the cold water in the shower stall on full blast. The tile room was full of racket.

"That's to give us a sound-screen," he explained in a normal voice. "Doc, after you went up last night, I heard the noises again on your outer walls, just at window level—which is ground level outside. The tapping and scraping. I'm sure somebody was tapping in spike mikes. Know what they are?"

"No."

"They're contact microphones that pick up vibrations through solid materials, just like the ones on electric guitars. Only they're fastened to the blunt ends of metal spikes. These spikes are driven into walls and pick up voices through the brick or wood."

I was going to tell him he was nuts. But then I remembered the kid on the Boston Common with the parabolic microphone dish in his backpack.

"So what the hell do we do?" I asked him. He sat on the toilet seat and thought. I leaned against the sink, my arms folded across my chest. The shower blasted away, creating ambient noise that protected us in a sound shield.

"First," he said, "I'm trying to reconstruct what they overheard, assuming the mikes in the cellar are now operating. I'm hoping they didn't overheard me telling you the two names, Doc. If they did, then I'm afraid your life probably isn't worth a nickel."

My heart skipped two beats at this tidbit. I wanted a cigarette again.

"But the odds are they didn't hear it. I don't think they could hear anything until just about the time you went up to bed."

"Well, let's hope so. But we can't be sure. I just—"

I stopped in midsentence, because just then the door flew open. There stood Mary, her mouth open wide in surprise. While the running water had certainly masked our voices with its sound shield, it had also kept us from hearing her open and shut the front door and come up the stairway.

"Charlie! . . . *Emil?!*"

"*Shhhhhh!*" I said.

"What the hell *is* this, for Chrissakes? Charlie, did you call the police?"

"No. And I'm not going to. Sit down, Mary, and I'll explain this."

She looked at Emil sitting on the toilet seat. She looked at me in my robe. She flung open the shower curtain—her face was beyond bewilderment.

"What the—"

"*Shhhhhh*, Mary! We're talking in here with the shower running so they can't hear us."

"*Who* can't hear you?"

"The KGB, if you really *must* know," I said.

"The KGB? The Russian spies? If I really *must* know? In my own fucking house? If I *must* know? You bet your sweet ass I must know! Where are they? I want to talk to them. They've got no right to—"

"*Talk* to them? Are you nuts? Listen, Mare, let's go for a little walk in the back yard while Emil gets ready to go."

"Go? He's not going anywhere. You heard what Joe said. *Emil Haszmanay: you stay right there while I make a phone call—*"

"Touch that phone, and you're dead," I shouted. So much for secrecy. Mary glared back at me, then stomped out of the bathroom and into our bedroom, slamming the door.

Emil was frozen, a look of terror in his eyes.

"Where did she get her training?" he finally asked. I assumed he meant military training, or something equally rough.

"She didn't need any; it's in the genes."

We hustled downstairs. I told Emil to grab everything he needed in thirty seconds and meet me in the garage. He flew down the basement stairs. I rushed upstairs to the bedroom and grabbed my wallet and car keys. Outside, I moved the Scout out of the way and pulled the Audi into our attached garage. I clicked the control, and the automatic door swung down. I opened the inside door and went through Mary's atelier and into the kitchen, where I met a panic-stricken Emil emerging, bundles in hand, from the basement.

"Is she really calling the police?" he whispered, panting.

"If not now, soon. Let's go."

I put him in the back seat and made him scrunch down on the floor, then threw his overcoat and little grip on top. I told him to stay down no matter what. I opened the garage door. In seconds we were out the driveway and rolling along Old Stone Mill Road at a good clip.

"Where are we going, Doc?" asked a muffled voice from beneath the clothing.

"I don't know yet. Just away. Hold on a second."

I pulled into a parking lot in Concord Center and hopped over to the automatic bank teller, withdrawing all the cash I could. Then I had an idea and headed west, turning onto Route 62 toward Maynard. I parked in front of The Outdoor Store.

"C'mon, Emil. We've got maybe fifteen minutes. Maybe not even that much. We've got to get you some warm clothing."

He followed me into the store. I asked him under my breath if he still had his disguise. He replied yes, in his grip.

"Good," I said. "I'm thinking of a plan."

"Is it a good one?"

"It better be; it's all we got. Now: shoes first. We want ragg wool socks and insulated hunting boots. They must fit perfectly. While you're getting fitted, I'll get the rest. Tell me your sizes."

While Emil was being fitted for the boots, I bought him a down-filled sleeping bag, a down parka, a down vest, two sets of long underwear—one polypro, one Duofold—a woolen watch cap, some wool pants, chino pants, and assorted other clothing. I did not shop around. I paid no attention to color or style. I bought top-of-the-line stuff with plenty of pockets. The pile of dry goods on the glass-topped counter rose like a lava flow. While the clerk was toting it up, I added three items I saw beneath the glass: a Buck sheath knife, a pair of compact binoculars, and a souped-up butane survivalist lighter.

"You ever do any Boy Scout stuff?" I asked the small, wiry, white-maned man next to me.

"None."

"Well, you're gonna learn fast. By hook or by crook." I was surprised when the salesman tossed *Handbook for Boys* on top of the heap. One of the greatest books ever published.

"There you go, Emil. Maybe you'll earn a few merit badges on the way."

Then it occurred to me that Emil had nothing to put his new gear in, no way to carry it. I took him over to the back of the store and we selected an ultralight aluminum-framed backpack designed for mountain assaults. It had a roomy nylon compartment on top and a place on the frame below to tie a rolled sleeping bag. We hauled it back to the salesman, and I stuffed garments into the bag as he rang them up.

"That come to, uh, lessee, eleven sixty-eight twenty-four."

"*Huh?* You mean eleven as in eleven hundred? As in greater than a thousand?"

"Yes, sir. Here are the totals—"

"Okay," I said, snapping a plastic bank card down on the counter. The clerk moved toward the phone. I told him we really didn't have time for a phone verification. I snapped down two more cards and told him to call to his heart's content after we left—he could hold the cards for collateral until I returned later. I flipped him a business card. He said he thought he recalled my face. . . .

But we were scurrying out the door by them. I carried Emil's half-filled backpack, and Emil, carrying the rest, followed me. I looked everywhere at once as we went outside. Then we hustled over to the car, and I told him to drive.

"But where are we going?" he asked again.

"I don't know; I'm making it up as we go along."

"Okay. Just asking."

"I'll sit in back and keep an eye on the road behind us

while I finish packing your stuff. Uh, lessee . . . head for the airport. No—don't turn around; go right on through town, then head south on Twenty-seven. When you hit One-seventeen, take a left. That'll take us east to One-twenty-eight."

As we slid out into traffic, I scanned each vehicle behind us. Red pickup. Cream-white station wagon. Neither looked suspicious. But what the hell did that mean? I stuffed the parka, vest, pants, and the rest into the bag on the pack. Down garments are terrific because they compress into a very small space. Then they fluff up again when you put them on. Just don't get them wet. I finished packing the main bag, then rolled the sleeping bag up tight and strapped it to the tubular frame. I looked out the rear window. Pickup still behind.

"Faster, Emil. Then we'll head north up One-twenty-eight, back to Route Two, instead of taking the Mass Pike. That way we're going almost in a big circle. Anyone who takes the same crazy route is the enemy. Savvy?"

He nodded, eyes intent on the road ahead. I packed the rest of his gear in the small side pockets of the pack: Boy Scout handbook, binoculars, lighter, knife. Knife. Oh, Christ. Forgot about the goddamn knife.

"Shit! Emil, they won't let you board with the knife. If you want to keep it, you'll have to check this through baggage. That's no good because it'll take too long, and it might get lost. You really want the knife, or what?"

"Well, sure. I'd like—wait a second, Doc. What's the plan, anyway? What's happening?"

"Okay: we drive to the airport. I let you off at a major terminal—a big airline with a lot of flights—and you rush in and take a flight that's leaving in a few minutes. I'll give you the cash to buy the ticket. Just rush in and get on the plane. No baggage check-in, no waiting at the gate. If possible, select a flight that's already boarded—when you buy the ticket, have the clerk phone the gate and say there's one more passenger, and can they hold the plane. Well?"

"Sounds good, I guess. But Doc, I've got to be *here*. Don't you see? Whatever's going to happen in thirteen days—I've got to find out what it is. I know it's something big—"

"I know. But you won't find out anything if you're dead. If the enforcers from the KGB get you, that's it. Okay, here's One-seventeen. Bang a left."

We didn't say a whole lot for the next half hour. By then we'd gotten onto 128, headed north on that busy beltway, then taken the Route 2 exit east. When we got to Fresh Pond, I had Emil pull over at the Ground Round restaurant on the rotary.

"If you want to use the head, do it now," I said, scanning the traffic. "I'll wait maybe a minute."

"No, let's keep moving."

We switched places. I advised him to don the disguise and wear his big dark coat as well. "Stow your windbreaker in the pack with your new clothes. When you get to your destination, it might be smart to ditch the disguise and get a new one. Then take a cab back to the airport and fly back to Boston. Or maybe even to Providence, and rent a car to get back."

He sat in back, nodding and looking out the windows. He was worried, and I couldn't blame him. Even if we had managed to temporarily ditch the meanies, by this time Mary had called Joe, and he had no doubt alerted the state police, Chet Harwood, and the FBI, too. Great. But I didn't say anything. There was no need to remind my friend of the danger he was in; he knew it even better than I did.

I had noticed a teal-blue sedan, an Olds, I think, come into the rotary at Fresh Pond. Instead of going through the rotary, it had kept going around it, doubling back the way it had come. It didn't stop near us, but went up toward Alewife Brook Parkway and Route 2. I made a mental note.

We were on Storrow Drive when Emil told me he didn't like the plan.

"The more I think about it, Doc, the riskier it sounds. What if I can't get a flight that leaves right away? They'll corner me and—"

"No, they won't—not in a public place. Just *don't* go into the john, whatever you—"

"I just don't like it. I'm afraid I'll be so nervous I'll give myself away. And I *do* want the knife with me. And I *don't* want to leave Boston."

I thought for a minute and came up with a good alternative.

"I've got it. Listen: it starts like the other one—I drop you off at a busy terminal. Any one we decide on. I drop you at the upper level, that's departures. I get out, help you with your stuff, and visibly hand you cash. We shake hands, you go into the terminal. *But,* once inside, you do *not* proceed to the ticket counter. No: you find the nearest escalator and go straight down to the lower level, which is arrivals. You go back out through the door as if you've just landed, hail a cab, and scoot. How's that?"

"Great!" he said, beaming. "That's much better. I like it. It's the unexpected. I'll be in, out, and away again before they even know it."

Just past Mass General Hospital, we took the ramp up to the Expressway, heading south through the heart of the city. I was constantly flicking my eyes up to the rearview mirror. I saw a teal-blue sedan. I could swear it was the same one I had seen at the rotary. If so, it had doubled back yet again, following us. I kept quiet. If all went well, Emil would make a clean getaway and yet stay in the area. I would be out of the spy business and finally able to get back to some sort of normal life. But I would miss him.

"Since you can't come back to my place, how will we keep in touch?" I asked him. He didn't answer, and I turned to look at him. I was shocked to see that his face once again bore a look of terror.

"Emil? You okay?"

"Y-yes," he nodded quickly, speaking in a low voice. "I'm just thinking, is all."

I turned off at the Haymarket exit and swung a left under the expressway, and we found ourselves in that crazy, Dantesque horizontal funnel of seven lanes of cars merging down into two lanes, getting ready to enter the Callahan Tunnel, which runs beneath Boston Harbor and over to East Boston and Logan Airport. Just another of those traffic nightmares that makes driving in Boston such a memorable experience.

As usual, at the very center of the sloping tunnel, the tunnel guard was in his little booth on the catwalk. Poor guy. I'm convinced this is the ultimate punishment for the city employee who screws up the most each week, since a day thus spent, amid the fumes and noise, must lessen the human life span by ten years.

We emerged on the far side of the tunnel and turned off onto the airport access road. I again asked Emil if he was okay, but he waved me off and said "Wait," so I shut up.

"Any preferences?" I asked as we approached the airline terminals.

"Try Eastern," he said.

Eastern is one of the few airlines located in a terminal separate from the main complex. It was a good choice, since it made it easier to see who was behind us. As we went up toward the departures level, I looked and looked for a teal-blue Olds sedan. I didn't see it. I rolled to a stop in front of the Eastern terminal, my heart thumping. I'm sure Emil's was too. This was it. A uniformed Skycap stood behind a small outside counter, waiting for curbside check-in. Otherwise the place was empty. I switched on the emergency flasher, and we both got out. Whatever it was Emil Haszmanay looked like in his crude get-up, it was not Emil Haszmanay. I helped him tug the gear out of the car. We stood facing each other in the cold wind. The ocean breeze was gusty, and it whipped Emil's fake hair all around. Ordinarily, I would have found it funny.

"Doc, I can't thank you—"

"Skip it, pal. Time's a-wastin'." I drew out my wallet and counted out all the cash I had. About four hundred and eighty bucks.

"Doc," he said in a low, earnest voice, "listen carefully. You asked how we'd get in touch again. I've though of a way. You know I can't call you or use the mails. I can't hang around your house anymore. Tell you what: if I come back—and you know I may not—I'll find a place to hide near Concord. Then I'll leave you a sign."

"A sign?"

"Yes. You know our minds work a like. We're secret sharers, after all. I'll leave a sign for you near your home. It'll tell you—and nobody else—where to come looking for me. Goodbye, Doc. God bless. . . ."

He gave me a hug, flung his backpack up on one shoulder with a wiry strength, and walked through the doors into the terminal. He was doing his damnedest to be brave, I thought. But despite the outward show, to me he appeared old, scared, and very vulnerable.

14

I GOT BACK BEHIND THE WHEEL AND LET OUT A LONG, SLOW sigh. Was it sadness or relief? Or both? I felt my energy escape with the sigh. Suddenly, with the excitement and tension gone, I was a deflated balloon, and very tired. Somebody honked behind me. Okay, okay. I shut off the emergency flasher and eased down the ramp onto the circular airport road. I kept looking in the rearview. Was that Emil's cab behind me? And where was the teal-blue sedan? Traffic thickened, and before I knew it I was once again underneath Boston Harbor, in the roaring, rushing, honking mayhem of the tunnel—this time the Sumner Tunnel, which runs the opposite way.

I emerged from the tunnel and was back in the city again, and I wanted to head straight home and have it out with Mary. Her calling the police was, to say the least, unappreciated. Luckily, Emil and I seemed to have circumvented them, and I had actually gotten through the ordeal sooner than I'd expected to. But another ordeal was soon to come: the wrath of the law. Joe, Chet, and Brian would want my head on a pole. But that would be nothing compared with the wrath of Mary Brindelli Adams.

Perhaps I should go to the Y for a workout. With the fever it had been days since I'd run . . .

Forget it, Adams. You can delay it, but not escape it. Best to head right on over to Ten Ten Comm. Ave. and face Joe now. Might as well get it over with. So I made my way over to Commonwealth Avenue and headed west. I parked in front of Eastern Mountain Sports and crossed the street. I rode the elevator to the fifth floor and went to Joe's office. I peeked in. Kevin O'Hearn was there, leaning back in his oak chair, staring at the bent Venetian blinds in his window. Kevin O'Hearn was a nice guy. Laid-back. He wouldn't go for my throat. Maybe he would even have suggestions as to how to dispel some of the anger that was headed my way. I hailed him, and he spun around in his chair.

"Oh, hiya, Doc. Your brother-in-law just went over to the Greek's to get coffee and sandwiches. Too bad you dint put an order in. Oh, that's right; Doc Adams doesn't eat lunch. Forgot. Hey, sit down."

I slid into a gray swivel chair with cracked vinyl seat covers. The foam padding was leaking out. Aesthetics unlimited.

"So, what brings you here?" he asked me, chewing on a toothpick. His manner surprised me. Was it possible Mary hadn't called Joe after all? A floor of relief passed through me. Careful, Adams. Don't bet on it.

"Just passing by; thought I'd stop in. Any new developments on the Haszmanay thing?"

He snapped his fingers and leaned over, looking at me intently. I got nervous again.

"I forgot. Joe wants you to look at the stiff. The guy we took down off the pole."

"I'd rather not."

"Naw. Look inna guy's mouth. That's what Joe wants. Tell him everyt'ing you know based on the guy's teeth."

"Do I have to look at his face too?"

"Ha! Naw. We'll drape it. Wait, here's Joe. Hear that big stomping down the hallway?"

Joe came in and sat down. He didn't say anything much. But I had to know.

"Mary call you?" I asked.

"Uh-uh. About what?"

"About dinner."

He shook his head, unwrapping the sub that sat on his grease-stained blotter. So she hadn't called; she'd listened to her good sense after we'd left and decided at least to wait until we could have a talk about it. Good for her.

"What? You callin' it off, or what?"

"No. I just thought we might have you over tonight instead of tomorrow."

Joe came to dinner most Saturday nights. And sometimes he stayed on for dinner Sunday, after he joined us in church. I was proposing that he show up tonight, Friday night. "Ummmmm!" Joe said through clenched teeth as he destroyed the sub. He held up a finger, chewing.

"Pix!" he finally blurted out the side of his mouth. He kept chewing. When he finally cleared his maw enough to mumble, he continued. "Gotta show you the M.E.'s photos, Doc. Don't wanta see 'em before I finish eating. . . ."

I took a stroll down the hall, in the direction of the Major's office. Major John Mahaffey, boss of the entire Bureau of Investigative Services, and the detective bureau's liaison to the Feds. There was a pay phone on the wall. I called home.

"So you *did* help him escape! Sweet Jesus, Charlie! Where are you now?"

"I'm calling from Joe's office, telling you not to worry. It's over, Mary. It's all over now. Everything's back to normal."

"Hell it is, pal. You've got to tell Joe. Right now. If you don't tell him, I will."

"Don't. I've asked him to dinner tonight. We'll prepare him, then tell him after dinner."

"You listen to me: you better come clean with everybody tonight, Charlie. I'm not kidding around. You quit this goddamn sneaking around with spies and turning my house into a—a—"

She couldn't think of a word, so she left off and started calling me names instead. Dipshit and birdbrain were two of the cuter ones she began with. But then they got worse, as did the threats that accompanied them. It was all done with the subtlety that is the hallmark of southern Italians. For example, one of the less pleasant threats was the promise to rip off my genitalia and stuff the parts down the disposal. Subtle. Very subtle. . . .

"And when you get home, pal, I've got a few more unpleasant surprises waiting. . . ."

We finally ended the conversation, if such it could be called, and I left the pay phone wondering if indeed I was ever going to return home. Then I recalled Laitis Roantis telling me once that Mary sometimes made him nervous. Mary making Laitis Roantis nervous. Think about that one for a second. She *had* agreed, however, to cook a good dinner for Joe. "But it's all for *him*, not *you*!" she'd said. I went back to Joe's office, where he was just stuffing the sub wrapper into another styrofoam coffee cup. He belched and drew out a sheaf of nine-by-twelves. They weren't exactly after-lunch material. Or before-lunch, for that matter. Joe read from the M.E.'s report:

"Male Caucasian. Age: forty-nine to fifty-two. Height: five feet, nine point five inches. Weight: one hundred eighty-two pounds. Color hair: black with gray. Color eyes: unknown, presumed brown. Identifying makes and scars: on face and head, none discernible. Large burn scar on back, upper left. Condition of teeth—here's the part I want—"

"Wait! What was that?"

"Condition of the teeth. It says—"

"No. Before that."

"Large burn scar on back, upper left."

I grabbed the photos, flipping through them until I found a shot of the victim's back. It had been taken from above, about two and a half feet over the gurney.

"Let me see him," I said, getting out of my chair and heading for the door. Joe followed. We rode the elevator down to the lower level and walked through two sets of double doors and into the tiled, chilly morgue. They wheeled out the drawer for us, and I requested the attendant to turn the corpse over. He left to summon another aide.

"What's this all about?" asked Joe. "All I wanted you to do was look in the guy's mouth."

"Surely you had your state man do that. But I will, don't worry, after I get a gander at his back."

"What's this all about?" he asked again. "You know something I don't?"

"After dinner, Joe, we'll have a long talk."

"Dammit, we'll talk *now*."

"Come for an early dinner. I can't tell you what I don't yet know. Come for cocktails around five. How's that?"

I heard a growling and cussing from him as the two attendants rolled the body over. There is was, the mass of whorled tissue, lumpy, raised up—"proud tissue," as it's called. It had tiny endgrains in it, like the bird's-eye grain of fine pipe briar or the speckly, wartlike grains on a dog's paw pads. And, overall, the shiny, glassy smoothness of scar tissue. It looked like mica, the stuff they used to put in the windows of old coal stoves and which they called fireglass. I looked for some time, then had them turn the body over again. They draped the upper face, which was thoughtful of them. It took a while for them to find a retractor, but finally I inserted it and eased open the mouth far enough. I didn't care for the aroma that issued forth. Did *not*. I looked in at his gums and choppers.

"Right-handed," I said. "Tell that immediately by the differences in gumlines left to right. Right-handed person has more eroded gumline on his left, from brushing the teeth. Let's see . . . three steel fillings, four silver, one gold onlay. Hmmmm. Interesting. Two of the silver fillings appear to be the oldest, and they're in the six-year molars. Stainless-steel fillings newer. Therefore, he spent his youth in America or Europe, then lived in the Soviet Union or Eastern Europe for a while. The gold work's been added since he came back here. I'd concur with the age: close to fifty . . . I'll be damned, *torus mandibula*, I can feel the growths with my finger. I've got 'em, too. Only twenty percent of any population has them."

I paused to take a breather; I needed it. I like live patients better.

"I'd say this guy was recently better fixed than he was early in life—though not rich. Probably the direct result of returning to America. Oh, yes, another obvious point: he was a smoker. But not a heavy one. I also seem to pick up a vitamin C deficiency, and perhaps niacin, too, but can't be too sure, considering he's been dead over five days."

I stood up and went over to the sink. Gee, it was nice to get away from that smell.

"Wait, Doc. You're saying the guy's not a native Russian? You're saying he was born here?"

"I'd say so. Here or in Europe, where they use precious metals to fill cavities instead of stainless steel."

"Hmmmmph! Well I'll be damned; we had him pegged for a Russkie."

"He did spend time there."

"Hmmm. Well, we made the car, Doc. White Mercury Lynx. Three years old. Found it parked on a side road called Willow Springs Lane. Still haven't found any ID. We made the guy by the tag number on the vehicle."

"Huh. I know the road. But hell, it's a mile, at least, from my house."

"Figure it out. If you were trying to bump somebody off, would you park right near your hidey-hole?"

"What's the guy's name?"

"Frederick Stansul. Mac Cousins, who's also in homicide, thinks probably it was shortened from a name like Stansuleski, or Stansulcek. Anyway, he was a purchasing agent for Adrian Products, a small metal-fastener company in Somerville, where he also lived. It's a little apartment, the top half of a duplex walk-up. Our guys went over the place thoroughly. Nothing. The guy was well covered."

"That's all you got? Maybe the KGB guys hustled in there ahead of you and cleaned out the place when they found out he wasn't coming back."

"Yeah. We thought of that. Or maybe he was only a part-timer. He had a job and a pretty good life, compared to what he'd have had if he'd stayed over there. Maybe they just activated him for wet work whenever the need arose. But we're still following any leads. That's why I want to know why you're so interested in the scar on his back.''

''Come to the house at four, then, instead of five. Also, can you bring a debugger with you?''

''A what?''

''Whatever those electronic instruments are that find bugs so you can remove them. Somebody's bugged my house, and I want them removed.''

''What makes you so sure?''

''I heard tapping in my walls in the middle of the night, that's what. Can you bring some equipment out?''

''I'll bring two good men and all the sweep equipment they'll need. It better be a good dinner.''

I managed to see two patients later that afternoon. It seemed like ages since I'd practiced medicine. As I was leaving for home, Moe stopped in and commented on my raggedy appearance, saying he hoped I'd put the stress behind me. I said I had, and did not fill him in on any of the details of Emil's escape earlier in the day.

''How's the, uh, situation wid your, eh, *friend*?'' he asked as we walked down the hall, putting on our coats.

''I have no idea what you're talking about, Moe. And neither do you.''

''Oh, yeah. Got it,'' he said, and wished me a pleasant weekend. ''At least, better dan da last one. *Whew!*''

As I went into the front hall of chez Adams, I wasn't exactly sure that this weekend *would* be any easier than the last. When Mary gets thoroughly steamed, you can clear the decks. I walked softly through the hall and the living room, skirted the sun porch, went through my study, and peeked through the other side door into the kitchen. No Mary. Safe for now. I poked my head into that warm, aromatic room. A strong hand yanked my shirt collar, and I was dragged into the kitchen, spun around, and forced up against the wall. My fist had begun its arc toward my hidden assailant. But then I was looking into a pair of big browns, surrounded by olive skin and lots of dark brown curls. Mary bumped me against the wall a few times to get my attention.

"Do that again, asshole, and you're dead meat!" she said in a low hiss. But then she seemed to read a rising rage in my face, and she hugged me, crying.

"Oh Charlie, I'm so *afraid*!" she wailed. And I knew it was true. All human anger is born of fear. I hugged her until she relaxed and then said she was sorry about all the bad things she'd said over the phone.

"Except about ripping your balls off. That's really going to happen to you if you play secret with me again. Now, what's happening with you and Emil?"

"Look, hon, I've got to explain it to Joe when he shows up, anyway. Can you let me off the hook until then?"

"Will you tell all?"

"All of it—I promise."

"All right, then. At least you didn't get yourself killed. I'm glad of that."

After that she cooled down and seemed relieved to have gotten rid of the tension. She walked back to the stove and started singing to herself as she swayed back and forth in front of it. That's something I'll never get used to with her: that Latin temper that rages and then falls placid within seconds. She flashed the big browns at me, then back down to the manicotti shells she was stuffing with ricotta cheese.

"Why don't you make a batch of your ACE salad dressing? You know how Joe loves it." She was arranging the tubular pasta shells in a Pyrex baking dish that had a little olive oil on the bottom. She rolled them around in it, coating them very lightly so they would stay moist during the baking and wouldn't stick. Then she was going to cover the stuffed pasta with a rich Bolognese meat sauce.

"What kind of salad should we have?" I asked her.

"How about a big antipasto plate we can share before, and just lettuce wedges afterward with the ACE dressing?"

Well, it sounded okay. I had requested the manicotti because I wanted Joe's mood to be as receptive and jovial as possible, considering the news I was going to lay on him after supper. I cranked open two bottles of Chianti classico and set them aside. The ACE dressing, my own concoction, is not for the faint of heart. I made up the name from the three main ingredients: anchovies, capers, and eggs.

I hard-boiled some eggs, then opened a can of anchovy fillets, draining off the oil. I put the anchovies into a blender with a little vegetable oil, beating them to a pulp. Then I added the eggs and two heaping teaspoons of capers, a dash of Worcestershire, a little Dijon mustard, black pepper, and the juice of a lemon and turned on the machine again. Into this maelstrom I added a half cup of olive oil, pouring it in a thin, steady stream.

This mixture is, to say the least, piquant. Even a Cajun crabber on the Atchafalaya might find it a bit much. So I cut it with regular Italian dressing, in equal parts. The result is not nearly so strong and fishy as one might suspect. I think the lemon and egg help cut the fishiness. It's still, uh, different and unforgettable. And it will never be wildly popular, largely because of those hairy little fish.

When Joe's unmarked cruiser swung into the drive behind our cars, the manicotti was ready in the oven. I met Joe in the hallway and handed him a big gin and tonic. House of Lords gin, Schweppes tonic, fresh jumbo lime slice—

"You're hiding something, Doc. I can sense it. You're about to drop a big load of shit on my head." He took the drink and guzzled half of it in four huge swallows. He held the glass out, admiring it. "Nice. You do nice work." Then he put the glass to his lips and tilted his head back again, killing it.

"Let's have an instant replay, sport," he said, handing me back the glass. I went into the kitchen to repair the drink. I heard a clumping and clattering at the front door as two men came in under Joe's guidance. They walked through the kitchen, where I was standing at the sideboard. They carried big cases, and one of them wore headphones and was holding an electronic sensor in his free hand. His friend unpacked an instrument that resembled a miniature carpet-sweeper with a meter on the handle. Joe told me it was a "boomerang nonlinear junction detector." That's nice, I said.

"Getting something," said the first man. "Getting something already, Joe."

Joe's eyebrows raised as he took the freshened drink from my hand. "Hmmmmm. Looks like you weren't imagining it, Doc. Your place *is* bugged. We'll start with the basement and work our way up."

Mary and I made antipastos while the team swept the house. Joe stayed with us, testing the wine, setting the table, and cutting the bread and putting the garlic butter on it. He kept glancing in my direction. At six-thirty, the team came back to the kitchen and loaded the table with little doodads.

"Bugs?" Mary asked. "All those?"

"Bugs," her brother nodded grimly. "Your house has more goddamn bugs than a July picnic. And guess what? Your phone's been tapped, too. Wireless intercept, right on the drop-line. Somebody is real anxious to hear whatever you're saying around here."

"But why the bird-feeder?" she asked. "Don't tell me that's bugged too?"

Joe nodded grimly. "These are very sophisticated bugs. Steve and Barry here can tell you just how sophisticated. They're state of the art, which leads me to believe they've been placed by an intelligence agency—namely, the KGB. See this little cylinder? We found it hidden in the living room. Okay, no bigger than half a pencil. Well, in this tiny cylinder is a complete integrated system: microphone, battery, and transmitter. This bug, like all the others on the table here, is wireless. There's a listening post—probably in a car or van—within half a mile of here that picks up the signal and amplifies it. I've already made a few phone calls to have the area canvassed. But there's not much hope we'll find it. Like I said, it was probably a car or a van, and it's probably gone by now."

I tapped my feet nervously on the floor. I remembered the sound of the car door slamming when Emil and I were in the coal bin. I picked up a long, thin plastic tube about eight inches long.

"Is this a spike mike?" I asked, twirling it in my fingers.

The manicotti was beginning to smell great, but my appetite was waning by the second.

"A tube mike. First cousin to a spike mike. Both types are driven through walls. We found these four tube mikes embedded in the foundation walls of your cellar."

"Now, the bird-feeder," he continued, holding up the small, Plexiglas seed tray we had recently bought for outside the dining-room window, "is a beaut. A real beaut, right, Barry? See the suction cup that holds it to the outside of the windowpane? Well, it's not standard issue. They've replaced it with a suction mike that picks up every vibration of the glass. Underneath the feeder, kept dry and safe by the Plexiglas, is the transmitter and a big alkaline battery. See? And this silver wire, running along inside the base, is the antenna. What's the megahertz range on this, Barry? What would you guess, based on antenna length of two inches?"

"It's between forty and five-twelve megahertz, the pro frequency," said Barry, packing up his gear.

"I was afraid of that," said Joe. "This unit has a lot of sensitivity and power. The eavesdropper could hear every word spoken in your dining room and hall from a mile away."

"Bastards!" Mary fumed. "Those bastards, Joe! And now Charlie's got something to tell you. Don't you, Charlie?"

"In a minute," I said. "When we're alone. . . ."

"I'm all ears," Joe said. "Steve? Barry? You guys wanna go outside and check the cars for bugs and RDFs? Thanks."

"I was just going to say—" I began. But I couldn't finish the sentence. Joe had told them to check the cars. Check the cars. Check the goddamn *cars*!

"Doc?"

"Joe, can the cars be bugged too?"

"Oh, for sure. They're easiest of all to bug. They can plant listening devices and direction-finders on them in a flash."

"Direction-finders? You said RDF. Is that like a marine navigation RDF?"

"The very same, Doc. A radio direction-finder. Just like the one you've got aboard the *Ella Hatton*. They're also called 'bumper beepers' in the trade. The good ones enable an agent to tail a car and stay way out of sight."

I sank down into a chair. Now I could fit the pieces together. The mystery of how I was tailed into Boston when I went to see Roantis was solved. But worst of all, if the cars were indeed bugged, it meant that every word Emil and I had spoken during the ride to Logan Airport had been overheard. That meant that they—whoever they were—knew about our plan of the fake plane flight. If the blue Olds *had* been following us, then whoever was driving it had heard it all. And when Emil came out of the arrivals level after I let him off, he'd probably had a reception committee waiting there for him.

"Doc? Hey, Doc?" Joe was shaking me by the shoulder. Just then Steven and Barry came back inside, bearing another handful of electronic goodies. They confirmed my worst fears: both Adams vehicles, the Audi and the Scout, had been bugged to the hilt. Listening devices, powerful and sensitive, were wired to the electrical system of each car. Using the car batteries for power, they could last a lifetime. Bumper beepers, magnetically mounted on the undercarriages. Flick a switch, and I'll follow you anywhere, Adams.

Son of a bitch. All was lost. I put my face in my hands and groaned.

"What is it?" asked Joe.

"Tell him, Charlie. Goddammit, you don't, and I *will*," Mary said.

"They've got him," I said.

"Who's got who? Who's got whom?" asked Joe.

"The KGB. They've got Emil Haszmanay. I tried to help him escape, but I blew it. They've got him now, and he's probably dead."

Joe got the Thousand-Yard Stare in his eyes. He got up and went over to the phone.

"Who you calling?" asked Mary.

"Everybody," he sighed. "But I'll start with Chet Harwood."

"I bet he already knows, Joe," said Steve, taking a cup of hot coffee from Mary. Joe looked up from the phone, puzzled.

"Whadduyuh mean?" he asked.

"That phone tap? Recognize it anywhere: it's a Fed tap. Can't say for sure who placed all these other devices, but the phone was tapped by the Bureau."

"Oh, bullshit, Steve. Chet woulda told me—"

"He's right," said Barry, lighting a cigarette. "It was the good ol' *effa bee eye*."

15

Chet Harwood kicked the bottom stone step of my front stoop. Joe and I sat there and watched him. It's dumb to kick stone when wearing canvas tennies, and he hurt his foot, which made him even more furious. It was the next morning, a Saturday, and Chet had showed up at my place early, fuming and cussing. He was also mad because he hadn't been able to contact his partner, Sid Wanzer. Chet was wearing a knit pullover and slacks. He was dressed for leisure. I guess we'd wrecked his weekend, too.

"Jesus Christ, Adams. *Jesus Christ!* We would've had this guy, at least for preliminary investigation. We had him right where we wanted him, and what do you do? You hide him out in your cellar for a couple days, then take him to the *airport*, for Chrissakes, so he can flee the country!"

He leaned over close and talked to me through clenched teeth.

"You trying for the Order of Lenin? Huh? Zat it?"

"Okay, Chet, okay. So Doc screwed up—"

"You're not doing so hot yourself, Brindelli," said Chet, drawing back his foot for another go at the stone. Then he thought better of it. He sure had changed from the smooth, calm professional I'd seen nearly a week earlier in Joe's office.

"What's that supposed to mean?" asked Joe.

"It means what it means. You come out here on an electronic sweep and ruin my intercept, that's what."

"You should've told me you tapped his phone. Or at least told Brian. It's S.O.P. for a federal agent—"

"Bullshit! Screw the S.O.P., Joe. This is not—*was* not—S.O.P. We're talking *spies* here. We're talking national security. Defense technology. Leaks. The whole nine yards. Of *course* I didn't tell anybody the tap was in place. It's not like I'm trying to bust up some half-assed interstate hijacking ring."

"I can tell you where the leaks are coming from, at least at Lincoln Labs," I said.

Chet spun around fast, and his eyes drilled into me.

"You? How? Haszmanay tell you?"

"He told me the name of the person he was certain was leaking information to the KGB. He told me to tell nobody, but since I assume he's now dead, or in custody, I might as well let you know."

Chet glowered at me, rattling the coins in his slacks pockets.

"I think, considering what you've already done, it'd be a good idea," he said softly.

"The leak's name is Roland Williamson. He works in the same department Emil does. Did. Roland Williamson. Emil intercepted a microdot on a company memo sent by Williamson. The memo was inconsequential; it was the microdot, appearing to the casual eye as a period at the end of a sentence, that was the gem."

The two men were looking at me intently now. Chet eased down and sat on the step. Joe leaned against one of the columns, looking at the gold maple trees with their big black trunks. The trees swayed and hissed in the breeze.

"Yeah?" said Joe. "So what did the microdot say, or didn't Emil find out?"

"He found out. He had a microdot reader at home, from his days with the Soviets—"

"You're assuming he's no longer with the, uh, 'Soviets'?" asked Chet, with irony in his voice.

"Yes. But before we get into that, just listen. The message in the dot mentioned a date. The date is October twenty-eighth, a Thursday."

"Thursday after next," said Joe. "So what is it? What's going to happen twelve days from now?"

"We don't know. We just know the date, not the time, not the location, not the event. Emil figured that this was the second of two messages, or the last in a series, because presumably all the other information had already been conveyed. But he figured it dealt with something at the lab, although he wasn't positive. Finally—and Chet, you'll find this interesting—the microdot was supposed to be sent to a man with the code name TALIN. Ever heard of him?"

He sat there, immobile, as if trying to remember. Apparently the name was not in his foremost thoughts. He ran his hand through his hair, then scratched his head.

"I'm thinking . . . ," he said slowly. "I'm thinking I recall that name from some time ago, like maybe in the seventies or even the late sixties. But I haven't heard it in a long time. I think he was supposed to be some sort of Russian heavy. But I vaguely recall . . . I think that even then, a lot of us thought it was a hoax—that the guy never existed. And the name hasn't come up since, which is why I had trouble remembering. That amount of time passes, we generally assume the guy's dead or has been replaced. Or never existed. A better guy to ask would be Victor Hamisch, who's with the Agency. Vic would know. Goddammit, where the hell's Wanzer? He's never where he's supposed to be." Chet fumed and looked at his watch again.

"Well, Chet, I've got news: TALIN is real, and he's now dead. I saw his remains with Joe, yesterday afternoon at the state morgue."

"*That* was him? The guy on the pole?"

"Right. Emil said TALIN could be identified by a burn scar on his upper-left back. Now you know why I was so interested in looking at his back once I'd seen the pictures. So if what Emil says is true, TALIN is now dead. That's probably the only good thing to come out of this."

Chet was smiling at me. His face wore a wide grin.

"Did I say something funny?" I asked.

"Tell you in a little bit," he answered, holding up his hand. "Go on, Doc."

"Well, that's about it. I just thought you'd at least be glad that TALIN is dead. It's gotta be a big setback for the KGB."

Chet stood up, scuffed his feet on the flagstones, and looked down at them in thought, rattling the change in his pockets again.

"Well, fine," said Chet. "If that's what really happened. Trouble is, I've been in this screwy business just long enough to know that things aren't always as they seem. In fact, what you see is hardly ever what you get. Now, I don't want to rain on your parade, but let's just make a weird assumption for a second. Let's assume that the guy in the tent on the pole wasn't TALIN, or even any sort of KGB operative. Let's instead assume he was a CIA marksman."

Joe and I stared at him.

"Aw, come off it, Chet," said Joe.

"No. I'm serious. I'm a hundred percent serious. I know the Company wants Haszmanay. They did not say they wanted him dead. Did not say that. But who knows? And if they do want him dead, do you think they'd tell us peons at the Bureau? Or the Senate and House committees? Or the Joint Chiefs, or the NSC? Or even the President? Shit, no. Not on your life, they wouldn't. Sure, we want Emil Haszmanay at the Bureau. We want him alive, and we want him to come clean. We're forgiving. We can be lenient. We work with the Company on surveillance and apprehension of enemy agents inside our borders. Outside the country, it's all the Company's show. We're the Company's legmen in America. The special forces and other military types are their hit men abroad. That's the way it is. But nobody outside the Company knows what the D.D.O. does, or what its plans are. Nobody."

"So what's the D.D.O. ?" I asked. "Or can't you tell me?"

"Sure, I can tell you. The CIA is divided into two main departments: the D.D.I. and the D.D.O. D.D.I. people are overt. That is, they say they're with the Company. They're up front about it. The D.D.I.—Deputy Directorate of Information—collects and processes data. They gather and analyze information. Period. No covert operations, no agents, no rough stuff. They examine aerial photos, listen to secret tape recordings, crack codes and ciphers, process information given to us by all sorts of agents and other sources—that kind of thing. Okay. Then there's the sister department, the Deputy Directorate of Operations. That's where you find the heavy stuff: foreign—and domestic—assassinations, coups, clandestine operations, sabotage, the whole shebang."

"So the D.D.O. does the nasty stuff," I said. "The stuff that we read about in the papers but don't believe. . . ."

"You got it. And believe me, as closely as we work with the Company, there's precious little we know about what's going on in the D.D.O. Precious little."

"But why would the Company want to kill Haszmanay?" Joe asked.

"I'm not saying they do want to. But if they did—for whatever reason—they sure as hell wouldn't tell us. And if the hit were botched, and their man killed, they sure as hell would want everybody to think that the killer was KGB, not CIA. Follow?"

"Christ, what a nasty, filthy business."

"You just said a mouthful, Adams. On both sides of the global chess game. The Bureau can be nasty, but we're pure as the driven snow compared to the D.D.O."

He came over and clapped me on the shoulder. For the first time I detected a trace of human sympathy in the bureaucrat. Maybe it was because it was Saturday, and he wasn't wearing his suit.

"Let me tell you my side—*our side*—okay? Our information indicates that, yes, there have been substantial leaks at Lincoln Labs. We have strong indications—not just idle speculation, but evidence—that Haszmanay is the one responsible. We're convinced that until very recently he was still working for the Russians, Doc. Now, I know the guy in the lineman's tent wanted to kill him. And he could indeed have been a Soviet agent. Or, as I say, he could have been something else. Maybe we'll never know. We do think that very recently Emil's been in hot water with the KGB. He did something to really piss them off, and now we're pretty sure they want him dead. The Bureau wants him too, but not dead. We could make a deal with him that would be far more attractive than the life he's been forced into lately. You follow?"

I nodded. Chet paced in front of us, brow furrowed earnestly, his hands working with the words, as if directing his own little string quartet.

"So my question now is," he continued, "*the* question is: *why the hell hasn't he come over to our side,* eh? *Why not?*"

I couldn't answer it. I shook my head a little.

"You see? You can't answer that obvious question. You can't answer it for the obvious reason: Emil Haszmanay hasn't leveled with you, Doc. He has something to hide. Personally, I wouldn't be too surprised if he's in Russia right now, waiting to get the Order of Lenin pinned on him."

Joe and I sat there, taking this in. It wasn't exactly what I wanted to hear. Chet sighed, put his hands on his hips, and stared out across Old Stone Mill Road at the fall colors in Dean McCloed's orchard.

"Where the hell is Wanzer?" he said.

He paused, then stamped around on my flagstones again, smacking his fist into his palm. I looked down at the moss in between the flagstones. I wanted to say something in Emil's defense, but I couldn't think of anything. Then Chet continued.

"I'll tell you why Haszmanay hasn't approached his contact in the Company. It's because if we interrogated him, we'd find that he was the leak. And he'd be facing life behind bars, that's why. And that's why I'm mad at you, Adams. You blew it. You got taken in by him and blew it. Sure, I planted that tap. And my ass is in a sling, too, because it was unauthorized. That's why I'm not screaming my head off to my superiors, and why you're off the hook. I figured he might phone you and we could intercept him. He was more clever than I thought. But he won't last—not if the KGB really wants him dead."

"Or the CIA."

"Or them. But you better not tell a soul I even suggested it. Same with you, Joe."

"He was so convincing. I don't see how he could have faked it. The cold, the shivering . . . the fear—"

"Oh, he wasn't faking the fear. You can count on that. He's got plenty to be afraid of. See, once one of these double agents starts burning the candle at both ends—trying to keep the intelligence networks of both sides happy—he ends up burning all his bridges too. Then both sides mark him for a traitor, and he's got nowhere to hide, except maybe in the basement of a well-meaning neighbor who gets taken in."

"Well, shit. He's dead anyway by now. I don't see any way he could have gotten out of that airport without being tagged. We both read the script over in the car beforehand. And they must've heard it. We practically told them what to do."

"And I think that bit about TALIN was meant to throw you off, Doc. Like I said, nobody's even heard that name in years. If the marksman was KGB, then I say there's a chance Haszmanay knew the guy. Recognized him when he climbed up there to have a look at whoever he'd drilled. Don't forget this is before the crows pecked the guy's face off. Haszmanay recognized the guy, knew of his scar, and made up a bullshit story for you to chow down on. A clever guy. But he would be. He was trained for it."

I got to my feet and went inside. Needless to say, I'd felt better. I still had some reason to think—based on all my hunches—that Emil was a square shooter. But certainly Chet had punched some big holes in his credibility—had all but destroyed it, in fact. So it now seemed plausible that Emil, having used up his luck and good will on both sides, had come slinking to my basement like a rat in search of a hole. And he had fed me stories about a mythical event involving national security and a mythical assassin with a hideous scar, as well as the myth that we were heroes together against evil bureaucracies—that we were secret sharers.

It made me sick. And so did the other thought: that if by

some chance Emil had told the truth, he was now probably dead, or about to die.

Well, it was over, anyway. I'd done what I could at the time, for better or worse. Shows where extending a helping hand can get you. Murphy's Law again. Good old Murphy, who said, among other gems: "No good deed ever goes unpunished."

Mary brought a big pot of coffee out to the terrace in back of the house where the three of us now sat. She gave me a quick look of sympathy, then beat it back inside.

"Now that I've told you all the reasons why we distrust Haszmanay," said Chet, taking out his notebook, "and the reasons why you should cooperate fully next time, I think we should get to the other matters. Because, in a sense, they are important, and they support what he told you."

"What are you saying now?" asked Joe. "That maybe he told Doc the truth?"

"No. I for one think he told Doc a lot of lies to get sympathy, a place to hide, and a head start. I think the stories about Thursday the twenty-eighth, TALIN the executioner, and Roland Williamson are all ruses to get us to look the other way."

He wrote some notes in the book with a silver Cross pen.

"But there's no denying the array of electronic devices inside. We didn't place those; somebody else did. Somebody good. It probably was the KGB. So, Doc, we're going to tap your phone again, if you don't mind. Dammit, even if you *do* mind. I'm also going to lace a few bugs of my own this afternoon. And there are liable to be surveillance vehicles and personnel around your neighborhood for a while, in case Haszmanay surfaces again. I mean, whether or not you now believe him, chances are he thinks he can still count on you, right? Therefore, if he isn't dead or in Russia, he might come back."

"And I'm to call you."

"Yes. Yes, yes, yes. Immediately."

"How will I know if the surveillance vehicles belong to you or the KGB?" I asked.

"You won't. So ignore them and keep your nose clean.

And even though I think Emil's stories were bullshit, it's my job to check them out. So I'm going to follow up on this Roland Williamson, for one. Joe, maybe the two of us had better put together a working list of all known public events scheduled for the twenty-eighth. I can check with our security people, see what they show as coming up that would make an appropriate Russian or terrorist target. Can you check with your people and with the *Globe*?''

Joe nodded.

''Good. Then, when the list is compiled, your people can meet with mine, and we'll go over everything to see which events look the most likely.''

''What about Lincoln Labs? Emil seemed to think it had to do with—''

''Yes, I know,'' said Chet, holding up his palm. ''I'm going to be in touch with the lab people, at the highest levels. I'll do that myself, mainly because they won't let anyone else in. And I also—Where the hell have *you* been?''

We turned around and saw Sid Wanzer sauntering around the side yard to the terrace. He gave us a casual wave, then sat down in one of the chairs.

''Well, how 'bout it? I called your home, I tried the beeper, I even called the office. Not that I expected you to be *there*, for Chrissakes.''

''Yeah, well, I was buying some shrubs. Forgot to take the beeper with me. Sorry. But when's the last time you wanted to get me on a Saturday?''

''It doesn't matter, Sid. The point is, that's the reason we have the beepers. So I can find you anywhere, anytime. And that's—hey, wait a sec. *Shrubs?* What do you want with shrubs? You live in an apartment.''

''Yeah. Well, I was with my brother. I dint know until Evelyn told me you called. So what's up?''

Chet filled Wanzer in quickly while Joe and I speculated on what events, if any, would be likely candidates for an undercover operation in the Boston area in two weeks. We didn't come up with any. Surprise, surprise.

Then Chet put down his coffee cup and asked me to retell

the story about TALIN so Sid could hear it. When I got to the part about the scar on his back, Wanzer started chuckling.

"This some kinda private joke?" Joe asked, wiping his mouth. "You two gonna fill us in, or what?"

"Shit, Chet, I got to admit you hide it well. If I hadn't run across the accident report, and the medical history in your file, I never woulda suspected. . . ."

Joe and I looked at each other.

"Go ahead, show 'em," said Wanzer. "They got strong stomachs."

"Scar on the back, eh?" said Chet, "you guys want to see a scar on the back? Here."

He crossed his arms over his stomach, grabbing the tails of his knit pullover. Then he drew up the shirt, turning around so his back faced us.

"Oh, Jesus—oh, my God, Chet . . . ," I said in a whisper.

Chet Harwood's back-muscles were half gone. In their place was a wavelike furrowing of shiny pink scar tissue, covering almost the entire area. Standing out above the rest were four huge diagonal slashes—raised ridges of proud flesh.

"Know how that happened, Dr. Adams? It was, lessee, maybe sixteen years ago—"

"Propeller?" I asked.

"Hey, right you are," he said, lowering his shirt again and resuming his seat. "I was snorkeling in Mexico. Hell, if I'd been scuba diving maybe the tank would've saved me. Anyhow, Joe, that's what happens when you're floating face down on the surface and a powerboat runs over you. Damn near bled to death. I was in surgery for four hours and in bed, on my stomach, for six weeks. Hell, Doc, scars on the back are everywhere. I know a guy who waited too long to have a big mole looked at. When they did the biopsy, it was melanoma, stage four. Know what that means?"

I nodded.

"What it means is they take off half your back. Hell, his back looks almost as bad as mine."

We finished the coffee and walked Chet out to his red Saab. As he eased behind the wheel, he looked at me again.

"It's not your fault you got taken in," he said. "You were only trying to be a nice guy. But next time, don't be fooled. And don't just go around looking for guys with scarred backs. There're too many of us. Remember: Emil shows up, give me a holler. We'll give him a much better break than the other side."

He drove off, and Joe and I walked back inside. Mary had fillets of red snapper laid out on paper towels. She was going to make Cajun blackened fish. My appetite was returning. I was putting it all behind me now. I was going to be fine.

Oh yeah.

16

JOE AND I WENT OUT TO THE DRIVING RANGE TO HIT GOLF balls. He thought it might allow both of us to release some tension and loosen up. I had suggested the pistol range, but Joe had declined. I guess it reminded him too much of work. And it was nice out there in the cool air, whapping those little balls off the rubber tees, watching them soar up where you didn't want them to go.

"Still think Haszmanay was telling you the truth?" he said as he planted his feet. I was right behind him on the next tee, scuffing my driver over the rubber mat, getting the feel of the club.

"I don't know anymore. Two days ago I would've sworn he was the most honest guy on earth. But hell, he was trained as a spy. Lies and deception are basic tools of the trade, right?"

Whack! I saw the little white sphere sail up in front of Joe's tee and curve way off to the right.

"Shit!" he said, placing another ball on the tee. He looked off over the field of white dots. "Well, Chet's a real pro. He's always in the field, chasing after this guy or that group. He takes it very personally when anything like this happens in his jurisdiction. And sometimes he's a bit too gung ho, like planting that phone tap. But he's as good as they come in the Feds. And straight. Straight as a Kansas highway."

"So what would the KGB do to Emil if they caught him?"

"Hard to say," he answered with a shrug. He took a slow backswing. *Whack!* "That's better. 'Course, in a place like Logan they couldn't do much except just abduct him. Get him in a john or some corner and stick a needle in him, then call for one of those skychairs—those wheelchairs they have. Just wheel him out semiconscious after the drug takes hold. Tell everybody's he's sick. That's what the IRA did two years ago to Duane McPhail. Remember Duane McPhail? The Provos said he betrayed them over in County Sligo, remember? So Duane hops on a plane over to here. Can you imagine? Trying to give the Provos the slip in *Boston*? Ha! Witnesses said later they just saw Duane being wheeled out of the Aer Lingus terminal by his family. Some family. They found Duane four days later under a pier in Scituate Harbor. Free dinner for the crabs . . . on him."

I clobbered a ball, pretending not to have heard this last remark.

"Now Haszmanay, once they'd got him clear of the airport, then they'd either interrogate him on the spot or sneak him off to some safe house, where they could do a more thorough job."

"They'd make him reveal everything?"

"Oh, yeah, and everything he told you, too." He turned around and watched me addressing the ball. "See, that's what worries me about this thing. Think back. Did he tell you anything so sensitive that it would endanger you if word got out you knew it?"

"I told you and Chet everything. That's it. He deliberately told me as little as he could get away with. The reason he gave me was the same one you just gave: he didn't want to endanger me or my family. Now, after what Chet said, I wonder if maybe he was just bullshitting me, hooking me on the stories, making them vague and sketchy on purpose."

"What do you think about Chet's idea of wiring your house again?"

"I think it stinks. Do I have a choice?"

"Oh yeah. That's why I brought it up. You don't have to let him just because he wants to. Of course, he could go higher up and get some power behind his request. More than likely he'd just sneak in and do it anyway, you know? No way you could stop him, really."

"With you and your sweepers, I could. Listen—if he wants to tap the phone again, fine. But nothing else, okay? Let's tell him it stops with the tap."

"Good idea."

"And can I ever meet Victor Hamisch? I'd like to ask him a few questions, if he wouldn't mind."

"I could probably arrange it. But Chet could do a better job."

"I want you to do it. I want to ruffle as few feathers as possible."

"Can I ask why you want to talk with him?"

"One of the last things Emil said was that he was afraid to go to the American side because something was out of place in the Company. Then he dropped it. I don't know what it means, but I'd like to talk briefly with this Hamlisch guy."

"And what makes you think you could unravel it?"

"Nothing. Nothing makes me think I can. But I think I should do it. Something may pop into my head. Hell, I don't know. I just don't like simply waiting around with all this sneaky shit going on. It gives me the creeps. I've got to do something."

"Well, for my two cents' worth, I think what you should be doing is minding your own business, which is pulling teeth and fixing mouths. But . . . I'll call Vic's office Monday morning if you really want me to."

When Chet returned to the house late in the afternoon with a van full of electronics, we laid down the law. He fought like hell at first but relaxed a little when we said he could reinstall the intercept on the phone line.

"Okay then," he said, "but I don't like it. And Joe, if you're going to keep sweeping the place for my bugs, make sure you take any other bugs out, too."

"Word of honor. Where're you off to now?"

"I've just come from Roland Williamson's place. He and his wife are out—maybe for the weekend—so I'll try again tomorrow night. Right now I'm going home, after I stop at the office to begin the list. Remember the list?"

"Uh-huh. Well, I'm staying out here with Doc again tonight. If by chance Haszmanay comes back, he won't leave."

Chet and his van whispered off down the road. Joe and Mary and I went out on the terrace with drinks and enjoyed the chilly evening. Squirrels were busy gathering acorns. Three skeins of geese sailed over at treetop height, honking in V formation en route to the Great Meadows Wildlife Refuge. Danny and Troubles, the two hunting dog, looked up at them and whined, twitching their black, wet noses and wagging their tails together like a pair of windshield wipers. The cool air washed over us, and the maples and oaks sighed and dropped showers of red and gold leaves that hit the grass spinning like tops.

"Dinner . . . ," mused Joe, tapping his fingers on the arm of his director's chair. "What're we gonna do about it?"

We finally decided on the Peking Garden over in Lexington. After an evening of Mai Tais, pot-stickers with hot sesame oil, spicy beef and broccoli, shrimp and snow peas, Moo Shu pork, and Tsing Tao beer, I was in near-paralysis on the way home. Joe was scarcely better off and, after he managed to settle himself on the living-room couch, promptly fell into a doze. Mary disappeared into her atelier to roll some clay slabs. I sat under my student lamp in the study, pipe in mouth, thinking. Okay: assuming Emil had told the truth—an assumption that seemed increasingly dubious—what kinds of scheduled events should be checked out regarding "D-Day," October twenty-eighth? I drew up a broad list of categories, as follows:

1. holidays, ceremonies, special events
2. lectures, guest appearances at universities
3. economic/industrial events
    a. ship dockings, launchings
    b. presentations, unveilings of new products
    c. precious cargo shipments

  d. high-tech demonstrations, test flights, etc.
  e. banking transactions/money transfers
4. political rallies, parades, demonstrations

That seemed to be it; I couldn't go beyond number four. The thing to do then would be to approach, say, the business and financial writers at the *Boston Globe*, the university public-relations people, city hall, the state cultural and industrial departments, various industries, banks, and other "grapevines" to see what they had planned for that day. With the list of specific planned events in hand, Joe and Chet could then develop a coordinated plan of attack.

I sat back and puffed, pleased with myself. For about three seconds. Looking back at the categories, it all seemed stupid, since it was predicated on scheduled events—foreseeable occurrences. I had a strong feeling that the whatever-it-was was not scheduled. For two reasons. One: events such as the ones I'd listed might be the target of terrorist groups or gangs of hoodlums, but it was unlikely that they'd be the focus of an effort by the intelligence agency of a major power. Everything I had ever witnessed and read about the KGB told me this. Two: the message—if there was one—originated in a hidden code on a memo in a high-tech research laboratory. Who had written the note? According to Emil, a research scientist. Who worked there and in similar corporations? Research scientists. What was Emil? A research scientist. What would it be, then? A heist, a theft of some invaluable American technological secret. And it was the heist, and the heist only, that would happen Thursday after next.

Yeah, could be.

Except, why schedule the heist? Why announce the date, instead of just walking off with the secret at the first opportune time? Why?

And, on the other hand, the KGB might be interested in either kidnapping or assassinating somebody who was going to visit Boston. In that case, an arrival date—or perhaps a strike date—would have to be well planned in advance. . . .

"Oh, the hell with it," I said to myself, and turned off the light.

* * *

"Don't bother him, Joey. Can't you see he's in postcoital depression?"

"Dudn't look like it to me," said Joe with a yawn. His lower face was blue-black with beard stubble. He sat down on the foot of the bed and ran his fingers through his hair, looking up at the ceiling. He was wearing only his undies.

"C'mon, you two," I said, "you're forgetting my WASP upbringing. We WASPs don't do tacky things like parade around other people's houses in our underwear."

"*Hmmmf!*" Mary said, "you don't even parade around in your *own* house unless you're fully dressed. Boring, Charlie. *Boooooo*ring."

"It's the WASP way, honey."

Joe yawned again. "There are many overrated things in this world," he said reflectively, "but I'm convinced the chief one is WASP culture. Now, more importantly, what's for breakfast?"

It was cappuccino and croissants, which we ate on the terrace. Then we went to church.

When we returned, Moe called and asked about a game of chess. An hour later he appeared—this time with samovar—and we sat out underneath the birches again and sipped hot tea in the cold air and played chess, with balalaika music on the little tape machine. Mary and Joe were inside cooking and talking about their Schenectady childhood. Moe was up two games already. I didn't care. When he'd won a couple more we'd go inside and eat and watch the Patriots game with a fire in the stove. It was lovely out, and getting colder by the second. I caught a whiff of something seafoody from the back of the house. Smelled more like shrimp or shellfish than fish. Shrimp Creole? Bouillabaisse? Cajun seafood gumbo? What? Any of them would be just fine.

Emil Haszmanay and the KGB were miles from my mind.

17

MONDAY MORNING, JOE CALLED TO SAY THAT VICTOR Hamisch wouldn't see me.

"He says don't take it personally, but they're very busy at the agency office, and could you put your thoughts in writing for him."

"What? Who the hell does he thing he is?"

"Victor Hamisch, Yale fifty-three, head of a regional office of the CIA, and a busy man. Mind telling me what specifically is on your mind?"

"Well, I was going to repeat what Emil told me and—"

"Yeah, but see, Doc, he already has that information, because Chet forwarded it to him."

"But Chet didn't tell him about something being out of whack in the Company. Remember, that's what Emil said."

"I know. But somehow it doesn't sound that impressive, or pressing, especially third hand. Know what I mean?"

"Hey, Joe, last night I got to thinking. I was thinking about TALIN and his scar. Here's Chet also with a scar on his back. How do we know he got it skin diving, eh? How do we now he didn't make that up?"

"Are you saying—assuming there's even any truth to the TALIN story—that Chet could be him?"

"Well, it's a crazy business. Chet said so himself. How

do we know he was really skin diving? Isn't it worth a check?''

''No. But tell you what. I do happen to be going over to the Bureau office at the J.F.K. building right now, as a matter of fact. I also happen to know Chet isn't there. I'll be meeting with some higher-ups there, and it wouldn't take long to verify Chet's story. I'll check on his medical history, and I'll do it discreetly so he won't find out and get pissed off. I'll do this if you'll stop asking for favors. I mean, I got work to do, and I'd like to keep a few professional friends. Okay?''

''Deal. Except I don't understand why Hamisch won't see me.''

''Well, he did say that if in a few days you still feel you must talk, you could call him on his private line. If you've got a pencil, I'll give you the number.''

So I wrote it down. That night, while Mary and I were having dinner, the doorbell rang. It was Joe, who demanded strong drink and food. While he sated his thirst and appetite (no small task), he suddenly flung down a folder on the dining-room table. In it were Xeroxed copies of pertinent papers and certificates from Chester R. Harwood's medical and personal files. I only had to skim them to see that they unquestionably verified Chet's skin-diving accident in Veracruz, Mexico, and subsequent hospital stay in Mexico City under the surgery and post-op care of one M. R. Pentalba, M.D. The report was signed and dated by the doctor, and his medical license number was included, all on hospital stationery. It was dated March third, 1969.

''They gotta do all the details. Being Feds, they gotta have everything sewn up tight as a mosquito's ass. How do you feel, Doc? Feel like a jerk?''

''Kind of. Gee, I hope Chet doesn't find out. He'd really be pissed.''

''You're not kidding. I told the Bureau brass if was for me, and that it was strictly procedural. They'll keep mum. If any word leaked out, Chet would never forgive me. My working relationship with him would be ruined. See how far out on a limb I crawled for you?''

"Thanks, Joe. Now I've got to decide if I want to call Victor Hamisch."

"One thing at a time. Take a good look at those papers again, then I'm going to tear them up and put them in the wood stove, *capisce*?"

So I did, and he did. Then he and Mary both told me not to call Victor Hamisch. That I had already made a big enough mess of things.

"Listen to Joey; he's right," said Mary.

"Listen to Mary; she's right," said Joe.

After that, two or three days slid by, the way so many of our days seem to: as dun-colored, Muzak-filled, no-risk capsules of boredom. They bring to mind treats like flat beer and those cellophane-wrapped cheese crackers in vending machines.

To cut the gloom and monotony I immersed myself in my work, which shows how desperate I was. Actually, that's not fair. I had two good surgeries, a string of brave and financially responsible patients, the lovely Susan Petri, the irascible and infinitely wise Morris Abramson, and, well, that's more than enough. Sometimes, when things go too smoothly and I get restless and bored, I have a tendency to gripe and fret about it. And then it's time for me to consider the other extreme, which is crisis and panic, and then I remember to count my blessings.

And there were a couple of memorable events in there, too. Brian Hannon corralled me in my office and chewed me up, down, and sideways for harboring Emil without telling him.

"But that won't happen again, Doc. Know why? Because Chet Harwood and I are undertaking a joint surveillance of your residence, starting right now. He's got the equipment, and I've got the know-how."

"He's relying on your know-how?"

"Correct."

I replied that every chain has its weak link. A little levity to smooth things over. But Brian didn't appreciate my humor; he got steamed and said I could consider myself a watched man. "You are going to be under surveillance as a potential threat to this country," he said. Well, I threw him out. That was just the kind of shit I did not want to hear, especially from a so-called "friend" like B. Hannon, Chief of Police.

So I stomped around the office, mad, and went home rather down. I went out for a run, but after three miles felt tired and bored with it. The sauna felt good, though. First nice thing in a while. I was toweling off and thinking about my postsauna beer, a half-liter stoneware mug of Spatenbrau, when Mary called around the corner, informing me that Chet Harwood was there to talk with me. I wasn't exactly eager to see him. I mean, I felt foolish enough about checking up on his accident. What if he'd gotten word I'd done it? I dressed quickly. Three minutes later we were sitting in the sun porch. He had his little notebook out.

"It's now fairly certain that Roland Williamson has fled," he began. He worked his hands nervously, took off his horn-rims and polished them, put them back on, twisted his Cross pen, brushed his coat sleeves—all the displacement activities ever invented.

"Gone? Flown the coop, you mean?"

"Apparently so," he said, looking at me intently. "Which means he somehow found out about our impending investigation."

"It also means something else," I said. "It means that he is, indeed, guilty of passing secrets. Which, by extension, means that Emil was telling me the truth, at least about Mr. Williamson."

"Uh . . . not necessarily. It could mean that Williamson is not as involved as Haszmanay, but fears implication."

"Well, have it your way. I for one don't think an innocent man would skip the scene. No. Somebody tipped him off that you were on his tail, and he took off."

"Right, Doc. Which is why I'm here. Do you have any idea who might have tipped him off?"

"No. Not me, if that's what you're thinking. But don't forget: the last night Emil spent here in my cellar he told me about Roland Williamson. Later that same night, we heard noises in the walls and a car door shutting outside. Next morning, Emil was silent as a Buddha, worrying about spike mikes. So they could have overheard us then."

"I thought you told me the spike mikes were placed *after* you two finished talking."

"Well, how did we know? There could've been one there beforehand. Also, remember that Emil was probably intercepted and abducted at the airport. If the KGB—or whoever it is—didn't know before, they sure as hell knew later on. All I know is, I told absolutely nobody about Roland Williamson except two people."

"Who are?"

"You and Joe. Now I'm going to tell you something else. Emil gave me another name at Lincoln Labs: Howard March. Said he was a hundred percent reliable and honest. If you haven't spent much time at Lincoln Laboratories yet, you might interview him in depth. Maybe you can see the whole thing from a different angle."

"What do you mean, different angle? You mean you want me to believe Haszmanay is a straight shooter? That he didn't pass any information to the Soviets?"

"C'mon, Chet. He admitted to me that he had passed information to them. That's part of being a double agent. You still don't think Williamson's splitting the scene gives Emil any credibility?"

"Okay, a little. Yes, it does make me, uh, shift gears a little. And there was the man who was found on the pole. That makes me shift viewpoints a bit."

"Does it alter your viewpoint enough to think about Thursday the twenty-eighth?"

"Frankly, I didn't get much support for that at the office. The general reaction was that it's a cock-and-bull story to hide something else. And from what I hear from Vic Hamisch's office, they're even less impressed."

"How is old Vic these days? Busy busy?"

"No. Not too busy."

"Well bless his little hard-working Yalie heart."

"Huh?"

"Forget it."

I handed Chet my small list of possible events, which he

folded and put into his pocket. It wouldn't have surprised me to find out he threw it away the first chance he got.

"By the way, Doc, you are guilty of harboring a murderer. I'm not saying that to scare you. I'm saying it because there will be a hearing. Homicide is homicide."

"Well, I'll handle that when it happens. Has there been any positive ID of the utility-pole killer?"

"You mean, is he—was he—TALIN? Don't know; we can't get beyond his assumed identity of Frederick Stansul. The Russkies are getting better and better at long-range planting. The IDs and legends acquired by their agents now take months to crack."

"Legends? What are legends?"

"*Legend* is an intelligence word for phony background. Here's Frederick Stansul, purchasing agent, presumably American. Only, we know that, at least for several years or more, he was in Russia. So he not only has a fake ID, but a false, detailed personal history, or legend, to back it up. His legend would account for all his previous life, from childhood through adolescence, and so on, up to the present. He could probably have told you his legend in his sleep."

"So then what was Emil's legend?" I asked.

"The one he described to you in your cellar: displaced Hungarian refugee, a victim of Soviet tyranny. See how the legend plucks at our heartstrings? In reality, of course, he was a shrewd scientist and agent, ready to be activated whenever Moscow gave the word. He admitted as much to you."

"Seems to me the legend and reality could intermingle. Eventually, it would be hard for anyone, even the agent, to distinguish between his real past and his . . . legendary one."

He sighed, tapping the closed notebook with the silver pen. "That's right, Doc. That's the bitch of it. It's a schizoid life. From what I've seen of spies, I'd say the weirdness is as debilitating as the danger."

We walked to the front door. "I'll be going back to Lincoln Labs," he said as he ambled down the front steps, "and I'll look up Howard March. By the way, if we don't get anything interesting over your phone tap in another ten days, we disconnect."

"Good. What about Emil, and October twenty-eighth?"

He paused and turned around, looking up at me with a grim and tired face.

"I told you about the twenty-eighth; the reaction at headquarters is ho hum. Still, we'll keep checking. And about Emil—I consider him gone. Beyond reach. He's either being interrogated somewhere or he's at the bottom of a bog."

"Ah, but you no longer think he's in Russia getting medals pinned on his chest—"

"I—*shit*—I don't know what I think anymore."

He lumbered off toward his car. I could feel his fatigue.

"Get some rest, Chet," I said, and went to get my Spatenbrau. I tripped in the dark and landed on my knee, which didn't feel good on the cement floor. Turning on the light, I saw I'd made the same mistake that Emil had the previous week: I had tripped over the damn cat box. By its lack of aroma, I knew it was still unused. Should I finally pack the thing up and forget it? I pondered this as I pulled two jars of Mary's home-canned tomatoes off the shelf, then took them upstairs to her.

"What were you swearing about, Charlie?"

"I tripped over the cat box and spilled the gravel. I'm thinking we should get rid of it."

"Why not?" she said. So I went back downstairs and into my workshop to get the broom. The broom that, for ten years or so, had always been kept right behind my workshop door, leaning against the wall. The broom wasn't there. I looked around the room. Where was it? I checked in the furnace room, then the laundry room, then the wine room. No broom. I yelled up at Mary, who answered, over the sound of sizzling meat, that she hadn't see it.

I went back into the hall and turned on the light. Then I saw that the litter box wasn't the only object there. Off to one side of it were two paint cans, stacked one atop the other. On the other side, flat on the floor, a yardstick.

"Charlie! Charlie? Can you come up and open this jar for me?"

I went up and twisted open one of the Mason jars, then checked for the broom in the pantry. No broom.

"Well, it couldn't have walked off," I said, "and what are you going to paint, anyway?"

"What? Paint? I'm not going to paint anything. Why do you say that?"

"There are paint cans downstairs. And a yardstick, too."

"Well, I'm not going to use them."

"Well, I'd just like to know who—"

Then there was a moment of quiet—I believe it's called a pregnant silence—while I stared at the stove.

"Charlie?" Mary said finally. "Charlie? Are you all—"

"Hmm? Am I all right? Sure. I just . . . thought of something. I've got to go back downstairs for a second."

In the basement hallway, I looked more closely at the objects on the floor. Cat box with the clay gravel spilled out. But had I tipped it over? No. I had bumped it a little but not tipped it over. Yet there was a lot of gravel on the floor. And why had I kicked it, anyway? Because it had been placed out in the center of the hallway, that's why.

Who had moved the cat box? Perhaps Chet or his men, in their haste to set the phone tap, had moved it. No; they'd done their work days ago, and I'd been in the basement hall since then.

Why move a cat box? And why take paint cans from my workroom closet and stack them right alongside the litter pan? And the yardstick? What was it doing there? And where in blue blazes was my broom? Somebody had moved the broom—taken or hidden it. Why? Apparently, so I would not clean up the mess. . . ."

I heard Mary come down the stairs. Her heels clicked on the cement floor behind me. I heard a sigh.

"Honey, you really are so strange at times. . . ."

"You didn't do this?" I asked, pointing down at the floor.

"No. I told you, I did not."

I'll leave you a sign, Doc. . . .

So I went back upstairs and ate, or tried to. Mary kept looking at me in a peculiar way. I couldn't blame her. Afterward, I cleaned up the kitchen, and she went into her studio to fire some pots. I returned to the basement hallway, this time with a camera. I took several shots of the arrangement from directly above, one from a low angle, and one from the opposite side at a similar angle. Then I squatted down and began sweeping up the gravel with my hand. When I took my second handful of clay gravel from the center of the spilled pile, I saw I was holding a small white cylinder.

A cigarette butt. A Camel.

Mr. Neat had left behind another telltale mess, just like the one I'd found on his upstairs study desk. *Tch. Tch.*

The butt had been buried just beneath the surface of the gravel, right in the center of the pile. I placed it on top of the clay so that it was visible and then snapped a few more pix. I finished cleaning up, shaking my head slowly back and forth. Just before returning upstairs, I decided, on a vague hunch, to peek inside the coal bin. There, on the floor where Emil had slept, was the broom.

"Thanks a lot for the sign, Emil," I muttered to myself. "I need it like a hole in the head."

18

NEXT MORNING, AS I FOLLOWED MARY OUT OF BED, I STILL couldn't believe it. Emil alive and well? Emil free and back in Concord? How had he done it? For he had done it—nobody else could have left those items in my basement hallway, and the broom in that telling place in the coal bin.

Mary held on to me in the bathroom, and I kissed her.

"Charlie."

"What?"

"You know."

"No. I'm not going to. I shouldn't have told you about it. All my instincts told me not to, but I did anyway. Now I'm sorry."

"But last weekend you swore to Joe and Chet that you'd let them know if anything happened. And now something's happened."

"Well I'm not sure it has. . . ."

She didn't say anything, just finished dressing and went downstairs to make coffee. But she was steamed; I could tell.

It certainly was a strange sign he'd left. Of course, on the spur of the moment, and taking a big risk to come back, how else could he do it? He couldn't very well leave a note. But the whole thing was too . . . "touchy-feely," as they say in art class. Who would pay any attention to it? I didn't think

Chet would, since he'd already pretty much discounted Emil's warning about the twenty-eighth. What would he say if I told him I thought Emil Haszmanay had outwitted the KGB at the last minute, returned to town, and left me a clue to his whereabouts that consisted of paint cans, a yardstick, and a spilled box of kitty litter? What would a guy like Chet—a lifer bureaucrat and FBI agent—say to that?

He would not say anything. He would simply call the state facility at Bridgewater and request that I be confined.

So much for telling Chet. But I might tell Joe. What would I tell him? If I hadn't a clue as to what the objects represented, how could I help him? Or he help me? So the first item of business was to figure out what the hell Emil was trying to tell me. On my way to work I took a detour to a photo lab in Lexington, where I dropped off the exposed color film. Had it been black-and-white I could have done it at home, but I wanted these shots in color. All day, as I yanked at molars, made casts of teeth, examined X-rays, and measured the insides of mouths, I contemplated the basement hallway. Couldn't make hide nor hair of it.

The next day, the prints were ready. There were six of them. Two I kept in my study desk. Two I put in my wallet. The final two I fastened to the Scout's sun visor with rubber bands. I figured that if I kept looking at them constantly, something would spring to mind.

It didn't. And then I realized it was now Friday. Exactly a week ago, Emil and I had fled the house for The Outdoor Store and the airport. That left only six days until the twenty-eighth. Time was getting short. If Emil had really needed help, he should have tried a less circuitous route to get in touch. By nightfall I was getting desperate to figure out the sign. Desperate and frustrated.

"The hell with it, Mare," I said, wearily shuffling four of the prints through my hands. We were sitting in the sun porch with a predinner glass of red, looking out at the almost-bare trees and remarking how early it was getting dark.

"The hell with what?"

"Me trying to figure this out. I'm telling Joe about it. Maybe he won't laugh the way Chet would. I'll keep an eye peeled as I buzz around town tomorrow on errands. Maybe something will ring a bell. But if I don't get anywhere, I'll let Joe in on it when he comes for dinner."

"That's a good idea," she said. "And Brian, too."

So the next night at eight-thirty found the four of us in my study with after-dinner espresso. We'd all tucked away a sinful feast of eggplant Parmesan that Joe had fixed. Earlier, I'd told Joe about a theory I had . . . and a plan to find Emil. Joe was reclining in one of the overstuffed chairs, his feet propped on an ottoman, shuffling through all six color prints, with Brian peering over his shoulder and sucking on a Lucky Strike.

"Hell, it's easy," Joe said. "Goddamn piece of cake. Mary, I'm surprised you didn't get this, considering Pop's business. Brian, what you've got here is a lumberyard. See? Paint cans, gravel, yardstick. Look, the yardstick even says Wilson's Lumber right on it. What could be easier?"

"They sell gravel at lumberyards?" asked Mary.

"Shame on you!" said her brother. "When's the last time Mom took you to visit the store? Brindelli's sells sand, gravel, hardware, paneling, power tools—"

"We're not interested in your family business in Schenectady, Joe," growled Brian, snatching the photos. "We're tryna figure out what the hell this means, and where the hell Emil's holed up. Assuming he's even in town. And also assuming this means anything. I personally think it smells like the biggest crock of shit I've sniffed in a long time. Pardon me, Mary."

"S'okay, pal," she said, patting him on the back, "I kind of agree with you."

"Then why did you want me to tell these guys?" I asked her.

"Because I wanted you to keep your word about letting them know if anything happened—even if it seemed minor. Also, and I want you all to hear this: I don't want the KGB in my house. I don't want the FBI in my house. Or the CIA. Or an agent. Or spike mikes. *Or anybody or anything I haven't invited in. Is that quite clear*?"

We all nodded. Mary was wearing that look that made you

nod in agreement. You'd nod even if she'd just condemned you to die under torture.

"Hmmmm," Brian said, leaning against my desk and swiveling the student lamp slightly for more light. "I'd say a lumberyard's a good bet. Good as any to start with. Then, if we strike out, we can try hardware stores and material yards. Doc? Joe said earlier you had a plan?"

"Yes. That's why I'm having coffee this late at night. And it's not as harebrained as it sounds, either. Emil told me himself he spent a night in a lumberyard last week. So, I say we stake out any nearby. Joe, you game?"

"Yeah. I'll give it a shot until the wee hours, anyway."

So Brian got on the phone and talked with the lumberyard owners, then with his officers on patrol for that night. Saturday night is always the busiest in any police department, so finding men for the lumberyard stakeouts was tough.

"Wait a sec," I said as we climbed into Brian's car. "I just want you to remember that a man's innocent until proven guilty. If we find Emil—and it looks like we might—I want no guns. No rough stuff. I have betrayed his trust by telling you this. He should be treated civilly."

"Fine, Doc. But remember: he's killed a man. Maybe justifiably, maybe not. But he still nailed him. And Chet says he's a national threat. We won't start any rough stuff. But if he resists, or flees, it could get a little rough. That's just the name of the game."

Twenty minutes later, with a sinking feeling, I settled myself on a bag of insulation in Concord Lumber's main shed. The owner had given us his permission to stake out the place, and Brian had only consented to my taking part in this action because I was the initial contact with Emil. Dressed in longies and wool pants, parka and insulated hunting boots, I knew I'd be warm enough. I carried no gun, although, with my Massachusetts gun permit, I was allowed to (*concealed*, yet!). But I didn't fear Emil. No matter what anybody told me, I *couldn't* fear him. So I sat there, knowing that two patrolmen were in a parked car not fifty yards away, waiting to rescue me from a hundred-forty-pound, sixty-some-year-old man who'd crawled into my basement in the hope—apparently false—that I wouldn't betray him.

Despite the warm clothes, a chill went up my back.

Swell, Doc. You've done everything but get the knife out. Too bad it's not March fifteenth, and this joint isn't the old Forum. Hey there, Adams. We're so proud of you—know what we're going to do?

What? I found myself asking myself.

We're gonna have you *bronzed*.

19

BRIAN CLIMBED UP ON THE PILE OF INSULATION BAGS AND grabbed my ankle, hard. He shook it.

"You awake?" he asked.

"Yeah, now I am."

"We been lookin' for you, Doc. Let's get out of here. We struck out, big time, all over the place. Nothing at Wilson's yard, nothing here. No Emil Haszmanay. Good thing we didn't tell Chet."

Freezing, I slid off the pile and down onto the cement floor of the warehouse. I jumped around to get warm, but I couldn't feel my feet. My breath came out in big steam-clouds. It had not been a fun night. My jaw was trembling from the cold.

"I want to go home and get into bed," I said.

"You're not the only one. Well, this turned out to be a dumb idea. Not the first you've had."

"Nor the last."

We walked out into the morning sun, which felt good hitting my face. I blinked at its brightness. "Gee, Brian. I don't know. I mean, Joe seemed so sure about the lumberyards. How about staking out the ones in Lexington, Acton, Maynard—"

"How about you shut up? How about we go to your house and have Mary fix us breakfast? How about that?"

* * *

Joe tucked into the sausage and eggs with his usual delicacy and restraint. We all had to rush to get any from the platter. I'm trying to give up animal fats—for breakfast anyway—and eat cereal grains and fruits instead. But I was cold that morning, and the air had a chilly bite to it. So I helped myself. We had fresh o.j. and two pots of coffee: Italiano and "regulah." After the meal was over and the men had cleaned up, we all went back to the study. Joe and Brian lighted cigarettes, so I opened a window.

"Well, a washout, looks like," said Joe, yawning. "I'm going to take a short nap up in the guest room. Is it okay if I spend the rest of the weekend here?"

"Sure, you're more than welcome, Joe," I said. "I appreciate your help last night. Maybe if you're up to it we can nose around the outskirts today and look for likely hiding spots. If you don't want to, I'll understand."

He said he'd be glad to help for a couple of hours, and trundled off to the upstairs sack. Soon afterward, Brian departed. Mary and I had another cup of coffee while she examined the photos for the ten-millionth time. I grabbed them from her hand and threw them down on my desk blotter.

"Jerk!" I said.

"Oh yeah?" she said, squinting at me.

"I don't mean you; I mean Emil. He's a jerk. If he wants help, he should step forward and ask for it, for Crissakes. Take whatever consequences are due, and then get on with it. This hide-and-seek stuff is starting to piss me off."

"You really are irritable without a decent night's sleep, aren't you, Charlie?"

"Uh-huh. I'm going up for a bath and nap."

I did this and woke up at eleven, feeling refreshed. I went for a long run, doing eight very slow miles in the fall air. Felt great. Returned home. Sauna bath, shower, and repeat. Afterward, had a big chilled German ceramic mug of Gosser beer on the terrace and a sandwich of cold roast beef with thin-sliced tomatoes, lettuce, and horseradish sauce. I sometimes make exceptions to my no-lunch rule on weekends. I belched gently, feeling the refreshing sting of horseradish and beer inside my nose. Mary came out and joined me, bringing the dogs. Flack put his feet up on my leg, so I hauled him onto my lap, where he sniffed at me with his black button nose and tried to lick my hands.

"Put those damned things away," I said to Mary, who was looking at the photographs again. She shook her head.

"Listen Charlie, I've been thinking. Just because Emil used these objects for his little sign to you doesn't mean you can find him near paint and yardsticks. I think these things are symbols for other things, maybe giant-sized things. The reason he used paint cans is because that's what was immediately available in your workshop."

"Well, that's sort of what I thought at the beginning. But then Joe—"

"Joe took the objects too literally. That's what I think. I mean, when he was young he practically grew up in Pop's store. Naturally he figured Emil was pointing to a lumberyard."

"Okay, then, what do you think these things stand for?"

"I don't know about the cans or the gravel. But I have a hunch about the yardstick. I bet it's a road. See how there's even a line down the middle of it?"

"Could be," I mused. "Or maybe even a railroad track, when you consider all the increment lines on it. The symbol for tracks on maps is a line with crosshatches. Emil mentioned railroad tracks once, too."

She nodded. I looked over her shoulder. Then I was inside the house and out again, carrying a map of Concord with me. Mary isn't as dumb as she looks. And she doesn't look dumb in the first place.

We spread the map out. In an instant, I could see what Mary was driving at. The truth is, Mary is very, very bright. We turned the map this way and that, placing the color prints next to it. Nothing leapt out at us, but that didn't mean we weren't on the right track. Joe appeared at the upstairs window of the guest room and asked what we were doing. We told him to hustle down and help us. He did just that, but after almost an hour of fiddling and fussing we were still no closer to any kind of hypothesis. So Joe and I took the map and the pictures with us and got into Mary's Audi for an extended tour of the town and environs. We cruised the side streets and the main roads. At every hardware store, building-supply house, or materials yard we passed, Joe insisted on getting out and looking the place over. He spoke to the owners or managers and asked them if they'd seen anybody lurking around the premises. Negative, all around.

We went out into the country, which, in New England, is within town boundaries. We stopped at every railroad crossing, got out of the car, and looked around.

"If what Mary's saying makes any sense," Joe said softly as he swept his gaze over the horizon, "then next to the track, or the road, or whatever it is, there should be some gravel, or some big cans or something. Like maybe oil storage tanks."

"Hey, yeah! Oil storage tanks. Maybe big diesel-fuel tanks."

Well, that got us going again. Put fresh wind into our sails, so to speak. We went to the nearest Yellow Pages and looked up fuel companies. One of them, Patriot Heating and Oil, was located right on Lowell Road, not far from my house. We sped over there with racing pulses, because I told Joe I remembered seeing a big pile of gravel there, too. We hopped out of the car and scouted around. There was no railroad spur nearby, but Lowell Road was one of the major routes running through Concord, leading—as the name suggests—to the city of Lowell, twenty miles north.

"Look," said Joe, pointing to the rear of the building. "Oil tanks. See?"

Sure enough, there, set horizontally in racks behind the office shed, were six big silver tanks. Since the place was closed, we were free to amble around at our leisure. But after half an hour's examination, we saw nothing unusual. Of course, that would be Emil's way. We ranged twenty yards on all sides of the fuel company, hoping to find a down sleeping bag in the weeds or in a shed. No luck. We headed back home, but I had decided to return after dark and wait.

This I did, after a light dinner, forgoing all wine and drinks and taking two mugs of coffee. Joe and Mary stayed home and watched a movie on the VCR. I spent the night hunkered down under the oil tanks in my parka. At three-forty-five in the morning, with the temperature somewhere in the low thirties, I gave up, walked the hundred yards to my car, and went home. In the kitchen, I doffed parka, poured hefty hooker of Glenlivet into glass with dash of soda, and sipped. Opening the stove, I was chagrined to find what I expected: dead ash. Still shivering slightly, I made my way upstairs and into the sack, where I pressed against Mary for warmth. She rolled over and hit me, cursing.

"Jesus, are you cold! Get away!"

"Sorry, hon. Guess what?"

"He wasn't there."

"Uh-huh. Hell with him, anyway. I'm definitely giving up."

She sat up and turned on the light, drawing up her knees under the covers and folding her arms around them.

"Don't," she said.

"Don't what?"

"Don't give up. I've been thinking again. The Patriot Fuel Company wasn't the right place. For one thing, you said there were six tanks there, not two. Secondly, they were on their sides, not upright. Also, the cans Emil left behind were stacked one atop the other. Remember? The fat one underneath, the tall skinny one on top of it—"

"Yeah, yeah, yeah. Christ! If he wanted to tell me where he was, why not leave a note? Why all this hocus-pocus?"

"Because someone else might have found a note. Emil wants you to find out, Charlie, and only you. Now, I insisted you tell Brian and Joe about the things in the cellar. Okay. You told them. You've all worn yourselves out trying to find him, and now Brian and Joe have called it quits. Fine. They're probably too embarrassed to tell Chet Harwood. Fine. So everything's taken care of. You've fulfilled your part of the deal. Now you can keep at it till you find him. See what I mean?" She rested her head on her knees and crossed arms, and her dark brown hair cascaded around the sheets. Knockout.

"Still, why didn't he say he'd leave a note taped underneath my table saw? Or stuffed into the flour canister? Huh?"

She was silent a minute, then spoke.

"Remember when you found out the car was bugged? You were certain that he'd been taken, because your plans for the fake plane flight were overheard?"

I nodded.

"Ah! But he wasn't taken. Somehow he slipped through the net. I say he may have realized, during the final leg of the ride, that the car might be bugged—he *is* a spy, you know. So he remained silent, as you said he did, as you approached the airport—"

"Right, Mary! Brilliant! And he was probably thinking fast. Thinking of a way to switch gears and get away."

"And the last thing he said was that he'd leave you a sign. So I say give it one more day. Sunday's a free day."

"What about my promise to Chet? And aren't you afraid of Emil? Don't you think he's a national threat?"

She sighed and rubbed her eyes.

"He may or may not be a national threat. I feel certain he is *not* a threat to Charlie Adams. So, if you find him, see what's on his mind. Just don't get into anything that'll land you in the slammer. As for Chet, I'm sure that if Joe feels it's necessary, he'll tell him."

I leaned over and kissed her.

"You're not as dumb as you look," I said.

"Oh, thanks a wot, you big stwong man. I jus *wuv* to be told how—"

"OW!" I yelled. "Let go!"

"But if you're such a big, stwong man—"

"OW! OW! Please! Mary! Let go!"

Finally, she let go.

"Say that again, fathead, and you'll be singing soprano the rest of your days."

There was a pounding rush approaching fast down the hallway. Two seconds later Joe burst into the room, panting and squinting, his service Beretta in hand.

"What's going on?" he said. "Who's hurt?" Sweat soaked

his face. His chest heaved and his eyes were squinted into slits at the sudden light.

"Nothin', Joey," said Mary. "Just a little foreplay. Charlie needed some discipline."

He left shaking his head and mumbling. "C'mon, it's the middle of the night, for Chrissakes. Cut it out, sis. You're reverting, I swear. This reminds me of the old days."

He stumbled out of the room, shut the door, and walked back to the guest room.

"Old days? What old days?" I asked.

"Hmmm? Oh, nothing, Charlie. Besides, I don't think you could take it if I told you *everything*. I mean, you're too WASPy and possessive. You might have a convulsion or something. Night, hon. . . ."

Then she fell asleep, or pretended to. She started snoring awfully soon.

"What old days?"

Snoring. Fake snoring.

"Goddammit, *what* old days?"

20

JOE LEFT EARLY SUNDAY MORNING. HE DIDN'T EVEN STAY for church.

"I'm going back to Pinckney Street and read the *Sunday Globe*," he said. "Then I'm going to watch the Pats get their ass kicked. Then I'm going to amble down to the Charles Restaurant for a huge dinner of pasta and calamari. Then I'm going home again for a movie and early to bed."

"Are you going to tell Chet Harwood about what's happened?" asked Mary.

"Yeah. Figure I've got to. Unless you want to do it yourself, Doc."

"No, I'll pass. Do you think he'll take it seriously?"

"No. 'Cause I don't. So why should he? And don't get the feeling I don't want to stay here, either. I like the idea. But Doc, you've been up in the cold two nights in a row. You just got over the flu. I mean, enough is enough, right? I think we should all rest up today. *Arrivederla*."

Mary and I were left alone with the French toast and coffee.

"Old days," I said. "What the hell were the old days? And what did you do during them?"

"There were no old days, Charlie. It's a joke. A gag between Joey and me. So forget it. There were no old days."

I breathed a sigh of relief.

"Except for that summer I spent in Juárez . . . ," she added, and glided into her workshop.

I went outside with the dogs and walked over to Emil's house. Sure was a nice house. Could he be hiding back here? I looked for cans stacked up, for gravel, for anything resembling a road or yardstick. Nothing. I walked back to the terrace and sat down. I should go for a run, I thought, but I decided to take a final cruise around town, looking for the elusive landmarks that would reveal Emil's hideaway. So at ten I climbed into the Audi and made a tight circle in the turnaround. A quick knocking came at the passenger window.

"I wanna come too," Mary said. So we eased out the driveway and cruised the towns of Concord, Bedford, Maynard, and parts of Acton. Mary rode shotgun, my binoculars in hand, scanning everything in sight. No luck. We eased over toward the Bedford-Lexington line, near the Lincoln Laboratories. We got as close as we were allowed and took turns with the binoculars looking at the complex of buildings with swarms of dishes and antennae on the roofs. It seemed that most of the dishes were pointing straight up. Were they sending and receiving messages from outer space? Wouldn't surprise me.

"I don't think this is the place," Mary said, walking back to the car. I agreed, and we started home. She put the binoculars back in their case and sighed.

"Well, we did our best. If Emil really needs you, Charlie, he'll come openly, no matter what the risk."

I nodded in agreement. As we rolled into the center of town, past the Civil War obelisk on the green, Mary suggested we make a short detour out to the seafood market in Acton.

"It's closed. Today's Sunday."

"Uh-uh. It's open. Folsom's is a restaurant, too. Remember?"

"Hey, you're right. We could get a dozen oysters and some

flounder. Or maybe even a couple live lobsters. Whadduyuh think? Will lobsters cheer you up?''

So we swung around the green and went west, out to Great Road. We bought two dozen oysters, two lobsters, and two pounds of shrimp for freezing. On the way back, I watched the road ahead and tried to think of pro football and seafood. To hell with Emil Haszmanay.

''CHARLIE!''

I almost ran off the road. Checking the rearview mirror, I put on the brakes as quickly as I dared and pulled over. Mary was pounding my shoulder with her fist.

''Charlie! There they are! Look!''

She was pointing at the horizon, at the cloudy sky far off over the basin of the Assabett River.

''Huh? Where are what?''

She pointed again, and I saw, in the distance, two water tanks. A short fat one and, probably sixty yards away from it, a tall skinny one that stood slightly higher.

''But they're not stacked on top of each other,'' I said. ''They're side by side.''

''Drive on a ways and keep watching them.''

I put the Audi in gear, and we continued slowly down the road. Cars behind us honked, then zoomed past us. I kept glancing at the tanks.

''They're getting farther and father apart,'' said Mary. ''Okay, maybe I was wrong.''

''Oh no you're not; let's turn around.'' So we headed back toward Acton again. The tanks seemed to grow closer and closer together, and it was then obvious to me that the tall, skinny, higher one was behind the shorter one. They inched together from this angle, and I slowed to a stop, pulling off onto the shoulder. Mary handed me the binoculars with a triumphant grin. I looked through them. There they were: the tall tank was standing directly behind the squat one. It appeared to be resting smack-dab on it, just like the two paint cans in my basement hallway.

''What do you think?'' Mary asked.

''As I said before, you're not as dumb as you look.''

I stood on the shoulder, with Mary right behind me.

"I'm thinking that the alignment is important, wouldn't you say? I mean, it seems to me if we keep the two tanks stacked in a line, we'll then be on the proper heading to the . . . whatever."

"Uh-huh. But I hate to tell you, there doesn't seem to be anything right here. Just some houses and woods."

I raised the binoculars again and stared, transfixed, at the faraway tanks. The near one was silver, the taller one behind it was pea-green. They shimmered slightly in the heat currents. The near one had a bunch of crows sitting on it. Or were they pigeons? Couldn't tell. There was no longer any question in my mind that these water tanks were what Emil had intended to symbolize with the paint cans. Question was, where was the gravel? And what about the yardstick?

"Let's go home for a sec," I said. "I need a few items." We stopped chez Adams just long enough to stow the seafood in the refrigerator. I put the oysters in salted ice water in the sink and went into my study for a USGS map of Concord and environs, a military-style compass, a ruler, and pencil. I grabbed a Plexiglas cutting board from the kitchen counter on my way out. Less than forty minutes later, we were back on Great Road (which is really Route 2A), looking at the water tanks. I placed a folded blanket on the hood of the Audi and the cutting board on top of it. Then the map, aligning it with the compass so that north pointed true north. Then I put the sighting compass on the map and drew a bead through the crosshair at the tanks. The bearing read 162. I transposed this to the map, drawing a pencil line through the two tiny dots on the map that represented the water tanks. Now the pencil line ran through roughly the center of the map in a more or less north-south direction. To see the tanks as stacked, therefore, one had to be along this line, on either side of them. Right now we were on the north side, and, it appeared, too far away.

We studied the map and decided that if Great Road was not the yardstick, then perhaps Route 2, further south and running parallel to 2A, was. So, back to the rotary near the prison in West Concord, and back out onto Route 2. Drove along until the tanks were aligned again and got out of the car. Walked into a cornfield. No dice.

"Let's go home now," Mary said. "I've got stuff to do; you can go out on your own. After all, I gave you the start you needed, didn't I?"

I told her that this was indeed true. After going over the USGS map carefully at my desk, I finally decided that the best bet was to try a third road, this one being much closer to the tanks than either of the others. It was Laws Brook Road, running west from Concord to the town of South Acton. I got back into the car, glancing at the map as I drove, noting where my pencil line intersected Laws Brook Road on it. Almost two miles out from West Concord, near the intersection of Laws Brook Road and School Street, I looked up over my left shoulder and saw the tanks again, this time much closer. And they were stacked in perfect alignment. I eased onto a wide, sandy shoulder and stopped.

I left everything except my binoculars and walked along the road, looking sharply from left to right. Yardstick? Kitty litter? There were thick pine woods on both sides of the road. I saw a sandy road off to the right. As I walked down it a short distance, I saw ahead of me a huge gravel pit. My heart was thumping like a jackhammer as I went down into the wide expanse. A gravel pit as big as twenty football fields. A gravel pit to beat the band. And Emil's Camel stub had been placed right smack-dab in the middle of the cat litter that symbolized it. So to the center of the open place I walked. I stood there, turning round and round, trying to see . . . something.

But all I saw was sand and gravel. Gravel, gravel, everywhere . . . I swept the edge of the pit slowly with the glasses. Nothing but woods.

I waited around in the gravel pit for almost an hour before heading back to the road. Sixty yards farther up, there was a big road off to the left. A sign, far enough back in the trees that it was not readily visible from the road, said:

McCLOUGH MASONRY PRODUCTS, INC.
Acton Sand and Gravel

The old ticker started revving up again. I walked up the company's road. There was a big iron bar extending across it, blocking all vehicles. I ducked under and went inside. Beyond the bar gate and the high wooden fence that fronted Laws Brook Road, the place opened up into a field. It was a gravel yard, and all around its edges were giant mounds of sand and gravel—pyramids of white, tan, buff, and gray.

Behind the mountains of sand and crushed rock, past the far reaches of the gravel yard with it parked skip-loaders, bulldozers, and heavy dump trucks, up above the intricate lacy ironwork of the conveyor-belt housings and gravel crushers, loomed the two water tanks, one seemingly atop the other. .

This was the place. The tanks, the gravel, and the road behind me that the yardstick on the floor—all pointed here.

"Emil," I whispered to myself, "you clever guy, you."

But the place was scary. Late on a Sunday afternoon, with the long, slanting shafts of golden sunlight illuminating the pyramids of rock and casting deep shadows on the giant furrowed tracks in the sand left by the heavy vehicles, it was eerily silent. I could imagine the hustle and noise of the place when it was operating: the roar and growl of the big diesel engines as the skip-loaders, trucks, and bucket cranes lifted, hauled, and pushed tons of rock and sand to and fro. The big crushers that banged and howled, spitting out newly broken rock. The sound of rushing rock on the belts, the sound of it falling into steel truck beds . . .

I could hear the swallows twittering overhead in the dying light.

I wanted to explore the place, but its stillness unnerved me. Where was Emil? I saw four buildings. Two of them were garagelike structures with pumps outside for fuel, and one of them had a big window and a truck scale as well. Another building looked like a small office for the foremen and crew. The biggest building, in the back, probably held the main office. Between these buildings were strung long neat stacks of gray cinder blocks. Near the dispatching shed these blocks were stacked on skids, or pallets, so the lift truck could put them on flatbeds. Four big trucks with half-cabs and hoppers as big as swimming pools stood parked in formation. Each group of sand and gravel pyramids had its own skip-loader. All were vacant and silent. Watchman? Where was he?

I walked purposefully over to the nearest building and knocked on the door, then tried the knob. Locked, as I had assumed it would be. If anyone asked me what I wanted, I would indignantly reply that I wanted to purchase some cinder blocks. What else? Never mind that it's four P.M. on Sunday. I want my goddamn cinder blocks. I mean, for Crissake, you guys in business or what?

Tried the next building. Locked. And so on. Walked around the buildings. Windows closed and locked. Tiny fuel shed or pump-house near middle of field. Made a beeline for it. Locked. Looked inside: old pump. No Emil.

Standing all alone on the chewed-up sand was an old steam shovel. At least, we called them steam shovels when I was a kid. Actually, I'm sure the old contraption was diesel-powered, but it had the old-fashioned, forward-facing bucket that was raised by a scissors beam in front. The newer backhoe types have the bucket facing backward, toward the operator. It was clear that this clunker hadn't been used in ages. Drawing closer, I saw that its green and yellow paint was splotched with circles of rust. I went up to it and saw that each rust-circle had a sharp dent in its center, and a hole. Bullet holes. Kids had been sniping at the old derelict shovel with twenty-twos. Why had the company kept this old wreck, and out in the center of the yard, to boot? I hopped up and sat down on the big steel treads of the lint belt, swinging my feet idly. I glassed the entire yard and was convinced I was the only person there. There might be plenty of places to hide in the stacks of blocks. But would Emil do that, and stow his sleeping bag and gear in there, too? How long before somebody would find it? Not long.

The sun was lower now; the shafts of golden light forced out long, grotesque shadows from the parked trucks and cranes. The tall gravel crusher and conveyor belt stood stark against the sky, a long-legged, giant iron heron with its head cut off. And underneath the tip of its truncated neck grew an ever-replenished mound of gravel that spilled from the lip of the belt.

I felt like calling out. But I didn't. Two ducks flew low over the trees with that frantic, rapid wingbeat that makes them look like they're just learning to fly. They were headed for Warner's Pond, over near the prison.

And if nothing happened soon, I was heading home.

Emil's Camel butt had been placed right smack-dab in the middle of the cat-litter heap. And I, sitting on the old, wrecked steam shovel with all the windows shot out, was likewise right smack-dab in the middle of—

I stood up on the treads and looked at the machine. I side-stepped over and peered into the cab. Through the broken windows I could see the operator's seat—the stuffing pouring out of it—and the levers and pedals that controlled the beast. Big deal. I walked back along the treads and saw a half-destroyed vented window toward the rear of the machine. It was covered with bent metal slats that let air in to cool the engine. The metal slats prevented me from looking inside. I hopped off the big steel treads and walked around to the rear of the steam shovel. There was a blown-away door there on the back side, high up. Over the doorway's lower lip, I could see the top of the big diesel engine and several huge winches wound with cable that controlled the arm and crane. I almost didn't bother to walk around the far side. But I did. And stopped dead in my tracks.

The far side of the shovel housing had a small door instead of a vented window. The door enabled the operator or a repairman to enter the engine compartment. The door was closed and fastened. But what drew my attention was the object stuck in the doorway between the metal door and the frame. It was tiny, but even from where I stood, at ground level, I could see it clearly. I jumped up on the treads again and yanked the paper-and-foil package free. There was the camel, all right, and the pyramids in the background. And, of course, the famous caveat on the back of the pack that I remembered so well: *Do not look for premiums or coupons, as the cost of tobaccos blended in Camel cigarettes prohibits their use. . . .*

I rapped softly on the door.

"Emil. Emil, it's Doc. . . ."

No answer. I rapped again. Still no answer. I drew in a deep breath, braced myself, and yanked open the door.

Nothing inside but the big engine and winches. I scanned the place quickly—and almost swore when I saw the arrow on the metal floor plate.

It was drawn in chalk. Blue mason's chalk. I'd seen hunks of it lying around the yard. And the lines were thick and straight. The arrow pointed toward the front of the cab but about fifteen degrees to the left. Since there was nothing inside the machine that I associated with Emil, or anything remotely related to him, I stood directly behind the blue arrow on the metal floor and sighted along it. Standing straight up behind the engine and the winch drums, I could see over them and out through the cracked and shattered windows of the cab. The arrow pointed to the woods beyond the yard, directly between two tall pines.

I hopped down onto the sand again, grabbed a handful of it, and returned inside the machine, where I dumped the sand on the chalked arrow and scuffed it back and forth with my foot, obliterating the mark. Then I shut the metal door again, jumped down, and walked straight toward the gap in the tall trees ahead.

As soon as I left the factory yard, the ground sloped gently upward. I walked between the tall pines and took a glance backward to make sure I was still lined up with the old derelict steam shovel. I crept forward like a stalking cat. The woods were getting dark now; only occasional streaks of gold slanted down through the boughs. I walked on and felt the ground sloping down again. Ahead, through the trees, I saw water. Very still water. A pond. What was this? Emil hiding underwater? What was going on here? I came to the junction of the woods and water and looked across. On the other side of the pond, which was very big, was the town of Maynard. I recognized the enormous mill building—the largest single mill building ever built in the world—that was now the home of the Digital Equipment Corporation. Before that—way before—it had been the home of Union Knitting Mills, which made almost all the army blankets for Union troops in the Civil War. And that, I thought idly as my eyes scanned the distant shoreline, was why the North finally beat the South. We had the factories, the people, and the railroads, and they didn't. They had the Courage and the Gallantry and the Tradition, and all that Honor done up in bunting. But it wasn't enough.

I sat at the water's edge and sighed. So where was Emil? Was he across the water, over in Maynard? Was I supposed to swim across? What the—

Disgusted, I flung a rock out over the water, skipping it, then turned to go. As I turned, my eyes swept past a dense alder thicket at the pond's edge, twenty yards away. The low shed within the copse was almost invisible. But there it was, perched right over the edge of the pond like a sunning turtle. I approached softly and could see more and more of the structure as I walked through the dense brush. I saw the low foundation of fieldstone and noticed that the shed's stone wall went right to the water's edge. There were no windows in the wooden walls. Then I heard the whispery, sighing rush of water. As I came up to the place, I saw the stone channel behind the house and the little flowing river within. Half speed. This was an abandoned sluice-gate house. The big one that now controlled the water level was further down the pond, right off Powder Mill Road. I knew because I had visited it.

How to get inside the little house? From the water side only, it seemed. I walked toward the narrow stone ledge, the lip of rock inches above the water, which went around to the pond side. But before I'd even inched my way there, I heard a voice. A hoarse whisper. A familiar voice. It said:

"Dr. Adams, I presume?"

21

I FOLLOWED THE ROCK LIP OF THE FOUNDATION AROUND TO the water's edge and saw that the old sluice-gate house was open on the pond side. In place of protective walls were very wide eaves. There was a raised wooden plank floor at the level of my chest. Below it were some vertical beams descending into a stagnant pool at the pond outlet. I knew there were big, heavy concrete or rock slabs underneath that controlled the flow of water from the pond to the channel in back.

Above the floor were the old wooden walls on the other three sides, with little chinks in them here and there, that let in some light. But most of the light was coming from my direction; it was the setting sun reflecting off the still water of the pond, which was now gold. A short figure scurried over the plank floor, and soon I saw Emil's face, bathed in golden light, looking down at me.

"Hop up, Doc," he said in a low voice. "Use that rock step to your left. There!"

I climbed up onto the old planks, and Emil left me momentarily to scurry back to the far wall and peer through the narrow chinks. Then he came back and sat down on the floor, which was covered with a thick layer of straw. I sat down too and looked at him. He looked happy and healthy. He leaned over and gave me a hug.

"Good old Doc!" he said. "He who never fails. How are you?"

"Well I've been better, let me tell you . . . ," I replied irritably. As is so often the case when you finally see someone whose absence has pained you, my initial reaction was anger. All the frustration of the past few days, all the work and worry over him, surfaced in the form of resentment.

"For Chrissake, Emil! Couldn't you let me know where to find you in a slightly more sensible way than leaving those damn things in my cellar? Shit! I've been chasing all over town, sleeping outside—I'm sick and tired of this whole thing."

"Nice to see you, too, Doc," he said. There was a moment of silence, then he sighed. "Well, I suppose I could have been more direct. But then somebody other than you could have found me. And that would never do, would it? So I did as I said I would: I left a sign, a sign I was confident you'd decipher. Guess it was a little trickier than I imagined."

"Mary's the one who figured it out," I admitted.

"Mary is smart. You are a lucky man, Doc."

"I'm aware of both. Now, quick: tell me everything. What the hell happened at the airport? I was sure you were captured there. You know why? The car was bugged! I was sure you were—"

"Yes. Sit down, Doc; you're jumping around!" He scolded me in a harsh whisper. I realized that in my agitation I had jumped up. I sat down again.

"Tell me, Emil. Tell me everything."

"All right, Doc. Whatever you say. Just let me light a cigarette. I have to be careful with all this straw. . . ."

He lighted the cigarette and flipped the match into the pond.

Tsssssst!

"Well, I was lucky," he said, after a big bluish lungful. "Because just before we went into the tunnel, I thought about the car being wired. The thought just struck me. Remember, as we were approaching the airport, suddenly I was quiet as a mouse?''

''Uh-huh. You looked as if you'd seen a ghost.''

''Yes. Well, I realized all at once there was a good chance that if your house was bugged, so was the car. We spies are supposed to know these things. So, if that was true, then every word we had said had been picked up. Therefore, your idea of the walk-in, walk-out plan was also overheard. They'd know right where to wait for me to walk into their hands. It was no good. So what I did was this: I decided even before I got out of the car to go with your original idea if I could—''

''You mean, to take a flight out of town, then come back?''

''Exactly. So we got out, you handed me the money, and I went inside. If anyone was waiting for me at the arrivals level—and I think they were—they were disappointed. And, once again, I was lucky. I found a flight to Rochester that was just boarding. I paid cash, gave a false name, and took my ticket right to the gate. I was the last one on the plane, and nobody got on after I did. You can't imagine how good it felt, Doc, to lift off over Boston Harbor, knowing I'd given them the slip.''

''And I was positive you'd been collared, Emil. That's why I told everyone about it—''

He groaned and sat up.

''No! Doc, why did you?''

''Because I figured you were dead meat, that's why.''

He shook his head sadly and continued. ''So anyway, I stayed at the Rochester airport for about two hours, after disposing of the disguise in the trash basket of the men's room. So in my natural identity, I waited around in the airport lounge. Nobody seemed interested in me. So then I took a return flight to Providence. Waited around again. Nobody even noticed me. Rented a car and drove up here. I was back in Concord by Saturday night. I spent the next four days hunting for a place to hide out. I wanted it on the western end of town, near the railroad tracks.''

''Why?''

"Because I think they'll figure in the event that's coming up Thursday."

"Four days from now. Well, what is it? What's going to happen?"

"I can't tell you now. For one thing, I'm not sure. And it's an important thing. Secondly . . . and . . . I thank you so much for your help, Doc. But I . . . I'm not sure . . ."

"If you can trust me?"

"Sort of like that, yes. Not that I think you're against me, either. I've just been thinking. You see, you're in an impossible position. I mean, here you are, your brother-in-law is a state police detective. Your close friend is the chief of police in Concord. You have these loyalties—"

"Yes. But you haven't mentioned the two most important ones: my family and my country."

"Ah, yes, of course. But you must realize, you must believe, that what I've been doing for the past several weeks is in the interest—the vital interest—of your country."

"You said 'your country.' You didn't say 'our country.' "

"*Hmmmmph*! What do you mean by that?"

"I don't know. Emil, when we talk together, I'm so sure of your motives and your allegiance. But then I hear Chet Harwood talk about you—"

"Who is this Harwood? This Chet Harwood?"

I told him. And then I told him everything Chet had told me regarding the Bureau's view of Emil Haszmanay and the tricky, heart-clutching way that Soviet illegals operated. Through it all Emil listened without a single word, nodding slowly, a sad and resigned look on his face. Then I finished.

"Well, that is one viewpoint, Dr. Adams. Mr. Harwood has claimed that I spied against the United States. That is true. If you remember, I have already admitted as much to you, in your basement. He claims that I am still passing information to the KGB. That is also true. But the fact is that the balance is tipped far, far in favor of your country over the Soviet Union. As I've already told you, I must pass them *some* information to keep credibility. Surely Mr. Harwood and his associates know that. That is the way it works."

"But there have been serious leaks from Lincoln Laboratory recently. From your department, Emil."

"I know," he nodded, "and I mentioned to you the name of Roland Williamson as the man who is responsible."

"Right. I mentioned Roland Williamson to Joe and Chet. I told them because I assumed—I knew—you wouldn't be coming back."

"Well, what did they say? What did they do then? Do they have him in custody?"

"No. Afraid not, Emil. Before Chet and his team could throw a net around him, he took off."

"Achhhh!"

He let his face drop onto the sleeping bag and lay there motionless. Maybe a minute went by with neither of us saying anything. Seemed like an hour. Just the slow, steady rush of the little waterfall in the rock channel beneath us.

"Sorry, Emil. Under the circumstances, I thought I was doing the only thing I could."

"Don't be sorry for me, Doc. Be sorry for . . . for what might happen now."

He was silent again, then spoke.

"Ah, well. Maybe it's not too bad you told them. Williamson was close to flight anyway. I could sense it. He would finish this last big assignment—the biggest in his life—and then get away fast. In fact, maybe it is a pity you didn't tell them sooner. Maybe they would have caught him. As for me, my cover is blown with the KGB anyway. The fact that they tried to kill me is proof enough—"

"Emil! I almost forgot to tell you: I think the man in the tent who tried to shoot you was the man you call TALIN."

His jaw dropped and he stared at me, the swirls of golden light from the water's reflection dancing on his face. It looked as if he were wearing a halo. I explained the lab photos at Joe's office. He listened, rubbed his forehead in thought, and remained puzzled.

"Then either TALIN his been given lesser assignments or else this thing is ever bigger than I initially thought."

"Well, at least he's dead. That is, I *think* he's dead."

"What do you mean?"

I explained to him Chet's doubt about the legend of TALIN, and the fact that there had been no word of him in years.

"TALIN is not a fabrication, Doc. And if the man I shot was TALIN, then it is a wonderful thing indeed that he is dead. But if he wasn't, and TALIN is still alive, he is extremely dangerous. Take my word for it. The fact that he has not been heard of recently means that his cover has been excellent. It means, if anything, that if he's alive, he's more dangerous than ever. You see?"

"And there's even another theory, or possibility. Chet suggested—half seriously, I think—that the man in the tent could have been a CIA hit man. What do you think about that?"

"I think," he said wearily, "that is it not as ridiculous as it sounds. In fact, it is too possible to be remotely funny. . . ."

"But why would *they* be after you? Why would the Company want you dead, Emil, if what you've told me is true? I mean, somebody's lying here. . . ."

His sad eyes looked up at me. He lighted another cigarette.

"Doc. I know that you and your friends in the police and the FBI have been wondering why I haven't contacted my supervisor in the Company and told him everything."

"That's exactly right. Just the other day, in fact, Chet asked me that very question. I couldn't answer it. So now *you've* got to answer it. Or I'll go to them myself."

He seemed to realize that I meant it and that he no longer had a choice. He hesitated only a second or two before replying.

"The reason I was forced to hide in your basement, and the reason I am having to hide here now, Doc, is that somebody in the Company wants me dead."

"Who?"

He shrugged his shoulders. "I don't know, that is the problem. My supervisor, the operative who oversees me, is named William Hasslin. You should never mention that name to anyone. He has grown colder, more distant over the past several months. He claims I am under increased suspicion by many in the Company. He overstepped his bounds just by telling me. I don't know who in the Agency is responsible for this. I know the Company is now convinced that it is I, not Williamson, who has been sending information to the Soviet agents. The fact that Williamson is now gone means my hope of clearing myself is now also gone. Someone warmed him just in time. And now it is fairly certain that both sides want me dead."

I remembered what Chet had told me about double agents—how finally, in a futile attempt to placate both sides, they burn all their bridges and have nowhere to go.

"Can you try to find out who it is? Who has turned on you?"

"Perhaps, if I had the time. But I don't. And if I made a mistake, if I revealed myself but identified the wrong person, it would be the end. I must do it perfectly or not attempt it at all. There is no second chance in this game. I think all that's left for me to do is what I've been doing since I came to you. I must act on this event Thursday. If I can stop it, and catch somebody in the net, then I will have proven my loyalty to the Company once again. You see? And that's why I have been so reluctant to tell you anything."

"Well, goddammit, you can't leave me in the middle, holding the goddamn bag, Emil. I won't stand for it! I've helped you more than enough in this shitty mess, and you're going—"

"*Shhhhhh*! Doc, you're shouting! Please!"

I stopped, and the silence was loud. I was breathing hard. Yes. I had shouted; I was mad. I was ready to slug the old man a few times.

Emil was off his sleeping bag, walking stooped over beneath the low roof to the far wall. He crouched down still lower and peered out through chinks in the old wood.

"There's nobody out there," I said. "There's nobody within two miles of us. And I won't shout anymore. I just want you to come clean with me."

He returned, walking bent over like an elf, scratching his head, brow wrinkled. He grabbed his chin, rubbed his nose, and sat down.

"When did you first contact your brother-in-law about me?"

"Friday night. After I dropped you off at the airport."

"Mmmmmm. So you told nobody about me until after we went into Boston together, which meant the bugs—and the spike mikes in your basement walls, too—were placed before you told anyone."

"Absolutely."

"Mmmmmm. Right. And then when did Roland Williamson disappear?"

"Can't say when he disappeared. But when Chet and his men went to move in on him Saturday—the day after we took off for the airport—he was already gone. He was away with his wife. They assumed he was gone for the weekend, and waited till Monday morning. By then it was too late."

"Ah, yes. He took a weekend's head start."

"Listen, Emil, if you want to be alone on this investigation of yours, why include me now? You're safe. Why leave me the sign in my cellar in the hope I'd find you?"

"One: I was—am—very grateful for what you did for me, Doc. You must believe that, if you believe nothing else. I wanted you to know that I was safe, that, at least for the time being, your efforts on my behalf weren't wasted. And two: I still need your help."

"Forget it. Come clean with Chet or forget it."

Emil was over looking through the chinks in the wall again. In the faint light, I saw his body tremble.

He came back, sat down again, and patted me on the shoulder.

"I know how you feel. I have felt the same way for months now. It is tiring and aggravating. All I can promise you is this: it is almost over. After Thursday, no matter what the outcome, you will be rid of this burden."

"Are you going to tell me what it is?"

"Yes. But not tonight. I cannot. Mainly because I'm not sure of the details yet."

I leaned back and propped myself up on one elbow, looking around. There was no sense in rushing Emil or trying to get tough with him. He would tell me when he was ready.

For my part, I would do nothing more, for or against him, until he did. I thought I'd change the subject for starters.

"Well, Emil, you seem to have almost all the comforts of home here. It's nice. Where'd you get the straw?"

"I stole it. I had to. It is a shame, but being a fugitive forces one into crime. I'm getting good at theft. The brick factory you walked through has many bales of straw. They use it for packing when they ship the finished blocks."

"How's the sleeping bag? You warm enough? It's been cold."

"I'm fine at night. That's a good sleeping bag. If I ever get out of this, I'll repay you."

"Don't worry. Let me look around a little before it gets totally dark out."

I gave the place a quick once-over. Projecting up through big slots in the floor were three huge geared wheels of black iron. I peeked down one of the slots. In the near-darkness, I could see the two massive parallel transverse beams of oak below, each twelve by twelve. The ancient iron gear-works rested on top of these beams and raised or lowered the heavy concrete sluice gates by means of a series of cogged wheels working against upright six-by-six beams of oak that had notched iron plates bolted along one side.

The vertical beams were halfway down, and the gear-works locked in place with ratchets. I doubted they'd been moved in thirty years. The big gate slabs that rode in their notches kept the pond-flow to the channel at a steady soft splash. Emil stretched, yawned, and flipped a rock into the pond just in front of the gates.

Plooosh!

The ripples eased out from the splash, jostling the old tires and the two plastic Coke bottles floating above the mouth of the gates. The slow exit current had brought them there. Tires can float; they float by hanging in the water upright with air trapped under the tread. You learn something every day. I had also learned that an abandoned sluice-gate house makes a dandy hiding place. Shielded by a copse of alders. No windows. No doors. Just a stone walkway at the water's edge, at the water's level, and then you hopped up onto the wooden planks four feet above that and there you were. It was house like the Water Rat's in *The Wind in the Willows*. Plenty of light came into the gate house's upper level. Swirling, spider-webby strings of light flickered all around the walls.

After a few minutes, Emil seemed relaxed enough to continue.

"Doc, the reason I still need you is this: once I put all the pieces together, I'll need someone to summon help at the last minute. Someone who has high credibility with the police. Understand? That person is you, not me."

"You're saying that once you put your finger on exactly what's taking place Thursday—and it's right near here, even I can figure that out—you'll get in touch with me so I can alert Joe, Brian Hannon, and Chet to put out the roadblocks?"

He nodded, a slight grin trying to form on his face.

"And once the mission is accomplished, and the bad guys are in the bag, then you'll hand yourself over to the good guys for all the interrogation they want to throw at you?"

"Exactly."

"You're nuts. I believe—for now, anyway—that you're on the level. But you are nuts. And now you want me to be the legman. I won't do it. There are several good reasons why not. One: my credibility is not what you think. In fact, it's at an all-time low right now. Two: if you've almost got the puzzle solved, why not go to Chet now with the pieces you've got? His machine is infinitely bigger than yours; he'll have the puzzle solved and the bad guys wrapped up lickety-split."

He sighed.

"Well, it's obvious you don't know much about your Bureau," he said. "Yes, they're big. That's just the problem. They would jump in with all three feet and scare off the people you like to call the 'bad guys.' And, what's more, they would notify the Company. They'd have to; it's their duty. And when they did that, the one turncoat—or maybe there is more than one—would move in on me before I could stop them."

"Well then, sorry. I guess I understand your predicament,

Emil, but count me out." I rose and walked to the edge of the floor.

"Please wait, Doc. Please. Just give me a little more time. Trust me a little longer. Please."

"I can't. I'm already guilty of near-treason."

"But you've told the authorities about me. You've done your part."

I jumped down onto the stone lip.

"All right, Doc. I'll make a bargain with you."

I turned and faced him. He looked desperate, like a cornered fox gone to ground.

"First, I'm going to tell you what I already know, under the condition that you tell nobody until you see me again, here, tomorrow evening."

I hopped back up onto the wooden floor and sat down. His eyes were panicked. He wasn't lying; I knew it.

"The way Lincoln Laboratory works is this: the operation is divided into departments. Many departments. For security's sake, they are highly specialized and compartmentalized. Most consist of less than half a dozen scientists, with a support staff roughly the same size. I shouldn't even be telling you this, because the arrangement is kept secret."

He paused to light up, and throw the match into the still, dark water below us.

"Now, it is a dismissal offense to discuss projects from one department to another. Therefore, if a major project involves, let us say, twelve departments, then you can see how difficult it would be to sell the project or steal it from the lab."

"Yes. Because even if an entire department became turncoats, which I cannot see happening, they would still only have a small piece of the puzzle."

"Precisely. But you see, as the project draws nearer and nearer completion, it becomes more vulnerable, because the pieces from the various departments begin to be fitted into place."

"Uh-huh. I see . . ."

He let out a deep sigh and scratched his head, as if he were about to take a deep plunge.

"I mentioned before, I think, that my department had been working on the final phases of the Strategic Defense Initiative, or Star Wars project. I told you of my deep suspicions about Roland Williamson, a member of my department, who was sending microdots to the man called TALIN, who is now probably dead."

"Is there a chance your worries could be over?"

"No. Not a chance; by now the entire KGB apparatus has been alerted. Also, you remember the name of Howard March, the man in whom I had great confidence."

"Yes."

Emil took out a small notebook and pencil. He scribbled on a page and tore it out, handing it to me. Then he tore out the blank page underneath it, tore it up, and let the pieces fall into the water. "Here's Howard's address and phone number. Keep it. You may need it if something happens to me. Now, within the various departments of the lab, as each phase of a system nears completion—drawing its component parts from other various departments—the system as a whole becomes nearly finished and therefore, as I said, is more vulnerable to espionage. The project I have been involved in is not a ray gun. Nor is it a fancy spy satellite that aims the laser. It is, actually, a highly sophisticated computer and software program that interacts with these devices."

"Sounds like a dime a dozen," I said. "I mean, there are computers everywhere nowadays."

"Ah, but not like this one. It is a special-purpose parallel processor, in which the equivalent of twenty thousand microcomputers are linked together. This allows the machine to absorb and analyze over forty-six million data bits each second—"

"Sounds nice. But it means nothing to me."

"There has never been a computer like this before—and not likely to be another for a long, long time. It is light-years ahead of anything the Soviets could hope to develop."

"And this supercomputer flies around in space?"

"Oh, no. It stays on the ground. It interprets signals from the radar-sensor satellites and will tell the hunter-killer satellites whether or not to fire at approaching signals."

"You mean, it's sort of a decision-maker? Go or no go?"

"Yes. That's exactly what it is. And it must be both sensitive and discriminatory, but not overly so in either direction. The alpha and the beta errors must be effectively eliminated."

"What?"

"Well, as the decision-maker about 'go or no go,' the computer must not interpret incoming data to arrive at a false positive—that is, interpreting a meterorite shower as a flock of hostile ICBM missiles, thus setting off a nuclear exchange for no reason."

"Right. I understand."

"Likewise—or conversely, to be precise—it should not make the equally horrendous mistake of misreading the data from a real attack and assuming that the approaching missiles are just a flock of geese."

"I see what you mean. To err either way is disaster."

"Right. Both the false positive and false negative—the alpha and beta errors—must be infinitesimally small. We could compare it to a firearm, since that is something we both know about. Suppose you have one firearm on which you rely almost totally for defense. Now, if it has eight safety devices, each of which must be switched in sequence, and the trigger is very hard to pull, the gun will be considered safe—"

"Yes. But slow."

"Right. Too slow to be effective in defense. So therefore this 'safe' gun really is not safe. On the other hand, if the gun has no safety devices, and a hair trigger as well, you have a dangerous weapon indeed. One that might fire prematurely, or at an illusory target. You can imagine the consequences when the firearm is actually a nuclear arsenal."

"I can. So you've been developing this computer, which is the decision-maker, and which controls, I take it, the whole strategic defense system. How close is it to completion?"

"It's finished. All the pieces are in place. I don't know how much you know about computers, but the software is more important than the hardware. The program that directs the machine is essential and extremely complex—"

"I know basically what software is. That's about it."

"Well, what makes this project unique is also the fact that a lot of what we would ordinarily refer to as software—that is, the guiding program that directs the electronic components in making decisions—is actually an integral part of the machine's structure. I guess you could say that much of the software is built into the hardware."

"How?" I asked.

"Ahhh! Wouldn't you—and everyone else—like to know, eh? That is what took so very long to develop, and, of course, I don't have the whole answer. I just have impressions, based on my work on a small but vital part of the project. Actually, I'll tell you how we got the idea for it. One of the team leaders is an enthusiast for a puzzle that was quite popular a few years ago. It was a manual puzzle invented by a fellow Hungarian. Do you recall Rubik's Cube?"

"Oh, sure. Could never work the damn thing, though. My kids were pretty good at it—"

"Yes. Well, Rubik's Cube was of course many cubes within one. The structure was arranged so that whole banks of cubes could be rotated. The rotation was on both the horizontal and vertical planes, allowing for a wide variety of combinations of spatial placement and therefore a vast number of combinations of contiguity for each small cube. Do you follow?"

"Uh, sort of. . . ."

"Well, each minicube on the big cube's surface could interface—be neighbors—with three, four, or five other minicubes at any one time. Not only that, but the cubes could be placed in numerous different combinations by manipulating the various movable planes. The mind boggles merely at the number of combinations possible. But that's only the beginning. No minicube in Rubik's Cube had more than five operative faces—that is, faces *without* colors on them—and some had only three. Now, if you imagine that each little cube of the Rubik puzzle is a computer, but with electronic interfacing capability on *all* of its six sides, able to rotate individually, you can get a rough idea as to how many supercomputer combinations can be made by rearranging the banks of minicomputers in this device."

"I see. The whole machine is made of little machines that swim around and join up with each other in different combinations. Hmmmm . . . more complicated than I thought."

"That's the understatement of the year, Doc. Of course, the components don't actually move around—the interfacing is done electronically. But you understand the principle. Well, all the pieces are now in place, as I mentioned. Most of the thousands of components came from eighteen separate departments at Lincoln Laboratories. Many more were made in four departments at MITRE, our sister laboratory in Lexington. Another batch arrived two weeks ago from a developmental research lab in Princeton, New Jersey. It's now ready to go."

"Go where?"

"Good question, Doc. That is what I have yet to discover. But go it will. It will not stay at Lincoln Labs. And the day they let it out the door, which is Thursday, that's when the KGB will come."

"You mean they'll try to steal it?"

He shrugged his shoulders again.

"Steal it or destroy it. And if they destroy it, we'll only build another. So they'll try to steal it. Steal it for long enough to disassemble it and take the components. If they do this, they will unravel it, since much of the decision-making logic is built into the circuitry. But they must have the object. They must have the machine itself, because all the drawings, photographs, and typed sheets in the world won't be sufficient. It would be like trying to solve the Rubik's Cube puzzle without getting your hands on it. You see? So, in this case, microfilm won't do it for the Soviets. They need to get their hands—if only briefly—on *ARGUS*. That, and that alone, will reveal the strategic thinking of the U.S.A."

"That's what this thing is called? ARGUS? If I remember right, Argus, in Greek mythology, was a thousand-eyed monster that stood guard. That's a pretty clever name."

"Yes, that's one Argus. There was another who built Jason's ship, the Argo. Remember Jason and the Argonauts?"

"Yes. So why's it named after him?"

"It isn't named after either. There was a third Argus: a dog. A dog that belonged to Odysseus."

"A dog? I don't remember anything about his dog. He take it with him on the voyage?"

"No, Doc. Like the computer that stays on the ground, the dog Argus stayed in Ithaca. And when Odysseus returned home to his island after wandering for twenty years, he disguised himself as a begger . . ."

"I remember that part. He put on an old cloak so he could sneak inside his own house and kill his wife's suitors. He did it, too."

"Yes. And his disguise fooled not only the suitors, but Penelope, his wife, and Telemachus, his son."

"So?"

"But one of the household was not fooled by the disguise—"

"The dog. Of course! He would recognize his master's scent."

"Yes. You see? The machine's function is not to detect incoming missiles; that task is the job of the spy satellites. Nor does it aim or fire the laser guns that will shoot them down—we have other computers to do that. ARGUS's job is to interpret all the incoming data so it can distinguish friend from foe—to discriminate between false signals and real danger in the skies."

"And, like Odysseus's dog, it alone can make a clear distinction between signals that are harmless and those that are lethal. . . ."

He nodded, and I gazed out over the shimmering pond, now almost dark. It seemed to rock and tilt before my eyes. Why me? Why had I been drawn into this mess? With the future of the world practically rubbing elbows with me? I groaned and felt a soft hand on my shoulder.

"Jesus, Emil. I wish I were in Muscatine."

"Muscatine? Where's that?"

"Muscatine, Iowa."

"Why? What's happening in Muscatine, Iowa?"

"Not a damn thing. That's why I wish I were there."

"Are you going to help me?"

"Let's see: you know the day, and you know the object. What you don't know yet is the exact location of the event and the exact time. And when you find that out, hopefully tomorrow or Wednesday, then you're going to have me blow the whistle at the last minute."

"That's exactly my plan. That's the way it must be, Doc. Trust me. And you know why I'm afraid of calling in the FBI too soon. So, here is the bargain: give me at least until tomorrow midnight. If I'm no closer to the solution then, we'll both go together to see the authorities. And you have my word on that."

"Great."

"But until then, tell no one what I've told you. I told you these things so we could strike this bargain and so, in the event that something happens to me, you'll have something to start with."

"What about Mary? I can tell her, can't I?"

"I wouldn't. If the secret had to be kept a long time, I would relent. But it's only for a day or two. Good night, Doc. May this all end happily for us on Thursday."

"Goodbye, Emil. Sleep well. I'll bring you hot food tomorrow night."

He waved, and then I was on the narrow rock lip that led back around the gate house and into the dark woods. I had started toward the leafy darkness when a nagging doubt that had been bothering me surfaced again with renewed force.

"*Psssst!*" I said at the wall. I heard a scuffling from within as he approached it.

"What is it? Is somebody out there?"

"No. I wanted to ask you again, was it phosphorous that burned TALIN's back when he was a Russian soldier?"

"That's what I heard. A phosphorous grenade fragment when he was in *Spetsnaz* training. Why?"

"Just curious, is all. You think the man you killed was TALIN?"

"I can't be certain. But I sure hope so. What do you think?"

"Well, it was a burn; I'm sure of that. If it's not TALIN, it's a hell of a coincidence. . . ."

"Well, whoever it was, he wanted to kill me. I'm not sorry I got him first. May I be as lucky tomorrow. Goodbye, Doc."

"Yeah. Bye, Emil. Be careful."

And then I went back into the deep woods again. No bird sang.

22

I DIDN'T GET HOME UNTIL AFTER EIGHT. I DELIBERATELY drove around Maynard and Acton for a while, trying to think what I was going to say to Mary. Emil didn't want me to tell her, but I wanted to. After all, she hadn't called Joe that day Emil and I skipped the scene. But the question was this: if I did tell her, would she become so afraid for my safety that she'd call her brother out of panic? If she did, he'd have to call Chet, and Chet would have to call Vic Hamisch . . . and there you go: things all gone to hell as far as Emil's plan was concerned. Also, there was the danger. If Mary found out about ARGUS, she'd be a sitting duck.

And then, of course, I considered as I maneuvered through the gentle S curve where Route 62 cuts underneath the B&M tracks on the way into Concord Center, she might be a sitting duck even if she didn't know. Why? Because somebody might just assume that she did know, and that she therefore had to be dealt out of the game. So the best bet was to tell her. To level with her completely, and then perhaps get her to leave town before the fireworks started.

"Well, bullshit, Charlie. I am *not* leaving town just because of a little danger. I've seen these little fixes of yours through before, and believe me—"

"Wait a minute. Wait. This is not a little danger, Mary. This is a great big danger. When the spy network of a superpower comes calling with blood in its eye, it is definitely *not* a little danger. Now, the Cape is really nice this time of year. Our favorite time. And uncrowded, too. I was hoping you and Janice could—"

"No. I'm not going down to the cottage. I'm staying. And personally I can't wait to meet one of those KGB guys. I'll make him sorry he was ever born."

"No. No, you won't. I'm not kidding now. Remember what it felt like the night after you picked up that pellet? Remember?"

She sank down into the easy chair and looked at her hands. She looked as if she might cry.

"So. We shouldn't even be talking here. The house is probably bugged again, remember?" she said.

"Oh, my God. C'mon, up to the shower."

We went into our own bathroom instead of the boys', but the procedure was the same: run the shower water to mask the conversation.

"But why's this computer—ARGUS, it's called?—why's it so special? I mean, hell, there are fifty computer companies around Boston. They make computers to do everything now, even feed gas into the carburetor. Why is this one so secret?"

"Emil explained that it has to do with alpha and beta errors and the software program being built into the mechanism in a special way. Anyway, it took years to develop and will be the heart of our new defense system. And it's one of a kind."

"And the Russians—the KGB guys with poisoned-pellet guns—really want to get their hands on it."

"Absolutely. Bet on it. And they'll go through anything and anybody who's in the way. Including Mary Brindelli Adams."

"So that's why you want me to go to the Cape with Janice?"

"Yep. Whadduyuh say?"

"No dice. Now let's go down and have a big drink. I've

been completely recovered for a while now. No more Prussian blue, and I can have a drink if I want. And I *want*."

"Okay, but be sure not to mention anything touchy. Know what Joe told me? He says there are some phone bugs that work when the phone is still on the hook. Anything you say in the same room as the phone can be picked up. How do you like that?"

"I don't. I'm sick of it."

"Yeah. Me too."

So we went down, and she had a hefty gin and tonic. I had a Scotch and soda.

"I'm hungry," she said. "Neither of us has eaten. What shall we have?"

"How about lamb chops with basil, garlic, and lemon?"

"Sounds okay. White beans?"

"Uh-huh. And marinated eggplant. Do we still have any left?"

"Four jars."

"What kind of wine?"

"Barbera. We'll need a strong one."

"Can do. Hey, Charlie, you sure it's a good idea not to tell Joe and company about . . . our friend who operates the steam shovel?"

"Maybe not a good idea. But a deal's a deal. It's only one more day."

"And who do you believe? Him or Chet?"

I held my finger to my mouth. "A little of both, I think," I whispered close to her ear. "I mean, I think our bureaucratic friend is telling us the version he really believes. But I'm not sure that the version he's telling us is totally right. Remember, he's been trained to think that way. That's his whole career."

"Yeah. Jeez, I hate this. I can't wait till it's over."

"You and me both."

The next day, Monday, I fussed and fidgeted at the office. I took a longish run at noontime, but it didn't help much. Then I got a call from Joe when I returned at two. He told me over the phone that he and Chet were going to have a short meeting about Thursday the twenty-eighth, and Chet said that if I wanted to sit in on it, it was okay with him.

"Hmmmm. You mean he's taking Emil's prediction more seriously now?"

"Yeah, guess so. Apparently there's an event scheduled at Brandeis University Thursday, and Chet and his staff think it fits the bill perfectly. We're going to have the meeting there, at the auditorium. Four-thirty. You want to come?"

I said yes, I would, although I couldn't get there until after five.

"S'okay, Doc. We'll still be there."

It was actually five-fifteen when I found a parking place and walked across the campus to the Spingold Theater at Brandeis. All the lights were on inside, which seemed silly because the place was practically deserted. Joe, Chet, and four other men—who I assumed, correctly, to be people on Chet's staff—sat in the front row, looking at the empty stage on which a speaker's podium had been set up. Chet was scratching his head and cussing when he saw me. He motioned me over with waves of his arm.

"What gives?" I asked. "It seems as if you're taking Emil's strange pronouncements a little more seriously."

"Well, sort of. It seems the Company has had a little change of heart about this thing. After Williamson fled, Vic Hamisch requested a follow-up."

"What we did was," said Joe, "we contacted the *Globe* and all sorts of media and PR people around town to come up with events that would be likely targets. This appears to be one of the best bets."

"A speaker?"

"Uh-huh. Ever hear of Hannah Lubinsky?"

"She sounds Jewish. And Russian."

"Exactly the point," said Chet. "And she's been written up in *Newsweek* and what have you. An expatriate from Russia, now an Israeli citizen—"

"Oh, wait—wait. Yes, I've heard of her. Strong feminist? Ardent Zionist? Doesn't say very nice things about the Soviet Union?"

"That's her. That's Hannah. Needless to say, the Russkies

hate her guts, since her writings, though banned, have stirred up a lot of domestic trouble in Russia in the last few years, particularly in the Ukraine. They would dearly love to see her dead."

I sank down into one of the seats. "Aw, come on, you guys. The Russians aren't going to pull a public hit in this country. I mean, they're nasty, sure. But they wouldn't risk the flack from an assassination on American soil."

"I agree. We're not saying they'll do it. We're saying they could easily have a stooge do it: some fanatical Arab or hopped-up Angolan. See, this auditorium is the fallback site in case of rain. The address is scheduled for eleven o'clock out on the quad. Hannah will be a live target out there."

I glanced around me at all the Feds busily making sketches and taking notes. Now and then they conferred in excited whispers and pointed to various corners of the theater. Probably picking out vantage points for the agents, so they could watch the crowd for any sign of an assassin. And they would no doubt confiscate or search all parcels, briefcases, and so on. Probably even check out guys walking with one stiff leg. And while you're at it, fellas, be on the lookout for a one-legged old guy with a metal crutch. Or haven't you read *Day of the Jackal*?

"I don't know, Chet. How sure are you about this event? To me, it's not the kind of thing Emil meant at all. . . ."

He turned and faced in my direction, the official Bureau look drilling into me. The black-framed glasses, the short haircut, the white shirt with starched collar, the gray suit. The whole shebang. Well, so much for Chet Harwood, the sensitive, sympathetic pal who had visited my house earlier in his slacks and pullover. He'd changed right back into the Bureau Monster again. The clothes. That's what does it: the goddamn clothes. Put on a uniform, and your mind, conscience, and soul take a hike. No wonder, then, that the sharpest-ever resident of Concord, Henry David Thoreau, warned: "Beware of enterprises requiring new clothes."

"Oh really?" pursued Chet. "Not what Emil meant at all? Well, Dr. Adams, maybe you can tell us just exactly what Emil Haszmanany *did* mean."

" 'Course I can't. He didn't intercept the entire message, remember? Just the last part of it. The part that mentioned the date."

"Then why are you so certain we're on the wrong track here? We've checked and double-checked the known scheduled events. This one comes closest to fitting the mold. If you've got a better suggestion, then let's hear it."

"Well, it seemed to me that Emil pretty much confined his last searches to the vicinity of Concord and Acton, not Waltham. Now, as you know, he gave me no details, for my own safety. But it seems to me that you and your staff would be wise to cover a few bases out in that neighborhood as well as here."

"But, other than the general area, you've got nothing specific?"

"No. Except Lincoln Labs. I mean, that's where he intercepted the microdot. And he mentioned the security leak there. You yourself went to snag Roland Williamson, and he came up missing."

"And I've been over to Lincoln Labs, too. Inside and out, top to bottom. At all levels, I'm getting no indication of anything major occurring there this Thursday. But you raise a good point. As it so happens, before you arrived I was telling Joe that on Thursday I may or may not be here, depending on last-minute developments."

"That's the way Chet always works," said Joe. "He's his own flying squad."

"That's right. I'll be here, there, and everywhere, depending on what goes down at the eleventh hour."

"You alone?"

"Alone or with a few of my agents."

"Sid Wanzer. Where *is* Sid?" I asked.

"Sid? I don't work with Sid anymore. We didn't get along. Besides, just between the three of us, he was never where he was supposed to be. Always late, like he was at your house, Doc. Or else turning up in strange places. Unprofessional. Last week he requested to work on his own. I thought it was rather sudden, but I can't say I miss him that much."

"Figured not. And where's *he* going to be?"

"I don't know, Doc. Why don't you ask him? Now, I've got plenty of men for this thing. I mean, the best we can do is cover as many bases as well as we can, then be flexible enough to move anywhere the action is at a second's notice. Assuming, Doc, that anything happens at all. Frankly, I've still got my doubts, even about this event here."

"So do I. About this event here. But why the sudden turnaround? What persuaded you that there might be something substantial in what Emil told me?"

Chet rose and walked up the aisle to the exit doors. Joe and I followed.

"I already told you, it wasn't me," Chet said over his shoulder. "It was Vic Hamisch. I guess he was persuaded by all the strange shit coming down as much as anything else. Haszmanany *is* wanted by the KGB, we know that now. Just because he's also wanted by us doesn't diminish that fact, which adds to his credibility. And then there's Roland Williamson. So, all in all, the Company—and the Bureau—now feel we should at least do a thorough follow-up on Thursday. Put it another way: if something big *does* happen, and it turns out we haven't paid any attention to the warning, then we're asleep at the switch. Get it?"

"What you're saying, Chet," I said. "is that it's a 'cover your ass' operation as much as anything else."

"You could say that," he answered, under his breath. "*I* would never say it. But *you* could."

"That's exactly what it is," added Joe, a sagacious, world-weary look on his bloodhound face. "Doc, let me tell you: when you're in the public service, ninety percent of what you're doing is covering your ass. It may be a shame, but there it is."

"There it is . . . ," repeated Chet, and then we were outside on the main quadrangle, where the workmen of the buildings and grounds department were unloading scaffolding for the bleachers from trucks.

"Now let me ask you something, Doc," said Chet, his eyes boring into mine. "Have you seen Emil recently?"

"No."

"Didn't think so. I guess he's gone for good. Now, what

are *you* going to be doing this Thursday? Hmmmm? Pulling teeth or playing secret agent?"

"I haven't decided yet. I do have some appointments, but I have some free time too."

Chet Harwood looked up at the trees and along the roof lines of the campus buildings, jingling the change in his pants pockets with his fingers. He let out a deep breath of air through a slit in his mouth. It sounded like a whale surfacing about a mile away. He rocked slightly back and forth on his heels and toes.

"Doc? Stay out of it. Please? You know there's a good chance that I know more than I'm telling you about this business. I'm not saying I'm a goddamn know-it-all. But I'm not totally in the dark, either. I mean, there's always a chance that Emil planted this story about Lincoln lab so that you'd tell us—which you have—and we'd all be looking in the wrong direction on Thursday. Know what I'm saying? And as long as we're on the subject of planting bullshit stories, Doc, try this one on for size: what if the *date*—next Thursday—is a bullshit story of its own? A ruse to make us let our guard down so the thing can then be pulled off Friday or Saturday? Huh? How about *that* one?"

"Well, hell, Chet, you could go crazy trying to think of all the possibilities."

"Exactly," he said, scuffing his black shiny shoes angrily on the campus walkway. "Think about it."

Then we walked over to the parking lot. Chet seemed to have the weight of the world on his shoulders; each step he took was plodding, methodical. He looked exhausted.

"Didn't sleep last night?" I asked. "You look tired."

"I slept. But not well. I haven't in over a week. Yes, I'm tired, Doc. Tired of this whole thing. I wish that if Emil's alive, he'd turn himself in and come clean with us. If he's dead, then I wish we'd find his body—wherever it is—and then at least we'd know. As it stands, there are too many loose ends. And that's tiring, by God. For somebody trained to work systematically—and that's me and all the Bureau, I admit it—loose ends are a roaring pain in the ass."

Then we were standing at Chet's Saab. He got inside and seemed to sink down into the seat.

"See ya," said Joe, bending low and looking in at Chet. "Hey, get some sleep. Whatever happens, it'll be over and done with Thursday night. And maybe it's nothing. Think about that, and you'll sleep fine."

"Yeah, sure," Chet said, and turned the ignition key.

Joe and I walked on to his car and leaned against it. There was something I had to ask him.

"I know what you're going to ask me," he said wearily. "Why haven't I told Chet about the paint cans in the cellar. Right?"

"Right."

"Well, simple: I didn't want him laughing at me. Thinking I was nuts. That's why. I mean, we didn't find Emil, right? So I'm not going to stick my neck out and say, 'Hey, Chet, Doc and I found these paint cans and kitty litter in Doc's basement. We think Emil came back in the dead of night and'—Well, if you were Chet, what would you think?"

"I'd think you were off your rocker. And maybe recommend you take a leave of absence."

"Uh-huh. See? It's what I said earlier, Doc. Cover your ass. Always cover your own ass. Listen, you never found him, did you?"

"No. By the way, Joe, are you going to be home tonight?"

"Yeah, sure. Guess so. Why?"

"Just wanted to know. Why don't you get some sleep too?"

"Not a bad idea. Say hello to Sis. Bye."

He walked on a few steps, his leather soles crackling on the gritty pavement. He stopped and turned to me.

"Hey, Doc? Where will *you* be tonight?"

"Around, I guess."

I watched his cruiser pull a tight circle in the lot and head off toward Boston. I felt all alone, and not totally honest.

I was walking back to my car, my head down, when a tan sedan pulled up beside me. The window came down, and the driver, a distinguished-looking man with gray hair and a neat, blue worsted-wool suit, inclined his head slightly out and said in a low, precise voice, "Charles Adams, I'm Victor Hamisch, and I would like you to please come into this car with me for a minute."

23

I GAZED AT VICTOR HAMISCH SITTING BEHIND THE WHEEL. Nondescript car. Nondescript, clean-cut, executive-type man driving it. Appears trustworthy. Looks like a banker. Well groomed; probably scrapes underneath his fingernails twice a days. But how about the toenails? The ones people can't see?

"Do I have a choice?"

"Of course you have a choice, Dr. Adams; I'm not a policeman. I'm a public servant. You have a choice. The important thing, I think, is for you to make the wise one. And from what I hear, you are a wise man. If you could just join me for a few minutes."

Realizing that, despite what he said, I probably didn't have a choice—in the long run, at least—I went over and hopped in next to him. He offered his hand, bone-dry and firm.

"Emil Haszmanay," he said. "Tell me about Emil Haszmanay, Doctor. What's important about him? What are your impressions?"

"As for his background, you know more than I do. As for my impressions, I believe he is—he was—telling me the truth. Mainly."

"The truth . . . mainly. Heh! I see you are a friend of Mr. Twain's. Yes, many of us tell the truth . . . mainly. It's the rare bird amongst our race who tells the truth . . . wholly. Agreed?''

''Most of the time it's probably not a good idea to tell the whole truth.''

''Well said. But I think in this case, considering what's at stake for the national security, it's best to put all the cards on the table. Now, please. Without feeling that you're stripping yourself naked, so to speak, and exposing yourself to severe invasions of privacy, could you please give me more specifics?''

Unctuous. That's what Hamisch was. I had been trying to think of the right word. . . .

''Well,'' I said, ''he came to me because, according to him, he had no place else to turn.''

Then I told him everything that had happened, except, of course, what had happened after we went to the airport. I said nothing about the return of Emil Haszmanay to Concord, or about anything else he'd told me. But I did take a wee chance and dropped a hint about betrayal in the Company.

''So through everything I was wondering to myself, 'Why doesn't he just go to the Company'—he called you the Company—'and tell them everything?' You know?''

''Precisely. That's exactly what we're wondering, Doctor. And frankly, it's what makes us uneasy, and suspicious of him.''

''Well, I keep thinking about this too. The only thing I can come up with is that there is somebody in the Company whom he didn't trust. I'm talking about a traitor, I guess. What do you think?''

''I *think* . . . What I *think* is, he was lying. But so what? That doesn't mean he was. I can't think of anyone in my organization who would be a candidate for traitor. But, as I said, that doesn't mean it can't happen. It's just that I must go on the evidence and on the most logical explanation. These both imply Haszmanay is the traitor. But the evidence does not say that overwhelmingly; it merely suggests it.''

''Now let me ask *you* a question. Do you think the KGB is friendly toward Emil, or do they want him dead?''

"They want him dead, of course, for collaborating with us. They tried to shoot him, didn't they?"

"Did they? Or was that one of your men?"

His head jerked back, and he frowned in surprise.

"Who told you that?"

"Nobody. It's just a thought I had, and I don't know who I can believe anymore."

"No. It wasn't anyone from my organization. And I can say the same for the FBI as well. And the method they employed, that dreadful poisoned pellet . . . I heard your wife was a victim as well. We're sorry. Surely you've been through enough, eh?"

"Yes, I have. I want to be shut of the entire thing. But whatever happens, it's not in my hands anymore. Emil Haszmanay is gone, and he isn't coming back."

"What makes you so sure?"

"Just a feeling."

"Well, for your information, we think otherwise. We have reason to believe he's alive, and hiding in this area. Now, if you see him, Doctor, I hope you'll do your duty and notify me immediately. Either me or Chet Harwood."

"Sure."

"Failure to do so warrants a lengthy prison term. I hate to sound harsh, you know. I really and truly do. But it's the situation that's harsh, not I. And there really is a lot at stake here."

"You know what it is, don't you?"

"I know a lot of things, Dr. Adams. That's my job. All I wanted to do in this little visit was to tell you sincerely that I sympathize with you and what you've been through. You didn't ask for your predicament. But for Heaven's sake don't let your compassion for your fellow man blind you. Do your duty as an American citizen first."

He paused with a formality I took as a signal that the conversation was over. I got out, shut the door, and looked back inside the nondescript tan sedan.

"Just two questions," I said. "One: if you ran across Haszmanay, would you harm him?"

He shook his head without hesitation.

"No. We would take him into custody for interrogation. Next?"

"Have you ever heard of a man called TALIN?"

I saw him stiffen slightly. It was barely noticeable, but it was there. And Hamisch was undoubtedly a man schooled and practiced in hiding his feelings.

"Why?"

"So you've heard of him. Is he real or a myth? If real, is he alive or dead?"

"Real. And alive, as far as I know. Alive and extremely dangerous."

"What does he look like?"

"Nobody knows."

"How do you know he's alive, then?"

"I can't s—" he began, then stopped. "Who told you about him?"

"Emil did. And I think TALIN was the guy Emil shot, up in the lineman's tent. I think TALIN's dead. Emil mentioned a scar he had, and the marksman had it. Right kind, right location."

"Then we'll all pray he's finally dead."

"Didn't Chet mention this to you?"

"No."

"Well, Chet thinks the guy's a myth, anyway."

"All the Feds do. But they don't know everything we know. Goodbye, Doctor. Take this, and call me if anything comes up."

He leaned over and handed me a card through the open window.

"I already have your number. Joe gave it to me."

"Joe? Oh, yes, yes. Your brother-in-law, I believe. No, that number's been changed already. This will do for the next few days."

Then he put the car in gear, eased down the drive, and was gone. I looked down at the card. On it was a phone number written lightly in pencil. Nothing else. It didn't even say *Lux et Veritas*.

24

Aren't you going to eat anything?''

''No. I can't.''

''You nervous?''

''Wouldn't *you* be?''

''But you're not going until after ten. It's only five-thirty.''

I looked down at the thick fillet of baked cod. I'd eaten only a third of it. I can generally eat a full pound of fresh fish. I'd eaten maybe four ounces and a little salad. I was on my third glass of wine, but even that had failed to slow my jack-hammer pulse and the general nervous rush of adrenalin I felt in every part of my body. I could have run twelve miles without tiring. My mind had told my body to gear up, and there wasn't a damn thing I could do to slow it down, even for dinner.

''Well, there's no sense trying to force yourself. I'll have a little of your fish and give the rest to Phoebe and the dogs. You want to take a walk?''

''Good idea. Great idea. I need . . . I need *motion*.''

So Mary and I took the two big dogs for a walk down Old Stone Mill Road in the quickly falling light. After about a mile, we reached Liberty Street, turned left, and entered the Old North Bridge park. We walked down the hill from the Buttrick Mansion to the river, crossed the Old North Bridge, and let Danny and Troubles swim in the Concord River for half an hour. In the darkness we could hear the ducks quacking and scolding at the dogs. I knew that Danny was trying to retrieve them. I've watched him retrieve tame ducks; he brings them in and sets them down on the grass, then watches them waddle back into the water, shaking their tail feathers. He never hurts them. The sound of the river was soothing and peaceful and almost made me forget my nighttime errand, fast approaching.

Mary and I got up from the riverbank. It was cold now, so we called the doggies and started back. We crossed Old North Bridge again, and I looked up at the bronze statue of the Concord Minuteman, now silhouetted against the night sky. It was cast by Daniel Chester French, a native son of Concord. He also did the seated Lincoln in the Lincoln Memorial in Washington. The statue I now gazed at portrayed a farmer with one hand on his plow, the other on his musket. He was a civilian who was ready to leave his field at a moment's notice to serve his country. He was a true hero. I was like him. He was like me. Ready to serve, even if death were the result. Sure. . . .

"Charlie? What's wrong? You look like you're about to cry."

"Oh, nothing. Let's hurry, Mare. I've got things to do."

"What things?"

"Just things, is all. Just things."

"Oh Jesus, I forgot to tell you."

"Tell me what?"

"That guy called for you today. That friend of Chet's?"

"Who? You mean Sid Wanzer?"

"Yeah, that's him. He called while you were gone. He said he'd be sure to get in touch."

"Well, did he leave a number?"

"No. Said he'd call back later. But he didn't."

"Well, if it's important, then he'll call me. Remember, Mare, I don't want to talk with any of those guys until after tonight."

When we got home I took a long sauna bath to relieve the tension. The effect was minimal, but it passed the time. At quarter to nine I took a warm shower. When I was toweling off, Mary came in. I saw her looking at my tattoo. The one of Daisy Duck I'd gotten down in North Carolina.

"Aren't you embarrassed by it, Charlie?" she said.

"Nah. I'm too old now to get embarrassed easily. Appearances no longer embarrass me. Behavior does."

"And you're not getting rid of it?" she asked.

" 'Course not. I kinda like it. Besides, the skin graft would look worse than the tattoo."

"You could have another tatto done over it," she suggested, "a nicer one."

"Yeah, but what could improve on old Daisy? Huh? C'mon, admit you're getting to like her. Right?"

"I've grown accustomed to her . . . face," she said, grabbing the doorknob. She opened the door and paused. "But not her snarl. Or her rifle."

Nine-o-eight. I took my Browning automatic pistol from its hiding place in the bedroom and went down into the study. I shucked and reloaded all three magazines, squirted them with WD-40 lubricant, checked the action, inserted a loaded magazine, drew back the slide and jacked a round into the chamber, decocked the pistol, put on the safety, and stuck the two spare slips in my hip pocket. Busy Busy Busy. Nervous Nervous Nervous. Stuck the sidearm down in my pants out of sight, pulling down Norwegian wool sweater over pistol butt. Didn't want to alarm Number One. Now I was pacing back and forth along the rug while Mary worked in the kitchen, heating up Emil's stew. One, two, three, four, turn around. One, two, three, four, turn around. Let's see. Portable tape recorder. Should I take a portable tape recorder so I wouldn't miss a word Emil told me? No. Dumb idea. If something screwed up, then the wrong people could get their hands on the portable tape recorder. Portable tape recorder is stupid because the—

"Charlie! You're mumbling to yourself!"

"Oh. Sorry, just thinking out loud. . . ."

"Why don't you have a great big drink? Won't that calm you down?"

"I don't think so. It'll just make me fuzzy, is all. I'm going to lie down."

And I did. The last thing I expected was to fall asleep. But damned if I didn't. The nervous exhaustion had worn me out. Mary woke me up at ten-fifteen, and I was up, shoes on, reaching for my light jacket in the closet before I was fully awake. Then she ducked into the kitchen to get me a mug of coffee and the wide-mouthed thermos filled with beef stew for Emil. I had promised him hot food, and I—"he who never fails"—would deliver.

"Charlie! Is that a pistol in your pocket?"

"No, just glad to see you," I said, kissing her on the cheek. I told her I'd be back at midnight, or maybe one at the latest, and went out and got in the car. But she followed me.

"Level with me, Charlie. Is this dangerous?"

"Absolutely not. I'm the only one who knows where Emil is. Everybody else thinks he's long gone. Tonight he's either going to tell me what's going to happen where and when, in which case we devise a plan, or else he's going to admit defeat and have me arrange for him to have a meeting with Joe."

"Joe? Why not Chet?"

"Because Chet's mad at him; Joe isn't. And, it won't hurt Joe's career any to be the liaison, know what I mean? But mainly, if we go through Joe first, I think things will go more smoothly. Chet's sometimes a bit too gung ho."

"This is your idea?"

"Uh-huh. Joe doesn't know it yet, of course. But I checked with him earlier—he'll be home tonight, so if I need to reach him in a hurry, I'll be able to."

She leaned through the car window and kissed me. I pulled out of the driveway and headed for Laws Brook Road and the Acton town line.

I didn't park in the same place on the shoulder I had used the previous afternoon. It was too suspicious. And then I remembered what Vic Harnisch had told me earlier: they suspected that Emil wasn't dead. They had a strong hunch he was back and in the area. How on earth had they found that out? And what would Emil say about it when I told him? I went farther up Laws Brook Road to a new housing development and parked opposite a well-lighted home, locked the car, and hoofed it back down the road carrying the big thermos bottle. I went slightly past the locked entrance gates of the cinder-block factory and skirted the big clearing, walking steadily and quietly along the trees that bordered it. I went in between the two tall pine trees and hiked toward the millpond. When I reached the alder thicket I waited and watched for ten minutes, then went around the tiny rock lip at the edge of the still water and hopped up onto the plank floor of the gate house. Emil wasn't there yet, but his sleeping bag was rolled in a corner under a pile of straw. I unrolled it and lay down on my back, staring at the roof over me. The time was quarter to eleven. I stared at the water and dozed, then awoke again and looked at my watch. Eleven-thirty. I let my eyes wander over the big iron wheels and the geared uprights that held the gate slabs. Looked back at the pond, dozed again, and so on.

At one-fifteen, I realized Emil wasn't coming back. He had told me to wait one more day. Had he, like Roland Williamson, used that twenty-four hours to take off, getting a head start? No. Whether he was still around Concord was hard to say, but something told me he was not coming back to the gate house. Either he had lied to me about everything he'd told me the previous night, or else he'd run into trouble spooking around in the dark doing his reconnaissance. Or it could be some incongruous combination of both of these. But in any case I wasn't waiting around all night for him; I'd done that twice before. I left the hot stew for him and took off.

I hopped down from the raised floor, took a last quick look around the gate house, and walked around the lip back into the alder copse. Half an hour later, I was back in my car and starting for home.

Mary was asleep in her chair when I came in. She popped open her big brown eyes and jumped up. "Well?" she asked. I told her.

"Oh, well, you did all you could, Charlie. Let's go up and get some sleep. You've got a full day tomorrow. You going to tell Joe?"

"Yes," I answered. "After all, that was the deal."

I finally fell asleep sometime between two-thirty and three. As fatigued as I was, I swore I wouldn't be able to get out of bed for work the next day, which was Tuesday the twenty-sixth. But a funny thing happened. At five o'clock I was wide awake, staring at my ceiling. My pulse was racing, my mouth was dry, and my tongue tingled. Why? What had awakened me? It was an image, an image of the gate-house interior. And now I was trying desperately to put it into shape. Had I really seen this, or only dreamt it? When I had swept my gaze around the gate house's dim interior, had I really noticed something different? Something out of place?

I slipped out of bed silently, dressed, and went downstairs to the garage, being sure to stick the Browning back into my jacket pocket. When I pulled onto the shoulder of Laws Brook Road, opposite the gravel company, it was still dark out. I hurried across the road and the clearing, not taking the time to skirt it but walking quickly right across the open field of packed sand and crunchy gravel.

Ten minutes later I was walking around the rock lip of the gate house, my ears cocked. There was no sound from within. I poked my head around the wall and peered inside. It was empty, exactly as I had left it a few hours earlier. But now there was enough faint, predawn glow on the quiet water of the millpond for me to see the gear-works inside. Sure enough, I had not imagined the image that had startled me awake. It was real: the central upright geared beams were four feet lower than the others. Somebody had lowered the central gate all the way down.

I climbed onto the rough wooden floor and kicked the straw aside. I grabbed the big iron wheel in both hands and pulled along its rim. It moved more easily than I had thought it would. The metal ratchets fell into place along the big gear teeth.

Pink-pink-pink-pink-pink . . .

I pulled on the wheel for what seemed a long time, yet I

noticed that the upright oaken beams had only moved up a little over a foot. It was obviously geared very low for maximum mechanical advantage, since the concrete gate slabs that filled the sluice were enormously heavy. I labored there in the dark, my breath coming faster and faster, until I had raised the big slab two feet. I hopped down onto the stone lip and looked underneath the gear-works. In the dim light I saw a pale object near the slab, to one side. I took out my pocket flashlight and swept it over the area. My heart sank.

Suspended there over the dark, scummy water, as if waving to me in freeze-frame, was a human hand.

I stared, transfixed, at the horror of it, not making a sound. Then, after a look into the woods all around me, I went back up onto the raised floor and cranked at the big wheel again. Finally the middle upright beams were raised up as far as the others. It was now daybreak, and light reflected off the pond water, flooding the interior of the sluice house. As I cranked I blinked away my blurry vision. The wheel had little wet spots on it. I swung down onto the ledge again, and this time, when I looked back into the shadowy cave underneath the timbers, over the water of the pond, I saw Emil. His head, minus the ever-present glasses, sagged sadly forward, his chin rested soddenly on his chest. He looked paler than ever, and his white hair, matted close to the side of his head, made him look tiny indeed. His body was wired to the rock slab. It appeared drawn up and horribly twisted, frozen in a convulsion of agony. How had he died? I saw no marks or wounds on him. But as I looked down through the water, I noticed that his legs terminated in two pale wavy blotches. They should have been dark wavy blotches; the boots I'd bought him were dark brown, not white. His shoes and socks had been removed. I was pretty sure why and didn't want to crank him all the way up to check the bottoms of his feet.

I grabbed the rock foundation wall with one hand and swung far out over the pond to touch the side of his ice-cold head gently in a gesture of farewell. And then I saw, just inside his open shirt collar, the tiny wound at the base of his neck. A round hole, no wide than a dried pea, that went deep into the tissue. And then I knew what was there inside him and had done its horrible damage, what had caused the agony and the convulsions. The poison pellet; revenge weapon of the KGB's Department Five.

Moscow Metal.

I climbed wearily back up onto the floorboards. I sat there in the dark, legs drawn up and head resting on my knees, for maybe twenty minutes. I wasn't sure; I lost track of time.

I couldn't stay there in the gate house any longer. I had too much to do, and Emil wouldn't want me to remain inactive. He also wouldn't want me to grieve over him. But I couldn't help it.

Finally, I rose and walked sadly over to the gear-works one last time. I was so sad I could hardly move my limbs. What I was going to do went against everything I felt in my heart. But I had to do it. I had to do it and get on with the job at hand, because there wasn't time for anything else now. I eased the wheel slightly forward, freeing the ratchet. I flipped the metal lever over. The wheel now floated free, able to be moved in either direction. I released my grip on it, and there came a soft, low whine of well-greased metal as the wheel groaned into an ever-quickening spin. It shrieked twice, where the grease was too thin on the beam plate. But mostly I heard a soothing whir as the gear-works spun, driven by the descending weight of the gate slab beneath, which eased back into the pond.

I sent Emil back into his cold, watery tomb.

I left the gate house. They had found him out and murdered him. Tortured him, too. That meant he had probably told them everything he'd told me, which was considerable. It meant, most importantly, that Emil Haszmanay had not lied. ARGUS was real, and likewise the threat to it. His story was true—even, sadly, the end he had predicted for himself.

I had two days to find the missing pieces and put everything right. My eyes kept blurring. I saw the tree trunks in the dawn's light waver and swim, then stand clear and straight when I blinked.

By the time I reached the car, the sadness had turned to rage. I was filled with bile, pus, and old stale sweat. In my dry, bitter mouth was the gritty dust ground from the fangs of dead pit bulldogs. I thought of what I would do to the people who had done this to Emil. They were not thoughts that a physician who's taken an oath to help and heal should ever, ever have.

25

I WAS AT THE TOWN SQUARE WHEN I CHANGED MY MIND about going home. Mary might be up and about and missing me. And she would ask questions. And I knew that in my present state of mind, I couldn't hide this latest development. What then? She would get hysterical and insist I call Joe. Maybe she would call her brother herself. No good.

So instead of taking Lowell Road north from town, I swung out on Route 62 eastbound, past Sleepy Hollow Cemetery, on through Bedford, and onto Route 4-225. I was bound for Lexington, where Howard March lived. I dug out my wallet and took Emil's note from the billfold. On it were March's address and phone number, but not his name. The address was 121 Follen Road, which branched off Highway 2A. My watch now said 6:40. I doubted that March left his home before seven, since Lincoln Labs, also located in Lexington, couldn't be more than a fifteen-minute drive.

I swung onto quiet Follen Road as the sun was coming up. I pulled right into the driveway, blocking it. I figured that Howard March could choose not to see me. He could even decide to call the law. But until I had my say, he wasn't going anywhere—in his car, at least. I hopped out and rang the bell. A trim man with a white crew cut and an impeccable tweed sport coat answered the door. Why do all these scientist/accountant types still wear crew cuts? I told him who I was, for starters.

"You are a Concord physician? A friend of Emil Haszmanay's?"

"Yes. I'm going to tell you, Howard, that I've seen Emil very recently and spoken with him. He trusted me with some very sensitive information because I helped him. He gave me your name as someone who can likewise be trusted. And now I need your help. It's not exaggerating to say *America* now needs your help. Can we talk a minute?"

"Certainly," he said, opening the door all the way. I said I would prefer to talk outside, away from all buildings and walls. He seemed immediately to understand, and led me around to the back yard, where we stood underneath a red-gold maple in the faint light of early morning.

"Has anyone else been to see you about Emil?" I asked.

"I'm not sure I should answer you, Dr. Adams, I trust you . . . I think . . . but I'm no ultimate judge on these things. You must understand our policies—"

"Has Chet Harwood spoken to you about Haszmanay?"

"Uh . . . why? Is that important? I mean, I'm not sure I should answer you. Why do you want to know?"

"Because he told me he was going to visit the lab. You'd be a natural person to ask about Emil, since I gave Chet your name."

"He never mentioned you. He wanted to know if I knew where Emil was hiding. I answered I didn't know, which is the truth. I've already told you much more than I should have. I hope you understand my reluctance."

"Perfectly. But I'm afraid we don't have a lot of time. Now listen, I'm going out on a limb here, but urgency forces me to tell you certain things. Here's the deal: Emil told me about ARGUS. I know basically what it does, or is supposed to do. I also know that something related to it will happen this Thursday. Now if you can—"

I stopped in midsentence. Howard March seemed to weave before me in a fit of anxiety. He reached up and rubbed his furrowed brow, taking little nervous steps with his feet.

"I can't tell you anything, Doctor. Nothing. Not only because it is top-secret, but because I don't know. I know nothing of what is to take place."

I paused for several second, wondering what to do.

"Okay. I understand your position. But now I going to tell you something important that you should keep to yourself for security's sake. I'm telling you because Emil said you could be trusted absolutely. Emil Haszmanay is dead. He was murdered last night by the KGB. That is, I *think* it was the KGB. There's a good chance the Soviets now know whatever it is that you don't know or can't tell me. Think about it."

He reached out and grabbed my arm to steady himself. I led him over to a stone bench, and we sat down together. He rubbed his palms down his pant legs, as if to dry them.

"We should contact the authorities," he said at last.

"No, we shouldn't. Not quite yet. I have three men I can and will contact immediately when the time is right. But for now I'm more than a little curious as to how the KGB found Emil so easily. In fact, I'm afraid that I'm the one who led them there."

"Then what should we do?"

"You should begin by telling me all you know, or can surmise, about the moving of ARGUS the day after tomorrow."

He sighed. "He told you that, too?"

"Yes. He had to, really. And now, of course, he's probably told his interrogator as well. You see the fix?"

"Frankly, no. If we called in enough people—"

"No. It won't work, Howard. I know what you're thinking. I thought that, too. But Emil was convinced that there is a turncoat somewhere in the Company. He was adamant about not calling in the Feds or the CIA until he had everything buttoned up."

"And look what happened to him. . . ."

"I know. But I think it only proves his point. There are some questions of my own that need answering first anyway. Then I'll go to the law, and pronto. Now, as to the event on Thursday—is there any particular place that comes to your mind?"

"I don't know, and I couldn't tell you if I did. Can you tell me about Emil, please? Can you tell me where he'd been, what he'd been doing?"

I told him virtually everything that had happened in the past two weeks. March listened intently, anger and sadness alternating on his keen features. When I finished, he stood up and paced to and fro, muttering and swearing.

"Tell me about your interview with Chet Harwood," I said.

"The man from the FBI? He didn't interview me. He barely saw me. Just asked if I knew where Emil might be hiding. He went higher up—to my supervisor and the directors. The people he saw know more about this project than I do."

I took a quick step backward and looked up at the trees.

"What's wrong?" he asked.

Now I was the one pacing to and fro on the lawn.

"Hell, if Chet went over to Lincoln Labs and saw the brass, then he must know everything already."

"No. Not if they didn't tell him."

"You mean they wouldn't tell the FBI?"

"Absolutely not. The Feds are always poking around, trying to find out what we're doing. And the Agency's not much better. Do you know there are more Company men in New England than anywhere except Washington? Mostly the excuse they give is 'advising on security matters.' Or sometimes, as in the case of Emil Haszmanay, they say they're 'tracking down a suspected insurgent.' Of course, that's not always a lie. Four years ago the Agency and the Feds nailed a top GRU agent right in the lab, with two subordinates. We're still trying to live it down."

"So you're saying that the FBI might know, and might not."

"Right," he answered. Then he thought a minute. When he spoke, his words surprised me.

"Now, I said I didn't know the details of the ARGUS move," he said in a low, low voice. Lower than a whisper. "But I have heard rumors—"

"Rumors? You mean a place like Lincoln Labs has rumors?"

"My dear fellow, every place has rumors. Rumors are part of the human condition. Now, the rumor is that ARGUS will be transported west on Thursday. Rumor says that the ultimate destination is NORAD, in Cheyenne Mountain. Know where that is?"

"Yes. I've been there. Just outside Colorado Springs. That's the nerve center of our defense system."

"Yes. Anyway, rumor has it that ARGUS will get there by rail. With no guard."

"What?"

"Rumor only, Dr. Adams. But we've been extremely successful with this approach before. No military transport planes or truck convoys. No platoon of commandos. They attract far too much attention. And what we're moving is not that big, either. Just a canvas-covered object on a flatcar with two industrial transformers. Nobody will pay it much notice."

"Ah. I see now. And, relying on secrecy, it's entirely safe, unless someone discovers the secret."

"Exactly."

"And what are the odds that the Feds and the Company know about it?"

"I have no idea one way or the other. In any case, it's all rumor at my end."

"And also, Chet doesn't know that Emil came back. He thinks Emil has gone over or been killed by the KGB. Which, ironically, has turned out to be true."

"And so, what do you think? And what will you do next?"

"I wish to hell I knew. I just know Emil was telling me the truth all along, and I've got to follow up on a few questions that are still nagging me."

I walked out the driveway to my car. He went with me and handed me a card. "Here's my number at the lab. If you need me, call. All the lines are monitored, so say something about a golf game before the weather gets too cold. I'll know it means for me to go out to a pay phone and return your call."

I thanked him and left. It was now seven-thirty. I went home this time and met Mary as she was coming downstairs. I took her up to the boys' john, turned on the shower, and told her everything. She half collapsed on the edge of the tub.

"You're calling Joe right now, Charlie. Right now!"

"Not just yet; there are a couple more things I've got to do first. Please don't talk to him until I do, okay?"

"But whoever killed Emil is probably after you now."

"Maybe. Maybe not. Maybe Emil never mentioned me before he died."

She buried her face in her hands.

"The thing I'm wondering is how much Chet knows. Emil's best pal at Lincoln Labs, Howard March, says Chet interviewed all the brass there. They could've let him in on the ARGUS secret, but maybe they didn't. The fact that Chet's making all those elaborate security preparations at Brandeis makes me think they didn't tell him."

"So what are you going to do?"

"I'm going to work, for starters. You're not on at the hospital, are you?"

"No. Not until next week."

"Then finish getting dressed. I'll drop you off at the DeGroots' on my way out. No arguments this time; we've only got two more days to go."

Two hours later, with Mary safely stowed at Jim and Janice DeGroot's and my first patient behind me, I went up to the second floor of the Concord Professional Building and rapped on the door of Aaron Schindler, Dermatologist. After a thirty-minute talk with him, I left the building and drove into the center of town, where I stood at one of the open pay phones near the square and made a lengthy call to Chicago, speaking to an old family friend named Martin Higgins. Marty had recently retired from the *Chicago Tribune*, which is, incidentally, the world's greatest newspaper. Its readers are assured of this because it says so right on the front page of every edition. Higgins is an extremely well-connected man, in government, politics, the military, and just about everywhere else.

"And you want it *when*? Ha! ha! ha!—as they say on those joke posters—"

"I'll need it today, if possible. No later than tomorrow around noon. It's going to involve some international calls, but I'll reimburse you."

"Not to worry about that, Doc. I just don't know if I can make all the calls in time. What if some of them are out? I mean, like out of the country?"

"Then do your best, Marty. I can't stress too much the importance of this, even though it may sound crazy."

"Not coming from you, it doesn't. That is, not any crazier than normal. Bye."

In the afternoon I had six patients, back to back. I canceled all the appointments, to the astonishment of Susan Petri.

"I can't explain now, Susan. Just tell them I'm sick again. And while you're at it, you might as well cancel them for tomorrow and Thursday too."

"Can't you tell me what's going on?" she asked, blinking her big, liquid eyes.

"I just can't . . . right now."

"And you've just been sitting there, Doc, looking out the window. What are you thinking?"

"I was thinking about tattoos. Something Mary said about my tattoo."

"*You*? Oh, I didn't know you had one. Let's see!"

So I showed her, and she oohed and ahed. I thought she was just doing it to be polite. But then she admitted she had one too.

"Yeah. It's a little rose, is all. Cost a lot to have it done, though. It's in color."

"Well, c'mon, Susan, let's see it. I showed you mine."

"Ooh! I don't know . . . it's in, like, a . . . personal place. . . ."

"Oh, really? Well, this gets more interesting all the time. Where specifically is it? Or is that too personal?"

"No. It's on my . . . left bun."

"Ah!" It was all I could think of to say.

"I suppose you'd like to see it?" she asked, arching her eyebrows and grinning mischievously.

"Well I, uh . . . why, sure—"

"Fat chance," she said, and glided out of the room.

I sighed and called myself names. Dirty Old Man. Old Fart. Jerk. There were others. . . .

I stopped down the hall to see Moe. He asked me how everything was going, and I was as noncommittal as possible. As I left I shook his hand.

"Be seeing you around," I said, heading for the door.

"What's dat mean? You going somewhere?"

"I've got some items to take care of around town for the next couple of days. I should be back by Friday, or maybe Monday."

As I went back outside and got into my car. I sure hoped it wasn't going to be the last time I ever saw him. But I had shaken his hand, just in case.

26

WEST BY RAIL. THAT WAS THE SCUTTLEBUTT AT LINCOLN Labs. ARGUS was going west by rail. I thought about this as I drove out toward the Acton line again. Trouble was, there was no railroad spur near the lab. I was familiar with the area, and there just wasn't any. So that meant that ARGUS would ride the first leg of its westward journey on a truck. That did not seem very safe to me, but truck transport would have to be the mode, even if ARGUS were to be guarded by the Marine Corps. But there wouldn't be any Marines, March had told me; that would attract undue attention.

Just a truck taking the computer to some kind of loading ramp or railroad spur. Hell, I hadn't a prayer of finding it. How many tracks led out of the Boston Metro Area for points west? Five? Ten? And how many spurs and ramps did each one have? Fifty? Two hundred? Say just five rail lines, with fifty loading sites on each. What was that? Two hundred and fifty possible sites. No way, Adams.

And if somebody wanted to hijack ARGUS, wouldn't they try to intercept the truck instead of the train? By taking the truck, they could drive to points unknown with their precious cargo. Or perhaps ditch the truck in some hidden spot, dismantle the ARGUS, and take the parts in cars to wherever they wanted. Or . . . well, they could do a million things.

I didn't have a year to find out; I had a day. And I needed help. I needed police help. Except I knew that if I went to Joe—which was the same as going to Chet and his boys—it would ruin everything. What had come down so far told me that loud and clear.

I stopped at a shopping center and went to another pay phone. I called Joe at Ten Ten Comm. Ave. He was out. Probably over at Brandeis getting the sharpshooters ready. Chet would be there too, setting up checkpoints and walkie-talkie codes, making sure all his guys were going to wear their Kevlar vests—the kind that can almost stop a .357 magnum.

I told the switchboard to patch me through to Karl Pirsch, and in a few seconds I heard his raspy voice, his Teutonic, accusatory tone.

"Yes? What is it, please?"

"Karl, this is Doc Adams. I'd ask Joe, but he's out in the field. Has there been any identification of the marksman, a.k.a. Frederick Stansul?"

"I am not authorized to tell you, Dr. Adams. But I know your brother-in-law will tell you anyway. As a matter of fact, I have a copy of the R and I report on the counter right in front of me. Yes, Records and Identification made him as Alfred Stansiewicz—Polish-American, Roman Catholic—who was born and raised down in Brocktown. Identification was confirmed by birth records, which included a footprint."

"Do you have anything else? Living relatives? Employment records in the area? Anything?

"He has a sister. Married. She lives in Marlboro, and was shocked indeed to hear that her baby brother was recently alive."

"Ah! You mean he faked his own death before he went over to Russia?"

"No. His sister told us he just disappeared. He was out of work for some time—this was in nineteen fifty-eight—and just being a vagrant. A bum, as we say. When he disappeared, she just thought he had taken off. She had assumed he was dead by now."

"And so he is . . . now. She very shaken up?"

"I don't know. You must ask Joe—"

"I will. But I'd really like to call the sister now, and just ask her two questions—"

"Impossible, Doctor. It is against the rules. I forbid you to call Mrs.—ehhh—Dolores Beck, in Marlboro. Goodbye!"

I had to go into the shopping center to get more coins, which I promptly pumped into the pay phone for a brief but important call to Marlboro. The call confirmed some of the elements of my earlier discussion with Dr. Aaron Schindler, the dermatologist. Now it would be interesting indeed to see what Martin Higgins in Chicago could come up with. Circumstances being what they were, I had been lucky to catch Mrs. Beck at home. The old ticker was racing again and seemed to skip a beat now and then. Nerves and lack of sleep—that combination will do it every time. That and anticipation.

I followed Powder Mill Road toward Maynard and pulled over onto the shoulder right near the old Powder Mill, which manufactured gunpowder for the Union troops in the Civil War. The Boston & Maine tracks were right next to it. It was not only what Howard March had told me that was making me look here, but Emil's mention of railroad tracks as well. Taken together, these references couldn't be ignored. And since I would not notify Chet or Joe about any of this until after I'd heard from Higgins, I had almost twenty-four hours to go looking on my own for some connection.

I left the locked car and hoofed it up the embankment to the right-of-way. The tracks were old but pretty well maintained. The rock ballast was packed down tight between the ties and was just about level with them, which made walking between the rails down the center of the eastbound track almost a breeze. The rail tops wore wide, shiny bands on top of them, which told of their frequent use. The oak and crushed rock that I was using as a footpath was stained with oil and grease. I kept my eyes moving, trying to notice anything interesting or unusual along the right-of-way. I saw nothing but woods and an occasional signal gantry above me. Twice I crossed small bridges with lots of steel latticework overhead, spanning lazy brown streams twenty feet below. I walked at a speed of four miles per hour, so after fifteen minutes of strolling, I knew there wasn't anything of interest—that was noticeable, anyway—on the first mile of track.

But how could I be sure I was following the correct line? I couldn't, of course. I was pretty certain, however, that the line out of Lexington wasn't the right one—even though it was obviously closer to the lab and more convenient than this line—because it swerved north out of town and headed up to Billerica, then to Lowell, then across the line to Nashua, New Hampshire. That wasn't the way to Colorado. And most of the lines south of the one through Concord tended to dip down toward New York, New Jersey, and the Atlantic seaboard. No, this line seemed a good bet, especially since Emil Haszmanay had chosen to station himself near it.

The second mile took me fully out of town and through marshland and bogs bordered by woods. In any case, there didn't seem to be anything that suggested a loading area. There were some sidings, but no ramps or platforms at the track level.

But starting on the third mile, as I approached the town of South Acton, I saw many possibilities. There were a lot of sidespurs of track, for one thing, as there always are in towns. There was the old depot, which was still used as a commuter stop for the passenger trains that ran in rush hour. Concord has one too, right on Thoreau Street. There were several sidings that drifted past warehouses and old buildings that had once been factories. All these were possibilities, but not probabilities.

But just on the far edge of town, standing all by itself, was a long siding spur that bordered on woods. I assumed the B&M had put it there to shunt slow freights off the main line so that faster express trains could pass them. An earthen ramp led up to the siding. This was nothing unusual. What was unusual, I thought as I ambled past, watching the place out of the corner of my eye, was the work detail of six men with spades and rakes, and the bulldozer with the pusher blade shoring up the ramp. It caught my eye not just because of its isolated location but because both the work detail and the bulldozer seemed peculiarly idle. I stopped and stared at the men. They stared back. Behind them, past the big bulldozer and the road through the trees, was a van with its side door slid open. The work crew had been driven out to the site in it. I was glad I had seen the van, because I noted that on its front door were the letters GTE.

I walked on. Twice I looked back and saw the men staring at me. All of them. A van with an idle work crew in the middle of nowhere? Gee . . . I thought.

"No." I said aloud. *"Gee Tee Eee."*

On the track ahead of me a dark squarish blob with an undulating bright light in its middle told me to get off the eastbound track and stand clear. I did. The blob grew slowly larger and more distinct. As it drew closer I could see it rocking slightly, back and forth, a plume of oily smoke purring out the top. The air above the shape shimmied and danced. Heat waves. The noise the shape was making grew more distinct, too: a brassy rumble of high-compression diesel pistons as wide as bowling balls. It was moving slowly; I knew it was a freight. Pretty soon the big diesel crawled by me, painted the bright blue of the B&M line and sweating noise and heat. Big fans on its top blew hot air upward in geysers of waves and wiggles. You couldn't think for the racket. A thin gray man in glasses wearing a puffy, pleated engineer's cap with a long bill leaned out the open window of the locomotive's cab. He was perched up there higher than a basketball net. He must've had a great view. Dammit, it looked like fun. He squinted at me briefly and gave a short wave. As the engine passed me I heard the massive *thunk* . . . ka bump . . . *thunk* . . . ka bump of the huge wheels, shiny bright on their rims, dirty and grease-caked everywhere else. I watched the rails give way and compress onto the ties as each locomotive wheel passed over. Then came the freight cars, bouncing along hollow-light with a faint chuckle and click of the couplings over the reedy, ear-tickling screech of metal. But over it all came the steady click and clack of the truck wheels, in pairs, slipping over the rail junctures. They sang a little song. They sang a song of Mary and Joe's hometown: *Sch-nec-ta-dy . . . Sch-nec-ta-dy . . . Sch-nec-ta-dy . . . Sch-nec-ta-day . . .*

As powerful and dramatic as trains are, few people pay any attention to them anymore. Most young people now have never even ridden on one. Damn shame. I stared nostalgically at the departing freight as it grew smaller and quieter in between the green walls of woods. It was, in the jet age, a dinosaur, limping its way into extinction. But this was why the plan for ARGUS was a good one. Who would think a top-secret defense mechanism would ride such an archaic monster? A slow, frumpy, multi-colored caravan that squeaked and bumped its way west? A crazy-quilt jalopy, that made motorists wait at flashing wooden poles until it crawled past? Perfect.

I walked another two miles up the line. While I saw many possibilities, none were as isolated and promising as the one right on the edge of South Acton. I turned around and walked the westbound track toward home. I walked fast now, stretching my legs out and pumping my feet. Before long I could see the lonely stretch of straight track and the siding with its wide, earthern ramp. But the work crew appeared to be gone. When I was abreast of the siding, I left the right-of-way, walked over to it, and had a close look at the ramp. The work crew had not been entirely idle; it had widened the ramp and raised it. This was apparent from the freshly packed earth. I walked down it and onto the gravel-topped approach road that led out of the thick woods lining the right-of-way. The unpaved road, wide enough for a big truck, curved to the left, then swung softly to the right, straightened out, and headed off to join a highway. I sat down on the gravel and rested my legs. There was a marsh off to the right, and red-winged blackbirds clung crooked-legged to the upright cattails and marsh grass, swinging on the slender stalks and singing *konk-ta-reeeeeeee . . . check! check! . . . konk-ta-reeeeeeee!*

I watched the glossy black birds with their bright orange-red epaulets, feeling positively dismal. I was very alone now. As alone as the keeper of a wave-washed lighthouse. I didn't know whom I could trust—completely. Well, I knew three people: Mary, Joe, and Emil. But one of them was dead now, so that left two. What about the others? Chet was too conventional, the corporate guy with the corporate line. Vic Hamisch and his cloak-and-dagger crowd, with the Ivy League sheepskins and the worsted suits, gave me the creeps. He would have given me the creeps even if I hadn't known of Emil's suspicions. Howard March? Yeah, I guess I trusted him. I guess, things being what they were, I bloody well had to. And I trusted Martin Higgins, of course. The well-connected old Adams family friend. It would be interesting to see what he had to tell me.

But other than a few skinny leads, some vague hunches, and a great deal of fear and suspicion, I had little to go on.

"Hey!" I asked the birds. "What should I do now, you guys? Huh? Whadduyuh say?"

But they paid no attention; they continued to swing on the marshy stalks, thrashing their tails and fluffing their wings. Ignorance is bliss.

I left the place and headed back. Behind me I could still hear them.

Konk-to-reeeeee . . . check! check! check! . . . konk-ta-reeeee!

27

WHEN I GOT BACK TO THE CAR IT WAS ALMOST TWO. I WAS dog-tired already. I hadn't had much sleep, and the knowledge of what was to come seemed to work on me by suggestion. I drove to the center of town and stood there in front of the phones, in the shadow of the Civil War obelisk, trying to punch in my credit-card number after the tone sounded. It was difficult with all the pedestrian traffic, but I managed. Martin Higgins wasn't home. Damn! If I didn't hear from him by tomorrow evening, I would have to play it on a hunch, which would be dangerous, to say the least.

I hung up and then called DeGroots'. Janice answered.

"Can you tell me what's up? What the hell's going on, Doc? Jeez, Mary's sitting here gulping coffee and twitching like she's—hey!"

"Charlie! Where are you? What's happening? Anything?"

"Gee, Mare. Kind of rude to just yank the phone away from her like that—"

"You don't get over here pronto, I'll show you rude. Where are you?"

"Concord Center. At the phone booths."

"Well, you get right over here and—"

"Can't. I could be followed. Just stay there. Stay there, dammit, and don't go out. Where's Jim? Is he around?"

"Janice says he's on some deal up in Nashua. He's going to call here soon to find out what's happening."

"Good. Now, listen: when he does, you tell him to come home as soon as possible and stay with you both with the doors locked. I'll be in touch."

"Where are you going now?"

"To eat. I'm starved. And Mary?"

"What?"

"Don't talk to Joe. And don't tell the DeGroots anything. I'll come by this evening and fill you in on what's been happening. Goodbye."

Well, I figured they were safe for the time being, anyway. Jim could always take out his twenty-gauge and sit with them until things clarified. One thing: I did *not* want Mary at home. Also, I thought as I went back to the car, I shouldn't return home either. I drove to the police station. Up on the second floor I rapped on Brian's door.

"Who is it?"

"It's me, Doc."

I heard the ruffle of newspaper and the slamming of a drawer, then footsteps. He let me in, and we went over to his desk, where he sat down with a tired groan. He didn't offer me a chair.

"What is it? I'm pretty busy today. Hell, I had to put in overtime last night writing the column."

The column to which he was referring is "Police Blotter," which appears in the *Concord Journal*, the local weekly. Described therein are the heinous and grisly crimes that Brian and staff must continually deal with. Crimes such as: kids drinking beer in the Stop & Shop parking lot. Kids drag racing on Strawberry Hill Road. Shoplifting at the Tricorn Gift Shoppe. Kids drinking beer and parking for sexual reasons in the Great Meadows Wildlife Refuge. Shoplifting at the Johnny Tremaine Gift Shop. Burglars absconding with handfuls of ice and pearls from the mansions on Nahsawtuc Hill and Monument Street. Et cetera.

"It's tough, wearing a badge in Concord," I said, looking down at him. He was in his shirt sleeves, lighting up a Lucky.

"You said it, pal," he replied, dangling the ciggie from his lip and letting it flip up and down as he spoke through clouds. I had a hunch Brian was cultivating his "gumshoe" look. Next he'd add the fedora and a cradle phone. "Speaking of which, just the other day hadda patrolman disabled—"

"Upset tummy again, or that hangnail problem?"

He looked up at me, frowning, then slowly removed the cigarette and tapped it on the dirty ashtray that rested on his blotter. The smoke dribbled out his nostrils; he looked like a dragon in heat.

"Real funny, butt-wipe. So happens the guy's got a compound fracture."

"Well, I'm sorry. And Brian, I wish you wouldn't refer to me as 'butt-wipe.' Some people might consider it pejorative."

"What do you *want*, anyway?"

"I need your help on something very important."

"Well, you're not very good at going about it; you always seem to rub me the wrong way."

"I've never laid a hand on you."

He requested my departure. I went back to the doorway.

"Will you be here, or somewhere else I can reach you, later on this afternoon?"

"I will be here, Doc. Right here. After that, I'll be home. You know how to get me at either place. Okay?"

"Fine," I said, and opened the door. I heard the rustle of newspaper behind me. I knew what it was. He'd hidden it before I came in.

"Doc?"

"Hmm?"

"Uh, having some trouble here. This one's a bitch. What's an eight-letter word for sword?"

I thought a second. "Claymore."

"Shit! How'd you know that?"

"Why don't you come to lunch with me and find out? I'll buy you a clam roll at Friendly's."

"Already ate; it's two-thirty, for Gawd's sake. You're buying, eh? All right—"

We left the station, got into my car, and headed down to Friendly's. But it was crowded, so Brian suggested we go to the Willow Pond Kitchen out on 2A.

"Isn't that kind of a biker joint?" I asked.

"Yeah, but the food's pretty good, and it's got atmosphere. You like atmosphere, right?"

"Love it. Breathe it every day. Or do you mean *ambiance*?"

"I mean shove it up your ass."

"What's the theme? 'Great Harleys I have known'?"

"Don't be so huffy; you're a biker yourself."

"People who ride BMWs aren't bikers, Brian; they're motorcyclists."

The Willow Pond was just as I remembered it—basically a bar in a roadside building in the country with rafters strung with old muskets and farm tools and hunting trophies of the moth-eaten variety. It was practically empty; the lunch crowd had left and the after-work drinkers wouldn't appear for several more hours. We took a varnished pine booth in back near a window. We had settled down to our clam chowder when I excused myself and went over to the pay phone. I dialed Chicago. Nobody home at Martin's house in Evanston. Damn. Called the *Tribune*, where he still keeps a downtown office. No answer there, either. Goddammit. Had he forgotten? He's getting on in years, I thought. Had I failed to stress the urgency enough, and he'd just forgotten the little favor? My hands were sweating. A trickle of sweat slid down the side of my rib cage. When I returned to the table, my chowder was cold, our cheeseburgers had arrived, and Brian was busy tucking into his.

"Thouh eww dnmm eee lunth!" he said.

"What?"

He gulped a huge swallow.

"I said I thought you didn't eat lunch," he repeated. "What's going on."

"Well, I didn't have any breakfast, and today hasn't exactly been normal."

"What kind of help you want?"

"I want you to help me catch a spy and a murderer."

His jaw stopped moving. "Seriously?" he said.

"Seriously. Will you help? I can't call on Joe. Or Chet. I think it's you or nobody. Well?"

"Tell me all about it. Quietly."

"Not here. And not now. I don't have all the pieces quite together yet. By this evening I should have a clearer picture. Then I'd like to come over to your place and explain everything."

"This is about the Haszmanay business, isn't it?"

"What else could it be?"

"Has he been murdered?"

I waved the question off with my hands.

"I told you, I'll know more tonight."

"Listen, Doc: you better come clean with me right now. I know a little of how your mind works. I've seen enough to know it's not normal. You better come clean or—"

"Save it, Brian," I said, holding up my hand. "Just save the lecture, all right? Just trust me for now, and you'll be a hero. Now, I want to ask for two things. One: can you sweep my car for bugs? Do you have the equipment?"

"No. We're too small. But Joe—"

"Forget Joe. Remember? I told you Joe can't be involved."

"Dangerous, huh?"

"Not that. There are reasons that you'll soon know."

"I can get an electronic bug-finder. That what you want?"

"Yes. And, two: can you get a good pair of long-range walkie-talkies?"

"We got those."

"Long-range? I mean, this won't be the meter-reading calling the station house; this is three, four, maybe ten miles."

"We got 'em. What do you want them for?"

"To talk to you."

He nodded and sipped his coffee. I began to see he was taking this thing seriously.

We finished up, I paid the tab, and we went back to the

station. I followed Brian up to his office and asked him to call the Acton police chief.

"Why?"

"Do you know him pretty well?"

"Very well. Jim Borum and I are friends, in fact. So I'm not anxious to ruin the friendship."

"Just ask him if he's heard anything at all about repairs on a railroad loading ramp west of town. GTE's doing the work. You could say that a friend of yours is interested in a real-estate deal nearby and doesn't want a lot of traffic around there. Say he's curious about the possible traffic. Make the inquiry real casual."

"What the hell's this all—"

"Just do it, Brian. Please. I'll tell you everything later. You're not breaking any ordinances, for Chrissakes."

He made the call. Chief James Borum had not heard doodly-squat about any ramp near any railroad. But he did tell Brian that his friend shouldn't worry about a lot of traffic, road or rail. Brian then told me that Jim's reputation was very good; if there were anything fishy going on, he'd know about it. I thanked Brian and left, saying I'd be in touch within hours.

"Just don't go *anywhere*, Brian. I mean it." I looked down at the crossword puzzle. Hell, no problem about his leaving; there were tons of blank squares left. Tons.

Back to the pay phones again. Called Howard March's office, gave a false name and reminded him of our golf date, and left the pay phone number. Eight minutes later it rang, and he was on the line.

"What do you know about GTE around here? Do they maintain a railroad spur and loading ramp near Acton?"

Silence.

"Howard? Howard, you still on?"

"Yes."

"Well, have you heard anything? Anything. Even something that sounded unimportant at the—"

"Did you say GTE?"

"Yes. You know, General Telephone."

"Jesus, how did you know?"

"What do you mean?"

"The last time we moved something big, GTE helped us out. We used their vehicles and uniforms. The men were ours—"

"Thank you, Howard. Thank you very, very much. Sit tight."

"But how the hell did you find out?"

"Legwork."

28

I FELT A SHAKING AND A PULLING AT MY SHOULDER. I opened my eyes in the dim light to see Brian Hannon standing over me.

"Jesus, Doc. You dozed off again. You're real tired."

"Yeah . . . ," I said, rubbing my eyes. I could see the Scout descending off the hydraulic lift with a soft, steady hiss of escaping compressed air. I was sitting on a cushion on an old plastic milk crate against the wall of the town garage. It was warm in there, and the lights weren't bright, since it was after hours. I heard the squeak and clunk of tools, the hiss of air, and the *rrrrrrrrr-rrrreeeeeeeeeeeowww!* of air wrenches. Two overtime mechanics were working to get important town vehicles back on their feet. The sounds seemed to soothe my troubled soul; no wonder I'd caught a little uneasy shuteye. God, I was tired. Actually, I was sick and tired, just like Chet. My eyes wandered around the dim garage. There were squad cars, scooters for the meter-readers, and a fire department pumper truck in there. They were sick vehicles, getting fixed. My car wasn't sick, but I'd had the strange feeling it was loaded.

One of the mechanics came up to us and stuck out his hand, black with grime. Resting on the palm was a little RDF device, just like the one Joe and his men had found earlier.

''Bumper beeper, right?'' I asked.

He nodded and held up the sweeper device in his other hand.

''Somebody really wantsta follow you,'' he said.

''I'm afraid they already did. Where'd you find it? I looked under the car a couple times, but I couldn't—''

''Naw. You couldn't nevah have found it by just lookin','' he said, spitting on the floor. ''Wheah it was, it was way up onna side of the gas tank . . . only way to find it was with a sweepah. . . .''

Brian picked up the device and turned it around and around in his hands, frowning. ''Shit,'' he said, as if that settled it.

''Can you guys find out what frequency it's set for? I mean, could we rig it up so we could use it?'' I asked.

''I don't know,'' said Brian. ''But I could ask. By the way, Doc, it's nine-thirty. When the hell are we gonna have our little talk?''

''Soon. Listen, you find out about rigging this direction-finder so we can use it. Also get those walkie-talkies ready. Wait at your house, and I'll be back there a little after midnight.''

''So where the hell are you going?''

''To see Mary for a while over at DeGroots'. Bye—and thanks, you guys.''

It took me forty minutes to get to the back door of DeGroots'. I drove a circuitous route, parked almost a mile away, and walked through woods and back yards to their house. Mary hugged me hard, cried, cussed, threatened to beat the shit out of me for not calling, hugged me hard, cried, cussed, etc. Like a tape playing over and over. Finally she settled down, and we sat on the grass. I told her what the situation was. She didn't like it. Especially the part about not hearing from Martin Higgins.

''And then what?''

''And then call the cops. Then, but not before.''

''And you won't . . . you wouldn't call them now . . .''

''I won't call them now because I want to catch the rat in the net. Brian's going to help me.''

"Well, how about that other guy, the guy in the car? You wouldn't call him either?"

"Vic Hamisch? Honey, I said there's a rat. Emil was sure of it. That's why he played it so close to the vest. The way we're going to do it is the way it's got to be."

We sat there, then we kissed, then we lay down together. Then I felt her legs around mine. I told her I couldn't.

"Can't now, Mary. I'm too wound up. All my energies are directed at this thing. Hell, I can't even sleep."

"You're not going to be in direct danger?"

"Uh-uh. Don't worry; Brian will be right there. All I'm going to do is hide in the bushes with the walkie-talkie and tell them what to do.

"When are you going to tell Brian about Emil? Jeez, Charlie, it's so horrible just to leave him down there under the gate like that. . . ."

"It's not that horrible, Mary. I'm sure Emil's feeling no pain. It's like he's buried at sea. Sure, I'd like to get him out. But when Brian finds out, he's going to want to act on it. He'll storm on down to the pond with a crew and ambulance and . . . well, it might alert whoever killed him. I'd just like to wait until the last minute on that. Look, I've got to get going and get some sleep."

"Where will you be tomorrow?"

"With Brian or at the office. I'm going home briefly tomorrow to feed the dogs and—"

"Not alone!"

"No. Brian and a car will be with me. Although there's probably no need. I just put you here to be extra, extra sure. Where's Jim going tomorrow?"

"He said he'd stay if you really wanted. But this deal up in Nashua is very important, so he'd like to go on up—"

"Good! That's good. Let him take the two of you with him for the day. Great."

"Really?"

"Sure. Now, bye."

I kissed her, and she made me explain one more time how I would guard my safety. This I did, and then I led her to the back door.

"Gee, Charlie. This reminds of the summer we met at Cornell. Remember when we used to lie out on the grass at night? Then you'd take me back to the dorm?"

"Yep. Seems like yesterday."

"Like yesterday, and a thousand years ago, too."

I kissed her one last time and hiked back to the car. On my way through the center of town to Brian's house, I stopped at the liquor store and bought a half-pint bottle of Beefeater's and a quart of tonic, since I knew Brian wouldn't have any booze at his place. I arrived at his modest frame house on Brister's Hill Road at just before midnight. He was sitting up watching the late news with a mug of java. As soon as I came in he flipped off the tube, swiveled around in his chair, and gave me his strongest "I am the law" look.

"All right, Doc. The bullshit's over. We're having our little talk right now, and you're going to tell me everything, aren't you?"

"Oh, all right. If you really insist," I said, pouring a record G&T. I took the tall drink and sat opposite him.

"Where'd you get the Loudmouth?" he asked, looking at the drink.

"The booze? At the store. I knew you wouldn't have any. I'm going to get into sleep fast tonight and stay asleep until you wake me in the morning. Loudmouth? Where'd you get that name for it? I call it the Destroyer."

"Same difference. Bogie used to call it Loudmouth. Well, just don't leave it here; I don't want to get tempted and then wake up next month in a flophouse in Bayonne."

"Don't worry. Okay, I'll make you a deal: if I tell you where to find a corpse, will you promise not to go get it until tomorrow evening?"

"Get serious, Doc. C'mon, it's late, for cry'n' out loud—"

"Then forget it. Did you find out about the beeper?"

"Uh-huh. We can use it if we want. Do we want?"

"Yes. I've got a rather tricky assignment for you. I want you to affix that beeper to Chet Harwood's car."

"What?"

"Affix it to his car sometime tonight before daylight."

"Why?"

"Because I want to see where he goes between now and Thursday morning."

"You mean you suspect *him*? C'mon!"

"Well, I suppose I suspect everyone in the government after what Emil told me. Especially the people in the CIA. But there's a specific reason for keeping tabs on Chet. I want to know where he goes Thursday morning. He told Joe and me he would be his own flying squad; that he'd go wherever he thought the action would be, based on last-minute developments. Now, if he stays near Brandeis, it will mean he doesn't know about the real event. If, on the other hand, he comes out toward Acton, it will tell me he knows—that the brass at Lincoln Labs have filled him in."

"Doc? What in the holy jumpin' Jesus are you talking about?"

"Yeah . . . ," I sighed, "I guess it won't work with you in the dark, will it? I can't ask for your help without telling you everything, much as I hate to. . . ."

I went back into the kitchen and poured him more coffee, freshened up my drink, and went back to him, running my hands through my hair. Decisions, decisions . . .

"Okay, Brian, here goes. I'm telling you more, and trusting you more completely, than Joe, Chet, or anybody else. But you've simply got to do it my way. In a sense, you've got to promise me you'll follow my orders. Okay?"

He shook his head. "Look: I know it must be important. But as a police chief, how can I place myself in that position? Tell you what: I'll do everything that's humanly possible—make that inhumanly possible—to go along with your scheme, provided it breaks no laws and provided you can convince me it's the only way to go. Otherwise, I'd be derelict in my duty. How's that? It's the best I can do."

"So you're saying if I tell you all now you'll do your best to go along with me?"

He nodded again, sipping coffee. "Now, let's get going, Doc. For Chrissakes, it's almost one. If we're going to be at our best in this caper, let's get started!"

I realized he had leveled with me, and that I really had no

choice. So, feeling I was placing my neck on a well-worn chopping block, I took a deep breath and told Brian Hannon every little last detail from the time Emil Haszmanay dropped into my cellar, and my life, like a sack of coal, until he dropped out of it, sliding slowly in the whirl of gear-works into the icy pond. And, of course, I told him everything that had happened since as well.

Throughout the narrative, he listened, spellbound, not daring to believe it. But then I got the surprise of my life.

Chief Brian Hannon—crusty, belligerent, defensive, irritable, and sarcastic Brian Hannon—said he'd cooperate completely.

I sighed with relief, knowing I was getting some real help without having to tell Joe and Company. Especially, not *Company*. I drained the last of the drink and got up off the sofa. I made my way toward the stairs, legs a bit wobbly from fatigue. As I lurched up the stairs to the spare bedroom, I could faintly hear Brian's voice on the phone.

"—that's right, tonight. A plainclothes operation, unmarked car, and I want . . . uh . . . I want an electronics guy—yeah, get Edwin. Right. Well, goddammit, wake him up! Have him call me here if necessary. Uh-huh . . . well, when he finds out how important it is, and—screw the jurisdiction, Frank. I'll take responsibility. Thing is, we need it *now*—"

Good old Brian, I thought as I crawled between the sheets. Now if only, if *only* I can hear from Martin tomorrow. . . .

29

I WOKE BRIAN AT FIVE-THIRTY. HE WAS UP, DRESSED, AND inhaling cigarette and coffee lickety-split. He didn't say a damn thing, which told me how much the upcoming events weighed on him.

"If I were you, I wouldn't make any more important calls from this house or the station," I said, pouring more java for both of us. The day was bright and sunny, October twenty-seventh, and the birds and squirrels jumped about and chatted outside the kitchen window. Bright rays of sun shot between the curtains and speckled the blue gingham oilcloth on the table. Brian stirred his coffee and grunted, lighting another Lucky.

"Reason is," I reminded him, "remember what happened at my house? Hell, doesn't take these characters long to wire anyplace they choose."

"Ummmmf! Good idea. Shit. I've got to check on the job Edwin did over in—"

He saw my hand over my mouth, and sipped nervously.

"Call Edwin at home from a pay phone, or a friend's," I whispered. He nodded back.

He leaned over and whispered very softly: "When the hell you gonna hear from the Chicago connection?"

"Don't know," I whispered back, scarcely able to hear

myself. "Before noon, I hope." He half nodded and looked blankly at the wall, like somebody in a Hemingway novel. Doubt and anxiety were written all over his face. I hated to think what mine looked like.

We left his house and drove in two cars to mine, where I fed and watered the dogs in their runs. They wagged their tails tentatively, muzzled and licked me cautiously, whining softly. Dogs always know. They can always tell when something's up. Then I went inside quickly and got a warmer jacket, a change of clothes, running shoes, binoculars, my Browning, and other overnight stuff, which I stowed in Brian's car. All but the Browning, which I tucked into my windbreaker. I set all the alarms, locked the house up tight, and followed Brian back into town. He split off for the station to get an early start, and I headed over to DeGroots', where I rang the doorbell enough times to wake everybody up.

"You mind telling me what the hell's going on?" asked Jim, blinking awake on his stoop in his bathrobe. "I mean, is anybody gonna come tearing down my door, or what?"

"No. It's just that I'll feel safer with Mary out of town for the next day or so. Can you take her and Janice with you up to Nashua?"

"Yeah. But then we had a better idea. The two of 'em are gonna drive up to the cottage."

The DeGroot cottage was up near Wolfsboro, New Hampshire, on Lake Winnepesaukee. It was a perfectly remote spot.

"Hey, great! That couldn't be better. When will they leave?"

"Well, thanks to you, Doc, sooner than we'd planned. They're already packed, and they're gonna eat breakfast on the road. So I guess as soon as they dress, they'll leave."

I went in and said goodbye to Mary again. She was too sleepy to be emotional. I had more coffee and waited for them to get into Janice's car, then saw them off.

"I'll call you tonight, honey," I said, kissing her. "Have a good time and don't worry."

She frowned at me as they backed out the drive, then blew a kiss.

Back to the pay phones near the village green again. Stood there, in the early morning chill, punching in my credit card number, then listening to the woman's mechanical voice. "Thaaank Youuu for using AT and T," she said. Phone rang and rang. Nobody home in Evanston. I looked at my watch; it said quarter to eight. What? Nobody home at quarter to seven? What the hell was—

I did the routine again, calling the *Tribune*. I knew they never slept. Phone rang and rang and rang. I let it ring. I was going to let the damn thing ring until hell froze over. Finally, a tired female voice answered.

"Martin Higgins? He hasn't been in his office for the past two days. I believe he's out of town."

"Out of town? OUT OF TOWN?

"Are you still there?" she asked.

"Yeeesss . . . ," I replied wearily. "Look, this is something really important. I've got to know where I can reach Mr. Higgins. This is an old family friend—"

"Oh, wait. Are you, uh, Dr. Charles Adams?"

The old ticker jumped and twitched.

"Yes! Yes, indeed I am! I am him. I am he—I—"

"Okay. Sorry. He's left a note here for you. Ready?"

"Yes. Yes, yes, yes—"

"Okay, here it is: *Doc, your lead is hot. Urgent go to Virginia to follow in person. Will phone details afternoon of ten-twenty-seven. Hang on. Our Country 'tis of Thee. Best, Martin.*"

There was a pause while I recovered from this barrage from afar.

"Dr. Adams? You still there?"

"Uh, yes. Would you mind reading that to me again, please?"

So she did. I rubbed my eyes and squinted at the Civil War obelisk on the green.

"Well?"

"Uh, thank you. May I ask your name?"

"Harriet Moore. I work the graveyard shift, and I keep messages for Mr. Higgins."

"Well thanks, Harriet. But there's a problem. I won't be

in my office today, or at home. So I'm wondering where Martin's going to call me. Did he leave an address in Virginia, or anyplace he would be staying?''

''No. Sorry.''

''Well, then I can't call him,'' I sighed.

My God, I thought, so near and yet so far. . . . Martin would call this afternoon and wouldn't be able to reach me. I thought and thought. Where was a phone where he could leave a message? I looked around. The drugstore? There were two, right across the street from one another: Richardson's and Snow's. I knew the pharmacists at both. They would be by the phones all day—

''Hello! Hel—*lo*-ohh! Dr. Adams?''

''Still here, Harriet. I'm just thinking . . .''

''Thought we lost you for a minute.''

—but the drugstores were crowded. I needed a phone in a quiet place, near the center of town, with someone I could absolutely trust. Who would be there all day. . . . My mind went through every building on the green. Town hall, insurance company . . . Colonial Inn. Colonial Inn? No, too crowded. . . .

''Harriet! Harriet? I've got a number for you. . . .'' I took out my wallet and flipped through it. ''When Mr. Higgins calls, tell him to please leave his message, as brief as possible, with Mrs. Sarah Heeney at St. Bernard's Rectory.''

''Rectory? Like a church? Mrs. what? Heeney?''

''Right. And if she doesn't answer, one of the priests will. Just have him leave the message so they write it down, and I'll pick it up.''

So I read off the number from the card in my wallet, thanked her, and hung up. Well, I knew this much: my earlier hunch had set the gears in motion, at least; Higgins's message saying that my ''lead was hot'' showed that. Question was, how close was I? My watch said 8:05. Jeez, like waiting for Christmas. I stood away from the phone booth—pardon me, phone *enclave*, as they call those miserable aluminum half-shells that you lean into—and felt the world sway slightly. Was I sick? No, just drunk on adrenalin. I sat down on the bench and breathed deeply. I waited almost ten minutes until the rush passed, then headed over to the police station. Brian would be needing help on the daily crossword.

But Brian hadn't even opened the paper; he was too busy. As soon as he saw me he motioned me over with waves of his arm. He was chain-smoking, too. I could tell by the bus-station aroma of the office and the nauseating gray and white mound in his ashtray.

"Harwood's on his way to Brandeis," he said gleefully. "I just got a call from Eric Demmon, one of our undercover guys. He's following the signals from the bumper beeper Jim Edwin placed on Chet's car last night. Thing works like downtown; we can track him anywhere."

"I must admit it feels kinda good snooping on the chief snooper. I like turning the tables once in a while. But Brian, how much did you tell these guys about what we're doing?"

"Demmon was simply told to follow Harwood because we want him to lead us to a suspect. It's a bullshit story, I know, but Eric was glad to get something away from the routine, so he didn't say boo. I just told him to stay out of sight and be cautious—that we could get into a lot of heat following the Feds. But don't worry, he's good; we've used him on a lot of drug busts. He knows how to stay out of sight."

"How about Jim Edwin? What did he think about wiring a Fed's car?"

He shrugged his stocky shoulders and lit up. "Not much, Doc. In fact, I think he liked it. Ed's not the kind to let moral imperatives interfere with his work."

"No moral imperatives, eh? Sounds like the perfect cop."

"Uh-huh. Or politician. Or lawyer. . . ."

"Well they better keep totally *mum* for the next twenty-four hours."

He nodded in assurance, then leaned over the desk, lowering his voice to a soft whisper. "Listen: late this afternoon, I'm sending a quiet squad out to the millpond to resurrect you-know-who."

"Shit, Brian. Can't you wait until Friday? I mean, we seem so close on this thing—"

"Don't worry. Three men in a police van. No flashing lights. Just a folding litter. One will take pictures and dust."

I paced up and down his spacious office, looking outside. The sun was bright, the wee animals still cheerful. But what did they know?

"What about your friend Higgins?" he asked. I told him.

"Well, Sarah Heeney's the one we got to worry about. Good God, she'll be on the phone telling everybody in five seconds."

"I'm trusting Martin's brains and discretion. Sarah won't think the message is that important. And I'm going to check on her constantly, so she won't have it in her hands for long."

"Good, then. I guess all we have to do now is wait."

"Uh-huh. The worst thing of all."

Since I can't stand waiting, I decided to go to the office until lunchtime. I told Brian I'd check in with him by pay phone to see what Harwood was up to.

"But the real test to see if the FBI knows the truth about tomorrow will be what Chet does early in the morning," he said.

"Uh-huh. Whether he heads east or west. . . ."

"Gee, Doc, you're playing worse than usual this morning."

"Which is poor indeed."

"Well . . . you said it; I didn't," answered Moe. "By the way, what's on your mind?"

"Huh? Nothing's on my mind."

"Oh, the hell it isn't. Whadduyuh think I am, a dummy?"

"You said it; I didn't."

"I can't tell you. But it'll pass."

He leaned over the chessboard, a sagacious look on his thin, bearded face. He talked in a very low voice.

"Does it have anything to do wid, uh . . . some of the strange occurrences of late? Know what I mean?"

"Never mind."

He resumed playing and took my rook.

"Whatever it is, don't do it," he said.

"Whatever what is? Don't do what?"

"You know. Whatever it is. Whatever scheme you're considering. Don't do it."

"You're nuts, Moe. How you make your living untangling people's troubled minds is beyond me."

"Takes one to know one. Don't do it. I don't wanna see you hurt."

"Well, I won't get hurt. I don't think."

"I can tell it's dangerous."

"How do you know all this?"

"I just do. I know it for the same reason I always beat you at chess."

True to his word, he beat me again. He really whipped me because my thinking was off. He wiped my ass all over the board. But I guess I didn't care. I set up the board again and walked over to the door. Moe, who'd remained ominously silent during the final phases of the game—make that the slaughter—now rose to his feet and pointed at me, shouting.

"All right, Doc! *Dats it*! You walk outa here and I'm gonna call Mary! I'm telling her what you're up to! I mean it!"

There it was, the ultimate threat. And then I knew Moe wasn't faking it. He was shaking like a leaf, and about to cry.

"You can't; I sent her out of town," I said in a soft voice. "But don't worry, nothing bad's going to happen. See you later."

I left the building, thrown even further off kilter by Morris Abramson. He affects me in strange ways sometimes. What a sap. A bleeding-heart sap. I don't know why I ever listen to him.

I made the call to Sarah Heeney from the pay phone outside the Concord Professional Building. She told me to come on over to the rectory.

"Don't you want some of my Irish soda bread while you're reading it, Dr. Adams?" she asked, leaning crickety-old over the kitchen table with her white frilly apron on. I smelled brewing tea along with the hot bread in the high-ceilinged room. I looked down at the envelope she'd handed me. I tore it open. Inside was a three-sentence message from Martin Higgins. Though it would have seemed unimportant to the casual reader, it rang our loud and clear to me.

Jackpot.

I leaned over and kissed a shocked Sarah Heeney on the cheek, scooped up a handful of her warm soda bread, and hightailed it over to Brian's office.

30

THE REST OF THE AFTERNOON WAS SPENT IN THE HOME OF Claire Montgomery, a neighbor and friend of Brian's who lived three houses down the street. We wanted to be sure of a safe phone. So Brian spent almost the entire time on the horn, calling various law-enforcement agencies and appropriate people, including many who worked for the Boston & Maine Railroad. Never a model of efficiency, in recent years, the railroad, in all its branches, offices, and manifestations, admirably lived up to this reputation.

''*Sonofabitch!*'' Brian growled as he slammed down the phone and turned to me. ''Problem is, they want higher authority. My word isn't enough. They want some big shot, like the governor, to tell them.''

''Well, we might have to contact him if it comes to that,'' I said. ''You know any chiefs of police in towns further out on the line? Maybe we could contact them and have them deal with it.''

''Hey, that's a good idea. I'm surprised at you, Doc. Yeah, I know most of them, in fact. Besides Jim Borum in Acton, I know the chiefs in Fitchburg, uh, Leominster, Gardner, and Greenfield. Maybe more.''

''Okay, screw the railroad then. Call these guys, one by one, and fill them in on the basics. That way, if they know the problem we're all up against, they'll understand why we can't blab it to the state guys or the Feds. I know it's risky, but time is short now; any leaks they may cause won't have major effects. Just tell them what we want done and that you'll be on the radio or the phone tomorrow to tell them which train it is and roughly when it'll pass through their jurisdictions. More than that we can't do."

"Right."

"And also ask them to have their men inspect the right-of-ways. Nothing too obvious, just casually. Have them be on the lookout for anything suspicious, especially something big or heavy that could stop a train."

So he got back on the blower, pumping the dial until I thought it would fall off. One of the men he called, an assistant chief in Gardner, had a brother who was a long-timer with the B&M. He promised us full cooperation. I felt a lot better after that.

We ate dinner at a restaurant called A Different Drummer in the old depot building on Thoreau Street. The food was excellent. And although I wasn't very hungry, I made myself eat a lot. But I can't remember what I ate. I picked up the tab, and we went back to Brian's house for the night. We sat in the kitchen. He fidgeted as he smoked. God, I wished the thing were over, if for no other reason than to escape the continual cigarette smoke. We tried to play cards, but our hearts weren't in it. We attempted television. No go. I said I wanted to go out and call Mary, and he wanted to come along.

"What are those for, Doc? You need binoculars to talk to Mary? You using semaphore, or what?"

"No. I want to cruise by Lincoln Labs late tonight and see what's going on there."

He smacked his fist into his palm a few times, considering it. Then he decided it was a dumb idea. After a brief discussion, I informed him that I was going anyway.

"Goddammit, Brian, I can't stand the waiting!"

"Yeah. Me neither. Let's go."

So I called the Boss and told her everything was fine. Brian took the line to assure her that everything would be under control. Then we left for the lab. We parked on a side road and hoofed it up through the pine woods and up the hill to the fence that bordered the place in back. There were no guard towers or vicious dogs, but we both knew the place was bristling with electronic sensors and alarms.

"Let's stop right here," Brian said when we were still twenty feet from the fence. "Any closer and I'm sure they'll peg us."

We took turns with the binoculars, looking at the cluster of big buildings and the yard beyond the fence. We kept our eyes on the big double doors, twenty feet high, at the far end of a tall building that could have been a fieldhouse or a hangar for a jumbo jet. But nothing moved. The yard and the grounds were quiet as a tomb. My watch said 11:35.

"Maybe it's not till later on. Maybe they won't even move the damn thing until late tomorrow."

"Yeah, or maybe they won't do anything at all," said Brian. "Maybe Chet's following the right caper after all, and nothing's going to happen here."

"We'll see. By the way, what did the bumper beeper tell you this afternoon? Where was Chet?"

"At Brandeis all day. Then back at his home in Belmont."

"Hey, look. They've turned on the lights."

The back of the yard was being slowly illuminated by those powerful vapor lamps that take time to warm up. As they grew brighter, we saw more and more of the big asphalt yard inside the fence.

"There it is," said Brian. "Way in the back. See it?"

I saw the truck's cab first, its bright red metal shining in the light. Then I saw the tall chrome vertical exhaust pipes on each side. The big tractor truck crept forward, pulling a long, drop center flatbed trailer. We could hear it groaning and grinding now, then the hiss of air brakes as it stopped and began to back up. As it did so, the tall doors of the building rumbled open on rollers. Inside, the big building was brightly lit. The truck eased back inside it. The doors ground shut again. The yard lights were cut.

We waited another forty minutes. Cars came and went. The yard lights came on again while a ground crew pushed a crane assembly around to the front of the yard. It was a small crane, like the ones you see on brick trucks, with an electric cable-winch. It rolled on a dolly with rubber car tires. The lights went off again.

"Well, we could stay all night, but let's get back and get some sleep," I said. And we did.

I finally fell asleep at two-thirty. At quarter to four I was up and dressed. I met Brian in the hallway. He was ready too. Outside, we checked the operation of the radios.

"You want a gun?" he asked.

"I've got one. Where are your men?"

"They'll be at the station, ready to go, at four-thirty. You know where I'll be."

"And you know where I'll be."

"Just stay out of sight, dammit. No heroics. You get wasted, Mary's gonna be on me like flypaper."

I got in the car and drove to South Acton. I parked on a side street as near to the B&M tracks as I could get, then locked up the car and hiked the rest of the way. I was wearing tennis shoes and jeans and a lightweight, dark-blue windbreaker. I carried my pistol, my binoculars, and my two-way radio. In the dark, I cut through woods to the tracks, then walked parallel to them in the cover of the trees until I saw a dim, pale outline ahead of me. It was the new gravel on the sloping earthen ramp. I slowed to a creep and forged ahead. I came up to the cleared passage in the woods and looked out in the direction of the marsh. It was silent and dark. The blackbirds weren't up yet. Nobody was on the road or near the place. There was no vehicle, no barricade, nothing.

Was the whole thing a pipe dream? No, I didn't think so. What told me more than anything was Howard March's reaction on the phone earlier. But one thing was certain: the lab had gone out of its way to insure that nothing was noticeable. I crossed the unpaved road, looking for a nice spot to hunker down in and go to ground, out of sight. I'd gotten pretty good at sneaking around in the woods thanks to the Daisy Ducks, who were pros at it. I found a nice hidey-hole in a copse of thin, densely packed pines on a small hillock that gave me a good view of the track, the long siding, and the ramp. If I rose to a half-stance and craned my neck around, I could look behind me and watch the approach road as well. That was as good as it was going to get, I thought, and wished I'd remembered to bring a thermos of hot coffee. On the other hand, my body seemed to be racing along just fine without it.

In the dark I drew out the pistol and laid it down on the pine needles right next to me. Same with the binoculars. I switched on the walkie-talkie and called Brian. He answered in a buzz and a whine.

"*Zzzzzt*! Doc? You in position? I'm here with my car now—*ssssssst*!—or what? Over."

"Can't hear that clearly. I think something's haywire with this thing. Brian? Yeah, I'm in good shape here at the ramp. Where's Chet? Any line on him? Over."

"Beeper says he's still at home. What time you got? Over."

"Five twenty-seven. You?"

"Sa—*eeeeeoww*!—the same. The men are set up on down the line. We better not talk too much. Somebody might pick up on the —*ssssst*!—and ruin it. Over."

"Okay. I'll sit tight and quiet. Over."

"Reach me at six, then every thirty minutes, okay? And talk louder; your voice is weak. You don't call, I'll send somebody down there. Over and out."

Well, the pieces seemed to be in place. Now to wait.

It was the third westbound train. There'd been a passenger train first, made up of those old Budd self-propelled silver passenger cars. It creaked and rocked its way past, stinking like a trawler and spitting soot. The train was damn near empty. Then there was a westbound freight, going at a pretty good clip. It was pulled by an Erie-Lackawanna engine. I didn't expect it to stop, and it didn't, just rumbled on past the siding saying *Schenectady, Schenectady*, and then groaning out of sight with the engine giving a final *ting ting ting ting* with its bell.

I had called Brian six times now. Half the time there was no response, so I had to do it over and over. So much for his excellent equipment. Each time we connected, he told me that Chet was still at home, which was strange.

"Maybe it means it won't happen until this afternoon."

"Or maybe it—*sssst*!—that he doesn't know, Doc. Over."

"Yeah. Hell, I don't know. And wouldn't he at least be at Brandeis? What the—Hey! Wait. Here comes one. I'll let you know. Bye."

It was a short freight, pulled by a big blue diesel engine of the B&M. It slowed as it neared me, rumbled past, then wound down to a squeaky, clunky stop way down the line. Its bell was going. It was now light enough to see clearly. A man jumped off the caboose steps and ran back down the right-of-way toward me. He stopped, leaned over, and pulled the big iron lever on the siding switch, then waved to the engineer. The train began to back with a thunderous growl and a big cloud of diesel smoke. When the train changed direction, all the couplings that had been stretched apart came together and went *thunk! thunk! thunk! thunk!* down the line. The trainman stood on the gravel, watching the big wheels grind past. I saw the cars scissor over the bend of track and ease onto the siding. The train consisted of the engine, three boxcars, an ancient, stained tank car, a flatcar, and the caboose. The flat car was carrying two huge contraptions painted dull battleship gray, one at each end, directly over the trucks. The big steel boxes had knobby projections and cooling fins. They were held onto the flatcar by steel cables fastened down to the sides of the car. I assumed they were the heavyduty transformers that March had mentioned. The middle portion of the flatcar, between the two transformers, was empty.

When the train finally squealed to a stop and the couplings thumped all down the line again, the center of the flatcar was directly alongside the ramp. The engine's bell stopped binging, and the engineer throttled back. The switchman swung the big switch lever over again. That was it. Then he walked back to the rear of the train and hopped up inside the caboose, presumably for a smoke or a cup of coffee. The big engine in front thrummed softly. Wisps of oily smoke peeled off its top and floated away in the morning breeze.

The ramp was still vacant. I eased up and twisted around for a look up the road. Also vacant. I called Brian on the walkie-talkie. No answer. I called again. No answer. So I just waited. I waited for another forty minutes before he called back, asking where the hell I was.

"Right here, dummy. I couldn't raise you. The train's here. It's in position on the siding. No truck yet, though. Nothing."

"Mr. Harwood is still at his residence in Belmont. How do you like that, Doc? Over."

"I don't. Some flying squad. He must know something nobody else does. Over."

Brian said he was getting antsy, and so were the men up the line. I said tough, so was I. And then I asked him to call me again in half an hour, at eight, since my radio wasn't transmitting well. Then I sat down to wait.

Just after he signed off, the truck showed up, whining up the gravel road in reverse gear. Almost before I knew it, it had backed right up to the ramp. I saw that the small crane had been affixed to the bed of the truck. Underneath it was a squarish bundle wrapped in canvas and fastened with metal strapping. It certainly didn't look exciting or important. But then, that was the plan. It was a rectangular block roughly the size of a subcompact auto, chained to the big wooden pallet on which it rested. The chains connected at the top in a big steel ring. The crane's hook was in the ring. ARGUS was all set to be hoisted off the truck and swung over onto the railroad car. Pretty slick.

The operation went fast, which showed how well planned it was. While I was watching the truck, the GTE van arrived and parked down the road. The side door slid open, and six men with GTE coveralls converged on the truck. Two stood watch while one operated the motorized crane. The watchmen carried big attaché cases. What was inside those cases? Not triplicate forms, that was for sure. The remaining three men steadied the load as it moved from semitrailer to railroad car. It didn't even look that heavy. The two watchmen with the heavy cases followed the bundle onto the flatcar and stood there while the others made it fast. Then all the GTE guys left the railroad car and went back to the big truck. But now there was another man on the scene, who seemed to have appeared from nowhere. Who was he? The van driver? He wore a wide-brimmed hat and dark glasses and was busy talking to the men. He showed them something in his wallet and shook hands with two of them, who nodded. I raised my binoculars. The man was Chet Harwood.

I picked up the walkie-talkie and called Brian. No answer. I called again. No goddamn answer. It was seven-forty. Brian wouldn't call me back until eight. In twenty more minutes. Now Chet was walking toward the flat car. He turned around and walked backward, waving to the men, who headed for the van.

How the hell had he appeared on the scene when he was still at home? Had Brian's men screwed up? Jesus Christ—

Then I glanced back beyond the van, and I had the answer. Chet had not driven his Saab; he'd left it at home. He'd driven another vehicle to the scene. It was a sedan. Looked like a late-model Olds.

Teal blue.

31

I KEPT TRYING TO RAISE BRIAN ON THE WALKIE-TALKIE, BUT I got no response. All the time, I was watching the train. Chet had gone into the caboose from the flatcar. He came back out shortly and returned to the work crew, talking with them and gesturing. Twice he pointed up the line, then resumed talking, writing in his little notebook. I expected the truck and van to leave, but they stayed put. The work crew paced back and forth on the side of the right-of-way and watched the train. No doubt they would stay there until it got underway. I kept glancing back at the teal-blue Olds. I was sure it was the same car that had followed Emil and me to the airport that afternoon. I had to let Brian know. . . .

Then I got the idea of rushing up to everyone trackside and blowing the whistle on Chet right then. But it occurred to me that some of the work crew were probably Feds or Company men. Hell, maybe they all were. Chet sure seemed to know them well enough. They looked too buttoned-up, too at ease with the attaché cases, to be associated with Lincoln Labs.

I felt very alone now. There didn't seem to be any way in hell I could let Brian know what was happening unless I could somehow sneak past them and get to my car. I left the walkie-talkie and the binoculars behind and crawled out of my hidey-hole, walking in a crouch. But after twenty feet, I realized I would soon be visible to everyone up there, a sitting duck. Just then something happened to make them all look eastward down the track, away from me.

There was a long, sonorous blast from a locomotive air horn. Way down the track a fast express was looming, its headlight whipping back and forth. And I moved. I moved real fast, only daring to glance quickly once. When I did, it was clear that nobody was looking in my direction; they all had their eyes glued to the approaching express. I ran up the embankment of crushed rock and slipped in between the old tank car and the last boxcar. I stepped over the near rail and climbed up onto the massive, waist-high coupling. I knew that now nobody could see me.

Just above the coupling there was a narrow metal catwalk that ran around the tank car. The box car had no catwalk down low. If there was a catwalk, it would be up on top of the car, and I sure didn't want to be up there. But the old tank car's frame, the metal on which the tank rested and to which the wheels below were attached, formed a two-foot-wide path of steel that ran all the way around the car a third of the way up from the bottom of the tank. To walk along it, you held on to tubular steel handrails affixed to the tank's middle. I stepped up onto this catwalk and sat cross-legged on it so my feet wouldn't hang down and be seen. There I hid, right between the cars. The big, dirty tank was between me and the flatcar and caboose. I was, for the time being at least, invisible.

Yeah, Adams, I thought to myself, clutching the pistol, you're in great shape. Great. How do you do it? How *do you do it*? Here you are again, up to your ass in alligators.

32

THE GROUND SHOOK AS THE EXPRESS APPROACHED. MY EARS rang with the blast of the horn. Then it flashed by, clattering in a rush of color, motion, and noise.

Then fade-away, and silence. I heard voices behind me, and a car door slam. Might be the truck door. Were they leaving? Well, I sat there, wishing the damn train would start and wishing I had a cigarette. But mainly wishing I were in Tierra del Fuego.

Then two things happened that nearly made me jump out of my skin. One was hearing my walkie-talkie come to life over in the bushes and call my name. I could hear the goddamn thing saying *"Doc! Doc!"* Jesus H. Christ. And I wasn't imagining it, either. I'd left the Receive switch on, and there was Brian calling me now. If the briefcase boys heard it, I was in big trouble. Then I heard footsteps coming toward me from the rear of the train, loud and fast, scuffing the crushed rock on the roadbed. There was no time to step around the catwalk to the far side of the car. I leaned back against the oily tank and squeezed the Browning in a sweaty palm.

The switchman walked right past me, not seven feet away. He walked with a detachment born of routine, puffing the remnants of a cheap cigar. I could see him perfectly, his dark hair in a crew cut, the diamond pattern of wrinkle creases on the back of his neck. The steel-framed glasses. . . .

He ambled on past. But I knew he would walk back. And when he did, he would be facing me. What then? Dare I poke my heard around the boxcar to see what he was doing? No, I daren't. You've been asinine enough for one morning already, Adams. What to do? Wait again. So I waited. I heard another car door slam.

—thunk thunk *THUNK!* thunk thunk—

I flew back and cracked my head against the tank as the car jolted forward.

Screeeeeeeeeeeeee!

I looked down and saw the crossties and crushed rock begin, ever so slowly, to slide underneath the car. We were moving . . . creeping off the siding onto the main line. As we gathered speed I stood up on the catwalk and inched my way around it to the far side of the tank so the switchman wouldn't see me. But I felt too exposed standing up; I stretched out on my side on the catwalk, peering back at the flatcar. I saw nobody on it. But I figured Chet was inside the caboose, along with the switchman, who'd swung back on board after we'd begun to move. There might also be a brakeman. Three men in the caboose. And if they looked out the cupola, or through the bay windows, they could see me on the catwalk even though I was almost underneath the edge of the tank. So I stood up again and worked my way back between the cars. I found a comfy spot where I could sit down on the catwalk and grip a short steel ladder that led up to the brake wheel. I looked down at the rails: two shiny lines that remained constant while the ties and crushed rock blurred past underneath the wheels below.

Ka-click . . . ka-*clunk* . . . Ka-click . . . ka-*clunk* . . .

The sound the wheels made revealed their tremendous weight. Now and then we would pass over a switch, and I would see extra-bright lines wave off from the straight rails and snake back and forth, and the wheels would chuckle and chunk through the rail points, making a very fast, loud clatter. Past the switch, the wheels would resume their steady song. We gained more speed, working our way up to maybe thirty-five miles per hour. Then the cars began that gentle side-to-side rocking that makes you sleepy. I was suddenly very tired. I was about to crash, and if I weren't careful I would doze off, loose my grip on the ladder, and fall under the wheels to a frightful death.

What was I going to do next? I knew that Brian would be waiting up the line in his car. But he'd said that if he couldn't raise me on the radio, he'd send somebody down. What if he decided to go himself? In that case, there'd be nobody to notice me on the train. I'd be all by myself with—

"All right, Adams. Don't move a muscle."

I turned and saw the muzzle end of an automatic aimed at my head. Then the man behind it: Chester Harwood, Special Agent. Quick and agile as a cat, he rounded the corner of the car. Then he stood next to me, one hand holding the ladder, the other the pistol.

"So you're not pulling teeth today. I was afraid of that. Listen, if you wanted a ride, why sneak aboard? You could get hurt. . . ."

I didn't say anything. As in other instances when I have been scared, the world took on a fuzzy, surreal quality. Chet was talking to me from miles away. He was hardly there. Was this my pathetic protection from this killer, to will him out of the scene, as a frightened child covers his eyes in the innocent belief that when he does, the world goes away? I saw the blurred wall of green behind Chet's hat as the trees rushed through the gap between the cars. I heard the loud thumping and chunking of the trucks below. *Schenectady . . . Schenectady* . . . I felt sleepy. Exhausted, in fact. I could fall asleep at any moment.

Chet leaned over as far as he could and rapped my windbreaker pocket with his pistol. He'd seen the bulge and sag there and was testing it. My gun clunked, metal to metal, and he told me to remove it.

"Take it out real slow, Adams. That's it. . . ."

I held the Browning by the tip of the butt, with finger and thumb.

"Drop it."

I did. It clattered briefly on the trackbed. Then he did

something that surprised me. He put his pistol back inside the belt holster over his kidney and motioned me with his arm.

"Come on, we can talk better back there, for Chrissake."

A bit stunned, I followed him around the catwalk to the rear of the tank car, then hopped over to the low, wooden deck of scarred planks that made up the flatcar. We walked its length together, just like two golfers on a fairway. We passed the bundled-up ARGUS, paying it no more attention than we would have a dumpster, moved on to the end of the flatcar, and sat down on the edge of the massive pallet that held one of the big transformers. We sat there, facing the head of the train, with the wind whipping our faces.

"What's up?" he asked me.

"What's up? A lot's up, Chet. You know that. Why the blue Olds? Where's your Saab?"

"That car is Federal property. We use it for special tasks. My Saab is in my driveway. Why?"

"You know why. That car followed me the day I took Emil Haszmanay to Logan Airport so he could get out of town. You were driving it."

He shook his head.

"I was not driving it. I was *not*. And I can refer you to records that will show I wasn't. I haven't driven that car in two months, until today."

"Then who was driving it?"

"Sid Wanzer was driving it, Dr. Adams. He's been using the car heavily the past eight or nine weeks. And not being where he was supposed to be. That's why he's now in custody."

"Custody? Who's in custody? Sid Wanzer's in custody?"

Harwood nodded, a grim look on his face.

"On suspicion of treason. I guess Vic Hamisch had a word or two with you?"

"Briefly. I thought it was secret, though. Just between us."

"Umm. Well, it was, until yesterday. Hamisch got some stuff on Wanzer that's pretty incriminating, I guess. Don't know all of it yet. Have you seen Haszmanay lately?"

"Why?"

"Why? Why do you think *why*? Everybody and his brother's been looking for him, for shit's sake. Don't ask *why*. Anyway, Vic was pretty certain Haszmanay had come back recently. He thought he'd been in touch with you. That's why he buttonholed you the other day. But anyway, new intelligence shows Wanzer may have murdered him. You know anything about this?"

I didn't answer. I was too overwhelmed by what he'd said to move. It had taken me completely off guard. What he said could make sense. *Could* . . . I sat there in the wind-rush, listening to the train wheels, watching the trees glide by making an endless green tunnel on both sides of us. Above the singsong clatter of the trucks and the rush of air, I heard the cawing of a crow overhead.

"Well, Adams?"

"I'm trying to think."

"Well, don't let it strain you. See, I don't know much about these recent developments; I just know what Vic told me last night, and it was rushed. I've mostly been busy getting this security thing set up."

"So you knew all along, didn't you?"

"About this? Oh, sure. Knew it for a couple of weeks. The higher-ups at Lincoln Labs finally trusted the Bureau enough to let us oversee this thing. I wasn't sure if you knew about it, but now it's clear that Emil Haszmanay told you after all. That bastard."

"Does Joe know?"

"No. Not unless you told him. As a matter of fact he's at Brandeis right now, probably wondering where the hell I am. So what did you suspect me of that you sneaked aboard with a gun? Huh? I mean, we spotted you right away from the caboose, huddled down on the side of that tank car. What's going on?"

"That doctor who sewed you up in Mexico City. Dr. Pentalba? Remember him?"

"Remember him? Sure, I remember. You can't be that close to death that long and not remember everything about the experience. But how did you find out his name? I know I didn't tell you."

"No. Your Bureau medical file told me. I had Joe snag it."

"Ah . . . I think I see it all now. You wanted to check my story about the skin-diving accident. You remembered the scar on my back and wanted to make sure I wasn't really TALIN, right?"

"Right. Your story checked out completely. The Bureau records show that everything happened exactly as you told us."

He smirked at me.

"And that surprised you? That an FBI agent would tell the truth? Jesus, Adams! That Russkie spy *did* brainwash you, didn't he?"

"But later on, I was still curious," I continued, "so I did some more snooping."

"What kind of snooping?" Chet said. His voice had an edge to it now. He sat motionless, looking at the large wrapped bundle in front of him. I saw his eyes narrow slightly.

"Well, I was curious about the doctor who treated you. As a fellow physician, I had a question I really wanted to ask him. So I asked a friend of mine who has good connections to get in touch with him. The doctor who sewed you up, Chet, and who watched over you for those weeks in the hospital? Know what happened to him within a few days of your release and return to the States?"

"No, what?" he asked. The words came through clenched teeth.

"He died, that's what. He died in a car wreck."

"Too bad. He was a nice guy and a good doctor too. Mexico needs more like him. Damn shame."

"Another interesting thing is that the nurse who helped him treat you died, too. Remember Helena Gutierrez? Well, I guess she was with him in the car when it was hit by the truck."

"What do you find so interesting about all this, Adams? And remember, you're the one who's got the explaining to do, not me. You're the one who's endangering a state secret; I'm the one who's guarding it.''

''Well, it's just that I was thinking the deaths might not have been accidental. I mean, that truck went across two lanes of traffic to collide with Dr. Pentalba's car. Big heavy truck, too; it was barely damaged. Don't know what happened to the driver. Nobody every found out. That's what my friend tells me, anyway.''

''Know what, Adams? You're boring me, that's what. You're boring the shit out of me. I think Joe's right. I think you're a little bit nuts. I'm sorry Dr. Pentalba and his nurse were killed. They were good people. But it's got nothing to do with me. And I resent the hell out of the fact that you had the nerve to investigate me. You've been nothing but trouble on this case, Adams, and I'm sick of it.''

I felt pretty unsure of myself after that little speech. Chet said, ''Now listen: I've got work to do. See that cable?'' He pointed to one of the steel lines holding ARGUS in place on the flatcar. ''See it shaking? It's loose. Guys from the lab were so damned concerned about security they didn't tighten all the cables. I'll have to do it myself. Now I could handcuff you to this pallet right here. God knows you deserve it. It might keep you from hurting yourself or something equally stupid. But I'm not going to. Know why? Because I know I'm clean, and no matter what bullshit theories you've got, the records will show I'm clean. If I were you, I'd keep my accusations to myself.''

He walked carefully across the moving car to where the cable was attached and began to work the turnbuckle, tightening it. I could tell by his face that he was pissed off. Very.

So I sat there, watching him, faced with the genuine possibility that the deaths of the doctor and nurse really had been accidental. That Chet Harwood really was Chet Harwood, FBI Special Agent and staunch defender of the United States. That would mean that Sid Wanzer had been the turncoat—that Wanzer was the one who'd finally caught up with Emil Haszmanay in the gate house.

''Hey, Adams, can you give me a hand with this damn

thing? It's too hard to turn without a lever. Maybe if you just grab it with me we can—"

He was grappling with the massive turnbuckle on the cable, his face flushed with the effort. I walked over and put my hands on the turnbuckle. Together, we turned it several turns, and the cable began to straighten out and tighten.

"I was just thinking about Miguel Pentalba, Adams. You know, he *could've* been murdered. When I was in his clinic, I found out he did illegal abortions right and left. And the nurse was his helper. The local priest and a lot of others knew what he was doing. They hated him. It could have been them who killed those two. They did have enemies."

"Well, looks like we'll never know. And I'm sorry I snooped on you, Chet. Just my curious nature. I hope you're not too hard on Joe."

"No, I won't be. But, shit, he could've just asked me. As for you, I think you should leave snooping to the pros from now on."

He grabbed the metal turnbuckle and grunted as he tried to turn it.

"Son . . . of . . . a . . . *BITCH!* This things tighter'n a gnat's ass. Can you lean over just a little and grab it?"

I knelt down on the planks right near the edge of the car and helped him twist the turnbuckle on the carriage frame. That tightened the cable nicely. I stood up and examined the cable, thrumming it with my hand. Then suddenly I realized that Chet could easily have shoved me over the edge of the flatcar while I was kneeling down. Shoved me to my death. I would have hit the roadbed headfirst at about forty miles per hour, shattering my skull or breaking my neck. But he hadn't. He hadn't done a damn thing but tighten the turnbuckle. I felt foolish. And now Brian would have something to hold over my head for months, maybe years, to come. How Adams had panicked and pointed the finger at the wrong guy.

I stood there in the breeze, hearing the rattle and click and feeling the rush of wind. I kept my eyes on the right side of the track line, waiting to see a gravel road and a parked car on it. Before long it came into view. There was Brian in an

Irish tweed hat and a trench coat, standing beside his car, with the driver's door open. He was smoking a cigarette, naturally. I looked up quickly and waved at him. I knew he was surprised to see me on the train; I was supposed to be back at the loading ramp with my radio. But when he saw me signal that I was okay, he jumped inside the cruiser to call his men. Chet, still kneeling down and fiddling with the cable, saw none of this. I decided it would be better not to mention it to him.

He grunted and asked me to lend a hand again, so I leaned over and awaited his instructions. As I leaned over the edge of the rocking car I instinctively steadied myself by placing my right hand on his shoulder. His left shoulder. Right on his scar.

Then I looked up at the woods and trees rushing by, trying to clear my head, trying to make my mind believe what my hand told me.

Because, in that instant, I knew that the man kneeling down in front of me was TALIN.

I looked down at him and saw him turn his face up. He was smiling, I think, but it wasn't friendly. He face, half surprise and half cold rage, told me that he knew I knew. I didn't like that look; I didn't like it at all. I caught a glimpse of the butt of his Walther automatic as it protruded from the small belt holster.

Quick as a wink I reached down and yanked at the little gun, tearing it from the holster and flicking it into the trackside weeds. And even as I did this, TALIN rose to his feet, swinging a wide, strong right hand as he came up.

The fist connected, catching me square on the left ear, and sent me spinning onto the planks. My head rested on the rough boards as I fought to stay conscious. Now the sound of the wheels below was very loud: *Schenectady . . . Schenectady . . . Schenectady . . .*

The world waved and tilted. I saw big feet running toward me. I got my arms underneath me and raised my head, moving it to the side—it seemed to take an hour—just in time to dodge the shoe that was aimed at my throat. Leather and shoelaces brushed by my cheek, cutting the skin. That woke me up, and I rolled away. Rolled fast, and stumbled up onto my feet. I was dizzy. I grabbed for canvas and got the steel straps over it that were sharp as tin cans. They cut into my hands. The pain helped clear my head.

"Brian!" I heard myself shout. *"Brian!"*

But it was too late. I was alone with TALIN. I realized I was running around one of the bundles of cargo. I stopped for a second to catch my breath and knew he would be coming for me again, even though I couldn't see him.

I pawed my way along the canvas and ran to the end of the flatcar. As I jumped over to the caboose, I almost fell into that clattery cavern between the cars. But I stumbled up and turned around. He was walking toward me. He was in no hurry now. He was calm and quiet as a tomb. He leaned over to tie his shoe. . . .

I shook my head to clear it and yanked open the caboose door. At least the switchman could help me. Even if he was old and thin, it would be two against one. And we could barricade the door.

I shut the door behind me and locked it. I looked out through the small window at the flatcar. Chet was pulling up his pants leg. I turned and called for the switchman, who was sleeping in his bunk. I called again, but he didn't hear me. He was curled up on his side, his back to the wall. I ran over and yanked his arm to wake him. I pulled him away from the wall and over onto his stomach.

He wasn't going to be any help at all. There was a butcher knife sticking into his back. Lower left side, right in the kidney. I knew he had never even screamed. I ran back to the door and looked out. Chet was taking a pistol from a leg holster fastened to his calf. The pistol was strange; it had a lever underneath the barrel that he pumped twice.

An air pistol. He pumped it twice more, then jumped over to the caboose platform and reached for the door.

33

By the time TALIN broke through the caboose-door window and reached in and unlocked it, I was out on the rear platform, the woods and countryside rushing past me, my heart thumping in time with the wheels. I stood on the jostling platform, watching his dark shape come through the car to get me. I thought he might be smiling. He held the air pistol easily in his hand, cradling its muzzle up near his head so he could snap his arm out straight for an accurate, close-range shot. And put that nasty pellet in my chest.

I looked down at the roadbed flying past beneath the platform and got ready to jump. I was sure any injuries I'd get would be better than a pellet of Moscow Metal. But the train was going fast now, the ties and switches scooting by lickety-split in the roar and clatter of hurtling steel. I changed my mind.

I grabbed the rails of the rear ladder and swung out onto it. Then I scooted up the rest of the way and stood on the flat roof of the old caboose. They'd removed the catwalk, but it was easy to stand up there. I waited for him to begin his climb up the ladder. I planned to run over the roof to the front of the caboose and jump down onto the flatcar, run over that and jump onto the tank car, and so on, until I reached the engine and found help. I just hoped I could do it fast enough.

But he didn't come up the ladder. I peered over the edge of the roof and saw that the rear platform was empty. Then I heard a faint squeak behind me. That squeak saved my life. I turned quickly to see TALIN prying open the rear cupola window. I made a life-and-death decision in the millisecond that followed and ran straight for the cupola instead of coming back down the ladder. If I'd gone back down, TALIN would have had me covered, up and down, from inside the cupola, and I would have been trapped in the rear of the car with no place to run anymore.

As I reached the cupola on a dead run, his arm, holding the pellet pistol, was snaking out the window frame. I kicked hard at it and heard him grunt and curse. He withdrew his arm in pain, but his hand kept the pistol. I climbed onto the cupola roof, watching it and both ladders. I patted my pockets. What did I have to defend myself with? Two spare nine-millimeter magazines, full. A small folding lock-back knife. Small, but very sharp. I opened it, holding it down against my leg, and waited.

There was a crash, and he lurched out the front cupola window. He must have leaped with all his might, because almost half his trunk was out the low window. He was turning around, trying to look upward and raise the gun. But I jumped down on him as hard as I could, landing on his back with my heels. Then I pulled the small knife-blade along his arm hard and fast, parting his coat sleeve and cutting him. He screamed in pain and swore at me, but still held on to the air pistol. He was turning it now, so I caught his forearm with my left hand and raked the knife along it again. Blood erupted from his upper arm, and TALIN bellowed. I raked the blade still further back, along his right shoulder, along the side of his neck. I wanted to cut his head off. But then he broke my grip on his arm and slipped back down into his snake-hole. I heard a heavy thump in the car below. He had fallen. I jumped back up to my perch on top of the cupola and waited.

I waited for ten minutes. It seemed like an hour. Where was he? Was he unconscious? Should I go back down?

Right. . . .

I waited, my ears straining for any sound I could distinguish over the rushing wind and the rattle and click of the carriage wheels below me. But none came. If I had severed his brachial artery, he could be dying already. But I wasn't about to leave my perch to check on him. I wanted no part of that pellet gun.

THUMP!

A bloody hand appeared on the rear edge of the roof. He was climbing up the ladder. For a split second I considered running up to the edge so I could kick him in the head. But that was too dangerous; he might grab my foot and yank me over. So I started for the front of the car, reaching the front ladder just as his face appeared above the roof. God, he was a bloody mess. I swung over the roof edge and dropped to the front platform. But instead of jumping onto the flatcar again, I ran back through the caboose as fast as I could, out the rear door, and onto the platform where I reached up high to slash at TALIN's upper leg. I was trying for the femoral artery, that thumb-thick, gristly rope of lifeblood that's the undoing of so many gored matadors.

I missed.

And that did it. He let out a bull-bellow of rage. It was less the injury I'd dealt him than the sneak attack that enraged him—since he obviously hadn't expected it. But enraged he was. And as he dropped fast down the ladder—so fast I knew his strength was ebbing—I realized that whatever the outcome, there could now be no quarter. I was in a fight to the death with TALIN.

But that was okay. That was fine. Because a strange new feeling dominated me. It was an emotion, a euphoria, that I'd been taught since infancy had left the human race.

Blood lust.

A black, atavistic barbarism that Bibles and pretty building, paintings and just laws had supposedly obliterated.

But it was not so: blood lust was real and just below the surface. I wanted TALIN dead. I wanted the murderer of

Emil Haszmanay to die. And I, Dr. Charles Adams, wanted to kill him. To kill him as surely and finally as the cave-man hunter wanted to slay the saber-toothed tiger or the great cave bear. And though I was the underdog, I had hurt him. I liked that. I wanted to do it again. I wanted to watch him die.

Shame, shame.

TALIN came storming out of the caboose with the butcher knife in his left hand, the gun in his right. He'd yanked the knife out of the dead switchman on his way through the caboose. He now had a short-range weapon, too. I had made my way over to the flatcar and around ARGUS, hiding from him. I figured if I could keep ARGUS between us, I'd be safe. But the air pistol was lethal for fifty yards at least. No matter where I went, I could never get out of range. Somehow I felt safer staying close and hiding. I heard him jump onto the flatcar, and I stepped sideways out into the open and threw one of the loaded pistol slips at him. It whizzed by him and thunked into the caboose. He didn't even seem to notice. His eyes were glazed. I jumped out again and threw the second one. It hit his shoulder. He just barely noticed it this time and came forward like a punch-drunk fighter who's lost count of rounds. Blood loss will do that. Then I heard him coming around the pallet, scuffling his feet. I stayed ahead of him. When I could tell he was on the opposite side of the big bundle, I grabbed the metal strapping and quickly climbed on top of ARGUS, my knife in my teeth.

I was panting like blazes when I rolled on top of the canvas, but I knew he couldn't hear me over the noise of the train. I belly-crawled to the edge and peeked down. There was TALIN, scuffling and staggering around ARGUS, looking to kill me. He didn't see me, so I jumped off and hit him on top of his head with both feet. Then we were down on the planks of the flatcar, tangled up and struggling. I don't know what happened to our knives; we were both fighting for the pistol. I had both my hands on his, which were wrapped around the grip. He still had a lot of hand-strength, and his hands were bloody and slippery. I grabbed hold as tight as I could. He was breathing in deep, ragged gasps. For an instant the ugly nostril of the bore came toward my face. I gripped hard and pushed his hands back, then grasped the barrel and forced it up.

PTOU!

The pellet went up between our heads. I drew back my fist to hit him. But he shrank from me, and I saw a look of horror come into his eyes. He dropped the pistol as if hypnotized, then clawed wildly at his neck, screaming. He sat down heavily, comically, on the flatcar bed and screamed and wept. He clawed and tore at his neck with his fingernails, as if his collar were way too tight. Bright drops of fresh blood soaked his shirt front.

Then I saw the small red hole there, right underneath his chin. I flung the pistol off the car and watched him.

He rolled and writhed around on the planks in agony for a long time, making all kinds of ugly noises before his convulsions flung him off the train. From where I stood I could see his writhing, flopping form on the tracks. I watched it until the green wall of trees hid it from view.

Schenectady, Schenectady, Schenectady . . .

34

THE GOOD GUYS STOPPED THE TRAIN AT WORCESTER, JUST the way we'd planned it, with Brian and his police buddies leading the way. After the big wheels underneath me crept to a halt with a reedy scream, Brian climbed up onto the flatcar and looked at me. I was sitting hunched over on the caboose platform. I'd been that way for some time. I felt too tired and drained to raise my head.

"Doc?"

I was still looking down at the track—at the shining lines the rails made.

"Doc?"

He walked over to me and put his hand on my shoulder.

"Hi, Brian."

"You okay, Doc?"

I said sure, why wouldn't I be? But he didn't believe it. He sat down next to me while a small parade of law-enforcement people and some guys in suits—probably Bureau and Company people—came up onto the car and surrounded us. They asked a thousand questions. I answered as many as I could. I told them about TALIN, and about our fight, and about his death. It was funny, but sometimes I had trouble talking. I couldn't catch my breath, and I was shaking a little. But I was okay. They said they'd already found TALIN's body in the weeds just off the track. He'd crawled into the weeds, they said, and died in a pool of blood and vomit. I wasn't sorry. And they had lots more questions, but Brian waved them off, saying I'd talk later, when I was recovered.

"But I'm okay, Brian," I said. "Just tired out."

"Sure. You're fine. Let's get the hell out of here and head back home. Mary called the station an hour ago. She's on her way home now. So let's get the hell out of here. Now."

"I miss Mary."

He walked over and took my arm and helped me to my feet, then half carried me down to the roadbed. I guess I had a third-degree case of rubber legs.

"Jeez, Brian. Look at my clothes. They're all bloody."

I heard another bunch of people coming up to us and saw Brian wave them off. We walked over to his cruiser. I had trouble walking. I felt sick, and my arms were trembling. Just the two of us got in, and he drove, ignoring the radio squawk. I have to admit that there are times when he knows exactly what to do.

"Well, a little more excitement than we thought, eh?"

I didn't say anything. Just sat there numb, listening to the buzz and squawk of the box.

"How you feeling, sport? Wanta stop for a beer?"

I shook my head and closed my eyes as the car lurched through the Worcester rail yards. Brian kept talking.

"Got a little piece of bad news, Doc. Sid Wanzer's body's been found in back of a bowling alley up in Peabody. Bludgeoned to death, then dumped there. We figure he was on to Chet, and he found out and iced him."

"Jesus. Yeah . . . so that's what he wanted to see me about. He wanted to warn me. Poor guy."

Brian fiddled with the steering wheel nervously, then changed the subject.

"The place they'd set for the heist was a long stretch of straight track right past Quabbin Reservoir. Woods and hills all around. No people. But you know the place; you fish there. The railroad people suggested that it would probably be an ideal spot for a heist, and so very early this morning a team had a look. Guess what they found in an abandoned sawmill lot?''

''Oh I don't know,'' I said, rubbing the bridge of my nose, then my temples. ''What did they find? What on earth could it be? How about Orson Welles reaching his hands up through a sewer main? Too heavy? Then let's try Annette Funicello and her Mouseketeer friends. . . . What do you want me to say right now? What?''

He looked at me quickly out of the corner of his eye before answering. He tapped his thumb fast on the rim of the steering wheel.

''Two heavy flatbed trucks, each with a wrapped bundle on it, *and*—and this is the kicker—a government-surplus helicopter.''

''A chopper? Didn't you know you could buy the damn things. Who'd they catch?''

''Two men, and they're closing in on a third. Two others, they may never get.''

We pulled out of the switchyard past a dispatcher tower and eased onto city streets. The clear fall day had clouded over. A light drizzle was falling now, making the streets shiny. I liked the whisper of our wet tires on the pavement. I liked the purr of the squad car's engine. I liked all those soft sounds, and the soft, hazy light, too. It would let me sleep. How much sleep had I gotten in the last three days? Nine hours total? No wonder I was tired. So tired. . . .

''Chet had to make sure had could stop the freight by himself with no screw-ups,'' Brian continued. ''Well, looking back at this thing now, we figure he was going to kill the switchman first anyway. So, Doc, you can't blame yourself for that. Then, see, he'd radio to the engineer that there was a sick crewman in back. When the train stopped, he could walk up to the engine cab and ice the two men in there.''

''But the chopper. Where the hell'd they get the chopper?''

''Standard-issue army-type is what I heard from early reports. About seven years old, they said. Either a Bell or Huey. Not huge, but big enough to stick ARGUS inside or dangle it from a cable underneath if they wanted. The state guys have examined it already and think it was bought at a government auction in Long Beach four months ago. Surplus item, just like a jeep. All armaments and military gear removed, of course. But works fine, and still wearing camo green. That could make any witnesses to the hijacking think it was some kind of military maneuver.'' Just then he swerved onto a side street and slowed the car. ''Want to get a beer now? You've been through it, pal.''

''Nah. I want to get home and see Mary. And Joe. And Moe. Even more of you, Brian.''

So we swung around and got onto 290, which would get us home in under an hour. I was very, very glad, and eased back into the seat. Brian said that one of the intercepted men—a professional criminal, not an agent—had already revealed the details of the plan, the genius of which was not simply the skyhooking of ARGUS off the flatcar, but what was to follow that. Having arrived at the stalled train, and in possession of ARGUS, the chopper was to fly at low level through the Quabbin wilderness area to the old sawmill less than six miles away, where the two loaded flatbed trucks were waiting, both with ''dummy'' cargoes sitting on their beds.

''Okay, the bird comes in low with the loot. Probably nobody but a couple fishermen have even seen it, and they think it's out of Fort Devens anyway. So far, fine. I mean, nobody from the goddamn *train*'s about to say anything—they're all dead. Sure, the dispatcher minding the control board back in Worcester knows there's a fuck-up, but still he's not worried because he doesn't even think there's anything worth stealing on the freight. Right?''

''Right.''

''Okay, so in comes the bird, puts ARGUS on one of the trucks, takes the dummy load, then soars off, way high up so a lot of people will see it. It's gonna head somewhere over cities and towns, and probably toward the coast, you know. When the alarm's given, a lot of people are gonna say they saw the chopper. So there's *one* decoy, right there—''

''Yeah,'' I said. ''And the other decoy is one of the trucks. . . .''

''Sure. Exactly. The second truck, with another dummy

load strapped to it, was to proceed south toward New York at a high rate of speed. Canadian plates. *Hot* Canadian plates. Can you beat it? Driver with heavy accent. 'I do note spik ze English so gude.' The whole nine yards."

"Maybe a bit overdone."

"Maybe, but there isn't a trooper alive who wouldn't think he was onto something stopping that truck. Meanwhile, the truck carrying ARGUS—get this—was to head right back here into Worcester, just a few miles away. Just boogie on into town here with all the other commercial vehicles and then quietly deposit the load in a rented warehouse. It kills me. By the time the decoys are getting into their acts, the treasure is here, practically in the bag. And then you know what they were gonna do with it once they had it?"

"Yes. Immediately disassemble it into smaller pieces. These could then be shipped out to various 'safe' locations, one at a time."

"Exactly. How'd you know that?"

"Emil told me. The only mystery to me was why Chet would hire common criminal-type hijackers for this super-important mission rather than seasoned agents. But now I know that too: they would be promised a treasure and be well paid in advance. Then, when ARGUS was safely in stow, they would be killed. Killed as shamelessly as the switchman on the train. Or Emil Haszmanay."

Brian nodded in silence. Finally, he said, "And that's why the guy talked, Doc, and told us everything. Once he was advised of the seriousness of the heist, he knew he wouldn't have gotten out alive."

"I killed a man. You know that?"

"Look, don't think about that now. The main thing is—"

"I'm glad. That's what I was going to say. That I'm glad I did it. He deserved to die. And I'm not sorry. Not one damn bit."

"Take it easy, kid. I know."

Then I looked down at my pants and shirt and noticed that they were soaked in blood. Had I seen that before? Or was that somebody else's clothes? I couldn't remember.

* * *

Two hours later we were all back at the house sitting on the terrace. I saw Moe coming across the lawn toward us. Mary was sitting next to me, but she wasn't saying much. She looked worried and kept grabbing my hand. I would be all right. Joe was just walking around on the terrace. I wished the boys were home. I looked up again at Moe, seeing a thin man with balding head and steel glasses, dressed in a powder-blue windbreaker. He was walking through Mary's grove of Russian olive trees. The sun had come back out—sort of—and it glinted off his high, straight forehead. He walked up slowly and seemed to wave and wiggle ever so slightly as he approached.

"Why's he walking through the garden? Why didn't he come up the walk?" I asked.

"Who knows?" said Mary. "Aren't you going to change your clothes, Charlie?"

"Why? Oh yeah . . . in a minute. So I'm sorry, Joe, about not letting you in on what I'd found out. I really am. It's just that you'd have been in such a bind, with Major Mahaffey and the Bureau and everything—"

"Forget it, Doc. You played it real well, I think. Real well. What made you decide to go back and try Mexico again?"

I looked down at the terrazzo stones under my tennis shoes and kicked the terrace wall lightly. I took a hefty sip of my drink. It felt good. Not good enough, but good.

"Well, it just seemed all along that the hidden hand was moving too fast. The bad guys—whoever they were—were way too quick on the uptake, even for pros. There had to be an inside leak. So then I began to suppose: what if the good guys and the bad guys are one and the same? The night before he died, Emil told me he had the same suspicion. After I cranked him up from the bottom of the pond, the thought just wouldn't go away."

"So you knew it was either Chet or Vic Hamisch or Sid Wanzer," said Joe.

"Well, Emil thought it was somebody in Vic's Company office. But after he was killed, I began to ask myself: who's been in the thick of it all along? Who would be in position to place all those taps and bugs?"

"Chet Harwood."

"Uh-huh. He was the only constant. And don't you see what great cover he had? What tremendous access to intelligence? It was Chet, in the dark of night, who placed those spike mikes in my cellar walls. It was Chet who shut the car door down the road and who followed us to the airport the next day, using his other car: the blue Olds he kept in a garage in town, under a different name, for KGB work. The KGB's gonna be sorry he's gone. I bet he was one of their best plants in the country."

I stopped and took a large swallow of whisky and soda. It didn't seem to be working.

"So," I continued, "What made me think of Mexico? Well, I got the idea initially from something Mary said about my tattoo. As you all know, Mary's not too keen on it and wants me to have it removed. I keep telling her that the scar from the skin graft would look as bad as the tattoo. But then the other day she said that maybe I could just alter the tattoo by having another one done over it. I got to thinking: it's the same way with scars. The only way to cover a deep scar effectively is to get another one—a bigger one—to appear over it. And I was also thinking about scars left by phosphorus burns. I remembered something from med school about their special characteristics, so I had a visit with Aaron Schindler, the dermatologist, to brush up on scar tissue."

"You didn't tell me that," said Mary. "What did he say?"

"Enough to set me thinking. The question I was going to ask the good doctor in Mexico City was this: did Chet Harwood really get run over by a speedboat, or did he come to you in good health, with a scar already on his back, and pay you an exorbitant amount to have you create a *new* scar on his back to hide the old one? But, as Martin Higgins discovered, I couldn't ask him that question, because he was dead."

"And then you knew . . . ," said Mary.

"Well, I *thought* I knew. I mean, the death of Pentalba and his nurse seemed more than coincidental. If Chet were indeed TALIN and had been penetrating the ranks of the FBI in the mid-sixties, then his telltale scar would have surely betrayed him at his first Bureau physical. Joe tells me the exams are very rigorous; there would be no way he could hide the scar or explain it away. The only solution would be to have another scar surgically implanted over the first one, exactly the way I described. And then of course his real sponsors—the KGB—would have to eliminate the doctor and anyone else who knew of the secret operation."

"I wish I'd thought of that," said Joe. "Hell, the files were enough to convince me."

"But when I mentioned all this to Chet to see his reaction, my little monologue had no effect on him. Chet wouldn't bite; he just kept fiddling with ARGUS's cable as if I'd said nothing important. So then I began to question my theory. It seemed entirely possible that the deaths of Pentalba and his nurse Gutierrez *were* coincidental . . . and that Sidney Wanzer was the culprit. And Chet made it sound so routine . . . so believable. I tell you, Chet Harwood was a masterful actor. It's what made him invulnerable for so long."

"I never would have suspected him even for a second," said Joe, a faraway look in his eyes. "Shows how good a sleuth I am. But what about our friend in the tent? What about Frederick Stansul? I mean, he had the scar, too. How'd you know he wasn't TALIN?"

"You mean Frederick Stansul, alias Alfred Stansiewicz. No, it wasn't him. From the start, I had a feeling the scar didn't look right for a phosphorus burn. I got his sister's number from Karl Pirsch and found out Freddie Stansiewicz's history. She said he got that scar on his back working in a factory when he was just out of high school, back in the early fifties. She said he was working as a steel-cutter in some now-defunct plant in Brockton. He fell into a burn table. Know what a burn table is?"

"No. Is it a place where they treat steel, like heat it?" asked Brian. "Or—what's it called—*temper* it?"

"No. It's a series of acetylene cutting torches that are suspended, nozzle down, on a movable rack. The rack sits over a slotted table. They put steel plates on this table, and the cutting torches move over it and produce curved pieces of steel by burning them out of the plate. Like a giant jigsaw. And the plate being cut gets hot as hell. Anyway, Stansiewicz's sister told me that one afternoon young Freddie tripped and fell onto that sizzling-hot steel plate, burning the living shit out of his back, poor kid. And guess what? The company that owned the factory gave him minimum coverage for his hospital stay, then fired him. Can you believe it? And he was burned so badly he couldn't find work anywhere. How do you like that?''

''Christ. Then it's a good thing they went bust.''

''Yeah. But that's what caused young Freddie Stansiewicz to become disenchanted with America. When he couldn't get any other kind of job, he was bitter and broke. That's probably when he started taking money from some Soviet illegal. One thing must have led to another, and then he was working for them big time. At least, that's the way his sister reconstructs it. I'd say she hit it on the button.''

''And Harwood—TALIN—knew of his scar, I bet,'' said Joe. ''He knew that if Stansul was ever killed, some of us might think he was TALIN and thus lay all suspicion to rest.''

''I think so,'' I said, reaching for the drink.

But Moe's warm, thin hand took my glass of Scotch and placed it on the terrace wall.

''You don't need that,'' he said.

''Says who?''

But Mary squeezed my hand and shook her head a little. So I let it drop. The drink wasn't working anyway; I still felt wound up.

''Okay, Doc, now we know all the research,'' said Brian, hunching his chair up closer to me, ''But what finally convinced you that Chet was TALIN? You said he didn't react to your accusation, so what did it?''

''What did it was my helping him tighten the cable. I leaned over and put my hand on his left shoulder to steady myself so I wouldn't fall off. I could feel the back-muscles through his shirt. My hand was there long enough for me to feel the deep fissures and pits beneath the top layer of scar tissue. There was no mistaking those deep wells of injury my surgeon's fingers felt through the shirt cloth. I knew what it was right away.''

''You mean, a special kind of scar?'' asked Brian.

"Uh-huh. The effects of burning phosphorus are devastating, mainly because it won't go out; it just keeps burning and burning right through flesh. Terrible stuff. Even before I drew back my hand from Chet's scar, I remembered the words Aaron Schindler had used to describe the scarring. Something like: 'massive tissue destruction . . . very deep wounds . . . automatic third-degree burns . . . sunken appearance . . . cobbled . . . hollowed . . .' In short, horrendous, deep scarring. It was then I knew who Chet really was. And he knew I knew it, too. That's when all hell broke loose. . . ."

"Charlie?"

I found I couldn't talk anymore. My throat ached terribly, and my jaw clenched and trembled.

I felt a sting on my forearm. I hadn't noticed that Moe had rolled up my shirt sleeve. He withdrew the syringe and clapped me on the shoulder.

"What's that?" I said, ready to slug him.

"Something to make you relax a little. Trust me, Doc."

In a very short time, I had an amazing change of heart. I decided I didn't want to talk about the past few days anymore. Anymore, ever again. The world became calm and lovely. Colors glowed fresh and bright. Sounds were sweet. I looked at each of my loved ones and smiled. They smiled back and nodded at Moe.

Then the air seemed to chime. Did I hear the faint *tink-tonk* of monks' bells on distant peaks? Did I see hazy-blue temples perched on glorious chasms far, far away? With prayer flags snapping in the wind?

No. I was just home again. But it sure felt like Shangri-la.

And then I saw that my pants were bloody.

". . . gotta change my clothes, Mare. Take a bath . . ."

She hugged me. Then, and only then, I knew I was going to be okay.

ABOUT THE AUTHOR

RICK BOYER'S previous Doc Adams' novels are: BILLINGSGATE SHOAL, awarded the Edgar for Best Mystery Novel of the Year, 1982, THE PENNY FERRY, THE DAISY DUCKS, THE WHALE'S FOOTPRINTS and GONE TO EARTH. A long-time resident of Concord, Massachusetts, Boyer currently teaches in Asheville, North Carolina.